NIGHTFALL

NIGHTFALL

Meri Elena

PROSPECTIVE PRESS

Winston-Salem

P ROSPECTIVE P RESS LLC

1959 Peace Haven Rd, #246, Winston-Salem, NC 27106 U.S.A.
www.prospectivepress.com

Published in the United States of America by PROSPECTIVE PRESS LLC

TRADEMARK

NIGHTFALL

Author photo by Guinevere Nease

Cover and interior design by ARTE RAVE

ISBN 978-1-943419-33-3

First PROSPECTIVE PRESS trade paperback edition

Printed in the United States of America
First printing, September, 2016

1 3 5 7 9 10 8 6 4 2

The text of this book was typeset in Alegreya
Accent text was typeset in Aquifer

This novel was previously independently published in 2014

Acknowledgments

Here we are again, and I still can't remember everyone who has helped me along the way. The Clump are the best of friends and fans, and they have remained loyal ever since the true first edition of *Nightfall*. Everything I write has a little something of you guys in it, except for Brunswick, which has a whole lot of you in it. I am also eternally grateful to my mother for her support and edits, as well as the staff at Prospective Press—Jason Graves, Chip Putnam, and intern Courtney Holder—who helped get this second edition ready. Especial thanks must go to Jason for mentoring me through my weird and wonderful authoring experience thus far.

1

R ichard McGill was keenly aware that he must be either stupid or crazy. There wasn't another reasonable explanation for what he was doing on the streets of Edinburgh, alone, at night, knowing full well that there would be werewolves on the prowl. The bright, round disc of the moon played hide-and-seek behind thick, dark clouds that threatened rain, plunging the entire city into shadow, and then bathing it in cool, creamy light once again. Richie cursed the impatience that had driven him out of the relative safety of the parking garage where he'd been crashing and into the perilous urban jungle.

A low, eerie howl reverberated through the damp air, sounding closer than Richie would have liked. Chills pricked at his spine, and he quickened his pace. This had to be the worst idea he'd had since running away from home to begin with. Desperation was making him reckless, and he knew it.

In every alleyway he passed, Richie thought he saw something slinking around in the dark. More than once, he darted past a pair of glowing eyes. On a night like this, stray cats and monsters looked about the same. Richie could feel the throb of his pulse in his temples and just hoped that nothing out there was listening for his heartbeat.

There was no warning growl—only snuffling and scuffling—and then something crashed into Richie's side like a furry torpedo. Richie hit the pavement, and the skin ripped from his palms as he tried to catch himself. The weight of the monster's body pinned Richie's torso and the breath was knocked from his lungs. He glimpsed dripping teeth in a snarling muzzle before a massive paw shoved his head to the side, its claws pressed against his face. Richie closed his eyes, waiting for those teeth to sink into the soft flesh of his neck. He felt the heat of the werewolf's breath and smelled the reek of its last kill, as its mouth dove for his jugular.

Richie heard a solid thud and the sound of breaking glass. A splash of liquid hit his ear, and the smell of alcohol filled his nose. The werewolf yelped and lifted its paw from its prey's head. Richie looked up to see a figure take the beast by the scruff and the tail and sling it aside.

Any ideas of gratitude were overwhelmed by the panicky impulse to run. Which he did. He scrambled to his feet, put the sounds of rending and snarling at his back, and ran in a random direction as fast as his legs could carry him. Richie kept going, heedless of where he was headed, until his body refused to go any farther. He collapsed against a wall on a side street he didn't recognize. His leg muscles spasmed. His chest burned. There wasn't enough oxygen in Edinburgh to satisfy his lungs. If the werewolf had won the fight, and decided to go find its escaped prey, Richie would be as defenseless as the day he was born. Every predator for a mile around could probably hear him panting. Richie forced himself to breathe more slowly and willed himself to calm down.

"Need I tell you what a moron you are? A kid like you, out alone on the night of the full moon? You were practically begging to get eaten."

Richie jumped clear out of his skin and looked around wildly to find the source of the voice. The labyrinth of buildings created deep shadows where anything could be hiding. A sweaty lock of his uncut cinnamon hair clung like a leech to his forehead, obscuring his view. Richie brushed it out of the way but still couldn't make out the speaker. Then, the man himself stepped into the mouth of the alleyway, hands in the pockets of his tattered jeans. He was bare from the waist up, which provided Richie an unobstructed view of the lean muscles rippling beneath his milk-white skin. A tangled mane of black hair disappeared into the darkness about halfway down his back. He looked human enough, except for the bright discs of reflection behind his brilliant green irises.

"Relax," the stranger said, followed with a short laugh. "I just risked my hide to save yours. No use killing you now." He stepped closer, and Richie pressed himself farther into the bricks behind himself, not quite ready to trust a glowing-eyed Tarzan, even if he was the one who had just saved his life—assuming this really was the same person.

"W-who are you?" Richie asked, the words sounding small and choked.

"Folks call me Jack," the half-naked man replied. "I have to ask: where the hell did you think you were going?" Jack crossed his arms over his chiseled-marble chest, his eyes wandering up and down Richie's short, scrawny form, not unlike the way that Richie was examining him. Richie cleared his throat, hoping to make his voice sound stronger this time.

"Why did you save me?" Richie asked, not willing to divulge his destination just yet.

"I...huh. I don't know." Jack furrowed his brow and looked down at the ground. "It's not something I do on a regular basis. Does it matter? You're alive, right? And you didn't answer my question."

"The Dog and Centaur," Richie said. He allowed himself to relax a smidgen.

"You're old enough for that?"

"Yes! I'm eighteen." Richie straightened up to his full height, forgetting his terror in the heat of his indignation.

"All right." Jack put his palms up in a gesture of surrender. "I believe you. Well, actually, I just don't care very much. Are you still headed that way or are you going to call it quits and go home?"

"I don't have a home," Richie said without thinking. Jack nodded, seeming unsurprised.

"I guess the pub it is, then. I know where it is. I'll walk you there. Safety in numbers. I could use a drink myself, anyway." Jack turned and walked out into the larger thoroughfare. Lacking a better plan, Richie coaxed his beleaguered muscles into following this odd man. Richie couldn't entirely shake the suspicion that maybe his savior only rescued him to kill Richie himself, or worse, but Richie had gotten hopelessly lost in his mad flight from the scene of attack. He couldn't stay where he was, so what choice did he have except to put a little faith in a stranger?

The Dog and Centaur was a place where werewolves in human form—as well as other bloodthirsty creatures—came to boast about kills and trade information. It was the latter that interested Richie.

Richie walked through the door so close behind Jack that he was in Jack's shadow. Now that he was there, he was unsure what he was going to do. He knew how to get people to talk, but these were not exactly run-of-the-mill people. He didn't have anything to bribe them with, or any leverage over them. Mulling over his dilemma, Richie mindlessly followed Jack to the bar and took the stool to Jack's left.

Belatedly he realized that this placed him right next to a werewolf patron. That was not a position he wanted to be in, but if he got up and moved that would be insulting.

Better to stay put.

Beside him, Jack ordered two scotches, which were delivered promptly. Jack slid one over to Richie, who downed the whole thing in a couple gulps before ordering a second. Jack sipped at his slowly. He held his little finger slightly away from the glass when he picked it up. Richie didn't think there were real people that did that. It seemed like the sort of overly-fancy gesture that would be reserved for movies and mockery.

"I've always wondered, do Scotsmen normally drink scotch?" Jack asked of nobody in particular. He stared fixedly into his glass while he spoke, as though he expected the amber liquid within to speak its wisdom to him.

"Sometimes..." Richie said after an awkward moment where nobody answered. Jack gave a seemingly meaningless grunt in reply and returned to nursing his scotch. Richie glanced over his shoulder, taking stock of his surroundings. Because it was a full moon, the place was mostly empty. That was why he had chosen tonight—any werewolf that wasn't out hunting would be of the less threatening variety, too sick or hurt to transform. A scrawny young man stared desolately at his table in a corner, stirring a tankard listlessly with his finger. Two women who looked like they had battled a chainsaw the night before sat in the middle of the room whispering to each other and looking annoyed about something, presumably whatever had scratched them up. And then there was the man sitting beside Richie. He looked dirty and grizzled. He also, Richie noted with surprise, looked old. He had never seen a werewolf that looked old before. Werewolves could choose to appear to be any age they wished. To live amongst humans they might chose to take on the look of aging, but they never looked old. This one had greasy, gray hair and a gray beard with a weathered face and tired eyes. Even though Richie didn't much like werewolves, the sight depressed him somehow. Richie realized he was staring when the old wolf caught his eye. Richie turned away quickly, embarrassed.

"It's all right," the old wolf told Richie. "I know how I look. My face is what I feel."

Richie turned his head farther in the opposite direction, trying not to engage. Jack, however, took the bait.

"What do you mean?" he asked.

In reply, the old wolf sighed dejectedly. Richie could tell he was gearing up towards a story. He supposed all old folks were the same. Feeling obligated to listen, Richie shifted his gaze back to the speaker as his second drink arrived. He saw the bartender roll his eyes and turn his back, evidently too sick of hearing the tale to feign politeness. The old wolf took a fortifying shot and then sighed again before starting.

"When I was young, I was the pride of my pack," he said wistfully. "I made the most kills night after night. I was a terror to every town I visited. I loved the violence. I reveled in the bloodshed. Those were good times." His eyes glazed over with nostalgia. It took all of Richie's willpower to keep his reaction from showing on his face. He glanced over at Jack nervously. Jack—leaning forward with his head tilted slightly to the side like an inquisitive puppy—was clearly engrossed in the story. It didn't seem to bother him that this old guy was a homicidal maniac. But then, Richie supposed that was fairly normal behavior for werewolves.

"A few decades ago—back in '58, I think—I stowed away on a ship bound for America. They say there's great hunting there because, you know, Americans don't believe in monsters. They're incredibly dense. And such good screamers! But that's not the point here.

"One night, I was hunting as a guest in a pack from the East Coast. We decided to pick a fight with a vampire clan. You know, just for fun. We thought we could take 'em, easy. There were just three, and there were six of us. We didn't know they were *primum* vampires. So—"

"What's a, um, what you said, a '*primum*' vampire?" Richie asked, absently swallowing the final dregs of his second scotch, raising his hand to get a third. Only then did he realize he was actually paying real attention to the story, which sort of surprised him.

"*Primum* are very strong vampires," the wolf said, looking rather irked that Richie had stopped him midstream. "They're almost impossible to kill, and they have wings—they knew we were coming and ambushed us from above. It's a lot harder to fight something that keeps flying out of the way. They killed my two mates. I managed to run away, but I'd been bitten. Vampire venom is toxic to werewolves." He directed this last statement to Richie, along with a look which clearly expressed that he thought Richie was ignorant.

"I know that," Richie said.

"Good. You need to know these things. Well, I'd been bitten so many times I should have been dead in ten minutes. I expected it. At some point I blacked out, but then I woke up. And I couldn't imagine how I'd made it. There was this woman, one of those cat people, standing over me. She said she'd saved my life. I never did figure out how she did it, but she did. It wasn't just me. Sally—that was her name—had other patients too, with all kinds of problems. I was there for a few weeks, saw her reassemble someone who had been disemboweled, cure a man of blindness, there was even this one guy that she sucked the hallucinations out of. I mean, sure, everyone knows cotus have powers, but hers were astounding. I bet there wasn't any ailment she couldn't heal."

Richie sat up attentively, and not just because their drinks had arrived. He wasn't sure what a cotu was, but he was afraid to ask in case the man got annoyed and refused to finish the story. Richie wanted to know where this healer named Sally was. He had been trying to find a cure for months, and no one could help him. Every mystic and sorcerer he had spoken to said you couldn't just take away something from out of your head. But if this woman could banish hallucinations, what *couldn't* she do? Between the desperation of months of failure, and the influence of alcohol, this sounded promising.

"After I got better, she started showing me around her town. It was an amazing place. Can't remember the name of it. It was sort of removed from the rest of the world, like a little bubble of a universe. There were all kinds of critters living there, on all the levels of about a hundred food chains. But there weren't any murders there. Everyone got along with each other: humans, werewolves, vampires, things I couldn't even name. It was surreal." The storyteller stopped to take another long swallow from his glass.

"Sally told me I could stay there forever. I could live in peace and never have to fight again. But I was too young and hot-blooded. I wanted to go right back out and get revenge on the vampires that almost killed me. She wouldn't let me leave until she was sure I was ready. I think she was just hoping I would change my mind. I started getting antsy, and one night I was out taking a walk, and ran right into a *primum* vampire. Not one of the ones from before—a new guy, but I attacked him all the same. Once again I got beat, but this time I wasn't hurt. Turned out he was Sally's boyfriend and didn't want to undo all her hard work. Instead of offing me, like he had the right to do, he threw me out of town, literally. Once I was outside the barrier,

I couldn't find a way to get back in. It was like the town had vanished.

"Well, I decided not to worry about it. I went home without looking back and returned to my old ways. Everything was great for a while. Just like old times.

"But then one day, a couple years ago, I started thinking. And I started wondering, what was I doing? Why? All I ever did was kill, for fun. Nothing against that, of course, in and of itself, but I started thinking that it was so *pointless*. I never really *did* anything or *got* anywhere. I realized that my life is meaningless. If I live a thousand years, I'll have nothing to show for it.

"In Sally's town, everyone did *something*. Great or small, everyone had a job to do, a reason to be. If I'd stayed, they would have given me one. I didn't think I needed a purpose then. My purpose was to enjoy myself. But then the joy faded away, and I wanted something more. Now that it's too late, I see that I made the wrong choice. So now I sit here every night, an old man, waiting for the end of this miserable existence." His well-rehearsed story ended, the old werewolf knocked back the rest of his liquor and sighed mournfully.

Richie was deep in thought. Finding this town and their doctor could bring exactly the kind of solution he needed. But how could he do that, he wondered, if the town was invisible from the outside?

"Um, if you don't mind my asking, what did Sally look like?" Jack asked.

For the first time, Richie noticed that Jack looked even more anxious and excited than he was. He was leaning so far towards the old wolf that he was almost in Richie's lap. The muscles in Jack's arms and bare shoulders were as rigid as the glass in Richie's hand. With no pretense of gentleness, he shoved at Jack to encourage him to exit the shared airspace. Richie's weak push was no match for Jack's iron body. In fact, Jack didn't even appear to notice. He continued to stare at the old man with wide, eager eyes.

"I don't know...brown hair, I think. I don't remember it very well. That was years ago," the wolf said, scooting over a bit on his bar stool to distance himself from Jack. He clearly hadn't expected such a high level of interest in his tale. "Oh! I do remember her having green eyes. Bright green. They really stood out in a crowd. Why?"

"Do you remember where the city was? Like, what state?" Richie asked. With a little help from the alcohol, he was feeling increasingly upbeat about his newest—and only—lead.

"No. It doesn't matter, you'll never find it," the old wolf said with a moan. He turned his body slightly to the left, away from his audience.

Having received the attention he wanted, he clearly wasn't planning on conversing any further.

Jack slumped back into his own seat. Richie, however, was too desperate and too inebriated to let it go at that. If some bird named Sally could fix him, then he intended to find her. It sounded like a great plan, except that it wasn't one. Richie had to admit to himself that he hadn't the slightest idea where to begin. Then he considered Jack's overenthusiastic reaction and wondered what he knew. At the same moment, Richie and Jack looked at each other. Richie could see his own hesitant hope reflected in Jack's eyes. What was Jack wishing for, that he thought Sally could provide? Richie suspected that Jack probably wanted some sort of healing, too. It hadn't escaped Richie what an advantage Jack was to have around. Whoever he was, he was strong and good in a fight, and Richie needed someone like that on his side. Did he really want to put his life in the hands of this stranger? He knew nothing about Jack. But he knew he wasn't likely to accomplish his quest alone. Jack interrupted his musings.

"You never told me your name," Jack said.

"Richie," he replied without hesitating. His rational mind screamed at him to stop, about-face, and back out before it was too late, but his intuition told him he could trust Jack. Or maybe that was just the buzz. Either way, at the moment it was convincing enough. He didn't feel inclined to bother thinking about it too much.

"Richie," Jack murmured thoughtfully, as though seeing how the name tasted. "Richie. You seemed interested in the story."

"So did you," Richie said, not yet committing to anything.

"Yes." Jack paused, running his tongue over his upper lip. "You want to find this town."

It was not a question, but Richie answered anyway. "I do."

"I could come with you," Jack said. "If you'd want me to. I could keep you safe, and I have information...." There was an undertone of begging to Jack's voice.

Richie forced himself to think before answering. He was surprised at how inclined he was to say yes. Sure, Jack had saved his life, which meant something, but who was he? You're homeless, penniless, and hopeless, said the thoughts crawling sluggishly through his brain. You can't go any lower, now can you? This is the first solution to your problem that you've found—maybe it will work, maybe it won't, but what is there to lose? Well, life, limb, and sanity, for a start, but what the hell. Richie had already talked himself into it.

"Where do we start?" Richie asked brightly. The corner of Jack's mouth turned up in what Richie thought might be a relieved smile.

"Let's get back to my place," Jack said. "We can talk there. Without, you know, people around." He inclined his head toward the bartender, who suddenly took a keen interest in the glass he was cleaning.

"All right. Let's go," Richie said. He hoped his optimistic impressions of Jack were right as Jack paid for their drinks with wadded up pound notes and led Richie out of The Dog and Centaur into the thick night air.

Jack's place was neither Jack's nor was it a proper "place." It was a small, run-down shack of a house with an ancient, overgrown *For Rent* sign in the front yard. Richie got the distinct impression that Jack wasn't paying anybody for the privilege of living there. There was a combination lock on the door and a broken padlock thrown down beside the doorstep. While Jack put in the combination, Richie stared at the discarded lock and couldn't help wondering what had become of the landlord. The lock opened with a click and Jack pulled back the door, rusty hinges squealing in protest, and held it for Richie to cross the threshold. Jack entered behind him and then allowed the door to fall shut. It did so reluctantly, taking a full minute to latch. Richie watched it every step of the way. After it had closed, he turned around to see the interior of the house. There was not much to it. A filthy stuffed chair sagged—deflated—in a corner. A sleeping bag, presumably Jack's, was unrolled in the middle of the room. One medium-sized, wheeled suitcase, its innards spilling onto the floor, lay beside it. A bedraggled towel, which might once have been white and had a golden K embroidered on the hem, flopped out of one end of the luggage. A red-and-black notebook was using the opposite side of the suitcase as a bookmark. Scattered wrappers, bottles, and take-out containers completed the mess.

"I wasn't expecting company," Jack said in apology, hurriedly sweeping the majority of the debris into a pile and shoving it under the chair. Jack surveyed the room and nodded, apparently pleased with his clean-up efforts, then sat cross-legged by the head of his sleeping bag and gestured at the floor in front of him. Richie sat in the indicated location, nudging a half-eaten chocolate bar out of the way with his foot. The walk to "Jack's place" had cleared his head;

however, as he looked around, Richie was beginning to wonder what he had gotten himself into. He felt inwardly itchy, like there were cockroaches crawling under his skin.

"So, Sally—the healer the werewolf told us about...I know who she is," Jack said. His left foot started to tap rapidly against the floorboards. Richie found it somewhat distracting, especially because that foot—and that foot alone—was clad with a lilac sock. As the only thing in the room not completely covered in grime, it drew the eye.

"I've been looking for her for a while now," Jack continued. "At least, I'm pretty sure she's the same person. Her name is Sally Kitch." Jack reached into the suitcase and pulled out a green, spiral-bound notebook. He tossed the notebook at Richie, who barely managed to catch it before it hit his face. Richie opened the book. On the first page was a drawing of a young woman from the shoulders up. She had brilliant green eyes and long, wavy hair the color of milk chocolate. Beneath the picture, the name Sally Madeline Kitch was written in fancy, but barely legible script. Below that was another drawing of something that resembled a purple-black furry creature with bat wings and round ears.

"What is a cotu?" Richie asked, looking at the strange animal.

"You...don't...*know* what a cotu is?"

"No, I don't. Should I?"

"Um...never mind. A cotu...well, cotus are to cats as humans are to monkeys. Another stage of evolution. They're thinking critters, felines, known for their shapeshifting. Usually they take the form of humans. Opposable thumbs, you know," Jack said.

"That wolf said he wouldn't have messed with that woman if he'd known she was a cotu. They've got to be pretty dangerous," Richie said, thinking that they ought to approach Sally with caution.

"Sure, cotus are strong, but it's a myth that we're all bad. We just don't—"

"Whoa, back up. You said 'we.'"

"Yeah, 'us.'" Jack squinted at Richie. "I guess maybe it isn't obvious to you. Okay, well, I'm a cotu. An ice cotu, to be specific. All cotus have some kind of elemental power, like fire or water or electricity; mine just happens to be ice," Jack said, acting as though it were no big deal. Richie felt a new twinge of fear. Jack must have seen it, because he quickly added "Hey, I said we're not all bad, all right? I won't hurt you. I promise." He made eye contact, pleading. Richie liked to think he was good at reading people. He thought Jack seemed sincere, but then Jack wasn't a "person" in the usual sense, so Richie couldn't be sure he was reading him right. Richie's throat worked as he tried to generate a response with which to fill the widening interlude of silence.

"You have a right to be suspicious," Jack said finally, looking away from Richie and down at his mismatched feet. "To be perfectly honest I don't trust you any more than you do me. But we have to trust each other a little bit if we're going to try and work together."

"I'll try," Richie said, hesitantly resigning himself to the fact that he didn't have another viable option. Jack nodded to the floor in response. Jack jerked his head up and looked over towards what appeared to Richie to be an empty corner of the room. But momentarily, he was gazing at Richie again, and talking. Richie couldn't shake the feeling that he had just missed something.

"Works for me. So, as I was saying, I've been trying to track her down. I've found plenty of records of her up till the mid-1960s, but then she drops off the grid. I think that must be when she went to this place we're talking about. Where the werewolf went. On the fourth page is a list of people I think might know where to find her. Old acquaintances and such. As best I can figure, those are some of the last people to see her before she checked out."

Richie turned to the indicated page, where a handful of names were listed, along with a line of pertinent information about each. "Mostly I've been working on compiling the list. I haven't hunted those people down yet," Jack said. "But I think it's as good a place as any to start."

"It's not a very long list. It's more than I have, though, so I guess we'll start here. Where does that put us, exactly?"

"I'm in Edinburgh following a lead that will hopefully get me an address on that first person. I was sidetracked tonight, but I'll try again tomorrow. If that works, we'll know where to go. If not...I'll cross that bridge when I trip over it. For now, though, I'm planning on getting some sleep. I suggest you do the same."

Richie had tried not to put much thought into how tired he was, but his eyelids were on the heavy side and his muscles were still sore from his narrow escape earlier. Sleep did sound inviting.

"You can have the sleeping bag if you want," Jack said.

Richie looked back and forth between the sleeping bag and the chair, trying to decide which was the lesser of the two evils. "No thanks, I'll take the chair."

"Right then. G'night." With that, Jack crawled into his sleeping bag and turned his back to Richie. Taking the hint, Richie walked over to the chair, wiped off the worst of the dust and dirt, and curled up on it. Although uncomfortable, it was a marked improvement over sleeping on the ground, like he had been lately, and Richie fell asleep instantly.

The first sleepy hint of daylight was visible over the city as Jack slipped into the largest, busiest convenience store he could find open at this hour. It really wasn't busy enough. Only four or five customers were wandering the aisles. This would be much better done in the afternoon, with more humans to shield him from discerning eyes or lenses, but Jack was on a mission to earn the kid's trust before he had time to realize that Jack was nothing like a trustworthy person.

Jack turned his back to a security camera and slipped a toothbrush and tube of toothpaste into the pocket of his hoodie. He hated wearing the thing—too hot, too itchy—but it sure was handy for shoplifting. He probably *could* pay for everything with that twenty in his pocket, but he was saving that for liquor.

What the hell are you doing? the voice of reason in Jack's mind chastised him. You can't even take care of yourself! Now you're going to babysit some homeless teenager? Do you want to get both of you killed?

"I can keep him safe," Jack said, arguing quietly with himself while stashing a bar of soap in the hoodie. He had taken care of his brother and sisters when they were little, and this wouldn't be much different.

Oh, yeah, because that's worked out so well before.

"I'll do better this time." Jack noticed another customer looking at him strangely and realized he was speaking out loud. He could feel his blood rising into his cheeks. He ducked out of the store before he could embarrass himself further. He could make the rest of his "purchases" somewhere else.

Once out on the sidewalk, in the open air with scarcely a soul in sight, Jack felt a little better. He snagged an empty cardboard box off the ground and unloaded his prizes into it. This was a complete waste of his time, but collecting necessities for his new partner was a nice thing to do, right? Even if he didn't need Richie to help him find Sally, Jack was sick of being alone, and the kid sure acted like *he* needed somebody, if only to keep him from being werewolf chow.

He doesn't need you, moron. He needs a "responsible adult." That ain't you, brother.

"Shut up." Jack spotted another shop that might be worth stealing from. He dropped the box behind a couple of trashcans and kicked it out of view of other would-be thieves. At this rate, he could gather everything Richie might require before the sun broke free of the horizon. A smile twitched at the corners of his mouth. If he could manage to keep Richie alive long enough, this whole partnership thing might actually be kind of fun.

Richie woke up disoriented and unsure of where he was. He opened his eyes to see a dusty, cracked window. A few brave rays of sunlight fought their way through the glass to illuminate the room. He turned his head the other way and saw the dirty, dilapidated room, and he remembered where he was. It was an unpleasant way to start the day. He had dreamed that he was home and, for a moment after he woke, thought it had been real.

With a resigned sigh, Richie sat up in the chair and flinched as the wooden base creaked dangerously with the motion. He hoped he wouldn't have to sleep on it much longer, because he doubted it would hold up. No wonder Jack slept on the floor. Speaking of Jack, where was he? Richie gingerly disembarked the chair and began wandering through the house. There wasn't much to it—just a kitchen, a space that might have been meant to be a bedroom, and a bathroom taken over by spiders—and no sign of Jack. For a second Richie feared that he had been abandoned after finally finding a strong, capable guide to lead him. The idea of being alone and vulnerable again quickened his heart and sent a chill down his spine. Richie hurried back into the main room to check that Jack's belongings were still there. To his relief, they were, along with a new addition to the clutter that Richie hadn't seen before. There was a small cardboard box, placed conspicuously in the exact center of the room, with a note lying on top. It must have been there all along, but Richie had been too preoccupied to notice. He walked over, knelt on the floor beside the mysterious parcel and took the note off the top:

> Dear Richie,
>
> Is that how you spell it? Or does it have a "y?"
> Anyway, I got up early this morning and obtained some necessities for our operation. Before you ask, yes, I stole them. I hope that doesn't bother you too much. I assume you've been living a similar lifestyle. By the way, there are some groceries in the kitchen cabinets. Packaged foods mostly, so not much to get excited about. Best I could do. And the electricity is off, but the rest of the utilities seem to function fine. Your tax dollars at work. I'll probably be out most of the day. You can do whatever you want. I would recommend taking a look at the Sally notebook, though, to make sure we're on the same page. See you later.
>
>   —Jack
>
> PS: The combination for the lock on the front door is 4-29-6, in case you need to know.

Setting the note aside, Richie opened the box. Inside were some basic toiletry items, a pocket knife, and a horseshoe-shaped neck pillow. Normally this would look like very little to Richie, but after several weeks of carving out a living on the streets, it was a treasure trove. And generous of Jack, even if he had stolen all of it. Apart from the clothes he was wearing, the items in the box were all Richie had to his name. He took each object out and placed them in a row on the floor, just staring at them, like he sometimes did as a kid on Christmas with his new toys. If this was how it was going to be, this was a partnership Richie figured he could live with.

Richie lay on his back on the floor, making good use of his new neck pillow. His breakfast, a bottle of water and a couple of packaged muffins, sat beside him. He broke a chunk off a muffin, brushing crumbs off of Jack's notebook as he ate. After taking a shower for the first time in longer than he cared to remember and otherwise cleaning himself up, Richie had decided to take Jack's advice and read up on this Sally Kitch. Only the first couple of pages listed information directly about her. She was an electric cotu of nobility, whatever that meant. She was born on October 31st, 1927. Her parents were Morris and Lightning Strike Kitch. What kind of names were those? Jack either couldn't get an address on them or hadn't tried, because none was listed. She had four siblings—Leaf Sun, listed as missing; Lily, deceased; and two brothers named William and Fireball, no other information given. She was an unlicensed medical practitioner, known both for assisting people who couldn't otherwise get medical care and for occasionally performing rather questionable experiments on live subjects. Sally was also known for combining the occult with medicine, apparently with great success, before she vanished around 1965.

From there on, the notebook contained a record of Jack's attempts to find her, although Richie found no mention of why Jack was looking for her in the first place. The detail and perseverance with which Jack attended to his search were more than borderline stalker-like. Richie had to admit to himself the possibility—nay, the likelihood— that Jack's motives were criminal. On the other hand, some of Jack's writings came across as protective. 'I hate to look so hard and turn over so many stones. What if one of her enemies follows my trail?' he had written a few weeks previously. Jack was turning out to be a thoroughly baffling enigma. Richie would have preferred to work with someone straightforward. But then he had never expected to have an opportunity to work with anyone at all, so he supposed he shouldn't complain.

The latest entry in the journal was dated two nights ago and detailed how Jack was coming to Edinburgh to see if he could find a werewolf who knew where a wolf named Clement George lived. Richie remembered that Clement George was the first name on the list of contacts he had seen on the fourth page. He flipped back to that page, reading and rereading the list to familiarize himself with who he was supposed to be helping Jack find.

KNOWN ASSOCIATES (short list):
- Clement George - werewolf - England - student of Sally's when she lived in the British Isles
- Ralph Laker - L.A. Medical Supplies - known supplier of Sally's 1937-1940
- Clara Hawthorne - West Virginia - witch? - known supplier and ally of Sally's 1935-1957
- Vlad Dracula - vampire - Carpathian Mountains - Sally's last known associate was his son, Alexandru

Richie had a hard time taking the last entry seriously. Vlad Dracula? Surely that wasn't a real person. Well, maybe it was. Sometimes people had weird names like that. Richie felt incredibly sorry for the poor soul that had to go through school with the name "Dracula." And on top of that, Vlad, of all things. His parents must have truly hated their son to curse him with such a name. Unless the entry referred to someone who had taken on the clichéd moniker after becoming a vampire, in which case it was merely tacky.

Richie closed the notebook and put it back in Jack's suitcase. He couldn't help seeing all the other notebooks in there. There had to be at least a dozen, of all different shapes and sizes, scattered amongst a collection of worn paperbacks. None of the notebooks were labeled in any way. It made Richie itch with curiosity to know what was in them, but he held himself back. They weren't his to read. More importantly, they were Jack's, and Richie didn't know how mad Jack would be if he messed around in his stuff.

He scooted away from the suitcase to remove the temptation. He sat there for a full ten seconds, staring at the wall, before it dawned on him that he had nothing to do. Jack's notebooks surfaced in his mind again, and Richie figured he had better find some form of amusement before he got himself in trouble. He thought about it for a minute and decided to be productive and do some more research on what Jack's notebook hadn't told him. He knew just the bookstore to find that information in, too. Assuming that the owner didn't eject him on sight, after that last incident.

Richie tried his best to look casual as he walked into Tony's Tomes, but unfortunately the door had one of those little bells on it. As soon as it rang, Tony looked up from his desk. When he saw Richie, his face turned a disturbing purplish red. Richie cursed under his breath.

"OUT!" Tony yelled, so loudly that they must have heard him in the space station. "OUT, YOU VERMIN! I TOLD YOU NEVER TO COME BACK HERE AGAIN!"

"But—"

"OUT!" Tony stood up and waved a fist. He was a scrawny little waif of a man, but he could out-shout anyone. Well, almost anyone.

"I'M NOT LEAVING 'TIL I GET WHAT I CAME FOR!" Richie yelled, winning the battle of lung power by a long shot. Tony shrank back a little, but stood his ground, crossing his arms and glaring daggers at the intruder.

"You manhandled me, ransacked my shop, cost me hundreds of dollars in damages, and you have the nerve to come back here again?" Tony asked.

"As a matter of fact, I do," Richie said. "Besides, it was your fault for saying you 'Don't serve riffraff' like me. You'd have been cross too if somebody insulted you like that. Now, if you'll just calm down, we can conduct our business like civilized men." Tony sucked in air to retaliate. "OR I can leave now, and come back later. With company. Either way, I'll get my information," Richie said, crossing his arms in a deliberate attempt to mock Tony. He was bluffing, really. If Tony gave him the boot, he would just ask Jack to explain things to him later. But Tony had made this a duel to prove who was boss, and Richie never turned down a challenge. The two sized each other up in silence for several minutes before Tony finally surrendered.

"What do you want?" he asked, deflating. Richie smiled triumphantly.

"Anything you've got on cotus," he answered. Tony nodded, and shuffled off into the stacks with Richie following close behind. He weaved among the aisles until he came to a bookshelf in the back of the room. Tony pulled a thin paperback from a row of identical books and handed it to Richie. It was a plain, sand-colored book with the title, *Smithfield's Encyclopedia of Cotus*, dead center on the front in black Times New Roman type.

"This is it?" Richie said. He flipped through the pages. It would do, he supposed, but he was hoping for a little more than fifty large-print sheets.

"That's the official book on cotus. Their government has a lot to hide, so they've outlawed any books about cotus other than that one," Tony explained.

"No wonder I'd never heard of them before," Richie muttered.

"Those little 'encyclopedias' are given away to all unorthodox booksellers such as myself for free, and we're required to let people take them for free. It's a publicity thing. Cotus are trying to change their image. Or at least the ones in power are. But if you've got any money on you, I may be able to find some books in the storage room on cotus that aren't, shall we say, mainstream?" Tony suggested. Richie deliberated for a moment, chewing his lower lip. He didn't have any money anymore, and he'd been so sure Tony wouldn't let him in the door that he hadn't thought about trying to get ahold of any. He could probably nick some from an unsuspecting passerby on the street, but that could be dangerous, and he didn't want to go to that much effort without knowing if Tony had anything that would be useful to him or not.

"Do you have anything on Sally Kitch?" Richie asked.

"Do I have anything on her? Of course I do. Almost all of the underground cotu texts have been written by her. One is a history of cotus that includes a wonderfully revealing autobiography and family history," Tony enticed.

"When did she write them?"

"During the '90s, mostly. There were only about fifty copies ever made, so you aren't likely to find them anywhere else. I happen to have the whole collection, however," Tony bragged.

During the 1990s. That was long after the last records Jack had on Sally. Those books could tell them where the unknown town was, or at least give him some clues. Or, Tony could be lying through his teeth. Still, it would be worth a large amount of hassle if those books were the real deal.

"How much would you want for them?" Richie questioned.

"Oh, about £6,500," Tony said nonchalantly. "Which is a steal, considering what they usually go for these days. I generally sell my illegal items for less than other merchants, to avoid being noticed by authorities."

Sixty-five hundred pounds! Nope, no way. Richie wasn't that good a pickpocket. "Um...is there any other form of currency you'd be willing to use?" Richie stalled, while simultaneously trying to think whether or not there were any alternate forms of currency in his possession. He couldn't think of any.

"Perhaps. Make me an offer," Tony said. Richie didn't have an offer. What did he own of any value? He wracked his brain, and could only come up with one, tenuous possibility, that maybe Jack owned something worth trading. He had a hard time believing that Jack would be living in the conditions he was if he had anything worth £6,500, but it could happen. It was worth a try, anyway.

"Will you hold the books for me until tomorrow?" Richie asked, shoving the complementary *Official Encyclopedia* into his back pocket.

"Oh, certainly!"

"I'll be back," Richie told him, suspecting even as he said it that it was a lie.

It took Richie about six tries to get the combination right, but eventually he let himself back into Jack's...living quarters. Richie couldn't think of the thing as a house. Of course, he reminded himself, he lived there now too, temporarily, so he probably ought to think better of the place. With the door ajar, looking into the central room, he tried to view it with some measure of fondness.

It didn't work.

Abandoning the effort, Richie entered the abode and flung himself onto the ground, leaning his back against his stuffed chair. He pulled the front cover back from his newly acquired volume and started reading.

He had intended to read every word in order to be fully informed, but he was never much of a reader and the encyclopedia was about as interesting as most books of that class. A brief, bland history said something about cotus originating in Australia, setting up a system of government, encountering the British, spreading all over the world, et cetera. Richie managed to discover that cotus reach maturity in ten years, before ceasing to age entirely, which explained the weird time line of Sally's life. After that, he reached a section written in impossible scientific jargon that seemed to explain cotu anatomy. Richie skimmed uncomprehendingly. The only part that managed to hold his attention to any significant degree was a section at the end that presented some common myths about cotus and the official statements on the matters. It seemed that the popular opinion about cotus was that they were vicious, animalistic creatures that infiltrated the ranks of other species by impersonation and were parasites to be feared and loathed. The counterarguments supplied by Mr. Smithfield were wonderful glittering generalities that Richie didn't find particularly impressive or convincing. "Cotus are civilized members of global society." Um, okay, so what does that mean, practically speaking? In Richie's opinion, it meant nothing. After he had read as much as he could take, Richie closed the book and tossed it away in annoyance seasoned with a pinch of disgust.

"Politics." He scoffed.

"What about 'em?" Richie whirled around to find Jack standing in the doorway. How Jack had gotten through that creaky door without him noticing, Richie hadn't a clue.

"Don't sneak up on me like that," Richie said with a gasp.

"I wasn't trying to, but, okay," Jack replied. He walked over and sat down in front of Richie. "Good news, by the way. I have the address I was looking for. We can leave for London tomorrow. Unless of course you have something to attend to first. And what were you chucking across the room?"

"'*The Official Encyclopedia of Cotus*,' the most useless reference book in the world," Richie replied.

Jack nodded knowingly.

"Which brings me to what I was going to ask you," Richie said, and launched into relating his misadventures. It took him the better part of half an hour—Richie was discovering that Jack had a habit of asking lots of insignificant questions—but he eventually got around to telling Jack about the rare books Tony claimed to have. Richie pointed out that, as far as he knew, Tony was the source for occult literature in Edinburgh, perhaps in all of Scotland. It wasn't a stretch to believe he might have books written by Sally Kitch hiding in his closet.

"So, what do you think?" Richie finished. Jack shook his head in a shell-shocked kind of way.

"Wow...I mean, I'd heard rumors that she'd, but, I never actually found...wow," Jack said, practically babbling. "That's a breakthrough I wasn't expecting."

"Yeah, I felt kind of like that, too," Richie said in agreement. "But, assuming that Tony's telling the truth, we haven't got anything to pay with. Not that I know of."

"I need those books," Jack said. "Or, we do, that is," he added, correcting himself. "Sixty-five hundred pounds. That's just over ten thousand American dollars, if I remember the exchange rate correctly. Damn. But if this Tony really does have his hand in the cotu black market, then maybe I do have something he would want. Worth more'n he's asking, probably."

"You do?" Richie asked, disbelieving. Jack nodded. He held out one of his hands, palm up. Richie watched with astonishment as a thick rope of gravity-defying silvery liquid somehow materialized and slid into Jack's hand from behind. It solidified and turned black and, within seconds of its original appearance, stabilized into a large mammalian tail with thick coal-black fur. Richie rubbed the back of one hand hard across his eyes and blinked several times, but the tail didn't disappear or melt back into liquid, so he assumed it must really be there.

"Cotus have what I guess you could call a stinger on the end of our tails," Jack explained. Richie checked quickly and saw that, indeed, the tail vanished from view behind Jack and appeared quite convincingly to be attached to him. Richie looked back towards the tail tip as Jack used his thumb to brush back the fur at the end, revealing a wicked silvery spine like a two-inch length of sharpened stainless steel. "They're extremely poisonous—or venomous, whichever it is—and make excellent weapons. People, mostly human people, will give up their first-born for that kind of power. You don't get many cotus just giving away their stingers, though, so they're rare, and worth a bundle. If Mr. Tony knows anything, I bet you he'll be happy to make us a trade."

"That's great," Richie said, trying his best to hold his gaze on Jack's face, rather than the anomalous tail. The lethal and inhuman weapon that hovered inches from his face was making him anxious, and distracting him from the task at hand. So he closed his eyes to consider Jack's proposal. "If it's such a powerful weapon, do we really want someone like Tony to have it? And do you really want to give away part of your body?" Richie thought about what he would do if his fingernails were made of gold or something. He decided that he would probably rip them off and sell them in a minute, but he doubted everyone would be so eager.

"Have you got a better plan?" Jack asked. "And why are your eyes closed?"

"Fair enough," Richie said, opening his eyes and deliberately not answering the second question. "Let's go first thing tomorrow morning and see about making a trade, then. But we'll need to be careful. He might try to double-cross us."

"Oh, don't worry about it. If that happens, I'll take care of it."

Richie opened his mouth to ask what Jack meant, then remembered the werewolf in the alley, and decided not to inquire further.

This time, when Richie came through his doors, Tony looked much more receptive.

"Well, you came back after all. So, what do you have for me?"

"This," Jack said, revealing his tail and stinger just as he had done for Richie the night before. Tony managed to look both terrified and thrilled in the way only a black market businessman can.

"So, you have our books?" Richie asked.

"Right this way," Tony declared, and hastened to the back room. Jack dropped his tail and followed. Richie brought up the rear, looking everywhere but the base of Jack's spine, though it was difficult not to stare. Richie still had a hard time wrapping his brain around how Jack could be perfectly human one minute, and the next sprout a tail. It was quite disturbing to him. Nothing against tails, but Richie wasn't accustomed to spending time with people who had them. He had always been taught that large, wild creatures with tails were something to be avoided, as they frequently interacted with humans in unpleasant ways.

It took Tony a few tries to fit his key into the lock. Finally, he managed to open the door and the three crowded into the tiny storage room. He picked up one of the many unassuming plastic boxes in the room and held it out to Jack and Richie. Richie took the box, which was heavier than it looked. A piece of masking tape on top labeled the contents as "S.K." Richie took off the lid to verify that this was what Tony claimed it was. His eyes were drawn to a colorful hardback that had obviously been designed in deliberate contrast to the official cotu encyclopedia. The cover was decorated in abstract rainbow swirls and a title in very curly, very girly, black script: *The Unofficial (But Vastly More Accurate) Encyclopedia of Cotus*, beneath which was the author's name, Sally Madeline Kitch.

Beside him, Richie heard Jack inhale sharply. Without a word, Jack brought his tail back into view, took the stinger between thumb and forefinger, and yanked it out. Jack barely grunted, but Richie heard himself cry out a little in sympathy. The way Jack had talked so nonchalantly about trading with this stinger, Richie had expected it to be something you could easily remove. Only then did he remember what happens to bees when they sting—removing their stinger kills them. Jack didn't appear to be in danger of expiring, but the stinger didn't come out smoothly. Jack didn't complain, though, just handed the bloody object to Tony, who snatched it gleefully, but carefully, not letting it pierce his skin. Jack thanked him with stiff politeness and ushered a stunned Richie back out onto the street.

"Um...doesn't that...hurt?" Richie asked, staring at the tip of Jack's tail, where it hung several centimeters above the ground, dripping thick red blood onto the sidewalk. Where the drops hit the pavement, they seemed to eat away at it. Even though it probably didn't make any difference to Jack, the fact that he was bleeding acid made the injury seem worse to Richie.

"Hell yeah, it hurts," Jack grunted through gritted teeth. "But I'll live. Let's get back to the shack. I want to see what's in those books."

Richie nodded and led the way. He was amazed at how few people seemed to notice anything unusual about Jack and him as they walked back to home base, even though Jack looked like a Tarzan who had grown a tail and tried to cut it off. There was one little girl who seemed concerned about Jack but whose mother pulled her away, and one businessman in a suit that cursed when he stepped on a drop of blood and found out what acid feels like on the bottom of one's foot. Other than that, everyone passed them by without a glance. Richie couldn't believe the supreme obliviousness of the human race.

"Hold still!" Richie demanded. Jack stopped squirming, but his tail continued to twitch, making it immeasurably harder for Richie to bandage it. As if trying to apply gauze to a wound that was bleeding acid wasn't hard enough. Richie couldn't imagine how he had failed to burn off his hands yet. He supposed Providence must be on his side. The only good thing was that Jack had the foresight to have stolen a first aid kit.

"There! I'm done," Richie said. Jack relaxed, tail drooping exhaustedly onto the floor. "Oh, so *now* you stop moving."

"Sorry." Jack's apology did not sound particularly sincere.

Richie rolled his eyes. "It's not a professional job," he said. "But I suppose it'll do. So, are you stuck with a tail until it heals, then?"

"Yeah," Jack answered glumly.

"I'll try not to step on it."

"Gee, thanks. I appreciate it. So, are we going to look at those books I went through all this for or not?"

"Right." Richie turned around and dragged the box in between Jack and him. Jack took the first book out with an expression almost of reverence, gently placing it on the floor between the box and Richie. Richie picked up the unofficial encyclopedia and turned it over in his hands while Jack continued removing the books out one by one and placing them in a row, precisely parallel to each other.

"So, I guess we have to read through each and every one of these now, don't we?" Richie said. Despite his burning curiosity, he didn't really want to do that.

"Yeah, I suppose so," Jack replied. He had finished arranging the books on the floor and had already buried his nose in one. Richie followed his lead and opened the encyclopedia. The copyright date was 1994. It was dedicated to William, *"The one who taught me to write and to be myself."* Richie remembered seeing that name in Jack's journal, and wondered if there was a lead there. If Sally had dedicated her book to her brother, then he must be important, and might know where she was. But then, surely Jack had thoroughly investigated her siblings. Richie filed the thought away and read on.

The Unofficial (But Vastly More Accurate) Encyclopedia of Cotus

Dear Reader—

I must warn you that the book you hold in your hands is probably quite illegal. I have every expectation that as soon as I start to disseminate copies, the International Council of Cotus and their Affairs (ICCA, pronounced ICK-uh) will ban it and try to destroy as many as it can. That is primarily because the contents herein do not reflect kindly upon ICCA, but then, that is rather the point.

Four years and some change have passed, as I write this, since the first edition of Jonathan Smithfield's ICCA-sponsored *Encyclopedia of Cotus* was published. Thousands of these little paperbacks have been printed, translated into six languages, that I know of, and given out for free in bookstores and on street corners to anyone willing to take one. Smithfield and I were contemporaries raised in the same cotu community, and I have to confess that I am somewhat disappointed in him. I knew he was never interested in being a revolutionary, but whether he meant to or not he has now become the face and instrument of ICCA and their publicity campaign. It is a campaign with which I cannot align myself, although, despite our past differences, ICCA has invited me to contribute to the coming second edition of the Encyclopedia. Smithfield is no scientist, nor, it would seem, are any of the members of ICCA, as evidenced by the paucity of relevant biological information in the first edition. Yes, I do want to publicize what is known to date about the physiology and anatomy of our species. There is very little information available on the subject, and I am in a position to know approximately how many cotus suffer and die from lack of medical care simply because almost no one knows anything about their biology. In the not too distant past, I almost lost a sibling because of such ignorance in the medical community. I have been trying to spread the word myself. The broad, deep network of ICCA would be valuable in this endeavor. However, I know better than most that ICCA itself tends to do more harm than good, so I declined their offer. The ICCA ency-

Sally Madeline Kitch — page xii

The Unofficial (But Vastly More Accurate) Encyclopedia of Cotus

clopedia contains very little information of merit and a deplorable body of twisted truths and outright falsehoods. I want no part in it. ICCA has never officially removed the price on my head. There is a distinct possibility that publishing something this divisive will renew interest in flushing me out of my burrow and silencing me at last. I have been living on borrowed time for most of my life. I accept the risks. My purpose in writing my *Unofficial Encyclopedia* is to both inform and correct ICCA's misinformation. ICCA aims to integrate cotus into human society and to shape the species into model "human" citizens in the process. Most of all, ICCA wants us to hide. It wants to stash away everything that has made cotus who we are. To erase the past is a dire mistake. You cannot learn from what you do not know. I openly acknowledge that my motivation is more of a personal vendetta than a professional disagreement. You may not be interested in the ways I feel that ICCA has wronged me, but I urge you to read on nonetheless. I promise that you will learn something, and I may be able to show you a new perspective on cotus and their affairs, one that I hope will give you the tools to build a better world for cotus and our human co-inhabitants. I will not apologize for the times when my less objective opinions slip through into the text. Everything I say that is factual, or not my original thoughts, is cited. I have provided ample references in case you wish to check behind me. And you should. Never cease to be skeptical. The more questions you ask, the closer you come to the truth, no matter how hard some people try to mask it. Let the unmasking begin.

Your co-conspirator,
Sally Madeline Kitch

Sally Madeline Kitch — page xiii

2

Jason slammed his hand onto his alarm clock, cutting the loud rock and roll off mid-screech. Normally he wouldn't mind waking up to AC/DC, but today he didn't want to wake up at all. He groaned and rolled over, hoping that everybody would just forget he was there and let him stay in bed.

"Good morning!" a cheerful voice said from outside his closed bedroom door. "Time to get up and get ready for school."

"Just a minute, Mom," he called, throwing off the sheets. He heaved his long, gangly legs over the side of his bed until his feet met the floor. Sitting up, he ran a hand through his golden blond curls and tossed his head to clear his sleep-muddled thoughts. Jason glanced across the room at his dresser mirror. His thin, pale skin was stretched taut across the delicate bones of his angular face. He looked as fragile and as ill as he felt, not in the least prepared to take on the challenge of a new school. Yep, this was going to be a great day.

By the time he got downstairs for breakfast, he had polished up and looked a bit less like a malnourished meerkat and more like an overdressed sixth grader. Since he was an overdressed sixth grader, that was a good sign, but his morale was not much improved. He slumped into a chair at the kitchen table. His mother smiled at him encouragingly and set a plate with two homemade cinnamon rolls in front of him. He thanked her, and then proceeded to stare at them morosely. Short of going to school, eating was the last thing he wanted to do—he was far too nervous. But he knew that his mom had probably gotten up at three in the morning to make him cinnamon rolls for the first day of school, like she did every year, so he forced himself to take a few bites.

"So, have you got everything packed? Your class list? Notebooks?"

"Yes, Mom," he said.

"Are you feeling okay? Your cell phone's charged, right? Because you know, if you get to feeling sick, you can call me anytime and I'll come take you home."

"I'm fine, Mom, I promise," he said. It was a lie, really. Stress always made his tangled tube syndrome symptoms worse, and this was the most stressful day he could think of in recent history. Beneath his skin, he felt like wire threads wound tight around a spool, which was not far off base, physiologically. It made him feel sore and somewhat queasy, but he saw no point in telling his mother that. She would gladly let him stay home, which would only have the effect of allowing him to spend more time stressing out.

"I have to ask these questions. It's my job," she said, joining him at the table. "I'm a mom, I worry about these things. But you don't need to worry. Everything will be all right today. You shouldn't fret. It isn't good for you."

"But I have to freak out. It's what I do." Jason poked delicately at his breakfast with one uninterested finger and thought with concern about how he worried too much.

"I'm afraid you must have gotten that from me. You didn't have the luck to get your fath—to not get that trait." For an awkward minute neither of them spoke. Jason glanced at the empty third chair where his father should be.

"It'll be fine," Jason's mother said, opting to trade the subject of the painful past for something more in the present. "School, that is. What is it you're afraid of?"

Jason shrugged. "Everything." That wasn't exactly true. When he thought about it, he knew there wasn't much he needed to worry about. He knew where his classes were. They were all on the same hall, so there was no way he could get lost. Schoolwork always came easy to him. The social aspect was sort of terrifying, but as long as he kept his head down it would probably work out all right. Mostly, the whole idea of going to middle school bothered him, even if the details didn't. He wasn't just a kid anymore. He was a middle-schooler. It was a major transition, and it frightened him. Jason was sure he was overreacting, but he couldn't shake the feeling of dread. Even so, he did his best to push it to the back of his mind and took another bite of cinnamon roll.

Alex. Aleeeex. Wake up! Sally's command pierced Alex's dreams. The murky nightmare images dissipated and his eyes blinked open. All right, all right, I'm awake, he shot back with his thoughts. Belatedly, Alex thought that he should have tried to preserve the dream, but why bother? For the last several months he hadn't been able to summon a single clear vision. He sat up and stretched, lean muscles rippling beneath his skin. Something important was happening today, wasn't it? Ah, right, school. Yuck. Sixth grade. Even worse. One-hundred and eighty days spent in an awkward pre-teen body.

Alex rolled out of bed and threw on some clothes. He was about to walk out the door when he thought perhaps he should turn the light on and check his outfit. And his body. After all, it was very important that he appear as the child he was pretending to be. He could see well enough in the dark, of course, but figured it was best to be thorough. He flipped the switch and walked over to the full-length mirror leaning against the wall. Black polo shirt. Long black pants. Looked dress code-appropriate enough. The form he had taken also looked suitable, he supposed. However, he lacked the true shapeshifting ability that could hide his build, which was too masculine for an eleven-year-old, or the canine teeth, which were too long and sharp for a human. He decided not to worry about it. He turned around and craned his neck to see his back in the mirror. Damn it. He had hoped the shirt would be enough cover. Sometimes Alex thought the disadvantages of having wings outweighed the benefits. A black leather jacket fixed the problem well enough, and Alex exited his room and walked up the stairs to the first floor.

"There you are. I was starting to think that I'd have to go and drag you up here," Sally said in greeting. She was standing by the basement door, hands resting impatiently on her hips. Her attempt at reverse-aging her adult body to look like a child had been more successful than Alex's. Then again, she was a cotu, and cotus are built for shifting. Alex was disappointed to note that she had even been able to reduce her feminine figure to appear prepubescent.

As soon as Alex cleared the threshold of the ground floor, Sally pivoted on her heel and trotted down the hall. Alex followed her to the kitchen. Only the light above the cooking island was on. There, Jenna was stoically doing some sort of food preparation. She looked sort of half-awake, still in her silky white nightgown and with her amber locks tangled and dangling chaotically. Sally appeared as her opposite, already showered, groomed, and dressed at 6:30 in the morning.

Her wavy hair was brushed to a shine and her brilliant green eyes were awake and alert. As usual, she was ready to take on the world before it had even come to life yet. She joined Jenna and removed a bagel from a bag on the counter.

"You want one?" she asked Alex, gesturing with the bread.

Alex shook his head. Instead, he pulled a thermos out of the refrigerator. He took an experimental sip of the red liquid inside. Still relatively fresh. He took a hearty slug and almost immediately felt energy creeping into his limbs. Nothing like a dose of vodka and B negative to start the day off right.

"Good morning Jen," he said in greeting. She mumbled something similar in response. "What are you doing up so early? You don't have to be anywhere until almost nine."

"I couldn't sleep," Jenna said, brushing a lock of hair out of her delicate, porcelain face. "Too much thinking. So I decided to get up and prepare breakfast."

"We're having bagels…what do you need to prepare?"

"I have to de-tomato Scarlet's," Jenna explained in a matter-of-fact manner.

Alex looked down at her hands and noticed that she was indeed removing hunks of tomato from a veggie bagel and placing them in a separate little pile on the plate.

"Why can't Scarlet de-tomato her own bagel?" Sally asked while rummaging through the pantry for a jar of peanut butter.

"She was out late honing her combat skills with several of the other werewolves last night. I decided to let her sleep in another half hour or so," Jenna replied.

"You're such a nice person. Unlike some people, Sally." Alex set his thermos down on the counter and let his eyes wander across the strange paraphernalia that lay there. There were three labeled folders arranged in geometric fashion: "Hope – Southern High School," "Jenna & Scarlet – JFK High School," and "Alex & Sally – Kendall Middle School." Littered around them were strange articles of witchcraft. A small red candle, an iron pentagram, and an intriguing bag of dried vegetation—obviously Hope's stuff. Alex picked up the plastic bag of plants for closer inspection.

"Alex…" Sally said in warning.

"I was just looking," he said, tossing the bag back on the granite countertop. Like he was stupid enough to smoke anything of Hope's again.

"Just because we're spending the day among children doesn't mean you need to act like one," Sally pointed out with mild disgust. Alex shrugged.

"There's nothing wrong with being young at heart."

"There could be something wrong with being stoned, however," Jenna said, her tone only half-jesting. "The Guardians could rise anywhere or anytime, so we need to be paying attention."

"Yeah, 'cause I've had such luck looking for them sober," Alex said. He understood that five people were limited in the amount of the universe they could possibly scan at once, but even so he was frustrated by the fact that they were only searching a specific population within an approximately twenty-mile radius, and had been for decades. "Every year, it's the same old schools and the same old result. Maybe I need a little Mary Jane to *expand my horizons* or something." They might attend one school for a couple months, and when nothing turned up try another, until the academic year ended. For Alex, the summer was usually an unending string of attempts to help Hope devise a Guardian-finding spell, while Sally kept scanning for omens in the news, Scarlet honed her various martial skills, and Jenna kept reading old books to see if something popped. Nothing was coming of it. What was the point?

"Hey now! I've very carefully determined the region and populace where we're most likely to find a rising Guardian," Sally said, stabbing the spreading knife into the peanut butter for emphasis. Alex groaned inwardly. He had started her off again.

"Texts show that the vast majority of heroes and such rise when they're between eleven and sixteen years old," she said, ranting, "or whatever the age of adolescence is for their species. And Brunswick is a central location in our universe, a hub of energies, where many different supernatural forces converge and mix. It follows that kids here would be most susceptible. My logic is sound." She spread peanut butter onto her bagel with unnecessary force.

"Yes, we know. Of course it is," Jenna said soothingly. "No one is questioning you. Alex is just grumpy because it's early. Right, Alex?"

Alex nodded vigorously in agreement.

"Okay. I'm sorry." Sally's hackles lowered.

Alex shot Jenna a grateful glance and then began rifling through the folder with his name on it. Sally prepared these folders whenever any of the five Guardian acolytes had a mission. Most of the information in them was the same each time, but it made Sally happy when the others read the notes she supplied because it made her feel useful. She and Jenna had started out as the crux of the operation, translating and dissecting the prophecies that they based their work on. But now the texts were yielding no new clues, and thus it was that Sally was obsessively printing out packets of info and Jenna was de-tomatoing bagels. And they were masquerading as adolescent humans to infiltrate the ranks of the candidate Guardians. All in all, Alex thought the effort was fairly lame, but he would never voice the full extent of his opinion out loud. Sally would be upset. And she might hurt him.

The folder contained each of the twelve prophecies, along with Sally and Jenna's explanations of each, and a detailed, multi-page map of the school he and Sally would be attending. He glanced over the illustration, refreshing his memory of the building plan. Kendall was a small school, which made scanning the students easier. It also always made blending in harder. The idea of spending another year amongst juvenile humans compelled Alex to take another long draught of alcohol-spiked blood. He had been against this idea from the get-go, but Sally had proposed the plan, and Sally won almost every argument. Especially with him.

Jason slunk into homeroom trying to be stealthy, which was next to impossible for someone who was nearly six inches taller than his peers. Fortunately, everyone else was busily catching up with old friends and meeting new ones. Being that Jason didn't know anyone present and was too shy to strike up a conversation, he chose to forgo talking and scan the room to find an empty seat. With people milling about everywhere, it was hard to tell. The only seats that were clearly vacant were those next to a guy who looked like the sort who you would find empty seats around. His hair was long and stringy and radioactive orange—glowing even more brightly against the backdrop of his all-black outfit. Jason thought he saw the glimmer of an earring in one of his ears.

This was just the kind of person Jason was afraid he would meet in middle school. Then again, orange-hair was also the only other person in the classroom who was not socializing, which made Jason inclined to like him. Sure that it was a bad idea, Jason walked over and took the seat to the left of the ginger biker. He tried not to stare, but it was a challenge. Now that he was closer, Jason could see that not only were this guy's ears pierced several times, but he also had a bar through one eyebrow and black-painted fingernails. Jason was seriously reconsidering his choice of seating, but then getting up would be offensive. Jason continued to argue with himself for a very long minute and a half before the scary guy took notice of him. He turned his head a fraction and fixed Jason with an icy blue gaze. Jason froze like a deer in the headlights.

"Relax, kid. I don't bite," the guy said with a chuckle.

His voice reminded Jason of someone he had heard before. The accent was from a foreign country, that much was obvious. "I—I believe you," Jason said lamely. Further conversation was cut off as the teacher entered the classroom, looking rather harried.

"Hello, I'm Mrs. Harold, and as soon as I find the roll, I'll take it," she said by way of greeting, while shuffling madly through papers on her cluttered desk. "Aha!" She held up a pink sheet triumphantly. "Here it is! Everyone sit down, we need to get this over with. Ale—" She stopped, bringing the page closer to her face and squinting through her glasses. "Alex—"

"Alexandru Alucard is here," the guy next to Jason said, wearing the same vaguely amused look he had given Jason. "And Alex is fine."

"Ah, yes, thank you, Alex. I'm afraid I'm not the best in the world with names. Now, Julie Armstrong..."

Jason made an effort to memorize the names as the roll was called, with limited success. He noticed that Alex seemed to be doing the same, focusing intently on each person in turn as they laid claim to their names. Perhaps he was having better luck learning identities. Once Mrs. Harold finished calling roll, she allowed chaos to resume, saying only that at 7:55 everyone needed to go to their first period class. Jason double-checked the class schedule that he clutched tightly in his right hand. First Period—Social Studies—Mrs. Harold.

"So you aren't going anywhere either, huh?"

Jason jumped. Alex pulled back, looking slightly surprised. He had been peeking at Jason's schedule over his shoulder.

Jason tried to relax, taking a deep breath that failed to be calming. "You scared me," he said in explanation.

Alex nodded once, slowly, eyes narrowing almost imperceptibly in an expression Jason didn't know how to read. He shifted awkwardly under the weight of Alex's gaze.

"I noticed," Alex said after a moment. The unreadable look vanished, and the relaxed, open feel came back to his face. "You know I really wasn't lying when I said I don't bite. Chill out, man." Alex held his hands up in a gesture of surrender. Jason felt guilty. Alex might be a perfectly nice person—no sense in making judgments based on what the guy was wearing.

"Sorry. I'm just jumpy today I guess," Jason said, apologizing meekly.

"Uh-huh. You don't know anybody at this school, do you?"

"No one. Everyone from my elementary school went to Jefferson, but I went here for the science stuff. How'd you guess?"

"I'm good at reading people," Alex said dismissively. "And I don't know anybody, either, or at least not anybody in my classes. I know one chick in another class, but basically I'm alone too. Guess that's something we have in common."

"Yeah." Jason remembered what he had been trying to figure out. "Bela Lugosi!"

Alex raised an eyebrow quizzically.

"Sorry," Jason said, feeling himself blush. "It's just I remembered w—who it is you sound like." Jason cringed, afraid he had offended his first middle school "friend."

Alex burst out laughing. "One of the greatest actors of all time. I'll take that as a compliment," Alex said as soon as his chortling subsided. "Except Bela Lugosi was Hungarian, and I'm Romanian. But I admit the accents are very similar."

"Dracula is one of my favorite movies," Jason said, starting to feel slightly less nervous. "I watched it all the time when I was a kid. It never scared me, because the special effects were so bad."

"Armadillo-rats all the way, man," Alex said, raising a fist into the air. Jason laughed. That was one of Jason's favorite parts of Bela Lugosi's Dracula—when the coffin chamber is first shown, there are vermin crawling all over the place, including armadillos, which were apparently intended to look like big, scary, scaly rats. Perhaps in 1931 people thought they did. Now it was just funny.

"You know there are Romanians who resent the Dracula legend?" Alex said. "I never understood that. I always thought Dracula was the greatest thing to come out of my country."

"Wasn't Bram Stoker Irish or something, though?"

"Whatever. We've got the castle."

"Hey, have you ever been to that castle?"

"What, 'Dracula's castle'? Yeah, once or twice," Alex said with a shrug.

"Really? What's it like?"
"Old, mostly. Kind of regal, in a dead and decaying sort of way."
"Cool..."
"I like you already, kid."

Alex frowned in concentration. With his eyes closed, the room was a black canvas covered with splashes of roughly human-shaped colors. Some were a cool, misty blue, some a warm, glowing pink, and others were spattered through different bands of the visible light spectrum. A few were even in colors not visible to normal eyes, but in the eye of his mind, Alex could see them. Even those were not extraordinarily unusual, though. Nothing about the room full of people seemed noteworthy. He thought perhaps he could sense a twinge of something. But then he couldn't see it anywhere. Alex let out a frustrated sigh, only then realizing that he had been holding his breath. He opened his eyes and the image vanished, the real world flooding back in. Somehow, Alex thought the school cafeteria had been more appealing the other way.

Glancing sideways, Alex saw his new friend looking at him curiously. Alex didn't answer his unspoken question, and his friend didn't say anything about it. That was one thing Alex liked about this Jason—he didn't ask too many questions, or at least not the kind of questions that would be hard for Alex to answer. Alex turned around sideways on his excessively uncomfortable plastic stool so that he was looking at Jason head-on. Alex found it amazing how familiar Jason looked. He hadn't decided who it was he looked like yet, but he was getting close. The eyes were different, a deep green with golden flecks. Whoever Alex was remembering had browner eyes. But the curly, golden hair; the tall, painfully thin frame; and tapering face— that was the same. Even his smell was familiar, both primate and feline, human and cotu. The way he carried himself, too, as though he was trying to curl inside and hide, and how his eyes wandered restlessly, never hovering on any one thing for more than a few seconds. It was so much like someone else he knew or had known. Now who was it?

"So, um, who was that girl you already knew?" Jason said, pulling Alex out of his reverie. The last sixth grade class had just entered the cafeteria. Alex gestured at where Sally sat at another table and momentarily switched his gaze to her. Half a second later he realized that this was probably Jason's objective, to get Alex to look at something other than him. Alex made a mental note to try not to stare so much.

"Sally Kitch," Alex told him.

"How do you know her?" Jason asked. He had a soft, hesitant voice—easy on the ears. Alex liked that about him too. Most people were too loud.

"We live in the same neighborhood," Alex replied, barely stopping himself from saying "The same house." That would have been awkward to explain.

"She has really pretty eyes," Jason said, sounding impressed. Alex wasn't surprised that he'd noticed. Sally's lime-green, vibrant eyes were her most striking feature. They were what had drawn Alex to her in the first place.

"That she does. Very pretty."

Kitch Manor was just far enough out of town to be the sort of place that people talked about. Alex had often heard it said that Kitch Manor was abandoned, or haunted, and once he had even heard someone say that an old crone lived there. That one had almost made him laugh out loud. No, for the past sixty years, it had been home to him and the girls. Before that, it really had been abandoned. Sally's obscenely rich parents had built it as a vacation home and used it all of twice before gifting it to their eldest daughter. It was an ancient construction, about a hundred and fifty years old, made of dark bricks with black roof tiles and black trimmings in a kind of Gothic-cathedral style. It was the sort of building that would have looked creepy even when it was new. Sally loved it. Alex had not been quite so enthusiastic about it when they had first moved in. Once he had lived there a while, though, he started to see its inherent charm and elegant beauty. It was a work of art, but more importantly, it was home.

The vehicular roar faded away as the black-and-chrome motorcycle came to a stop in the manor garage. Alex disembarked, Sally following behind, removing the helmet she insisted on wearing. He pulled the bike up onto its center stand just as a teal-accented Volkswagen bus pulled up beside him. Hope, the fifth member of their operation, opened the driver's door and jumped lightly to the ground. She was small and slight, sort of pixyish, with little figure in her adult form and none now that she had taken the appearance of someone much younger. To compensate, she accented her looks with short dresses, lots of sparkly jewelry, and so much make-up that her face was hardly visible. Even her faceted, multicolored eyes paled in comparison to the loud eye shadow surrounding them. Today was the first time Alex thought that her garb might be reasonable. Because she was doing her observation in a high school, the excessive ornamentation would fit right in.

'—and the science building is SO FAR AWAY from my history class, I just can't believe it! But it's okay, because I can cut through the catacombs to get there, and those are awesome.' Scarlet's telepathic monologue cut into Alex's mind space. On cue, she climbed out of the side door, followed shortly by Jenna. Scarlet looked out of place standing between Hope and Jenna, who were both slight and very feminine. Of the three, Alex thought she was the best-looking, second only to Sally, but in the society in which he had grown up she would have been considered grossly unfeminine. She was rough, tough, and had no need for men whatsoever. Her light blonde hair, streaked with natural darker lowlights, was cut short and allowed to hang down in her face, obscuring her sea-green eyes most of the time. Her skin was nigh impenetrable and as tan as bronzed leather from hours spent outside every day. Scarlet only wore shoes when forced and generally sported comfortable, but entirely unstylish clothes that suited her fancy and were fluid enough to abide her high-energy lifestyle. At present, she was wearing Crocodile Hunter khaki shorts and a homemade tie-dye t-shirt. Her sandals were nowhere to be seen. She'd probably lost them somewhere.

"I mean, what could be cooler than catacombs?" Scarlet blurted, finishing her train of thought in the physical realm. She grinned with childish glee at the idea.

"I can't imagine," Alex replied with a friendly smirk. Scarlet's exuberance was refreshing, if somewhat inappropriate. In the midst of serious universal peril, she could still manage to find something to be happy about. Her aura was pleasant too—a soft, undulating blue-and-green mist that seemed to have its own inner light, shining through breaks in the color.

"How'd we all get back here at the same time?" Hope asked of no one in particular, glancing at Scarlet with disdain. Unlike Alex, she was never pleased with Scarlet's immaturity. "Doesn't middle school get out an hour earlier?"

"I made Alex go grocery shopping," Sally said, brandishing a reusable fabric bag full of boxes and cans.

Scarlet became more serious while still sounding bubbly. "Sooo, how'd it go? None of us had any luck," Jenna said. She closed the book she was reading in order to participate in the conversation.

"Same here," Alex said. "I thought I felt something, but then I couldn't get a location. May have been wishful thinking. I'll keep trying, though, to make sure I don't miss anything."

"Obviously you found something, because there's a phone number written on your arm," Hope observed. Alex looked at where she was pointing.

"Oh yeah, I'd forgotten about that. That's this kid in my class, Jason. He looked kind of freaked, so I started talking to him. Turns out we have a lot in common. Relatively speaking."

"Good for you, Alex!" Sally said. "I can't remember the last time you made a friend!"

"Thank heaven for small miracles," he agreed, not sure if she was being sarcastic or not. Sally had a peculiar way of putting you down even when she was trying to be nice. "By the way, you remember Thomas, right?"

"Yes, I remember," Sally said unenthusiastically. That was an experiment that went rather horribly wrong. Even Scarlet's smile faded as everyone remembered how Thomas had misused all the skills they taught him.

"Did he ever have a kid?" Alex asked.

"Oh, yeah, he and his wife had a boy," Sally said, digging around in her purse. A second later she raised an arm in triumph, her key ring clasped between two fingers. "I saw him as a patient when he was young. You didn't know?" Sally turned the key in the lock and entered the house. Her four companions migrated towards the entryway after her.

"Uh, you didn't tell me?" Alex replied with thick sarcasm.

"Um...apparently not. Sorry?"

"That's all right. We've got bigger fish to fry." Alex couldn't help being a little upset, because he and Thomas had been good friends at one time. It would have been nice to know what went on with his life. Well, Sally wasn't known for her communication skills. Besides, like he had said, there were more important issues at hand. Something about Jason bothered him, though, and it was not just the borderline eerie similarity to Thomas. He shrugged and made a mental note to pay closer attention to Jason tomorrow. In the meantime, Alex was looking forward to spending the afternoon in the orchards, pruning, once his chore was out of the way. As the only resident fond of yard work, he got the privilege of doing all of it. No such luck today, however.

"Meet me downstairs," Sally whispered in his ear as she brushed past him on their way toward the heart of the house. Inwardly, Alex sighed. Whenever Sally wanted to discuss something with him privately, it didn't mean good things, not anymore. At least he wouldn't have to worry about it for a while yet. The first hour or so after school was traditionally when the girls had their down time together. As he had expected, today was no exception.

With business discussion out of the way, the four girls sat in a circle on the floor of the what they called the living room, a space that had been originally intended to be the foyer, and chatted like real teenish girls about school. Alex refilled his thermos, and then sat in his black beanbag to legally eavesdrop.

"—a kid in our class said that his brother had Ms. Trust two years ago. Supposedly, this brother would throw pencils and erasers at her and she wouldn't even notice. I thought he was making it up, until I met her," Sally was saying.

"She can't be that bad," Scarlet said, defending the spacey science teacher. "Not if she's teaching you about animals!" She grinned and wriggled as though wagging the tail that would only have been present on a full-moon night.

"Scarlet, what could she possibly teach me about animals that you haven't already told me a million times?" Sally asked.

"Well…not much, but it'll be fun!"

"My bio teacher said that we're doing a squid dissection this year. I don't think I can handle that," Hope said in despair. She paused in French-braiding her hair to give a delicate shudder.

"Hope, you've assisted Sally during surgery," Jenna said.

"But, *squid!*"

Okay, so maybe they weren't chatting *exactly* like normal girls. Alex chuckled softly to himself. Listening to them talk was always entertaining. He lounged lazily in his beanbag to watch the show, and for the next hour they put the fate of the world on the back burner and just enjoyed each other's company, the picture of harmony and friendship.

"I'm saying that our tactics aren't working."

"I know, Sally, but what do you expect me to do about it?"

Alex refrained from pointing out that most of the tactics in question were, in fact, hers. He was perched awkwardly on the only unoccupied lab stool in the basement, trying not to disturb anything in the room. Every other surface—floor, stools, and counters—was covered with strange objects and papers that held no meaning for him. Sally's arts were potions and biology, two things that Alex could not wrap his mind around. He tried to avoid Sally's lab, because every time he entered he just knew that he would mess up something she was doing. If there was one thing that made Sally madder than anything else, it was someone ruining one of her experiments, or whatever it was she was doing. That was why he was confused and slightly annoyed that she had made him join her in there to talk.

"We can only cover a tiny space," Sally said, continuing. "I still stand by my probability calculations, but honestly, what are the chances of us finding anything by staying in Brunswick? We need more people, Alex. You've said so yourself."

Well, at least that explained why they were having this conversation in the lab. Sally had been campaigning since the beginning to hire other people to help them in their search. Hope wouldn't allow it, saying that the more people they involved in this, the more vulnerable they would be. Hired workers are easily bribed by the other side. Alex understood her point. Hope would know that people can't be trusted. She had been the victim of witch hunts before, and it taught her to be suspicious. Alex didn't blame her for feeling that way, but at the same time, he was inclined to agree with Sally—five individuals couldn't feasibly search the globe for twelve people. Heaven forbid one of the would-be Guardians was from another world. It was one of those issues that Sally and Hope, as the powerhouses of the operation, frequently clashed over. Alex had told Sally that he agreed with her, but was afraid to say so publicly. It would increase friction in the group, and unity was vital to this operation. He should have known that staying silent would come back to bite him.

"You mean we should go behind Hope's back and recruit others to help us," Alex said, stating the idea for confirmation. Sally nodded. "You know how bad an idea that is. If Hope finds out, we'll be down to two instead of five. Maybe three. Either way, not a good situation."

"The loss of two or three could be counteracted by gaining dozens," Sally said. "Besides, if we keep going at this rate we'll never get anywhere. Something has to give. If it means alienating Hope, well, I hate to do that, but I will, if necessary."

"Let's just give it one more year. If school ends this time and we haven't found anything, we'll see about expanding our search party. Okay?" Alex pleaded, hoping to once again put off making the difficult decision. Sally thought about that for a moment.

"All right, but if June gets here and we don't have any leads, I *will* take matters into my own hands, whether you're with me or not," Sally said, finally agreeing. Tilting her head down a notch and raising her eyebrows, she fixed him with a gaze that left no room for argument.

"I'll be with you," Alex promised. "Always. I just think we shouldn't jump into this too quickly. Hope and the others are the greatest allies we could wish for, not to mention the greatest friends. I don't want to lose that."

"Me neither," Sally said quietly. She crossed her arms and leaned back, gaze drifting away and releasing its hold on Alex's face. The two of them stared out into space for a long moment, lost in their own contemplations. After a minute Sally walked over to an incubator on the other side of the room and began to take out petri dishes of fuzzy white cultures. Alex took the hint and gladly left the lab. He had his own work to attend to, anyway. He vaulted up the steps to the first floor, coming out onto the main hall. He passed the living room, catching a quick glimpse of Hope and Scarlet working diligently on opposite couches, and then started climbing the fancy, spiraling main staircase one silver-veined, black marble step at a time.

Many dozens of steps later, he emerged in the West Tower, his own private meditation space. It was a small cylindrical room walled in only with the bricks from which the manor was built. One rectangular window was set opposite the door, shuttered, but with slats in the wood that allowed in just enough light for a vampire to see by. The lone piece of furniture was a dark red cushion lying in the center of the black stone floor. This tower was where Alex came to focus. It used to be that he could project from anywhere, but lately he had been struggling to connect to the outside energy sphere. Once he could see the future and know the mind of everyone in the present, but something was weakening him, sapping his natural gifts. Trying to catch a passing vision these days was like trying to listen to the radio underneath a thunderhead—the signal was nothing but static.

The auras were still clear for now, however, and he intended to take advantage of that while it lasted.

He sat down cross-legged on this cushion and closed his eyes, focusing until the room fell away, and he was within himself, a floating spirit in a strange dreamscape. His eyes flickered beneath his lids as he allowed himself to drift free, out of his body, out of the tower, and into the town below, to search among the spirits for those that stood out from the rest.

3

Jason crouched at the edge of a small, murky pond, dropping in pinches of fish food. He watched as each flake vanished with a tiny splash and a barely audible plopping sound, leaving only a series of circular ripples spreading across the surface as evidence that it had ever been there.

"Whatcha doing?"

Jason looked over his shoulder. A familiar Brazilian-American face grinned back at him.

"Oh. Hi, Sammy. I was just feeding Vanessa."

"You know she'll never be able to fend for herself if you keep taking care of her," Sammy warned, dropping to his haunches beside Jason. Sammy was Jason's best friend, even though they were polar opposites. Where Jason was tall, pale, meek, and sickly, Sammy was short, dark, and radiated confidence, health, and strength. His dark brown hair had just the right amount of shine and his skin sported a perfectly even bronze summer tan, bolstered by the toned muscles underneath. Sammy was the only eleven-year-old Jason knew that could possibly be a swim-suit model. In fact, Sammy had done an ad for Star Player Sports Equipment once. He had the poster in his room to prove it.

"So...how was your first week of school?" Sammy asked, prompting Jason with an elbow to his shoulder.

"Some week. It was only three days. Whose idea was that, to start on a Wednesday?"

"You're stalling."

"Yes, I am." Jason sighed. "It was okay, I think. I mean, I have one new friend, Alex. He's the only one that's said more than two words to me. He's kind of different, though."

"Well, one's better than nothing. Actually, I'm kind of impressed. It took you, what, two months to ask me if you could play soccer with us?"

"Yeah," Jason said, and then laughed hollowly.

"And what do you mean by 'different'? I mean, you could say that I'm 'different,' too."

"You're not different like Alex is," Jason said. "No way. He wears black from head to toe and has like a dozen piercings, and he paints his nails. I like him pretty well, but he still makes me kind of nervous."

"He's just doing the pre-teenage rebellion thing. Everybody does it one way or another. Well, except maybe you."

"Rebelling really isn't me. I'd rather just not be noticed at all."

Sammy nodded in reply. Jason knew that Sammy didn't approve of his antisocial habits, but Sammy had long since given up trying to change Jason's nature.

For a few minutes neither said anything more. Sammy took a pinch of fish food from the plastic container in Jason's hand and held it just above the water level, slightly inland from the shore of the pond. Two gray-green webbed feet emerged onto the bank, followed by a smooth-skinned, steel-colored nose, sniffing for the food. After a few seconds the head emerged, an oblong shape, about the size of a large lemon, and the mouth opened expectantly next to Sammy's hand. Sammy placed the flakes on the creature's tongue, careful to avoid its sharp little teeth. The creature snapped its jaws shut and quickly retreated into the pond.

"What happened to 'she'll never be able to fend for herself'?" Jason asked, teasing his friend.

Sammy smiled sheepishly.

"I will need to find something else to do with her soon, though," Jason said. "She's okay here right now, but she'll get bigger. Fish food isn't going to be enough for much longer, and sooner or later I'll need to move her to the lake." He was talking more to himself than to Sammy. Thinking about moving Vanessa to the lake was difficult. Jason swallowed hard. "I hope she'll be okay."

"She's a lake monster, J.D. I think she'll be fine," Sammy said. 'J.D.' was Jason's nickname from third grade, when he'd gone through this phase where he didn't want to be called by his real name. Only Sammy still called him that.

"But there are other lake monsters in that lake too! What if they hurt her?"

"She's smart. She'll manage," Sammy said with his usual easy optimism.

Jason wasn't convinced.

"I wish I had a swimming pool. Then I could keep her, no problem."

Sammy gave him a vexed look.

"I'm just saying," Jason added defensively. "So how was your week?"

"Fine. I've been hanging with Tyler and Robin, you know, from our old school. My teachers have already pegged me as a trouble-maker that talks too much. The usual."

"I assume you'll try out for the soccer team this year?"

"Of course! Won't you?"

"Nah. We have this team called National Academic League, though, which I'm thinking about trying out for," Jason replied.

"Oh. Well. Sounds exciting," Sammy said.

Jason couldn't tell if he meant to be sarcastic or not.

"But you'll still come play soccer with the guys on Sunday afternoons, right?" Sammy asked.

"Wouldn't miss it for the world," Jason told him. He saw that the sky was beginning to turn pink behind Sammy's head, and checked his watch.

Sammy followed Jason's gaze. "5:30? That late already?"

"Guess we'd better get going," Jason said, standing up and screwing the lid onto the container of fish food. Sammy scrambled to his feet and turned towards his neighborhood, which was on the opposite side of the park from Jason's.

"See you tomorrow," Sammy said, and began sprinting for home.

"See you," Jason called back, then turned and walked at a more leisurely pace out of the park and across the street. As he entered his neighborhood, he passed a small, red brick wall with the words "Wolf's Run" affixed onto it, then walked past the scores of homes until he reached a two-story house with yellow vinyl siding and green shutters. He walked up the porch steps and through the front door, closing it behind him. The house number, in golden figures on the thick wooden door, gleamed orange in the fading daylight.

"Two-zero-five. Wolf's Run. That's where he lives."

"Are we sure it's him?"

"Yeah, we're sure."

"So why don't we just kill him now?"

"Because we're trying to avoid making a scene. Going after him at home is our last resort. It's dangerous and it would draw attention. We aren't ready for that yet."

"Will we ever be?"

"Soon. In the meantime, we lay low and follow orders. When the time is right, the Queen will tell us."

The Crossroads United Methodist Church, after years of debate, had grudgingly decided to start an early-morning contemporary service. Because Sally had been quite vocal in favor of this development, she made a point of getting her housemates up in time to be nearly an hour early for the nine a.m. event. The band was just beginning to set up the sound system when they arrived. Scarlet, always eager at the prospect of whatever she happened to be doing, crashed through the fellowship hall doors first. Sally and Jenna entered briskly behind her, deep in conversation with one another. Hope and Alex shuffled in last, sharing a look of sympathy for their mutual hatred of mornings.

The cavernous room had been set up the night before with a scattering of tables, because the fellowship hall typically had no need for pews. Scarlet flounced into a chair at a table near the front and her companions joined her, Sally and Jenna on one side of her and Alex and Hope on the other. Alex stared blearily at a stain on the tablecloth and half-listened to Jenna in an effort to stay awake.

"I had imagined it would be all meaningless violence, that's why I'd never read it, but what elegance! The story is a cruel one, but full of philosophical points and thought-provoking parallels."

"What are you guys talking about?" Scarlet asked.

"*Frankenstein*," Sally replied. "I finally convinced Jenna to read it."

"Oh! I know that book. We used to have a first edition in the glass case at Libelli! I don't know what happened to it when the shop closed," Scarlet said. Libelli was the name of the bookstore where Scarlet worked from her teenage years right up until the day she quit to be hired as Sally's personal bodyguard. Despite spending so much time among the stacks, she lacked the literary prowess of Jenna and Sally, having been unable to read before a werewolf bite at the age of eight unexpectedly cured her crippling dyslexia. Scarlet had read widely since, but could never quite catch up.

"You should read it when I'm finished," Jenna said, her voice lacked any hint of patronizing her undereducated friend. "It's from Sally's library, so there's no due date."

"Just don't, you know, chew on it," Sally added quickly. Alex stifled a laugh. The statement was rather silly, but he knew Sally was perfectly serious. Ever since Scarlet roughed up Sally's copy of *Call of the Wild* while in werewolf form, Sally was nervous about lending her—or anyone else—books.

"Sally, I think she's got it," Hope said, "so you can probably stop reminding her now." Sally stiffened a bit at being corrected, but conceded Hope's point and apologized to Scarlet. Scarlet, caught in the middle, both thanked Hope for standing up for her and insisted to Sally that she hadn't been offended.

Alex tried to remember when Sally and Hope had started pushing each other away. It was hard to figure. When the two girls had first landed on his doorstep, they were best friends. Sally enjoyed the company of an intellectual who appreciated her view of magic and science, while Hope adored the camaraderie and loyalty she found in Sally. Maybe they had fallen out when they stopped needing each other. That was it, Alex supposed. Sally began teaching her ideas to others, forming a network of like-minded intellectuals. Hope realized that being a witch was acceptable in many circles, and no longer felt like a heathen or an outcast. When they lost that element of necessity, their differences must have become apparent. Alex let the train of thought derail at that. This was too heavy for that time of the morning.

"I'm going to go look for a coffee pot," he said, pushing his chair back from the table. As he wandered into the church kitchen, following a waft of roasted grounds, Alex almost collided with a woman in an apron.

"Geez, I'm sorry, ma'am," Alex said. His acquired Southern politeness usually helped him escape sticky social situations. Fortunately, the woman was not angry with him. She favored Alex with a warm smile, and he felt as though he knew her from somewhere.

"It's quite all right," she told him. "Were you looking for something?" She was a few inches shorter than Alex in his current, adult form, with straight light brown hair and a kind, matronly presence.

"Yeah, actually. Coffee?" Alex asked. She pointed him into the kitchen.

"On the far counter," she said. Alex thanked her and proceeded to the coffee maker. He passed a kid, perhaps the apron woman's son, mixing orange juice in a drink cooler, and thought how glad he was that Sally's too-early service would at least provide a minimum of refreshment.

"Good morning," the kid greeted over his shoulder. At the sound of his voice, Alex did a double take. No longer focused on tracking the coffee, the boy's scent registered in Alex's brain, and he couldn't believe he hadn't noticed who it was the moment he saw him.

"Jason? What are you doing here?"

Of course, Jason couldn't possibly mistake Alex's distinctive, lightly Slavic speech. He spun around, narrowly catching the cooler before his momentum knocked it on the floor.

"Alex! It's so great to see you!"

Alex was surprised by Jason's exuberant response at first, but as Jason explained his presence in the kitchen it soon became clear. Jason was a lifelong Brunswickan, and until recently he and his mother had attended the only other church in town, Brunswick Baptist. A few months ago their church hired a new pastor so the previous one could retire.

"Mom didn't like this new guy," Jason explained, "and after a while we left. This is only our second week here. Mom is super-helpful, so she volunteered to do beverages and stuff for the early service. I thought we would be sitting all by ourselves again during service, but now *you're* here! You...wouldn't mind, right? Sitting with us? Unless you have other people..." Jason paused and narrowed his eyes, scanning Alex from head to toe. "Have you always been this tall?"

"What?" He had just realized that the woman was Pansy Drake, Thomas's wife, who Alex hadn't seen in over ten years. He looked at Jason and thought, which makes you.... "Oh, no, I guess I haven't. This is the way I normally look," Alex admitted, gesturing to his body in its full adult glory. "I use a glamour to look younger for school."

"Uh-huh. Why are you at my school at all, then?"

"It's, well, it's a long story," Alex replied, desperately trying to remember which cover story Sally told him to use under these circumstances. The revelation of Jason's identity was making it difficult to think.

"Hey, Alex! Who's your friend?" Hope trotted into place at Alex's side, looking much perkier than a moment ago. Sour notes of anxiety intertwined with her orange blossom perfume. Alex sent her a grateful sidelong glance. Whether she came into the kitchen to get coffee or to check on him, she had come to his rescue.

"Ah! Jason, this is one of my housemates, Hope McClintock," Alex said. "Hope, meet one of my new classmates, Jason Drake. We were just talking about why I have to go to middle school." Please, God, let Hope have an excuse that doesn't make me sound like a pedophile.

"Yes that whole private security isn't everything you thought it would be, is it?" Hope prompted, levelly meeting Alex's gaze.

At least one of them remembered the right lies.

"Well, there are only so many careers available to an uneducated boy from Eastern Europe these days." Alex turned back to Jason's confused countenance. "What can I say? Rich people are paranoid, and they pay well, especially for more safety than a human could provide."

"And you are…?" Jason glanced from Alex to Hope and back.

"Vampire, first class." Alex pointed a finger toward his sternum. "Hope is a witch. With a more glamorous job than me."

"I write spell books," Hope said, "and sometimes sell potions online."

"Wow. Huh." Jason looked down at the floor, nodding to himself. Alex couldn't tell if his wrinkled brow was the result of skepticism or information overload. Jason shifted his eyes upward again and tilted his head. "Sunlight. How?"

"The *vampirum primum* have nothing more to fear from daylight than sunburn," Alex quipped, channeling his father, a *primum* vampire as well. "It's convenient when you need to tail two spoiled human brats around all day." He figured that claiming two charges would prevent him from having to find someone he shared all of his classes with to name as his supposed employer's child, should Jason think to ask.

"Oh. Um, okay. I guess that makes sense. Sooooo, is it cool if Mom and I sit with you two during the service?"

Alex had forgotten how this conversation started. He eyed Hope. She shrugged. He knew Hope wouldn't like sitting with someone she didn't know, but Alex wouldn't feel right denying companionship to an old friend's shy, lonely kid.

"Of course you can," Alex replied. "As soon as I get my coffee." Hope nodded in enthusiastic agreement. A few minutes later, caffeine boosts in hand, Alex and Hope shepherded Jason to the table where their housemates were seated. Jenna and Scarlet were staging a war of hand spiders while Sally watched with some amusement.

"Hey everybody, this is Jason," Alex said. The three girls ceased their sport and turned to look at Jason. Jason gave an awkward wave. "These are our other housemates," he explained to Jason.

"Hiya!" Scarlet said with a chirp. Her trademark grin lit up her face. "I'm Scarlet. You're that guy from Alex's class, right?"

"Yeah, I guess that's me." Jason shifted his weight to his heels and clasped one forearm behind his back with the other hand. Alex read something like *socially blindsided* in the young man's stance. Oh well. Scarlet and Jenna could make anyone feel at home.

"The other two are Sally and Jenna," Alex said, pointing to each in turn. "We share a house Sally inherited from her parents. A mansion, actually. Kitch Manor."

"Whoa, you mean you're the people in the creepy house that never talk to anybody?" Jason asked, then abruptly blushed bright red and clapped a hand over his mouth, as though he might capture the words before they went airborne.

"The very same," Sally said, not offended in the least. "Alex, did you tell us that Jason lived in Brunswick and I just wasn't listening?"

"No, I didn't know, either," Alex said, palms held up in surrender. "'Cause, you know, we never talk to anybody or anything."

"Well, Mom and I kind of keep to ourselves, too," Jason said, "ever since my dad, um, disappeared. People judge, so we tend to avoid them."

"Your father. Would that be Thomas Drake?" Sally asked. She had recognized who Jason was immediately.

"Yeah," Jason said with a note of wariness. Alex suspected most conversations that started with questions about his father ended badly. Alex hated that. Alex had quite liked Thomas when he was younger. He had been a smart kid. He just made some bad choices. Well, terrible choices, actually.

"Interesting," Sally said. "Well, it's a pleasure to meet you, Jason." She extended her hand, and Jason shook it, his pale, bone-thin limb eclipsed in Sally's strong, vibrant grasp.

"Jason and I were wondering if he and his mother could join us at the table," Alex said. He glanced around. No one gave any objections. "Great! Come back as soon as you finish with the orange juice, okay?"

"Um...a chicken farmer in Iowa says all his eggs hatched snakes instead of chicks." Jenna lay on her stomach on the floor of the basement den, surrounded by every newspaper and fringe magazine she had been able to find that week.

"That isn't really all that unusual, Jen," Sally said, her eyes not leaving the computer screen. "It's a fairly common witch's curse. They can even make people give birth to snakes. Chickens is nothing."

Jenna raised her eyebrows. "O-kay, then. I learned something new today. Well, that's all I've found, except the usual rain-of-toads and alleged alien abductions." Jenna refolded the newspaper in front of her and began stacking up the unhelpful publications. "Anything on your front?"

"Just a wasp epidemic in Charlotte," Sally replied, leaning back into her rocking chair. "That probably has more to do with climate change than Armageddon."

"Do you want to call it a day? We've been at this since we got back from church." Jenna rolled onto her back, her long skirt enfolding her legs in pale yellow cotton. She set her reading glasses aside on the pile of paper nearest her.

Sally showed no such signs of being ready to quit, however. She kept her face glued to her laptop, not bothering to answer Jenna's question.

"Did you find something interesting, or are you just ignoring me?" Jenna asked.

"I'm just ignoring you," Sally replied, with a tiny smirk.

"Typical." Jenna gave a theatrical sigh. "Speaking of church, today was kind of exciting."

"The preaching was nothing special, so I assume you're talking about meeting the Drakes. Is a unicorn sighting in Belize worth following up on?"

"The last time I remember seeing Jason, he wasn't any bigger than a loaf of bread," Jenna said. "Don't bother with the unicorn."

"I suppose you're right. Even if they did see a unicorn, that isn't exactly an omen, either. Not that we have any clue what kind of omens go along with a rising Guardian, anyway."

"Come on, Sally. Gossip like an old lady with me," Jenna pleaded. "You work too hard. Unwind."

Sally rolled her eyes and closed the lid of her laptop. "Fine, fine. What do you want to talk about?"

"Jason, of course! Alex hasn't made a new friend since the turn of the century. This is big news!"

"I'm more surprised that Jason is even alive," Sally said, setting the sleeping computer down on the lamp table. "I was so sure he was dead when Thomas stopped bringing him to me."

"Well, it looks like you were wrong." Jenna shifted into a sitting position so she could look at Sally straight on. "What were you treating him for?"

"TTS...Tangled Tube Syndrome."

"Come again?"

"It's a birth defect of cotu hybrids," Sally explained. "Their extra-circulatory veins are laid down incorrectly during prenatal development. It usually isn't a problem unless the veins constrict or perforate an organ. Or knot up in an inconvenient place."

"Uh-huh." Jenna pondered for a moment. "Could we try that again with more English and less jargon? I'm really more of a humanities person, you know."

"The wiry bits on the inside poke holes in things and get tangled around important stuff."

"Ah. And that can kill you?"

"The internal bleeding can. Or the blood clots," Sally said. "Most of the time it's not that big of a deal, but Jason...well, miracles do happen. I couldn't fix him, but I guess Thomas and Pansy must have found someone who could." Sally shrugged, as if it didn't hurt her pride that another physician had done something she couldn't.

"Did you diagnose him yourself?" Jenna asked.

"Yeah. After six MDs claimed it was everything from colic to cancer." Sally said and snorted. "Imbeciles."

"How would the world ever get on without you?"

"Hey, watch it with that sarcasm," Sally said with mock indignation. "And I'm sure some classically educated physicians know what they're doing. It's only *most* of them that are fools. When we're done saving the world, I'll get right on that."

After a thousand years of existence, Alex thought he knew all about being bored, but Mr. Callahan's English class took it to a whole new level. It wasn't Mr. Callahan's fault, Alex supposed. The overpopulation of sixth graders at the school had led to the creation of an unnecessary second English class, the academic purpose of which seemed to be the learning of endless pages of vocabulary words. And perhaps if Alex didn't know all those words already, he would be more interested. He glanced across the table at Jason, who was doodling in the margins of his half-finished worksheet. Then again, maybe it really was just that boring.

Write a paragraph using all ten of these vocabulary words. Could there be a bigger waste of my time? Alex erased his first sentence for at least the fifth time. The abused paper tore under the rough machinations of the pink rubber. He growled softly in the depths of his throat as he pulled a fresh sheet out of his binder. School was so much easier when Alex had originally attended. Well, maybe not, but there was less to learn. When would he ever need to use these vocab words?

"I think my brain is melting out my ears," Alex whispered in complaint—a little too loudly. Mr. Callahan looked up from his computer to give Alex the teacher death-glare. Alex ignored him, choosing instead to take a leaf from Jason's book. He flipped over the infernal worksheet and started sketching mindlessly on the back. Jason, he noticed, had started working diligently the moment the teacher looked in their direction. So obedient.

Alex's pencil had created a handful of monsters and part of a bleeding black rose on the back of his paper when he heard a sharp, brisk knock at the classroom door. He paused only a moment in the shading of his rose petal, but out of habit allowed the sounds of the classroom to enter his ears in case the interloper was a hazard. One of his classmates got up and opened the door. Alex added a long, thin stem to his rose. A set of low-impact footsteps crossed the room. Alex drew the outline of a thorn onto the stem. A soft female voice said something to Mr. Callahan. Alex wasn't paying enough attention to catch her words.

"Of course," Mr. Callahan said in answer to the request. Then, loud enough for the whole class to hear, "Jason Drake, this lady would like to speak to you for a moment."

"All right..." Jason said, sounding confused. The legs of his chair screeched against the tile floor as he rose and approached the newcomer. The woman whispered something else, and two sets of footsteps walked out of the classroom. They brushed past Alex, and the woman's scent washed over him. At this, his pencil stopped scratching. She wasn't human. In fact, she didn't smell like any species Alex recognized. He did, however, recognize the smoky odor of magic. Glancing up, he saw a sparking web of arcane power twined around the stranger's midnight-blue aura.

Alex felt a creeping sense of unease as Jason left the classroom with this indeterminate. He had learned many times in his life to beware of magic. He looked away from the door and back to Mr. Callahan, now sitting once again at his desk. Alex's extrasensory sight revealed a tiny point of bright light whizzing in orbit around the educator like an erratic electron—the unmistakable sign of a spell. Alex's pencil hovered indecisively over the paper and the half-finished rose as he debated whether he should follow his instincts or not. After a few seconds, Alex gave in. He set his pencil down and left his seat. Alex walked out the door and down the hall, following the scent trail of the indeterminate creature, who was already far ahead of him.

With Jason.

Alex knew that Jason's business was none of his, but it wouldn't hurt to keep an eye on him. Mr. Callahan's indignant cry of "Mr. Alucard!" went completely disregarded.

"It's about your bus assignment, Mr. Drake," the woman explained, ushering him into her office and closing the door. She was a tiny woman, shorter than Jason by at least a foot, but also rather intimidating with her crisp business suit and her silence. She hadn't spoken a word to Jason the whole time they were walking from his classroom to the transportation office, which were at polar opposite ends of the first floor. It was incredibly awkward and only getting more so.

"I don't ride the bus, ma'am," Jason replied, as politely as he could.

"Your mother requested that we give you a bus stop, in case of emergency," she told him, rounding her desk and opening the top drawer. "You reside at 205 Wolf's Run, in Brunswick, yes?" She turned her head to glance at him, her wide, ebony eyes meeting his for a second. The woman quickly whipped her gaze away from Jason's, allowing a sheet of her coarse black hair to hide her face.

"Yeah, I do." Jason's eyebrows furrowed quizzically. He thought his mom would have told him if she had done something like that. She was usually very good about keeping him in the loop.

The woman didn't say anything further, only reached into the desk drawer and picked something up. She held the object carefully out of Jason's view. Her tawny wrists twisted as she toyed with whatever it was. *Shhhrrrrrk.* Jason stiffened at the sound. A memory flashed so vividly in his mind that for a heartbeat it was more real than the office around him: his father, reverently handling his favorite broadsword. Jason's memory-father grasped the sheath in one hand and gently slid it off the blade; the hissing friction of leather-on-metal echoed through Jason's recollection. His pulse quickened. Could he possibly have misheard? The sound was one he had heard too many times to easily mistake.

"C—can I go now?" Jason asked urgently, his leg muscles already stiffening to make a run for it.

The woman nodded absently. Jason took that to mean "yes." He got up to leave. His eyes fell to the woman's now-visible hands, and he saw the glint of sharpened steel. All doubts Jason may have had vanished. He whirled around and sprinted for the hallway. A throwing knife clanged off of the doorframe half a second after he passed through. Jason started to turn towards the office, judging he would find safety there, but he stumbled over his own gangly legs. In the moment that he was stumbling, something happened—it was like the air thickened around him. He tried to get up. His muscles contracted but couldn't move him. Magic, he thought.

"Relax, it'll be over soon," said the woman from behind.

Jason thought she sounded oddly sincere, but he was preoccupied with his futile attempts to move, and didn't dwell on it.

"You know, I thought this would be harder," she continued speaking. The voice was coming closer, and Jason's heart was beating faster by the second. "You're so dangerous that they won't fight you themselves, but one small spell was all it took. I suppose you are very young. Well, goodbye." The dagger swished as it cut through the air, but a ginger-and-black whirlwind passed Jason and collided with his attacker. The spell broke and Jason ducked out of the blade's trajectory. He rolled over in time to see his rescuer pin the woman against the wall.

"You talk too much," Alex said critically, and sank his teeth into her throat.

"What are we going to tell him?"

"What can we tell him? We don't know anything ourselves! We don't even know what attacked him!" Sally was pacing up and down the length of the living room, so agitated that she made the room crackle with static electricity. Alex stood in the middle of the floor, and Scarlet, Hope, and Jenna stood in various other places. Everyone was too frazzled to sit down. Downstairs, an even more distraught eleven-year-old boy was shivering on an old sofa, waiting for someone to explain to him what was happening.

"It would almost be easier if he was as ignorant as the rest of humanity," Jenna said. "At least then we could fabricate a plausible story about drug lords and gang violence, and he would believe it."

"I think he'd be too smart for that anyway," Alex said, contesting gloomily. For a while none of them said anything. "We've got to say something," Alex continued speaking, breaking the long silence. "I'll go down and talk to him. Can you guys go do your research thing, try to find out what the hell just happened?"

"Language," Sally admonished reflexively. "And yes, we certainly can." She abruptly changed her direction and marched down to the basement, with Alex and the girls trailing behind. Waiting for them at the bottom of the stairs was Jason, crouched on a scruffy sofa and wringing his hands. Sally nodded to him in acknowledgment and led Hope, Scarlet, and Jenna past the main room and down the hall to the library. Jason watched them pass, then turned his frightened gaze back to Alex. For a heartbeat they locked eyes, and then Alex dropped his.

"We got nothing," he said in shame, running a hand through his hair. "We can't figure out why or what or who or anything. I'm sorry. But we *are* working on it." Jason nodded. He was eerily calm, probably still in shock, but Alex could hear his heartbeat—so fast that the sound was almost a vibration, instead of a steady thumping.

"Does Mom know?"

"Yeah. I called her. She's on her way here." It had been a difficult conversation. Alex had only met Pansy a few times since the school year began. They had been acquainted somewhat when Thomas first started dating her, true, but Pansy certainly didn't know Alex well enough to expect him to deliver such frightening news about her son.

"Is she okay? No one went after her too, did they?" Jason asked, panic blooming in his voice.

"She's fine," Alex said, hurrying to assure him. "Confused, but fine."

"Thank God Mom's all right," Jason said in a gush. The silence stretched out. Alex rocked back and forth on his heels, feeling completely useless.

"You killed that person," Jason said, his voice unwavering but faint. Alex couldn't identify his tone. Jason kept his eyes trained on the worn beige rug beneath his feet, so Alex couldn't read his expression, either.

"Yes, I did. Does that bother you?"

"A little bit," Jason replied, nodding. "Not that I'm not grateful!" he hurried to add, snapping his head back up. "I am. Really, really grateful."

"You're welcome," Alex said, not knowing what else to say under such circumstances. Guilty thoughts flickered in his mind. I killed a person right in front of you and you'll probably be traumatized for the rest of your life. But you're welcome. "Anytime. Although I hope I never have to do it again."

"Same here." Jason paused, and a puzzled expression crawled onto his face from the forehead down. "You drank her blood."

"Yes...that is what I do," Alex replied. "You know that."

"You didn't know what she was...and you drank her blood?" Jason said again, his upper lip curling in disgust. "Isn't that some kind of food safety hazard?"

"Oh. Yes." Alex cleared his throat. "That may not have been my best decision. But, hey, I was hungry, and she tasted good. Like human, but not. Not like a witch, either. Sweeter. Kind of sugary. Purple, though, which is weird...and I'm totally grossing you out, aren't I?"

"Uh-huh."

"Sorry, kid. Didn't mean to," Alex told him.

Jason nodded noncommittally and switched his gaze to his hands. "Hey, Alex?" he said after a moment.

"Mmm?"

"This isn't the end, is it?"

"What do you mean?"

"This wasn't random. Someone wants me dead. Whoever it is, they'll probably try again." It was a statement, not a question.

"This would be easier if you weren't so perceptive."

"Yeah, I thought so. I'm not going to be safe for a while, then." Jason's voice shook as he shared his conclusion.

"I'll be watching your back," Alex promised. "Whatever this is, you won't be alone in it. I'll make damn sure of that."

"Jason's mother is here to take him home. I'm going with him." Alex had made the decision the moment he said that he would look after Jason. Someone had to be around at all times to keep him safe, and Jason would be most comfortable with Alex.

"Sounds good," Sally said, not looking up from the heavy leather-bound tome she was scanning. "Let us know if anything happens."

"I will. And tell me if you find anything out. I can question Jason some more, but I think we've got all the information we're going to get."

"Hey, what did you do with the body of the thing you killed?" Sally asked.

"Threw it in a dumpster in an alley behind the school. Why?"

"I'm going to dissect it. See what it can tell us. That may at least help us ID the species."

"I'll go get it," Scarlet said.

"Then we're all set," Alex said. "I'll talk to you later. Good luck."

"Right back at'cha," Sally replied.

Jason was scrunched into the back corner of his closet, flipping slowly through his collection. His father had given him the book for his seventh birthday. It was probably meant for those wallet-size photographs, but his father had put a limited-edition, collectible Rolling Stones guitar pick in the first plastic sleeve. Jason had been filling the pages with picks ever since. The book was about half full now. All of the picks had a piece of paper behind them saying where and when Jason had gotten each of them. That book held a lot of good memories, all of them connecting back to his father. It was where Jason turned when he was upset, or when he needed to think. Right then, it was a question of both.

Down a set of stairs and a few feet to the right, Alex was lounging on the couch, watching TV Land and making sure, Jason figured, that no one else tried to kill him today. He was pretty used to weird—he had grown up in Brunswick, after all, the town where the paranormal is normal—but even by his standards, today had been weird, not to mention mind-numbingly terrifying. He was having difficulty wrapping his brain around the idea that someone would try to kill him. He never picked fights, never got on anyone's bad side. Why him? It could be an enemy of his father's. Jason was old enough now to realize that his father had more enemies than friends. But if that was the case, why now? Thomas wasn't here to see it. It was senseless, which made it all the more frightening. Jason felt a little better having Alex around. He had seen the way Alex tossed that...whatever-she-was around like a rag doll and tore out her throat like nobody's business. The flip side was that Jason had nothing but Alex's word that the same wouldn't happen to him. But, of the two, Jason much preferred the devil he was acquainted with.

Alex wouldn't always be around, though. Sooner or later, they would get separated, and Jason would be vulnerable again. He knew how to fight to an extent—another gift from his father—but he didn't have the strength to pack much of a punch. And he didn't even know what he was fighting. Was this just one psycho, or was there some sort of conspiracy? And if his attacker wasn't a human or a witch, and Alex believed that she wasn't, then what was she? How could Jason defend himself? There were too many questions and not enough answers.

Jason almost jumped out of his skin as a sound ripped through the room, before he realized it was just the telephone. He exhaled with relief and curled back into his corner, waiting for his heart to stop hammering against his ribcage. It slowed down some, but not much.

"Hey, Jason?" he heard his mother whisper from outside of the bedroom door. Jason closed the book—it wasn't helping much anyway—and sequestered it back under a box of Legos.

"Yes?" he called back, picking himself up off the floor.

"Sally's on the phone, and Alex says you need to hear what she has to say."

"So, I cut into our culprit. It took me awhile, but I've figured out what she is. For the most part, she looks human, but for a few interesting anatomical anomalies, particularly of the intestines and forebrain. Well, and the royal purple blood. That's kind of a dead give—"

"The point, Sally?"

"Fine, fine." She said, biting each word. "You're so impatient. As I was saying, she's a genie."

Alex and Jason looked at each other quizzically.

"You mean the kind that you let out of a lamp and they give you three wishes? I thought those were a myth," Jason said.

"And I thought those were just exaggerated stories about witches," Alex said.

"Don't you two know by now that almost all myths have a basis in reality? According to several reliable accounts, genies, also known as genia, are a human-like, magic-working breed from North Africa and the Arabian Peninsula. They're small in stature, and the species is entirely composed of females. All of those facts are in congruence with Jason's story. What doesn't check out is that I can't find any record of a genie ever hurting anyone. Not so much as a frog. They seem to be a peaceful race. Keep mostly to themselves. Sometimes they're even helpful, hence the three wishes thing. I can't figure why one would try to knife a human, let alone a child. We're still looking, so we might turn up more answers soon. I thought you guys would want to know about the progress ASAP."

"Yeah. Thanks for helping," Jason said.

"You're welcome. Any friend of Alex's is a friend of mine. And I kind of owe your dad one. Or several. Right, so, that's everything. If you guys don't have anything to add, I'll get back to work."

"Wait, I have a question," Alex said. "You said they're all female?"

"Yep."

"Then how..."

"Alex? *Really*? Not in front of the kid."

"Oh. Right. Sorry."

"And I don't know. I wasn't looking for *that* information. Since, you know, we kind of have other, potentially life-or-death things to worry about?"

"Yeah. Of course. I'm focused."

"Uh-huh. Sure you are. Call if you need anything *important*. You too, Jason. You've got our number, right?"

"I do."

"Great. Later." *Click.* Alex placed the phone back in the cradle.

"One thing she didn't tell us is how to kill them," Jason said haltingly. The word 'kill' caught in his throat—never before in his life had Jason considered killing anything larger than a spider. His stomach turned and his extracirculatory veins tightened at the prospect.

"She said they're human-like. That means 'easy to kill.' The one that attacked you was. I don't think they're very strong, physically. It's the magic we'll need to look out for," Alex replied.

"What can you do about that?" Jason asked.

"That's Hope's field, not mine. She's a witch, you know. She can probably conjure up some sort of spell-shield for you once she knows more, but until then, the best we can do is be on our guard, and avoid getting close enough to get jinxed. I know it sounds...unimpressive, but we'll make it work. The girls make a great team. They'll figure this out. We'll keep you safe, Jason. And on the bright side, at least now we know what we're facing."

"What news do you bring me?" The room was small, lit only by a single candle on a square wooden table in the center of the stone floor. Wax melted onto an assortment of charts, maps, and scrolls that spread across the table and the floor. The creator of this orderly chaos sat in the shifting shadows behind the globe of light created by the flame, only her tented hands and the glint of her eyes visible to the messenger who came cautiously through the door.

"Sara has failed, my Queen. She did not realize there was a *primum* vampire guarding the boy, and that mistake cost her life. I am sorry," the messenger said, bowing her head in a mixture of shame, respect, and fear. She trembled a little.

"I was afraid of that. And please, do not shake so. I am not angry with you, Kell. You have served me well. It is not your fault that you must deliver unpleasant messages," the Queen said soothingly, with a voice like dripping honey. Kell relaxed, barely.

"I suppose our furry friend fared no better?" the Queen asked.

"No, he too was killed, by a rogue ice cotu, we gather."

"Pity. Well, the easiest way is always worth an attempt. Fortunately, I have another plan. And this one I have more faith in." The Queen rose from her seat. Kell hurried to open the door for her.

"Come with me," the Queen said to Kell as she walked out into the hall. "I favor you. I have even considered promoting you. As such, I am going to show you what our next move is."

"Thank you, my Queen," Kell replied, stunned by the display of generosity and trust. She obediently followed her ruler down the long hallway. The expanse of stone walls was broken every few feet by an alcove, occupied by a fist-sized violet flame, burning without any visible means of sustenance. A few doors were interspersed between the torches, some wooden, some iron, all sealed shut by a barrier of iridescence where they met the wall. The door at the end of the hallway was under even more magical protections, which the Queen breezed through. Tentatively, Kell followed, placing first one toe through the outermost barrier, then stepping through. The Queen placed her hand on the door, and it vanished, reforming after Kell had stepped past. The room on the other side was too dark for even Kell to see. One of the magical flames floated in the center, and it took a minute for her eyes to be able to see by its light.

It was a dungeon. Half a dozen prison cells arranged in a circle. Inside of each, a swirling mass of darkness, with two glowing spheres at its center. Kell got the eerie feeling that those spheres were eyes, watching her, and the hairs on the back of her neck began to rise.

"What are they?" she whispered.

"This is Phase Two," the Queen said, gesturing grandly at the things in the cages. They gave a low, moaning growl in response. The sound slithered around the room and made Kell shiver. "I have summoned these spirits to help us," the Queen continued saying. "They will succeed where Sara and the werewolf failed."

"My Queen....!" Kell gasped, in awe and trepidation.

"Please, my dear, call me Jasmine."

4

The darkness of the nightmare melded into a still, solid blackness. Was it over? Something was pressing onto his wrist. His arm jerked back reflexively, and the pressure slid away. He shivered. He must still be dreaming, to be feeling these creeping sensations. But it felt so...present. His brain was hazy and uncertain. The thing was back, now rapping against his ribs. *Thunk, thunk, thunk-thunk.* A growly complaint issued from his throat, but the thing was undeterred. It let his ribs alone and appeared again on his shoulder. It poked into the space between his clavicle and his throat—and it smarted. Richie snapped awake.

This wasn't a dream.

"Holy shit!" he yelled, screeching and squirming away from the thing and pulling the sleeping bag protectively to his chest. Accordingly, Jack toppled backwards, his hand jerking back from Richie.

"I—um, I...you're awake," Jack said in blunt observation.

"Yeah, I noticed." Richie seethed. "What the hell were you doing?"

"You...um...you kind of seized up in your sleep...yes, and I was just checking for signs of life," Jack said in a stammer.

Richie stared at him incredulously, completely at a loss for a response. Richie was well aware that he tended to thrash and do other strange things in his sleep—it used to drive his brothers crazy at night—but aside from that there wasn't the slightest indication of truth in Jack's poorly constructed story. On the contrary, Richie couldn't really think of any alternate logical explanation.

"Just...don't do it again," Richie said. "Never. Ever. Again. Or I'm so out of here."

"Okay, okay! Don't get all worked up about it. I apologize for making sure you were still among the living." Jack's attempt to look annoyed wasn't very convincing and his eyes avoided Richie's.

"Don't we have somewhere to be today?" Richie asked, trying to keep his mind from the disturbing territory it was entering. After several days with Jack and his obvious commitment to their cause, Richie thought there was a good chance that Jack really had recruited him as a partner, as opposed to, say, a snack. Still, he determined to not get too close to Jack in the near future. And to make sure he was always the one in the sleeping bag at night. He fought back a shudder.

"You're right, yeah, we do," Jack agreed with an enthusiastic bobbing of the head. He scrambled to his feet, slipping a little on his sock-clad left foot, and dashed over to his suitcase to shuffle through some papers and find the hand-drawn map to the residence of one Dr. George.

Dr. Clement George lived in a big, fancy house in an expensive neighborhood. The kind of neighborhood where a scruffy kid like Richie would be chased down the street by a housewife with a broom. He couldn't imagine what they'd do to Jack, especially since he was still sporting a tail. It was deemed safer to contact Dr. George at his practice, which Richie discovered, much to his surprise, was located in a far seedier part of town. Not that he was complaining. He was much more comfortable there, but it didn't make sense that a high-end doctor would work in the low-rent district.

"It's the kind of practice he does," Jack said in explanation, as they strolled down a cracked, crumbling sidewalk, stepping over all manner of debris, some of which was alive at varying levels. Richie nodded in response, watching Jack's feet closely to assure that he kept a comfortable distance away. "It's a special kind of medicine—he treats species that normal doctors can't handle. It was a field Sally pioneered, actually. Clement was one of the first practitioners. Oh, there's his office." Jack glanced down at the written address for confirmation.

"It looks a little...out of place," Richie said, coming to a stop several strides behind Jack. The trim, two-story, brown-brick building was situated amongst a sea of slumped wooden structures. It looked sensible and professional, two things that had little bearing in a neighborhood like this. But then, any office would probably look out of place here. Jack lagged a little behind as Richie approached the door.

An unassuming gold-plated plaque confirmed the building as the *Office of Clement George, MBBS, PhD*. Richie rang the doorbell.

"I'll be with you shortly," a muffled voice called from somewhere within. Richie fidgeted, not being the patient sort.

"You want to do the talking, or me?" Jack asked hesitantly. Richie shrugged. He certainly did not want to do the talking, but he wasn't going to admit to being nervous, or to any other weakness for that matter.

"Well, I guess, you know more about all this than I do," Richie said, hinting. He was trying for nonchalance, but operating on a night of little sleep and a morning of awkward occurrences his voice came out noticeably tight.

"Me it is, then," Jack said. He glanced at Richie from the corner of his eye, unconsciously twisting a strand of ebony hair around his fingers.

"Hmmm. Smells like blood," Jack murmured, his eyes abruptly choosing to wander from Richie back to the building before them. On that note, he strode in front of Richie to meet the doctor.

Right on cue, the door opened, revealing a tall, lanky man with messy brown hair. Only a name tag pinned to his dark gray turtle-neck sweater indicated his profession. Otherwise, he looked far too casual to be on the job.

"May I help you gentlemen?" he said politely, not looking at all surprised by the ruffians he found standing at his doorstep.

"We want to know whatever it is you know about Sally Kitch," Jack said. Richie glared at Jack in exasperation. Richie was sure that was not the way to broach the subject gracefully. Jack caught his look.

"Please?" Jack added. Richie rolled his eyes. This partnership was deteriorating rapidly.

The doctor's eyes narrowed. He scrutinized his visitors with an intelligent, perceptive gaze, making Richie shift uncomfortably. He resisted the urge to look away and risk looking more suspicious. Dr. George's eyes paused on Jack's face.

"Have we met?" he asked.

Jack shook his head. "Don't think so.". He hesitated a moment, brow furrowing as he pondered the matter, and then shook his head in confirmation of his statement.

The doctor contemplated the situation for a few seconds more, head tilted to the side. "Come in," he said at last, stepping aside. Jack and Richie slunk through, and the door was closed behind them.

"You can call me Clement," the doctor said, walking off down the hallway. His visitors followed him cautiously.

The office wasn't like any sterile, gleaming white doctor's office Richie had ever seen. It looked more like a home. The walls were a dark beige color, decorated with landscape paintings of open moors complete with families of rabbits. The architecture had an open, airy feel, with all the rooms having wide entry-ways and internal windows cut out from the walls. The main entrance opened into an abnormally comfortable waiting room and a library/study, giving the impression that the doctor would welcome you into his private space, as well as his practice.

Clement led them around the corner and into a room with a computer desk and some file cabinets. He closed the door behind them.

"I'm not going to ask who you are, because I know you'll lie about it," he said, sitting down on the edge of his desk. "But I do want to know why you're looking for Dr. Kitch." He folded his hands and looked at Jack expectantly. "Take care with how you answer."

"We need her help," Jack said, enunciating each word painstakingly. On the floor, his tail twitched like a large, nervous snake. "Not just because she's a doctor, but because of her experience, and the like. She knows things other doctors don't. It's hard to explain." His words came with the kind of awful slowness that comes from trying to say something and hide it at the same time. It took several heartbeats for Richie to realize that Jack wasn't going to elaborate. Clement was watching them with eyebrows raised, unimpressed.

"It's about me," Richie interrupted finally in order to salvage the situation. Like Jack, he wasn't inclined to spill his secret, but he couldn't imagine any other way to convince Clement that he and Jack were for real. "Er...I keep having these dreams, and then they come true, and I don't understand what's happening to me. Nobody else seems to, either. But I think maybe she will. This bloke, Jack, has agreed to help me find her." Jack was staring at him. Richie purposely didn't look back. Besides, Clement was sizing him up again, presumably looking for signs that Richie was lying.

"Hmmm. And why is Jack being so generous?" Clement asked, his tone demanding. Richie opened his mouth, couldn't think of a lie to fill it with, and closed his jaws helplessly. He turned towards Jack. Jack was focused on Clement, his eyes widened with a light touch of panic. Richie wished Jack would hurry up and say something convincing. Selfishly, he didn't care whether it was the truth or not—

Richie only hoped to get to Sally, regardless of Jack's motivation for helping him.

"Because…because I was a patient of hers, once," Jack said, choking the words out after an infinitely long moment. "And I believe I may have been prematurely discharged." He finished more easily, his eyes settling in line with Clement's. A manic series of thumps arose from the polished wooden floor. A quick visual search allowed Richie to identify Jack's besocked left foot as the source. Richie groaned internally. Nothing about Jack's spasmodic response inspired confidence. He was certain that the entire effort was ruined, and within seconds he would be back on the streets to beg for scraps of information.

"I see," Clement eventually said. To Richie's astonishment, he made no move to chase them off. He unclasped his hands and planted them on the desk behind him, loosening his rigid spine and leaning his weight onto his palms. "And when did this discharge take place?"

"1944," Jack replied, this time not missing a beat. "April, I think." An exclamation of surprise arose in Richie's chest, and he barely caught it in his throat. A small, strangled cry still managed to escape. 1944? He had assumed that because Jack looked like a twenty-something human, he really was twenty-something. The fact that Jack was alive in 1944 did not mesh with Richie's sense of what was right and normal in the world.

Clement, however, didn't bat an eye. "Where?" he asked.

"Hong Kong."

"Are you willing to tell me what she was treating you for?"

"I'd rather not, if you don't mind."

"I suppose you aren't with the ICCA law enforcement," Clement said, apparently reaching a decision. Jack and Richie blinked at him blankly, astounded that he took them seriously. "If you were, you wouldn't be so cagey, and you'd have your story straight," Clement said. "One more question, and this is for both of you: how did you find out about the good doctor?"

"We're from the same cotu community, in Appalachia. Everyone knew the Kitch family. I wasn't around when she first started practicing, but…" Jack said. His restless foot slowed and by the end of his explanation had ceased its insistent tapping.

"A werewolf told me," Richie replied in turn, after a kick in the shin from Jack brought him back from 1944. "In a bar. In Edinburgh. He said he'd seen her somewhere in America." Clement nodded, seeming satisfied with their answers.

"Well, the good news is, I'm sure Dr. Kitch could help you two, whatever your exact problems may be. As you must be aware, she is quite brilliant."

Richie's spirits began to lift—

"The bad news is," Clement continued speaking. "I don't know where she's gone any more than you do."

—and came crashing back down to earth.

"You don't have any idea, at all?" Richie asked with a small, sad voice.

Clement shook his head. "The last time I saw her was in 1959. She'd been teaching me her trade on and off for a few years. We were doing a dissection and she mentioned that she was going on holiday, but didn't say where. And then I never saw or heard from her directly again. I can't say I was surprised. She's like that. Always dashing off on some new adventure. She used to travel constantly, never staying in one place for long, but since she dropped off the grid, so to speak, I don't know what to think." Clement shrugged.

Richie stared at his hands, watching one thumbnail dig a trench around the other and trying to remind himself that there were three more names on that list.

"America sounds plausible," Clement continued speaking. "I seem to recall her having a house somewhere in that country—"

Jack shook his head, cutting Clement off mid-stream. "I found out where the house was, but there's nothing there now. Just an empty lot." Defeat rang hollowly in his voice.

"Oh dear. Well, I've heard other theories. There are all sorts of rumors going around in our medical community, but it's all friend-of-a-friend hearsay. None of us know for sure. I'll tell you what, though, ours is a tight knit professional circle. I can put out the word that the search is on, and see what kind of feedback I get, if you would like me to. Is there any way I can contact either of you?" Jack and Richie looked at each other.

"I've got an e-mail address..." Richie said. The enthusiasm had leached out of his tone. He rubbed the back of one hand across a tired eye. Several embarrassing revelations and a wasted day later, and he was no closer to any sort of relief.

"Splendid." Clement took a business card out of a holder on his desk and handed it to Richie with a flourish. "Send a message to that e-mail address, and I'll start sending you any information I get that might help you. Perhaps you'll get lucky. They say that she sometimes reemerges when an interesting case presents itself."

"Thank you, so much, Clement," Richie said, trying to sound grateful through his disappointment. He knew he shouldn't have expected immediate success, but he had let himself be hopeful. He needed to not let that happen in the future.

"You're welcome. I assume you can find your way out?" Jack and Richie nodded. "Good. And don't try to steal anything. I'll hear you." Another nod. "All right, be on your way. And good luck." They turned to leave. Richie was already in the hallway when Clement added one last comment.

"Oh, and gentlemen? I am inclined to think that you're genuine, but in case I'm wrong, I want you to know that if you have any intention of harming Dr. Kitch, it would be in your best interest not to find her. She can handle herself quite well."

"Yeah, we know," Jack said, and closed the door behind him.

"Well that was a waste of time," Jack said in lament, violently scratching a pen across Clement George's name on the list of leads. He and Richie were back at their London home base, a room in what was left of a foreclosed motel. So far, no one had noticed the two trespassers, or if they had, they didn't care. Although they had only been in London for about eighteen hours, the room was already a disaster area. Snack food packages and books by Sally Kitch carpeted the floor. It was a semi-purposeful mess, however. The progress in analyzing Sally's works had been minimal, but at least it was extant. The little they had read revealed nothing, which made sense, Richie had realized upon further reflection. If one was going to publish an illegal book, why would they give away their location?

"And so we're right back where we started," Richie said and sighed.

"It was a pretty weak lead, I suppose," Jack said. "Might as well just move on. Speaking of which, we've got to figure what we're doing next."

"We go to the next name on the list, I would think," Richie said. "I hate to leave London so soon, but we have things to do."

"It isn't such a great city. I've been here before. It's big, dirty, swarming with people, just like everywhere else. Some of the women were interesting, but that's about it."

Richie made an effort not to look too disappointed, but he didn't try very hard. Jack watched him mope for a moment and sighed quietly.

"Fine, we'll stay for a while," Jack said, conceding. "Go explore to your heart's content. I've got reading I need to be doing anyways."

"Thanks! I won't keep us here long. It's just that I've never been in a city this big before," Richie said. He felt immature and naïve saying so, but he couldn't help it. He'd grown up on a farm, far from any kind of urban center. London was an exciting prospect.

"Yeah. The only reason I'm agreeing to this is 'cause I know how you feel. First time I ever saw a big city, I thought I'd died and gone to heaven. The enchantment wears off pretty quick, though, I have to warn you."

"I know. I found that out in Edinburgh. But I'd hate to tell people that I went to one of Europe's great cities and didn't see anything but the slums."

"There are worse things you could do," Jack said, sounding a touch defensive. His reaction confused Richie for a second, but then he put two and two together.

"Don't tell me...that's all you saw when you were here before."

"It was all I could afford! And the uptown folk wouldn't have allowed me to dirty their streets anyways. The class divides were a lot worse back then."

"When was 'back then'?" Richie asked, wondering just what the lifespan of a cotu was.

"Eighteen-thirty–um, something."

"Whoa. You're old." The words were out of Richie's mouth before he could think them through. He felt his cheeks getting hot.

"Well, yeah, I suppose I am," Jack said, laughing a little. "I'm one-hundred and seventy-two. Or, maybe seventy-three. What day is it?"

"Uhhh, September? I think?"

"Oh. That doesn't help. Well, somewhere just shy of one seventy-five," Jack said. Richie tried to think what that would be like. He knew there were creatures that could live for almost two centuries or more, like vampires and giant tortoises, but he had never been familiar with one. His brain didn't seem to want to accept the information.

"Do cotus normally live that long?" Richie asked.

"No, they don't, actually. Most don't make it to a hundred. We don't age much after we finish growing, so we simply live until something kills us. So far, somehow, nothing has killed me." Jack shrugged. "I guess I'm just that lucky."

Richie thought he heard a thread of bitterness in that last remark, but he wasn't certain.

"It was lucky for me," Richie said, pointed out the benefit. "If you weren't old, I'd be dead."

"That is a strange way to say it," Jack replied, "but I appreciate the sentiment. You're probably the only person on Earth who would be thankful that I'm alive."

He was standing alone in the middle of the woods. The darkness was complete, the sliver of moon lost in the branches of the trees. Something was out there, circling him. He was terrified, but he couldn't run. A twig cracked behind him. He couldn't bear to look. He knew what he'd see. He closed his eyes, knowing this was the end. But wasn't it worth it, his life, to save so many others? Leaves rustled. It was drawing closer, taking its time. It knew he wouldn't try to escape. It knew it had time to enjoy this. Second after grueling second passed, and at last he couldn't stand the suspense a moment longer. He turned, just as it lunged for the kill, sinking in its claws—

Richie sat bolt upright, barely choking back a scream. His frantic heartbeat was plainly audible. Torrents of sweat rolled down his skin. It took a moment for him to convince himself that he wasn't in the woods, he wasn't dying.

It was just a dream.

"Just a dream," Richie mumbled breathlessly, trying to make himself believe it. But it wasn't true, and he knew it. It was never just a dream anymore.

"Are you all right?"

Richie jumped, scooting away from the sound. Then he realized that it was only Jack, in a sleeping bag a few yards away—and thankfully not prodding him. He was propped up on one elbow and looking at Richie, his eyes rendered as twin green discs by the dim light reflecting from behind his corneas.

"I woke you up, didn't I? I'm sorry. No, I'm fine, just, go back to sleep," Richie said and slowly unlocked each muscle-spasmed joint and falling back onto his sleeping bag like a forsaken marionette. But he couldn't possibly go back to sleep. He couldn't even bring himself to close his eyes, for fear that he would open them in the forest. He noticed that he was trembling, and couldn't seem to stop.

"That yarn you spun for Clement—it wasn't just a story, was it?" It was the first time Jack had mentioned it. Richie had been hoping that he'd forgotten.

"Definitely not a fairy tale," he said. "I don't want to talk about it."

"All right. G'night then." Jack flopped back into a prone position and curled up to return to his slumber. Richie stared at the opposite wall, still wide awake. His mind wandered to the first dream, and how terrified he had been then. As far as he could tell, time hadn't diminished the feeling.

"Hey, Jack?"

"Mmm?"

"Do you think Sally Kitch can...fix me?" The question had been floating around the back of Richie's mind for many a day, but he had been trying not to think too much about it, unable to consider that the answer might be 'no.' Sally was the last resort.

"I don't know," Jack replied, so softly that Richie could barely hear him. "I've been wondering the same for myself, and I can't say. But I do know that if there's a solution, she'll find it. Sally never gives up on anything."

"So you really do know her? Personally? I thought you made that whole 'patient' thing up on the spot."

"Well, I may have stretched the truth a little. She wasn't my doctor so much as my confidant. And lately I've realized that I need somebody to set me straight again," Jack said. "It's a long, sordid story. I might tell you sometime. When I know you better. We first met, what, five days ago?"

True, Richie thought. So much had changed in that time that it seemed to him to have been a far longer interval.

"That's not really long enough for trust, is it?" Jack asked.

"I don't know, I'm starting to trust you a wee bit." Although if I were a sane person, I probably wouldn't.

"You shouldn't," Jack spoke the warning matter-of-factly.

"Wha—? Why?" Richie asked, caught off guard completely.

"I can be...unpredictable. Bad things tend to happen to those close to me, and it's usually my fault, somehow," Jack explained, somehow managing to sound both troubled and off-hand.

"You're telling me this now? Why couldn't you have said something when you asked me to be your partner?"

"'Cause you wouldn't have accepted the offer. And I'm selfish. Tired of going it alone and of just talking to myself."

"At least you're honest," Richie said.

"When possible," Jack said in agreement.

For a long moment, he was silent, and Richie thought the conversation was over.

"You can leave if you want to, you know. Anytime. I won't stop you," Jack whispered. His brittle voice betrayed that he was certain Richie would do just that, and he wasn't happy about it.

"No, I'm staying," Richie said, deciding before his brain had the chance to hold him back. "No danger you put me in could be worse than what I'd get into on my own. And...I should tell you, the reason I left home was because my dreams were causing people I knew to get hurt. Someone almost died, once. So I'm selfishly putting you in danger, too, for the purpose of saving my own ass."

"Oh, good. We're even, then."

"Why do they need a giant clock?"

Jack and Richie stood on the London Bridge, staring out across the city. Richie was using an abandoned London Guidebook, nabbed from park bench, to provide a bird's eye view tour of the city's landmarks. Jack wasn't responding particularly well.

"Well...so everyone in the city knows the time," Richie said, guessing. He flipped back a few pages in the guidebook to see if it had a better answer. No such luck.

"But they've all got watches and those little phones. They all know the time."

"I think you're missing the point of sightseeing. Big Ben is *the* icon of London. It's something every tourist needs to see."

"It's a waste of space and money," Jack said flatly.

Richie sighed in exasperation.

"Now the Tower of London, I understand. *That* was built for a purpose," Jack said.

"You mean torture and murder?"

"Well, yeah." Jack leaned heavily on the railing, looking down into the dark water rushing beneath them. "Why isn't 'Thames' spelled anything like it's pronounced?" he said, wondering aloud.

"Why do you keep asking me questions like I know the answers?"

"You're the one with the guidebook."

"None of the things *you* want to know are in the guidebook."

"I can't help that," Jack said, taking a swig from a bottle of liquor he'd stolen earlier that morning. Richie closed the guidebook, giving up on the tour. He turned around, resting his back on the rail. He met the eyes of a girl on the opposite side of the bridge. She quickly looked away. Having been a notorious lady-killer in his hometown, that was something Richie wasn't accustomed to. But then his appearance wasn't what it had been. For the first time, Richie noticed the small bubble of space around him and Jack. People were avoiding them. Richie understood why—he hadn't changed clothes in a couple days, and his companion had a tail and no shirt—but all the same, he didn't like it. Richie had always been charming and handsome, the charismatic boy with deep brown eyes and a heart-stopping devilish smirk. Now he was a common ragamuffin who people circumnavigated when they passed on the street. He suddenly felt extremely self-conscious.

"Let's get out of here, Jack," he said, hurrying off the bridge. He ducked his head, feeling like he needed to hide his grime-streaked face. There was no one here to recognize him, but Richie had the impression that everyone around him was judging his ragged clothes and greasy, unwashed hair, and that provided shame enough. Jack followed him, looking thoroughly vexed, but for once not asking any questions.

Richie didn't stop walking until he had left the pretty part of London far behind. He had sort of been thinking about power-walking all the way back to the motel, but he had been traveling on foot all day, and had to give his legs a break. He sat down on the sidewalk for a minute to catch his breath, and to calm his thoughts. Jack, still right behind him, dropped to the ground by his side.

"I hate to interrupt your...whatever you're doing, but I think you should know that we're being followed," Jack said quietly after a moment.

"What?" Richie exclaimed, ripped from his thoughts.

"Young woman. Short. Long, blonde hair. She was on the bridge with us, and she's been following ever since," Jack said.

Richie stiffened. He looked about him, but couldn't see anyone.

"What should we do?" he whispered.

"Depends. Would anyone be following you for any reason?"

"I don't think so...although I suppose I am a missing person..."

"I don't think this is an officer of the law. So. Would you like me to go after her?"

"I guess so. But don't kill her! Unless you have to."

"All right. Stay here, and watch this for me." Jack plunked down his half-empty bottle, jumped to his feet, and took off running across the street and down an alley. Richie stayed put as instructed, even though he felt exposed, sitting by himself out in the open. He wrapped his arms around his torso for comfort, hoping Jack wouldn't be long.

Richie hummed to himself, taking little comfort from the effort. He staged a thumb war between his own two hands. Just when he couldn't stand the suspense anymore, Jack ducked back out of the alleyway. Richie stood up. Then he saw that Jack was alone.

"I couldn't catch her," Jack said, gesticulating as he continued the story. "I could smell her, and I was right on her tail, and then she was gone. The scent trail just stopped. It's like she vanished. And I think I tasted magic." Jack stomped back to Richie. He crossed his arms and hunched his shoulders, looking more humiliated than angry. "I hate magic," he grumbled. His eye moved to the bottle sitting on the paving stones at Richie's other side. "Give me that."

"What do you think she wanted?" Richie asked, handing the liquor over.

"She may have been after me," Jack replied. "I know it may be hard to believe, but I come from a pretty important family, if not a very well-liked one." Richie's eyebrows shifted up his forehead. He did find it difficult to believe that the ragged man beside him was from an important family.

"But I've been ignored for a long time," Jack said. "I find it hard to believe that someone's coming for me now..." His eyes lit up. If he were a cartoon character, a light bulb would have flared to life over his head. "Oh...maybe..."

"What? Why are you looking at me like that?"

"Your dreams come true. You said you thought they were causing things to happen, but if instead they're predictions...well, people like to know what's coming. I could be wrong, of course, but it's the only other possibility I can think of," Jack said.

"But...what does that mean? For me?" A thrilling thought popped into Richie's head. "Do you think they would take them away—the dreams, I mean?"

Jack hesitated before answering. "I can't say no, but probably not. I don't know who 'they' are, if it even is a 'they,' or what 'they' could do.

But I don't think any 'they' or 'she' or whoever should be trusted without being investigated," Jack said carefully. "This could just be some creeper who's only stalking you 'cause she can't get laid. Although, now that I think about it, that might not be a bad thing...but my point is, we don't know who she is. Or what's she's up to. No jumping to conclusions. You understand?"

"I understand," Richie said, but he couldn't help wondering. He had promised himself he wouldn't get worked up again, but the possibility was simply too tantalizing. Jack stared at Richie for a few seconds, thoughtfully chewing the inside of his cheek.

"We need to discuss this," Jack said in conclusion. "Let's go back to the motel."

Richie nodded in agreement. Jack stood up first, offering a hand to Richie. He took it, and Jack pulled him up. They walked back to the motel, side by side, their minds miles apart.

"If she wanted to help you, then why didn't she just say so, instead of sneaking around? I speak from experience when I say sneaking around never leads to anything good."

Jack's arguments were rational, but Richie didn't want to hear them. The more he thought about it, the more he wanted to try and find his stalker. He was sure that she, or whoever she worked for, could take his nightmares away. Deep inside, he knew that he was being unreasonable, but he pushed those thoughts aside. The idea that he might be *so close* to a full night's sleep, to being a normal person, to seeing his family—Richie could scarcely restrain himself from storming out the door and calling out his whereabouts for all to hear. And who was *Jack* to tell him he couldn't?

"You don't know that she won't help me!" He protested, his voice ratcheting up in loudness and his emotions in intensity.

"You don't know that she won't *kill* you!"

"It's worth a try, isn't it? It's a better chance than this ghost we're chasing! We might never find that town, or that Kitch girl, but this person is *right here!*"

"But we don't know who she is, or what she wants. Sally may be a long shot, but she's a good person. If she can help you—"

"IF! *If* we can find her and *if* she can help. *If* you're even being honest with me! There are a lot of 'ifs' in your plan, Jack, and I need more than that. I need answers. I need to know that I can be fixed." Richie was practically screaming, but he couldn't turn down the volume on his voice. He didn't really want to. Anger at a thousand different things bubbled over inside him. He was sizzling red hot beneath his skin.

"There are a lot of 'ifs' in your plan, too! You can't just assume that someone looking for what you have is on your side!" Jack's voice was raised also, and his upper lip curled in the slightest of snarls. He shut his eyes tight and took a deep breath, trying to bring himself back under control. His fingernails dug into the frame of the bed beneath him. Standing in front of him, Richie repeatedly clenched his hands into fists, trying to do the exact opposite and work himself up before Jack's logic could reach his brain.

"Look," Jack said in a gentler voice, opening his eyelids and meeting Richie's gaze. "I know a lot about the black market. I've dealt in it more than I care to admit. I've seen a couple of people with 'gifts' that got recruited by black market merchants. They'll tell you whatever you want to hear, to lure you in. Then they chain you up and auction you off, making you a slave to the highest bidder. They don't treat you well in the interim, either. It isn't pretty. I don't want to see that happen to you. And it'd be an easy trap to fall into."

"I have to try...I have to try something. I can't keep running after false leads. I need help, now." He babbled. He knew it, but he couldn't stop. "I can't...I can't do this. It's driving me crazy. Someone's going to die. I've dreamt it three nights in a row. I know it's going to happen. I felt it happen. But I can't do anything." Richie clamped his jaw shut and closed his eyes. He was seconds away from tears. Breathe, he told himself. Just keep breathing. For several minutes, Richie kept his eyes shut, trying to reign in his erratic emotions in.

Jack remained silent. "Richie...what if you could?" Jack finally said.

"Could what?" Richie asked, as soon as he was under his own control again. His heartbeat began to slow. He opened his eyes.

"What if you could do something?" Jack asked when he had Richie's gaze once more. "Have you ever tried to keep one of your dreams from coming true?"

Richie thought about it. "No, but I don't know when they're going to happen, or who to. In the dream, it's always happening to me. And even if I knew, in this dream, I'm attacked by something really big and really strong. What could I do to save that person? I'm not strong, I don't know how to fight."

"I don't know about the others, but we can work on those last two. I could teach you," Jack said.

"Even if you did, I'll never be strong enough to face off against that thing."

"Um...actually, I think you could be. There's, uh, something I think I need to tell you." Jack paused and inhaled slowly.

Richie stared at him, hopeful but baffled.

"I assume you recall the day I woke you up by, um, poking you."

"Vividly."

"Yeah, sorry about that, but I had my reasons. Your scent tipped me off, but I had to do a little experimenting to be certain. And now, I'm pretty sure you're a cotu."

Jack's statement hit Richie like a ton of bricks. It took him a few seconds to recover and comprehend. "I—no, that's not possible. My parents and brothers, they're all human. And so am I. I couldn't be—no. You're wrong."

"I am not. You scent as a cotu. It's a distinctive scent, I couldn't mistake it. Your heart only beats once at a time, not twice like a human's. Your chest wall, all bony-like, and that sensitive spot at the base of your neck...surely you've noticed something before. You were faster than the other kids, maybe? Quicker to heal, never sick?"

All spot on. He could outrun all of his friends, and even his older brothers and their friends. He'd never so much as gotten a head cold in his life. But—

"What about the age thing?" Richie argued. "Sally was a doctor at, like, ten years old! How come I didn't start uni when I was a toddler?"

"Cotus are masters of disguise, Richie. We don't even have to think about it," Jack said without hesitation. "You probably adjusted your form to match those around you automatically. It's happened before." Jack watched steadily as Richie's brain churned, hunting for some new argument to throw.

It couldn't be true, because if it was, then...

"My parents aren't my parents." Richie sank to the floor.

"Well, not biologically. But that doesn't mean they aren't your parents. Family is more than that, I think," Jack said. He knelt beside Richie. "And you're still yourself. Just a little different."

"A LITTLE? If you're right, this changes everything!"

"Okay, so maybe it does." Jack placed a hand on Richie's shoulder. "But maybe it'll let you use your dreams to save lives. Wouldn't that be worth it?"

5

Scarlet watched with quiet disappointment as her student attempted a roundhouse kick and managed only to flop gracelessly into the tall meadow grass. As a senior member of her pack, Scarlet was often given the tough cases, but this whelp might actually be impossible.

"I don't get why I have to do this, anyway," Tyler grumbled, scrambling to his feet and brushing grass-seed off his t-shirt. "Wolves don't use martial arts. And I'm going to miss Soccer Sunday."

"Yeah, sure, wolves don't fight with fists...or feet, but you might have to," Scarlet said, coming over to his side. She picked a dried leaf out of his messy blond hair. "Our pack has been keeping the peace in Brunswick for over fifty years. Passing our combat skills on to the next generation is important. Playing soccer isn't, so much." She could see her wayward apprentice physically fighting the urge to roll his eyes.

"Soccer is important to me," he said. Scarlet wondered if maybe they should have waited until he was a little older to start tutoring him in the path of the pack. It wasn't just him, though. The newer generations of werewolves couldn't remember a time when blood ran in the streets of Brunswick. But Scarlet couldn't forget. She considered Tyler for a moment.

"You don't have to do this, you know," she said to reminded him, as gently as one could say such a thing. Fear flittered across the young werewolf's eyes. He knew that if you didn't follow the rules, you had to leave the pack—an extended family that Tyler had been born into, unlike Scarlet. He had never known anything else.

"No, I want to! I just want to go to Soccer Sunday, too."

"Are you sure?" Scarlet tried to look stern. The expression felt weird on her face, but she could manage it well enough. Tyler nodded with vigor. Scarlet's scowl morphed into her more usual smile.

"Good! I can try to plan around your soccer schedule, but Sally has me on an assignment now that keeps me tied up most times when you aren't at school. Let's try that kick again. Trust me that this stuff will be useful to you." Well, maybe, she thought.

"An assignment?" Tyler asked. He assumed the Tae Kwon Do fighting stance and experimented with swinging his leg out at the hip in proper form, not yet willing to commit to another kick.

"Just a bodyguard kind of thing," Scarlet replied. "A friend of Alex's was attacked. Alex wants my help making sure this guy doesn't get hurt while Sally and Alex get to the bottom of it. It's no big deal. I don't think it's the kick that's getting you, it's the pivot. You aren't moving on your planted foot fast enough."

"It was probably a big deal if Alex thinks his friend needs personal security. Can he not take care of himself?"

Tyler finally attempted the roundhouse, shifting his weight onto his right foot and managing, just barely, to turn it in time to keep his balance throughout the entire motion.

"That's better!" Scarlet gave a thumbs-up, more for Tyler's effort than for his form. Then she thought about how to answer his question. Her athletic but hapless pupil was not likely to be the mastermind of the attempt on Jason's life, but Hope always said you never knew who might be listening. "Um, no, I don't think he can. He's only about your age and mostly human. Kind of sickly, too. You're still a little wobbly, so give a few more times before we iron out the wrinkles."

"How did he end up friends with Alex?"

"I don't know. It is a strange thought, isn't it? But Alex is a strange man. We like him that way. Speaking of Alex's friend, Sally wants me to start training him, too," Scarlet said.

"What?" Losing his balance entirely, Tyler plummeted to the ground once more. Scarlet blinked down at him, wondering why that came as such a shock.

"I've trained more than one at once before. I'll start training Darby soon, too." Scarlet proffered a hand to help Tyler up. He accepted and let the older werewolf pull him to his feet, the ropes of her muscles rippling under her leathery, beige skin.

"But you said he isn't a werewolf," Tyler said, arguing. "I hate to say 'he's not one of us,' but, he's not. What about 'passing our skills on to the next generation?'"

"He's part of the next generation too."

"That's not what I meant."

"Our job is to keep people safe, Tyler. If teaching him to fight helps keep him safe, then I'm doing my job." Scarlet glanced up at the sky to check the time. She had a watch once, but she must have lost it. "We've been at this for a while. What do you say we spar for a few minutes, and then I'll walk you home? Maybe you'll still get to play soccer with your friends."

Sally rubbed her right temple and stared at the fanciful illustration of genies in *Supernatural Beasts of the Middle East*. Despite being published over a hundred years ago and having a decidedly racist title, it was still regarded as one of the best books on the subject, which might have something to do with the paucity of other books on the same topic. The Middle East and North Africa were poorly studied terrain in terms of magic, and right now Sally wished somebody had noticed that sooner.

The faded image showed four genies near the entrance to a cave, surrounded by what appeared to be a haze of fairy dust or something, presumably an artistic license taken by the illustrator. One was braiding her sister's hair. Another held a small bird in her cupped hands, and the fourth was poking her head out of the gloom that led into their subterranean nest. They were all smiling serenely. The accompanying text suggested that this picture of harmony was in fact fairly representative of the species, which is what Sally had always been led to believe. What could turn a shy, peaceful genie into an assassin? A knock at the library door pulled Sally away from her frustrated thoughts.

"Come in!"

"Am I interrupting?" Alex stepped into the room. "Hope is watching Jason, so I thought I would see how it's going at this end. Maybe I can help with the research."

"Sounds great. Pull up a beanbag."

Alex snagged one of the amorphous cushions from the pile by the door and flopped down next to Sally on the floor, a little too close for coworkers—close enough for his musky, coppery smell to flood her scent glands.

She pretended not to notice.

"What's up?" Alex asked.

"Have you ever seen a beetle that's lost a wing trying to fly with the other, just spinning around in circles? Because that's what my brain is doing."

"And why is your brain a spinning beetle?"

"Everything I can find about genies says what I already knew," she replied, gesturing dismissively at the book on her lap. "They don't go out of their way to hurt people. Even if threatened, they prefer running away to inflicting serious harm, although Jason's experience and a few folktales here and there would imply that they are capable of it."

"One of them couldn't happen to be a psychopath?" Alex asked.

Sally shook her head. "I don't think so. They're like social insects—every individual works for the common good, and without the rest of their hive, they're lost. Normally they spend most of their lives gathering food for the queen and playing with their sisters."

"Could the queen have made her do it?"

"No." Sally flipped over a few pages to show him the illustration of the globular genie queen. Alex's lips curled in disgust. "It's pretty much a big sack of cells that occasionally produces genies to maintain the population. It doesn't speak or anything. The genies communicate telepathically, so when it needs something, they just know. But the queen isn't sentient." Sally leaned back against a bookshelf and shut *Supernatural Beasts*. "I don't understand."

"I guess I can help look through the books," Alex said without enthusiasm. Sally handed him one that she hadn't been through yet, and then dug back into the pages herself.

"I'm starting to think the answers aren't here," Alex said and sighed, tossing aside another tome that hadn't yielded them any helpful information on homicidal genies. "Maybe something changed recently. Then it wouldn't be in any of the books we have."

"You could be right. I'll try my luck on the Internet." Sally reached over a short stack of books to grab her laptop. Sally was the only computer-savvy team member, so it fell to her to dig for anything not found in their library. She opened the lid of the laptop, covered by a plastic case with a pattern of purple spirals, and started typing and clicking like machine gun fire. Alex glanced at the luminescent screen, all befuddling blocks of color and scrolling text, and resumed slowly working his way through the maze of books and papers, a task with which he felt more competent.

"You know another possibility is that we're looking for the wrong thing," Sally said, without missing a beat in her typing.

"How so?"

"We're looking to the genies, but maybe we should be looking at their target. If we know why Jason would be worth killing, then we might know why the genies are the ones doing it."

"He's Thomas's kid," Alex said, already knowing it wasn't a very good answer.

"Thomas was never that big of a fish in the sorcery pond," Sally replied. "Recruiting a peaceful race like the genies would be too much trouble. Besides, you go after someone's child if you want to hurt the parent, and Thomas has been missing, if not dead, for nigh on five years now, from what I've heard. Killing Jason wouldn't leave much of an impression on someone who isn't here to know it happened."

"Do you think Pansy has some sort of dark, secret past?"

"I highly doubt it. But I'm having Scarlet run a background check anyways, just in case. Which leaves only one option—there's something amiss with Jason that we don't know about. You've read Jason's aura, I presume?"

"Of course."

"So...what of it?"

Alex looked back on that first day of school, when he'd been searching everyone's auras. He knew he'd at least glanced at Jason's, but...

"I can't remember what it looked like," Alex said, thoroughly embarrassed and confused. He never forgot an aura, just like some people never forgot a face. But when he tried to recall Jason's, it just slipped away from him.

"Well there's your problem," Sally said in scathing conclusion.

"Yeah, maybe. I should be able to see him from here, though, if I try. Let me look again." And hopefully redeem myself in the process. Alex closed his eyes and concentrated on Jason's image in his mind. It would have been easier in his tower, where he didn't have to hear Sally's keyboarding, but he could manage. Before long, he was out of his body, and searching the town for Jason. It didn't take long. Jason was in the park near his house, with most of the other boys from his neighborhood it looked like. Alex homed in on Jason, trying to get a fix on his aura.

"That's funny," Alex murmured aloud.

"What is?" Sally asked.

"His aura is...muffled, like there's something between me and it." It was weird. He could see the aura, but only in a foggy way, like looking through dirty glass. No wonder he couldn't remember what it looked like—he'd never seen Jason's aura, not really.

"Can you break through?"

"I'll try." Alex enveloped Jason with his consciousness and began chipping away at the barrier. "Damn. Yeah, it's strong, but I can break it."

After a few minutes, he felt it crack, then give way. Jason's aura spilled free, mingling with Alex's for one amazing moment, before Alex's consciousness faltered, and the image was overtaken by blackness.

He couldn't believe the indignity of it all! Those little two-legged creatures, telling him what to do! He who could inspire terror in anyone or kill with only his eyes! The worst part was that he couldn't resist their magics, and he hated himself for it.

He crouched in the woods, shrouded and protected by the darkness under the full summer foliage, and watched the human pups running about, chasing that round, black-and-white object. What was the purpose of this nonsense? Not only the game itself, but why was he being made to watch? He couldn't even tell who he was supposed to find. They wouldn't give him a description. "You'll know him when you smell him," they said. Well, he didn't smell anything but human, witch, wolf-kin, and a touch of half-breed. So he watched, waiting for some sign that one of these pups was his target.

The fast one with the brown head-fur kicked the round object into the square device, and the female pups howled louder. What a strange game this was. The one with long yellow head-fur kicked the thing in the other direction, and the tallest whelp ran towards it, but stumbled. Then he knew.

A scent, the likes of which he'd never known before, washed over him. It smelled of power—like the heady perfume of cedar smoke with a citrus sting. A lot of power. It smelled ancient, even older than he was. A power from the beginning of time. The intensity of it scent-blinded him for a moment. He shook his head to regain his composure and subsequently realized he was the only one who had noticed the event. The game continued uninterrupted.

The small dark male checked in on the tall pale one, and then they both ran towards the round thing again. He didn't know what had happened, but he could still smell that scent, that delicious scent of old magic, and he could tell from which pup it emanated: that tallest one, the one who demonstrated the least ability, the weakest and clumsiest. It seemed unlikely that this frail pup would hold such power. He had thought it would be the strong brown-furred wolfkin, if indeed it was one of these whelps. But the ancient magics worked in mysterious ways; he should know, it was the stuff he was made of.

He had no desire to cause harm to a creature of the old magic like himself, but his new mistresses demanded it. Oh, how he hated them. Still, he had no choice. The fates willing, he thought it would be a long time before he had to do it. He certainly couldn't attack now. He needed the powerful one alone. He doubted there was anyone that could prevent him from killing the pup, but he wanted to be cautious. Maybe he could find a way to free himself and his brethren in the meantime, and he wouldn't have to do it at all. But in case he couldn't, he would need to have a plan. How to get the pup alone? He was told that the pup would be well-guarded at all times. There was a solution to that, though. A paws-off, but extraordinarily effective, method—the characteristic tool of his species—which he could implement to get his prize alone. It would take time, perhaps a few months even, but it would work. Unless he could free himself of his orders, the tall, yellow-furred pup filled with old magic would die.

The library blurred back into view slowly. Alex blinked, disoriented.

"...you all right?" he heard Sally ask.

"I'm not sure, to be honest," he replied. "Man, that was weird."

"You broke through, then?"

"Oh yeah, I definitely broke through. Jason's aura...I can't really describe it. I've never seen anything like it. I got an impression of immense power, blindingly luminescent, and then...it threw me back. *Man*, that was weird."

Sally set the laptop aside and stared at Alex. He could see the gears turning as she tried to understand what it meant.

"That could be a reason to want him dead," Sally said. "If he has that much power, enough even to overwhelm you, and somebody found that out before you did. Still doesn't explain the use of genies, but it does give a reason." A hopeful light dawned in Sally's eyes. "Alex, did you happen to notice the color of Jason's aura?"

"Kind of a deep yellow..."

"Is that a color you see often?"

"No, actually. I don't think I've ever seen yellow before. It's almost always a blue or red shade, if there is any obvious color," Alex replied, mulling the fact over in his mind. He knew Sally was going somewhere with this. He could see her chewing on her tongue like she always did when deep in thought.

"Hmmm. 'A golden light,' you could say. That would be a lot of ancient magic, don't you think?" Sally wondered aloud. "Even enough to daze a vampire of your caliber?"

For a moment, Alex was entirely confused. Sally's tendency to neglect to mention parts of her thinking had left him behind. But he couldn't mistake the line she had quoted—the first line of one of the prophecies. And after some consideration, he caught up with her.

"*Dumnezeule*...It's possible. Wow...that's not something I would ever have thought about Jason, but now that you've said it, it kind of makes sense." The two stared at each other in shock for a long moment. Sally was the first to break into a tentative smile.

"Alex, we did it." She started laughing, hesitantly at first, then with increasing mirth. "Oh my God, Alex, we actually did it! We found him!"

"Yeah, we did." Alex found himself drawn into the slightly delirious laughter. After all this time, *finally*, they had found a Guardian.

"Oh, gosh, okay, we've got work to do," Sally said after several minutes of uncontrolled levity. "Okay. Call the other three and tell them what just happened." She shut her laptop with a decisive *snap*.

"Who's going to tell Jason?" Alex asked, his grin fading as the gravity of the task at hand began to sink in. "And his mother? This is going to be hard for them to swallow."

Sally bit her lip. "Crap," she said in a huff. "All right, we'll do it together. Meet at their house so they're somewhere familiar when they get the news that everything is about to change."

Jason and Pansy sat next to each other on the sofa, fraught with anxiety as Sally settled onto the chair opposite them. Pansy rubbed a hand across Jason's back reassuringly. He took some comfort from his mother's presence, but very little. It was Sally's nervousness that bothered him most. If she wasn't so fidgety, Jason might have felt comfortable knowing that she was confident. A bit afraid to meet her eyes, Jason fixed his line of sight on Sally's hands, where one thumb was slowly tearing away the cuticles from its sister digit.

"All right, so, long story short, Alex and I think we know why Jason has been targeted, in a general sense," Sally said, directing her comments towards Pansy. "I still can't figure what genies have to do with anything, but we'll get there, I'm certain." She swallowed and interlocked her fingers, preventing her thumb from causing any more damage. Then, abruptly, her case of nerves vanished, replaced by the iron visage and clipped, commanding voice Jason was used to.

"Right then," Sally said, still speaking to Pansy rather than Jason. "By process of elimination, Alex and I determined that somebody either had a beef with you, or with Jason. I had Alex do some investigating. He has a special gift to be able to see and interpret auras. They can tell him about the species, personality, physical anomalies, and sometimes emotions of anyone he observes."

"Excuse me?" Jason asked, raising his hand by force of habit. "What's an aura?"

"Well, this is how Alex explained it to me: whenever a person occupies a place in space, their consciousness leaves an impact on the surrounding energies. It's like when you drop a rock in a pond, and it creates ripples. Some people, like Alex, can see the ripples. They're unique to each person, more so even than a fingerprint. Does that make sense?" Sally met Jason's eyes and held them until he nodded. She remained facing Jason as she continued, even while referring to him in third person.

"Alex did this out-of-body-experience he uses to see auras at a distance and looked in on Jason. There was some kind of barrier that kept Alex from seeing his aura. He's never seen anything like it. Alex broke the spell, or whatever it was, and was nearly knocked unconscious by the force of Jason's energy. The aura was also an unusual, golden hue. I imagine this makes little sense to you, so I will explain as best I can. Bear with me."

Sally paused for a moment, and then took up her narrative at a totally different point. "Hope and I found an interesting group of documents in my library a few decades ago. They're a set of prophecies. The story goes that in ancient times, the universe was ruled by semi-celestial beings called Infinites. It's not clear what exactly the Infinites were, only that their rule was all-encompassing, cruel, and oppressive. At some point twelve mortals, mostly humans with blood from more powerful species, came together and decided to take the Infinites down. They performed some sort of ritual, which unfortunately was never recorded, and successfully imprisoned the Infinites between the layers of the realities. In the universe's dungeon, you could say. When they did this, the twelve people, who called themselves Guardians, became gifted with immortality. Ever since, they have been working to keep the Infinites trapped. The first of the prophecies foretells that if the Infinites manage to kill all twelve Guardians, they will be able to return. But, in order to prevent this, the last remaining Guardians will appoint twelve new ones to take their places. Using the set of prophecies, twelve of which describe each of the new Guardians, Alex and the girls and I have been trying to hunt down the new Guardians as they rise, in the interest of protecting them. For years we had no success at all. Now, however, we think we may have found the first young Guardian. Jason, we believe that is you."

Jason felt as though his heart had stopped. Lost in the story, he had nearly forgotten that this was about him. He couldn't believe this. He couldn't be one of *those* people. He was nobody. He was happy being nobody. This was impossible. Dimly, Jason heard his mother voicing some of the same thoughts.

"How can you tell? What does this prophecy say, exactly?" Pansy asked. Her voice was confrontational, edged with hysteria. Normally, Sally would bristle at the slightest indication of a challenge, but this time she didn't retort or glare. Instead, she closed her eyes, and proceeded to recite the prophecy from memory:

"*A golden light*
Pure and blameless
Child of Earth and Stone
Torn from within
Born on the battlefield
To hold the army together
With his silken tongue."

The words flowed into Jason's chaotic mind, nestling in the muddled corners where he tried to decipher their meaning—not their literal meaning, necessarily, but what they would mean for him.

"When Alex told me how powerful and luminescent Jason's aura was, that first line came into my head," Sally said. "After he told me that it was a 'golden light,' I was pretty sure. Another clue is the third line. Pansy is human, a species commonly symbolized by the element of Earth in lyrical works. The word 'Stone,' especially capitalized, often represents cotus, and Thomas was clearly part cotu. Jason was born in Brunswick, which right now is very much 'the battlefield.' Technically this is all speculation, but it is really the only explanation I have found that fits with all the facts."

"What does this mean? For Jason?" Pansy asked, her voice low and fragile. Pansy looked over at her son, one hand held fretfully to her heart. Jason glanced at her out of the corner of his eyes, but kept his head numbly tilted down, unwilling to meet either woman face-to-face.

"In the short term, it doesn't mean anything we didn't already know. He's a target. The Infinites and their followers will want him dead. We, the Guardians' acolytes, have to protect him. And we will. The long term is more concerning. As long as some of the original Guardians remain, all Jason has to worry about is staying alive. Once they're dead, things will get more...complicated. I don't know just what trials he may face then."

"How many are left, Sally?" Jason interrupted. He finally looked up and met her gaze. This time, she didn't look away from him. "How many Guardians are left?" he repeated. Jason's voice sounded raspy and toneless, hardly recognizable to his own ears.

"They are difficult to monitor, but last I heard, there are four," Sally replied. "That was about three months ago, when a colleague of mine in Germany heard that they'd been spotted in the English countryside."

Jason nodded stiffly. "How much longer do you think it will be?"

"I really don't know. My best guess is somewhere between five and ten years. Maybe more, maybe less. I *am* sure that it will be a matter of years, as opposed to weeks or months. There is time."

"Not a lot," Jason said. He dropped his eyes to stare at a point on the carpeting.

"For what it's worth, you aren't in this alone," Sally said. "Everyone at the manor is here to support you. We're a rather motley crew, I'll admit, but we are ready for this. And there are eleven more new Guardians out there somewhere, or soon will be."

"If they're not dead already." Jason frowned.

"They aren't," Sally replied firmly. Reaching across the space between them, she put two fingers under Jason's chin and pulled his gaze back to her. The lines of her face were unflinching, and her intense green eyes pierced into him.

"There are eleven more Guardians, and we will find them. They are not dead. It's all starting now. You have been called. The Infinites have just begun to coalesce a fighting force. We are not too late, Jason. We're right on time." Sally retracted her hand, releasing Jason and the momentary connection.

"I'm doubling Jason's guard detail," she said, refocusing on Pansy. "Scarlet and Alex are in charge of keeping him safe 24/7. They will be here soon. I can provide assistance while he's at school. I'm also going to make my research more directional by trying to find out what the genies are capable of and seeing what other devotees the Infinites might have gathered." She proceeded to detail basic spell-avoidance tactics and other safety procedures to Pansy. Jason tuned them out, retreating inside himself to process the revelation. He found himself wishing desperately for a taste of the normalcy that he sensed he had left behind forever.

Jason and Sammy were the only kids out in the park that day. Scarlet was there as Jason's guard, frolicking in the grass some distance away trying to catch a cricket. It was really too cold to be outside—it was only early November, but a cold snap had brought a stiff chill to the air. Both boys were bundled up in coats and scarves. Everyone else was warm inside their homes, which made it the perfect weather for Jason to tell Sammy something no one else could hear.

"Wow...J.D., that's...I don't even know what that is. I totally understand why your head hasn't been in the game." Sammy shook his head in awe. Jason wasn't sure he should have told Sammy about the prophecy. He'd been agonizing about it for a month, but in the end Jason needed to be able to talk to his best friend. It was selfish and reckless, but he was glad he'd done it.

"That was kind of how I felt when they told me. I'm not sure I really believe it yet, to tell you the truth. My life's ambition was to get through it with as few conflicts as possible. Guess it's some kind of really backward karma. Now I'm right in the middle of 'the greatest conflict of our times,'" Jason said. He kicked a pile of fallen leaves that lay at the foot of his park bench and watched them get carried away by the cool autumn wind.

"I'm gonna go out on a limb and say that you're not happy about it."

"You've got that right. I'd love for it to all just go away…but then at the same time I feel obligated to do something, now that I know. Sally keeps talking about how many people would die if the Infinites won. Not sure how she knows that, but it just seems natural. Bad guys win, universe-wide massacre. No pressure."

"But all you have to do right now is just not die, right?" Sammy said, trying to see the good in amidst the distinctly negative circumstances.

"That may be harder than you'd think."

"You said no one's come for you since that—you called it a genie, right?—at school, though."

"They will. That's one thing we're sure of. We don't know what the hold-up is, but sooner or later they'll try again," Jason said. The wind began to bite harder, and he wrapped his arms tighter around his torso to try to warm up.

"You're being protected."

"They know that now, too. Their last assassin was going solo, and didn't make it. If they're smart, they'll try harder next time."

"Well, let's hope they aren't smart, then. I'll be praying for you, by the way," Sammy said soberly, looking Jason in the eyes.

"Thanks," Jason said, trying to smile. "I think I'll need it."

The nights were getting longer and more foreboding. The time was ripe for him to take action. He watched the sun sink below the horizon from the entrance of his cave. As soon as the blood-red orb dipped beneath the blackness of the tree line, he got to his paws and pulled himself out of the tunnel's mouth. He shook the dirt out of his fur and began to trot toward the lights that marked the town. It was late enough and cold enough for most people to be inside their caves of wood and red stone, but still early enough for some to be out of their dens. It was the perfect time.

Floating on silent paws, he crept to the edge of the town, slinking in the darkest shadows of the human structures. He didn't want to be seen before he was ready. He began in an area with little population, on the outskirts, where the human dens were poorly built and even more poorly maintained. He kept his nose on high alert, looking for the slightest whiff of man's smell. The moment he caught one, blowing on the icy wind, he followed it, loping with long, easy strides toward the source of the scent. It wasn't long before he found it: one lone, ill-smelling male human stumbling about in the dark. Now it was time for the show to begin.

He came as close to the unwary human as he could while still remaining invisible in the shadows. He crouched and began to growl. The human stopped walking and looked around for the animal that made the noise. He let the volume of his growl rise, slowly, then fall to silence, and then leapt from his hiding place into the path of his bewildered prey. He fixed his eyes on the man, remained for a few seconds, until the human's fear finally caught up to it, and he screamed, filled with the unblemished terror only a few beings were empowered to induce.

He ran soundlessly from view and back into the tree line. One was enough for tonight. He ran about thirty paces into the forest. He spotted a high hill and, on impulse, ran to its summit, tilted back his head, and let out his best bone-chilling howl.

6

Richie stared at the dry maple leaf in the palm of his hand, cursing quietly and feeling absolutely absurd. This was never going to work. Jack was wasting both of their time.

"You can do it…" Jack said, urging him and staring at the leaf with even more intensity.

"No I can't!" Richie said, barely resisting the impulse to crumple the leaf to dust in frustration. "We've been at this for hours, and NOTHING is happening—" Richie felt a curious sensation rush through his veins. It was like his blood was boiling. And yet, it didn't hurt. It felt… good. Really good. Almost intoxicating. Richie looked at the leaf in the palm of his hand, already knowing what he would see. The dry leaf was in flames. The logical part of his mind told him to drop the leaf immediately, but he didn't. This fire wouldn't hurt him. This was *his* fire, and this fire was him. His skin tingled warmly beneath the flame, and he could feel the fire seeping from inside of him and onto the leaf. It was an incredible sensation. He watched in awe as the little fire consumed every fiber of the leaf and then extinguished itself, without leaving a mark on his flesh.

"I was right," Jack said smugly. "Fire cotu it is."

Richie couldn't speak; his emotions were too conflicted to settle on a single sentence. He brushed the few remaining ash particles off of his hand and into the Danube River.

"If I am a cotu," Richie finally said, "then how come I never noticed? I guess I could have overlooked some things, but why haven't I ever, I don't know, set my eyebrows on fire?"

"You can't set yourself on fire. Fire can't hurt you. It is possible to do something unintentionally, but that typically happens only when you're angry or scared. Although, it's more likely now that you've already set fire to something once."

"Oh, so *now* I'm going to start torching eyebrows by accident. Just not mine. That's wonderful."

"Well, yeah, if you want to put it that way. But hey, if you ever get attacked by a werewolf in an alley again, you'll be set."

"It took me six hours to set a leaf on fire."

"Okay, after a lot more training, then you'll be set," Jack said in amended.

"You're an ice cotu. I can believe that you'll teach me to fight. I know you can do that. But what can an ice cotu teach me about how to use my fire?"

"I...had a brother who was a fire cotu." A shadow passed over Jack's face, but was masked by an expression of false nonchalance a moment later. "I learned a lot from him. But I probably won't have to give you much instruction. In case you didn't notice, you just referred to it as 'your' fire. Already you're getting the hang of it. You'll learn by yourself pretty quick."

"Okay," Richie said. He hesitated for a moment, debating whether or not to say what he was planning on saying next, and decided to go with it.

"I'm sorry. A—about your brother. I didn't mean to bring up anything painful."

"It isn't your fault. Truth is, he's been popping up in my brain ever since I first caught your scent. I think that might be why I saved you," Jack said.

"If you don't mind my asking, how, um, how did he die?" Richie knew he was probably broaching a topic that was best left alone, but now that the subject had risen, he was curious. It was the first time Jack had opened the door for Richie, and he wanted to take advantage of the opportunity.

"He didn't die...it was worse than that." Jack glanced at Richie, then turned to look at the ground of the river bank on which they sat. He picked up a small stone. "He killed one of our sisters," Jack finally said, weighing the stone in his hand. "Not directly, but, he let it happen. We haven't spoken since. Before that, we were really close." Jack cocked back his arm and flung the stone into the river. "Although I'm not much better than him," he added softly.

"You've got to be somewhat better than him. I mean, you saved me," Richie said, hoping to dig Jack out of the hole Richie had inadvertently pushed him into.

"That doesn't even begin to make up for the things I've done."

"Well, it's a start." Richie wondered what Jack could have done that he felt so guilty about.

"Yeah, sure. I guess so." Jack shrugged and tossed another rock into the water.

From: RichieTheGr8
To: ClemGeorge4755
November 9 at 11:02 am
Subject: You Know Who
Ok, so, here I am. I apologize for the delay in sending you a message. Jack and I have been busy traveling on €0 for a month. It's more work than you might think. I haven't gotten to use a computer in a while. Thank God for public libraries. And thanks again for your help.

From: ClemGeorge4755
To: RichieTheGr8
November 9 at 11:15 am
Subject: Re: You Know Who
Nice subject line. Even better e-mail address.
I don't know what use it will be to you, but here are some links for the websites Sally's been known to write for and/or communicate on. When I said I hadn't heard from her, I misled you somewhat. She's still active in the "medical revolution" that she started, but she's very skilled at concealing her location, even when she is quite open about her identity. Efforts to track IP addresses and other virtual information have failed. More traditional approaches, trying to catch her in a slip that would reveal where she's gone, have also come up dry. I doubt you'll fare any better, but it would be a start. I suggest checking out the Med Revolution website, the website for the journal *Vampirology*, and the chat rooms on Cotu Central. Med Revolution is an on-line hub for physicians hoping to bridge the gap in healthcare created by the anthropocentric bias of the medical community. Dr. Kitch is an enthusiastic supporter. She founded and, as far as I know, is still the Chief Editor of *Vampirology*. Cotu Central is an open forum for all things cotu, so it's a bit of a long shot, but it's the only one that doesn't require a login, and you have to become a paying member of *Vampirology*

to get into the contact information page. I will try to investigate
that avenue for you.
Good luck, my friend.

From: RichieTheGr8
To: ClemGeorge4755
November 9 at 11:28 am
Subject: Re: You Know Who
Thank you! But why didn't you just tell us about that to start
with?!? Might have saved some time.

From: ClemGeorge4755
To: RichieTheGr8
November 9 at 11:34 am
Subject: Re: You Know Who
I wanted to double-check that Cotu Central was still running. The
site was taken down for several years recently. Also, I didn't trust
your man "Jack." He said we hadn't met, but I am certain that we
have, and if my remembrance had been correct, I could have
safely said that he is not a good character. But I can't find any
evidence of our meeting, and the picture from my security camera didn't raise any alarms from my associates, so despite the
stirrings of my intuition I must conclude that my suspicions were
unfounded.

From: RichieTheGr8
To: ClemGeorge4755
November 9 at 11:40 am
Subject: Re: You Know Who
So how did you think you met Jack then?

Richie glanced at his watch. One o'clock. It was time to meet Jack to
catch their cargo train to Switzerland, and Clement *still* hadn't replied. Even though Jack hadn't shown any sign of evil intentions,
Richie still didn't entirely trust him, and if Clement had misgivings
then Richie wanted to know why. He growled deep in his throat, annoyed that Clement wouldn't answer. He quickly clapped a hand over
his mouth. Humans aren't supposed to make that noise. He looked

around, hoping there wasn't anybody around to have heard him. A woman in a flowery dress at a bookshelf a few yards away was looking at him kind of funny, but that might just be the mismatched winter clothing. Richie wondered, not for the first time, how often in his old life he had growled, or done something else inhuman. He cleared his throat and began to close the windows on his computer. He logged out and exited the library, flipping up his coat collar against the cold as he walked onto the busy Paris streets.

"I went to the sites Clement sent me. Nothing earth shattering there. I get the impression that Dr. Kitch really doesn't want to be found," Richie told Jack. "She's doesn't give anything away." Sally's remarkable ability to cover her tracks was beginning to settle like smog over their plan. Richie had to question what, or who, could have made Sally go into deep hiding. There was an unpleasant possibility that it was Jack she was avoiding so ardently. The thought had a bitter taste. Richie tried to console himself by recalling how often he had seen Jack driven to distraction, often by nothing that Richie could see. He also had a tendency to lose anything that wasn't attached to his body. Surely a man with such poor focus would not require much effort to put off. Of course, that was probably why Jack wrote everything down, so he *would* remember.

"So we're getting nowhere," Jack said. "Story of my life." He looked away from Richie and out at the landscape blurring by them. Richie followed his gaze, shifting his position to try and become more comfortable leaning against the doorframe of the train car. They had left the urban centers behind, and the view was rather pretty, if going by at too high a speed to really appreciate.

"I know that our situation is not the greatest, but this is still kind of exciting," Richie said. The whole idea of jumping a train felt dangerous and free. He loved it. Richie closed his eyes, relishing the sensation of the air rushing by on his face, tousling his hair. The corner of his mouth turned up in a smile.

"You're so lucky," Jack said softly, sounding both jealous and despondent. Richie opened his eyes and rotated his head in Jack's direction. Jack was still looking out of the car, with a faraway expression on his face, the one he usually got when he was thinking about something past, one of those things he wouldn't talk about.

"How so?" Richie asked.

"You can still enjoy it," Jack replied simply.

"Enjoy what?"

"You know, sun on your face, wind in your hair, life in general. That's all kind of lost on me."

"God, Jack, way to kill the mood," Richie replied, taken a bit by surprise. He was getting used to Jack's occasional bouts of darkness, but did he have to have one right now? This was fun.

"Oh. Sorry. I'm a little out-of-sorts tonight." Jack arched his back and stretched his arms up against the doorframe. "I could really use a drink," he murmured.

"Didn't you just finish off a bottle of wine before we got on the train?"

"Yeah, and that was the last of my stock, too. I wonder if there's anything on here worth taking?" Jack got to his feet and wandered off among the stacks of crates behind them in the car. Richie sighed. Sure. Train robbery. Why not? He picked himself off the rough wooden floor and followed his companion into the maze of other people's things.

"Jack, are you sure you know where we're going?"

"Of course," Jack said. He stopped to pull the map out of his back pocket. He looked at it, looked at the alpine woods around him, put the map back, swiveled precariously on one heel, and started walking forward again at a slightly different angle. As far as Richie could tell, there weren't any visible landmarks. Ever since they'd left the more civilized foothills and started hiking the wilder slopes, Richie was fairly certain that they were lost in the Carpathian Mountains. They'd been wandering aimlessly for hours, or at least that seemed to be the case. Richie was so desperate to get a firm heading that he would even have been willing to ask for directions, if they could find someone to ask. Someone that spoke English, instead of Romanian, preferably. But Jack swore up and down that he knew where they were going.

"Are you *really* sure?"

"Of course! I know exactly where we're going."

It occurred to Richie that Jack wasn't claiming to know the most important piece of information.

"Do you know where we *are*?"

"Not a clue," Jack replied cheerfully. "But I'll figure it out. No worries. Everything's A-okay."

"The only reason you're so chipper is because of that case of Jack Daniels on the train."

"Hey, you're the one who said you didn't want any."

"I just thought one of us should be sober while we wander around in the woods and wait for hypothermia to set in. Give me the damn map." Richie snatched the crinkled sheet of paper and squinted at the blobs and lines Jack had scrawled onto its surface. "Which way is up—er, north?"

"That way." Jack pointed at the edge on Richie's right, then moved his finger to the bottom edge. "Or that way. I don't really remember."

"We're going to die," Richie said and moaned. "We're going to starve to death out here—no, you will starve to death, after I've already died of frostbite—and no one will ever know."

"Nah, we'll be fine. Even if I can't find the castle, sooner or later we'll find someone. This is the modern world. Walk long enough you're bound to run into civilization. And shouldn't a fire cotu be able to keep himself warm?"

"I'm *trying*. It's not working. I think my fire's hiding. Can't say I blame it. It's freezing up here." Richie rubbed his hands together, half hoping he'd generate some sparks, and then stuck them back in the pockets of his oversized coat. Jack looked at him, eyebrows pushed down a few degrees on the inside corners. Richie wanted to interpret the expression as empathetic, but Jack was too hard to read.

"I guess you are pretty new at that," Jack said. "Well, it's getting dark, and I don't think we're going to find it before sundown. What do you say we bed down for the night?"

"Okay." Richie allowed his duffel bag to slump off his arm and sat down while Jack wrestled the sleeping bags out of their bindings. It was hard to gauge how tired he was because his frozen muscles were going numb, but Richie was sure that he was exhausted. He and Jack had been walking all day, and all of the day before that. They'd tried hitchhiking, but there weren't a whole lot of people willing to give a ride to a ragged pair like them. Richie wished he knew how to hot-wire a car. Of course, that would only work if no one pulled them over and asked to see a license.

Jack tossed Richie's unraveled sleeping bag at him. He caught it, more or less, and laid it out on the frost-hardened leaf-litter. It was probably the most uncomfortable place Richie had slept in yet, and the sleeping bag did little to protect against the cold, but after about a half hour of rolling around, trying to find the least painful position, he finally fell asleep.

Richie woke up in the dead of night. The moon was a thin sliver that gave off only a little bit of light. He sat up, watching his breath billow out in a silver cloud in front of him. What had woken him up? He vaguely remembered hearing something, he thought, but it was probably just in one of his dreams—

There it was again. A faint rustling. It didn't sound far off. Richie reached over and shook Jack's shoulder. Jack mumbled something and sat up drowsily. Then he stiffened, obviously hearing it too. The rustling got louder, then stopped, and there was a thump, as of something dropping from the trees. Richie whipped his head around to set eyes on the source of the noise. He watched in horror as a dark, amorphous shape began to grow and rise from ground level.

"What the—" Jack started.

"I was about to ask *you* the same," declared an indignant voice with a strong Slavic accent.

"Somehow I expected Dracula's castle to be, I don't know, spookier," Richie said. The entrance hall was well-lit with numerous wall-mounted electric lamps that clashed with the faded ancient tapestries hung beside them.

"I don't have to decorate like it's the twelfth century simply because I lived through it," said their host, a tall, pale, and stately gentleman with black hair and angular eyebrows. "Even the dead like electric lights. You have no idea how foul torches smell. Now, follow me, if you will."

"So is he really, you know, *Dracula*?" Richie asked Jack as they walked behind the vampire in question.

"Of course," Jack said. "Who'd you think it was?"

"I don't know what I thought, but the more important question is *why didn't you tell me*," Richie demanded, not hiding his irritation.

"I thought it was obvious."

"Well...okay, so maybe it was obvious, but it's *not logical!*"

"If you're expecting 'logical,' you are in the wrong line of work,"

Jack replied. Richie couldn't think of anything intelligent to say in rebuttal, so he sulked in silence until Count Dracula seated them in his living room.

"So, you said that the reason you were trespassing on my property had something to do with my son," Dracula prompted, sitting down in an easy chair across from Jack and Richie. He took a sip from a glass of a suspicious red liquid that sat on a nearby lamp table. The count was putting on the air of being calm and collected, but Richie had detected the anxiety underlying his hurried actions, ever since Jack had tossed out the name "Alexandru." It was a good thing Jack knew the magic word, otherwise Richie figured that Dracula would have ended them out there in the woods.

"You don't know where he is, then?" Jack said.

"No, I don't. I haven't had any notion of his whereabouts for years. Not since he left with that harlot," Dracula said, staring with undisguised hostility into his glass of blood. Richie saw Jack begin to bristle at Dracula's less-than-respectful description of who he guessed was Sally and quickly interrupted to keep Jack from saying something that could get them into a fight with a centuries-old vampire—a fight they would almost certainly lose.

"We think he's in America, somewhere in the southeast," Richie said. He shot Jack a look, pleading with him to keep his mouth shut. Jack glared, but took the hint and didn't interrupt. "We're trying to find a woman named Sally, and we've heard that she used to run with Alexandru. We would really like to talk to him, if you could please tell us anything about where he's been, or even just how he knew Sally."

Dracula nodded, accepting with dignity the disappointment that his guests knew little more than he. "Sally came to us," Dracula said, "along with a witch by the name of Hope. She told me that they were conducting some sort of scientific research on vampires, and wanted to interview me and my family. I didn't like the idea, but I made the mistake of being hospitable and letting those sirens stay the night. Right from the start Sally started reeling in my son. He convinced me to let them stay and do their research. We answered their questions, allowed them to poke and prod us, all on Alexandru's insistence. Then, after a couple weeks, they announced that they were leaving, and Alexandru announced that he was going with them. He'd wanted to get out of Romania for quite some time, and this was his chance at adventure. I couldn't stop him. He wrote back every once in a while, but about forty years ago he wrote his last letter. He said that he and

Sally were working on some sort of sensitive business, and that he wouldn't be able to communicate with me for a while. He said that if I needed to find him, I would have to get lost. No explanation. And that was it." Dracula finished his story by knocking back the last of the blood.

"The only indication I have," Dracula said after a moment, "is the name 'Brunswick.' Alexandru mentioned it in several letters, before his last—I believe he's been there, wherever it is, with Sally for most of the time. I've sent scores of slaves to every Brunswick we could identify, looking for him, but they have all come back empty-handed. Does that name mean anything to either of you?" Richie and Jack looked at each other and shrugged.

"No," Richie said.

"But it gives us something to look for," Jack said. He seemed to have put the 'harlot' incident behind them in the interest of progress, although he still wasn't looking at Dracula in a manner that was entirely friendly. "We already had a region, and now we have a name. Since we'll be covering a smaller area, we may have more success than you did."

"If we find your son, what should we do?" Richie asked hesitantly. He assumed that Dracula would want to know that his child was safe, but then Alexandru seemed to want to stay secret. Dracula creased his brow and appeared deep in thought.

"Ask Alexandru to send me a message," he said finally. "If he doesn't want me to find him, then I won't try anymore, but I need to know that he's all right. My wives and daughter have all been killed. He's the only one I have left."

Richie analyzed the photograph Dracula had given them. The date on the back was September, 1947. It was in color, despite the early date, and showed Dracula's son Alexandru alongside a woman Richie recognized as Sally Kitch and another who must be Hope. Alexandru had his arm around Sally's shoulders.

"Sally seems to have had a busy life before she disappeared. Mastering multiple kinds of medicine, writing books, training new doctors, seducing the son of a rich aristocrat—all between the forties and the sixties," Richie commented. He and Jack were holed up in a room on the second floor of Dracula's castle. The count had been kind enough to let them stay, despite his adverse experience with house guests, and plan their next move for a few days. It was the nicest place they had stayed thus far, possibly the nicest place Richie had ever stayed in his life, although it was a bit dank. So Richie was making lots of comments with the goal of prolonging the planning period as long as possible.

"And before that, she was a fugitive," Jack replied, looking up from his notebook to focus on the picture in Richie's hands. "From the time she was seven and a half—which is like teenage for cotus, since they only age until their tenth year—until 1936. Then for a few years people stopped bothering her, and she got to actually do some living."

"You sure did your homework," Richie said, somewhat impressed, even if Jack's vast and specific knowledge of Sally was a tad stalker-ish. "What was she running from?"

"Assassins. Sent by the cotu governing body, ICCA. She didn't like the way they ran things, tried to do something about it, and they accused her of treason and tried to kill her. After chasing her 'round the globe a time or two they basically got bored and gave up." Jack said it very matter-of-factly, but there was a tension in his voice.

"Well that's kind of...overkill. What did she do to deserve that?"

"Just the usual sort of rash things the children of rich and politically significant parents do," Jack replied with a short sigh. "She organized some protests, vandalized some property, shorted out the electricity in a couple of minor government facilities. Then she got more purposeful and dug up some dirt on the cotus up top. That was what got her in such trouble. She publicized information that cast them in a really bad light, and it started a movement that got several thrown out of office and possibly got one guy killed, although that's debatable. It wasn't good stuff, but ICCA had it coming. The council wants cotus to assimilate among humans at any cost."

"What kind of 'cost'?" Richie asked. Jack tensed, just barely enough to notice.

"Well, for one thing, they like to lock up people who have a hard time controlling their powers," he said. "They used to brand criminals and the insane. I'm not certain they do that anymore, but I know the law still says that if a cotu finds someone with a brand, they're to report the person to the council so they can be taken back to whatever hellhole they were being kept in. Oh, and they are doing their best to take out the remaining populations of 'wild' cotus. Killing them is frowned upon, so ICCA instead tries to take all their cubs and plant them into civilized society." Jack stopped, his forehead furrowing. "Now that I think about it, that might be what happened to you."

"Wait, what?" Richie had wondered sometimes about his birth parents and why they left him, ever since Jack revealed that he must have been adopted, but this was a thought he'd never considered. "You think I was *stolen* from my biological parents and given to my other parents? Why?"

"I think the idea is to force cubs to acclimate to human society so they don't have the chance to choose anything else," Jack said. "We think that might be what happened to my baby sister. But that doesn't mean that's what happened to you. If it was, your parents, your adoptive ones, probably wouldn't even know. Yeah, I know. Sick, isn't it?"

"It's worse than 'sick.'" Richie did his best to hold onto his temper while imaging someone snatching him away from his cat-like parents and deceitfully landing him with his human family. He loved his family, but that didn't make it right. "Why do you—er, we—let them get away with that?"

"Our species tends to not be very collaborative," Jack replied. "I don't think anyone likes the ICCA system, but no one has been able to cooperate well enough to organize a rebellion. Sally is one of the few who has done any damage at all."

"So are the government goons still after her now? That *would* be a good reason for her to stay hidden."

"I don't know. They might be. But Sally handed their ass to them several times over when they were actively trying to kill her. They might have given up, or they might be even more furious. They're hard to predict. Regardless, Sally's never been one to hide from a challenge. She might run, but sooner or later she'll turn around and fight."

Richie thought about the intro to Sally's encyclopedia. He had to admit, taking cover under a rock didn't seem like her. Which brought them right back around to square one, where they didn't know anything.

"How do they fit into all of this?" Richie asked, fluttering the photograph in his hand. "I guess Alexandru just fell for the wrong girl, but what about this other one, Hope? You haven't mentioned her before."

"I've never heard of her before tonight," Jack said, sounding as mystified as Richie. "There are plenty of witnesses to Alexandru and Sally, but no one I've talked to has said anything about Hope."

"So we're halfway through our list and no closer to Sally."

"Well, we do have that name. Brunswick. And Alexandru said something about getting lost. Either he really wanted to shake off his dad, or that was a clue. This means we've got two directions we can go. We can start looking up Brunswick, or keep looking into contacts and see if that narrows anything down. What's your opinion?"

"There's a contact in West Virginia, and that's on the right side of the country, if I remember my geography correctly," Richie said, glancing at Jack for confirmation. Jack nodded. "So we could go there, and see if we can get any more information. If we find out something new, great, we'll take it from there. If we don't, we can give up and start looking for Brunswick. Although we'll have to get to the US somehow, which is a problem. We can't exactly walk there."

"Perhaps I can help." Both Richie and Jack whirled around towards the door that they hadn't heard open. Count Dracula stood leaning on the doorframe. Once again Richie noticed how very unorthodox Dracula looked. He was wearing factory-ripped denim jeans and a black t-shirt. He had bushy, angular eyebrows, just like that guy in the old movie, but his hair was shoulder-length and dyed with purple and red highlights.

"I get the impression that you two are short on funds," Dracula said. "And unless you intend to find a discarded sailboat and pilot it across the Atlantic, perhaps you wouldn't mind if I bought us some plane tickets?"

"Us?" Jack said.

"I've changed my mind," Dracula replied. "Too long have I sat in this castle and waited for news of Alexandru. It is time I took action. I'm coming with you to seek my son."

"And bringing your checkbook?" Richie added hopefully.

"Of course."

"Welcome to the team!" Jack yelled.

A mote of light the size of a ping pong ball floated at an unhurried pace through the darkened forest. Kell followed clumsily, tripping over branches and tugging her hair out of the jealous grasp of thorns and branches. She kept thinking that if she was better at her job, she would have been done in London and not be spending hours stumbling around in a forest following a tracking spell that was much more mobile than she. But the ice cotu had turned on her and she panicked, and now here she was. She thought they would stop for the night hours ago, but the tracker kept going.

The light wafted through a massive tree trunk, and when Kell worked her way around to the other side of it, her tracker was hovering motionless in the air. She frowned. Tracking spells followed a person until they found it and then disappeared. She had never heard of one just *stopping*. Maybe something was in its way? Kell bent and searched among the leaf litter for a stick, praying she wouldn't instead find a snake. Luck was on her side. She closed her hand around a good-size stick and cautiously reached out with it to probe the space right below the stuck mote. It didn't hit anything. Kell waved it around for good measure, but felt no barrier. She dropped the stick and held out her hand in the same spot. Contact.

Something cool and fluid caressed her palm. Kell pushed on it, and it became suddenly hard and unyielding, like silk turning to marble. What kind of ward was this? Kell snatched back her tracker in her hand and reabsorbed the energy through her skin.

"Now what?" she huffed to herself. Somehow, her targets had passed through this point that wouldn't even permit a tiny tracker spell. She replaced her palm on the invisible surface and willed it to be opaque. Black streamed from her hand across the barrier. The magic ink spread in all directions, forming a titanic globe that stretched far beyond Kell's field of view. She dug into the dirt at its base with her shoe and discovered that the sphere curved away underground, as well.

Kell cursed under her breath. Someone or something had blocked the boy from her reach entirely. She tried for a moment to take stabs of energy to the wall like a chisel, but to no avail. It was too big, too thick, and too strong. What was in this fortress? She took out her phone, not expecting much, and was pleasantly surprised to find that she still had some battery life left, and the GPS was still just barely working. She recorded her coordinates, made a new tracker to take her to the nearest town, and abandoned the effort for one night. Once she determined what was hiding in the giant magic bubble, perhaps the next step would make itself apparent. If not, maybe there was another way to determine where they might go next.

"Rise and shine, my friends!" Dracula greeted enthusiastically, flinging wide the door to the room Jack and Richie were staying in. Richie blinked open his sleep-encrusted eyes. Across the room he could see Jack sitting up in bed, blearily rubbing a hand over his face.

"Whattimeizzit?" Richie mumbled.

"6:07 a.m.," Dracula replied. "The flight is at 8:30 this evening, but I would prefer to get there early to make sure everything is in order. And it'll take us most of the day to drive there."

"Don't you sleep during the day?" Jack asked.

"A *primum* vampire, limited by sunlight? I am insulted! What do you take me for, a common leech? Now come on, rouse yourselves! We have to get going! I've let you sleep too late already." Richie groaned and stuck his head under his pillow. He heard a dull *thunk* as Jack rolled out of bed and onto the floor.

Dracula insisted that Richie and Jack both look their best before he would be seen in public with them. This seemed to both annoy and completely baffle Jack. Richie had to admit that he understood the count's point.

"We need to get you a shirt. And...shoes," Richie suggested, looking his socially unacceptable companion up and down. His pants were a little worse for wear as well, but that wasn't as big of an issue. The hair, however, was a mess. But there wasn't much that could be done about that before they had to get to the airport.

"Why?" Jack asked, tilting his head quizzically.

"Wha—you mean why do you need a shirt? It's just what people do. They wear clothing. Over their whole bodies. In public," Richie said, trying to explain.

"Really?" Jack said. Dracula was staring at Jack, as though he couldn't tell if he was serious or not. In answer to the unspoken question, Richie gave Dracula a small nod.

"You don't get out much, do you?" Dracula said. Jack shook his head, still looking confused. "Well, fortunately I took the liberty of obtaining a couple sets of clothes for you two, for the sake of my reputation, at least. If fortune is on our side, they'll fit."

They did fit. The blue jeans were kind of stiff, but the mere newness of them made up for that. Richie couldn't remember ever having new clothes. He'd always gotten hand-me-downs from his brothers. And Dracula had even gotten his favorite color right. Granted, the red polo had probably just been at the top of the stack, but it still felt a little personalized. Richie was immensely grateful. After all, clothes are one of those things that aren't easily shoplifted, what with those little electronic tags on them that beep when you walk out the door with something you haven't paid for. Jack didn't appear to be as thrilled. He'd refused to change out of his single pair of black jeans, but he had grudgingly agreed to put a shirt on over them. Dracula was clearly not happy that the old, worn-out denim was still there, but he was willing to compromise. On one point he would not give in, however.

"OW!" Jack said in complaint, flinching away, which only made the brush pull his hair harder.

"Oh, get over it," Richie said. In the driver's seat of the black Ferrari, Dracula was chuckling softly at Richie and Jack's shenanigans.

"You know, it should really be *you* back here," Richie said in a shot at Dracula. "*You're* the one who insisted on getting these blasted tangles out." Richie yanked the hairbrush free, ignoring Jack's protests, and started brushing again from the top. After it got caught once again in the impenetrable carpet, Richie abandoned the brush entirely and started trying to work out the worst of the snags with his fingers.

"I'm sorely tempted to just set your hair on fire and see if that fixes it," Richie grumbled. Jack hissed at him and Dracula laughed even louder.

"Finally!" Richie exclaimed with relief, slamming the hairbrush on the table for emphasis. The other patrons in the diner were looking at him strangely, but he was too busy glorying in his victory to care. He'd labored for over two hours, until he and Jack were both close to tears, and Richie had gotten the last snarl out of Jack's hair. Dracula glanced up from the morning paper and gave Richie an approving nod.

"This feels weird..." Jack said, bordering on a whine, as he ran his fingers through his hair.

"Hey, quit complaining," Richie protested. "I've been working on that all morning, and don't you dare say it doesn't look good. I might still set it on fire." Jack glared at Richie, who looked the other way and took a sip of his chocolate milk.

"Here's your coffee, sir," said a blonde waitress, setting the steaming cup in front of Dracula.

"Ah, thank you my dear," Dracula said, looking up. His eyes fixed on her throat for a heartbeat, then turned back down as he opened a creamer and poured it into his coffee. The waitress blushed, clearly thinking that he'd been looking somewhere else, and retreated without a word.

"I thought you never drank," Richie said. "You know, 'I never dvrink,'" he added, trying to mimic Dracula's accent.

"The line you are referring to says 'I never drink *wine.*' Which is also a lie. Cinema puts words in my mouth often. And your attempt at Romanian pronunciation is terrible," Dracula replied, stirring his coffee.

"Hey, I'd like to hear your Scottish imitation."

"Touché," Dracula said, and took a swig of coffee.

"So how much longer are we going to be driving?" Jack asked.

"Another hour, maybe more. I don't usually drive this far, so I'm not certain. We're flying out of Budapest, which is on the south end of the country. About as far from my castle as you can get and still be in Romania."

"There aren't airports closer than that?" Richie asked.

"Didn't check."

"What? Why?"

"I'm familiar with this airport, I've always had good experiences there, and I see no reason to try another one," Dracula explained. Richie gave him a strange look, but before he could comment on Dracula's stubbornness, the blonde waitress delivered breakfast for Jack and Richie, and any chance of conversation ceased to exist. Dracula continued to flip through the newspaper while Jack and Richie inhaled the first real food they'd had in ages.

"One of my slaves is meeting us at the airport with your passports," Dracula said after a few minutes, not looking up from the news. "They'll be professionally forged. They'll even get you through U.S. security. I don't know what country of issue they'll be. You may have to be Romanian for a while, but that'll be all right. I can call you foreign exchange students. With me as your generous benefactor. Yes, I like the sound of that. Now, our Budapest flight will be taking us to Amsterdam, and we'll be there for an hour for refueling before we can fly for New York. I intend to spend that time planning our course of action for when we enter America. And has no one ever fed either of you before in your life?"

"It's been a looong time," Richie said.

"I haven't eaten anything that didn't come wrapped in plastic in at least five years," Jack added around a mouthful of eggs.

"Swallow before you speak," Dracula, his upper lip curling a little in disgust, told Jack.

"Thank you so much for paying for this." Richie shoved another forkful of sausage in his mouth.

"Apparently it's a good thing I did. Otherwise you might have starved to death," Dracula said, somehow managing to sound both sarcastic and dead serious at the same time.

Clement looked about the train station furtively. Everyone seemed to be watching him. He knew he was being paranoid, but then that seemed a good thing to be, these days. He checked the seat beside him for the fifth time in as many minutes, assuring himself that the laptop was still there. He praised the foresight that had told him to buy a portable computer, in case he ever needed to relocate quickly. On impulse, he opened the device and turned it on. He pulled up the Internet and checked his e-mail. There was something from Richie, but it would have to wait. Clement clicked the "Compose" button and put the *Vampirology* journal's contact e-mail in the address bar. It was the only way he knew to maybe send a message to Sally herself. He had last used it to mention that a couple potential patients were asking around for her, and he had received no response. Still, he had to try something. Clement typed in his message:

Watch yourself.

He considered adding more information, but decided against it. He didn't really have anything to tell her. The word in the underground was that the genies were becoming violent, and one was looking for two male cotus, who were looking for Brunswick. Clement had heard this from a patient, and remembered the genie that had been in his office not so many weeks ago, and cursed himself. She'd come in right after Jack and Richie left, pretending to be the mother of all hypochondriacs. To stop her worrying about catching something from the patients before, he'd assured her that his last patients had a cotus-only problem. He realized his mistake when he was e-mailing with Richie later, and had taken off immediately with the laptop. He thought maybe he would go to outer Siberia, or some other place where neither he nor his computer could give away any more information.

Clement hit "Send," and then sent an identical message to Richie. He was careful to make sure that he deleted the sent messages, and double-checked that Sally and Richie had been erased from his contacts. He shut down the laptop and replaced it on the chair.

The locomotive arrived and Clement boarded, his eyes flitting manically as he tried to make sure he wasn't being followed. It was late at night, or early in the morning, depending upon how you looked at it, so there weren't many people in the train station to survey. And, after all, this wasn't London. South Wales was a quieter place. There was only one other person on his train car. This made him a little nervous as well, but he took a deep breath and told himself it would be all right. Still, he made sure to take a seat in full view of his fellow passenger. After a few minutes, the train began to move out of the station.

Clement passed the first hour of the train ride fidgeting and fretting. He even found himself staring intently out the window, as though someone could possibly be running alongside. Shaking his head to bring himself back to reality, Clement shifted in his seat and stared straight ahead. The other commuter laid their head against the window and promptly began to snore. Well, at least *he* probably wasn't a threat. Clement hadn't slept in a day or so, and knew that he should, but he couldn't relax. Even though he hadn't seen any sign of a follower, he was sure someone would be after him. The paranoia did have its advantages. All the worrying left him little time to feel guilty about mistakenly helping set Richie's pursuers on his trail.

A new scent wafted into the car from the door leading to the car behind them. Clement sat straight up, sniffing. By the time he'd identified the smell, it was too late. The magic was working quickly, and just like the human passenger before him Clement found that he couldn't stay awake. He struggled for as long as he could, but werewolves were not made to resist magic. Just as he was about to lose all consciousness, he felt two small hands grab him under the arms, pulling him out of his seat and dragging—him—somewhere—

7

Jason splashed his fingers lightly on the surface of the pond. Heeding the call, Vanessa poked her head above the water with an eager squeak. He ran an affectionate hand over her warm, slippery head and neck, then tossed a handful of dried bloodworms her way. Vanessa pounced upon one of the slim, lifeless forms, as though the dead worm might consider attempting an escape, and crunched it between her teeth.

"Not playing with the boys today?" Jenna, with one long, thin finger situated between the pages of a book to mark her place, plopped down beside Jason. Though not part of Jason's protective detail, Jenna came to soccer Sundays on occasion as an extra set of eyes in the chaos.

"Nah, I don't feel up to it," Jason replied. He shifted his position, but the needling discomfort of the wiry veins constricting inside his abdomen was undiminished. What was more, he had woken up with one of the searing headaches that were part of his symptom set. Even if Sunday soccer was no contact—which it never was—the activity would be too hard on him.

"Shouldn't you be at home?"

"If I stayed home every time my TTS bothered me, I'd barely get out of the house," he reminded her, not without a touch of frustration. "Besides, I think the fresh air kind of helps, especially with the headaches."

"Well, all right," Jenna said. She didn't seem convinced, though. Rather than return to her usual bench and read, Jenna settled into the grass and turned her attention to the soccer game, keeping half an eye on Jason. Jason couldn't be sore with her for looking after him. He actually was glad of it, as he wasn't so sure himself that he shouldn't be at home resting. He just hated to miss the last normal socialization left to him.

A bit wistfully, Jason watched the other boys at their sporting. At the moment, Sammy and Tyler were locked in a battle of skilled footwork while the other players stood off to the sides, chatting and waiting with some impatience for the two sports kings to let someone else have a chance. Jason tossed Vanessa a few more bloodworms and watched the confrontation with the idle interest of someone not invested in the outcome. Sammy had possession of the ball, twisting and dodging to prevent his much more powerful adversary from stealing it. Tyler's strength was matched to his speed, however, and in this contest he prevailed, confiscating the ball and delivering a sound kick that even from midfield was too hard and fast for the goalie to risk catching. Tyler ran a victory lap, high-fiving every player in reach, including a few on the opposing team.

"Tyler sure is an intriguing character, isn't he?" Jenna observed. "He's so young, and already displaying almost perfectly the masculine stereotype."

"I've never heard it said quite like that before, but yeah, he is. Like I need another reminder of my total lack of biological fitness."

"I doubt that you are as feeble as you seem to believe," Jenna said, her voice as firm as she could manage. "You are one of the most powerful individuals in the known universe. Perhaps your strengths are not readily apparent, but they must exist."

"If I have some sort of powers, I've never seen them," Jason replied, wrapping a blade of grass around his finger. "How I'm going to trap any Infinites is beyond me. I'll have some help, though, so I guess it'll work out. But, um, no, I wouldn't consider myself very intimidating."

"Intimidating is overrated. There are other ways to show strength. I, for one, am impressed with how well you have withstood the pressures of both adolescence and a confusing, unwanted destiny. Or consider the creature in that puddle beside you. You have rescued and raised her all by yourself, even though you have to risk leaving the safety of your home to do it."

Jason couldn't help but smile at the praise. He supposed his lake monster was one thing he'd managed to do right.

Vanessa nipped his finger impatiently, pulling Jason back from the rare moment of self-appreciation. He laughed at her impetuousness, despite the beads of blood welling on his finger, and poured the rest of the makeshift lake monster food into the little green pond.

"Salvēte, discipulī," Mrs. Adair greeted her sixth period Latin class.

"Salvē, Magistra," the students intoned mechanically. Jason noticed that he didn't hear Alex, and looked at the desk beside him. Alex was fast asleep, head resting on his crossed arms. Behind Alex, Sally was eyeing him disapprovingly. She punched him between the shoulder blades, hard, and he jerked awake with a snort.

"My confidence in your protective abilities wanes by the moment," Sally whispered. Alex guiltily ducked his head and pretended to be busy pulling his Latin binder out of his scaly black shoulder bag.

"If you'll open your textbooks to page 52, we're starting a new chapter today. We'll be learning about the genitive case," Mrs. Adair said. Jason flipped through the large red book as instructed. A picture of a faded, broken Roman mosaic graced the top of the page. It looked like it must have been quite beautiful in its day.

"I hear there was another scare last night," Sally said quietly, casting her eyes about the room to make sure no one was eavesdropping. Although she wasn't specific, Jason knew what she was talking about. In the last few weeks there had been several reports of a monstrous black beast with glowing red eyes stalking around town at night. Strange things had happened in Brunswick, but nobody could remember this particular strange thing happening before, and the town was getting nervous.

"So do you know what it means?" Jason asked.

"Yes," Sally replied readily. "Well, sort of. I think what people are seeing is a Black Dog. Capital 'B,' capital 'D.' They're common in the global mythology. They spread terror and calamity. To see one is rumored to be a portent of death. Unfortunately, none of the books say how to banish them.

"What I did find was a ritual to summon and enslave a Black Dog. And with Brunswick surrounded by energy barriers, I would postulate that a spirit being like a Black Dog would be hard pressed to get here another way. I think you can understand my concern. Genie magic is pretty strong. It would be mighty easy for them to summon themselves a pet Black Dog."

Jason and Alex were silent while the idea of this new threat sunk in. As long as Alex was around, Jason hadn't felt afraid of the genies, or much anything else. But if this was something Alex didn't know how to kill...

Spiders of ice crawled up and down Jason's spine. "What do we do?"

"*You* don't go out at night by yourself, or at all, preferably, until we know whether or not this Black Dog is after you," Sally said. "The records agree that Black Dogs are strictly nocturnal."

"But what about everyone else in town? Do we know the Black Dog won't hurt them? I mean, even if it's not after me, we ought to do something."

"Scarlet and the rest of the pack are taking turns patrolling the town," Sally told him. "They'll look out for the civilians."

"You didn't exactly answer the question."

"Okay, then. I don't know what the Black Dog might do, but I think that the townspeople will be perfectly fine, as long as the pack is guarding them."

Jason supposed that would have to do. He shifted his attention back to the teacher, even though the others were still talking. However, with his life-or-death crisis being discussed right beside him, Jason struggled to concentrate.

"The genitive singular feminine ending is –ae, just like the nominative plural..."

"...not sure the genies have that kind of power. Black Dogs are pretty potent..."

"This pattern holds true for most of the endings..."

"...a really roundabout way, not to mention risky..."

"...copy the chart on page 54..."

"...Hope could try that spell..."

"Could you guys please shut up?" Jason yelled. Alex and Sally stopped talking immediately, staring at Jason in disbelief. A few of their other classmates turned to look as well.

"I—I'm sorry," Jason apologized hurriedly. "It's just—I'd really like to be able to focus on school, while I'm at school, okay?" He quickly returned to his note-taking to hide his embarrassment.

"Sorry," Alex said. He began copying the chart of endings, or at least pretending to. When Sally didn't add her voice, Alex whispered something sharp at her.

"I apologize, Jason," she said with thinly-veiled frustration.

"She wants the best for you, really," Alex said as he walked with Jason to their next class. "Sally just doesn't understand the desire to be normal. It was never an option for her."

"I know," Jason replied. "You've told me before. And I've seen how she acts. She's all business. I don't blame her for that. But it's hard not to blame someone…" He trailed off, looking across the hall. A group of eighth grade boys were joking loudly, pushing each other around and generally causing chaos. Without a care in the world.

"Your world has come apart, and someone has to take the fall. I get that. And if it makes you feel better, I give you permission to yell at me all you want. But Sally doesn't understand how you feel about it. She doesn't think the way the rest of us do. So, can you try not to take it out on her?" Alex asked, his expression pleading. Jason nodded, not looking at Alex. He heard Alex sigh softly, but Alex didn't say anything else.

"These Black Dogs," Jason finally said, as they were about to get to the band room, "what is it they do to people again?"

"I'm actually not sure," Alex replied. "I read over everything Sally found. The sources aren't real specific, or consistent, about anything. They can't even agree whether 'Black' Dogs are black, white, or yellow. In the stories, it seems like they scare people to death, which kind of sounds like BS to me. But we can't afford to underestimate them."

They reached the band room door. Without a further word, Alex went around to the back of the room, joining the other two percussionists in their fortress of drums and cymbals. Jason turned the other way, taking his assigned first-chair place, front row, right by where Mr. Lambert's conducting stand sat. Carrie, the second-chair clarinet with the French braids, waved at him from the other side of the semi-circle of front row chairs. Jason smiled back, blushing a little at the attention, even if she did flirt with all the guys. He quickly busied himself with putting together his flute.

"Hey, Jason! We're getting our Christmas Concert music today!" Cameron exclaimed with even more energy than usual. He flung himself into the chair beside Jason, even as its rightful owner came in and glared daggers at him. The chair rocked back precariously, colliding with a music stand and almost braining the trombone player behind. Cameron didn't notice.

"That we are," Jason said in agreement before playing a short scale on his flute to warm it up. The sound wasn't quite right. Jason turned the head of the flute a little bit to the outside and tried it again. While he experimented, Cameron continued to chatter beside him. Something about unicorns and matrices. Jason laughed a little, causing his high D to fail to take off. He never knew what Cameron was talking about, but the inane chattering always cheered him up all the same. Even if band hadn't been his favorite class, Cameron would have made it a highlight of the day. Him, and Mr. Lambert.

"All right, let's get started. Lin, pass out these sheets. Here's the first of the songs for the Christm—sorry, *Winter* Concert. Today we fail miserably at sight-reading it, and the other two songs that will be coming around shortly. Then we spend the next month trying to prevent it from being a disaster when we play it at the concert. I will be recording the concert performance, so that your parents can have a CD, so... Don't. Screw. It. Up. Now, let's get rollin'. Cameron, get out of Brooke's seat and put your trumpet on your face. Alex, if you don't stop playing with my drumsticks, I will beat you with them. Those are worth more than you are."

Cameron obediently ceded the chair to Brooke and took his designated seat beside Mickey, who was doing fingerings in the air with his mouthpiece in place, for he had once again forgotten his trumpet somewhere or other. Alex rapped the metal instrument cabinet with the mallets once more for good measure before sullenly setting them aside and reading over the sheet music Lin had just set on top of his snare drum. One of the tubas was attempting to play James Bond tracks, while Katie, the Trombone Mother, gave him her best reproachful sideways glance. Already it was shaping up to be a good class.

Alex found himself humming "Little Drummer Boy" while cleaning up the orchard for winter. It was somewhat annoying, and yet he couldn't seem to stop. Trim a branch here, *pa-rum-pa-pum-pum*. Rake the leaves up there, *pa-rum-pa-pum-pum*. Even with the song stuck in his head, he was rather enjoying himself. The work was hard, but he liked it, and this was a great day for it. Cool and cloudy, just the way he liked it. No sun to hurt his eyes. Sunlight wouldn't scald Alex's skin, as it did to weaker vampires, but he still preferred that the solar disk be well hidden.

Alex tapped his foot to the imaginary beat. Pile leaves around this tree, *pa-rum-pa-pum-pum*. He was so immersed in landscaping and music that at first he didn't register the subtle disturbance behind him. He stopped humming and froze. The noise came again, an ephemeral, barely audible crunching of the fallen leaves. Alex looked over his shoulder. There was nothing there but bare tree trunks and brown leaves swirling in the breeze...except, there wasn't a breeze that afternoon.

Alex leaned the rake against a nearby pear tree and slowly approached the area, his footfalls carefully measured and placed so as not to make a sound. He searched the better part of an acre, but couldn't find anything more alarming than a squirrel. Yet he had the nagging feeling that someone had been watching him, and perhaps that someone still was.

"Hello?" he called. His voice echoed like a wandering ghost among the trees, but otherwise there was no response. He looked around once more, putting his hands on his hips, and finally concluded that it must have been his imagination. Shaking his head, Alex gave up and went to return to his work. He happened to angle his head downward, and noticed something impressed into a patch of soft mud. He crouched to get a closer look.

It was a paw print.

He superimposed his hand over it, and a chill ran down his spine. It was at least half again as big as his spread palm, with smaller indentations a couple inches apart from the toes indicating long, wicked claws. Either someone had lost their pet Great Dane, or he'd just had a brush with a Black Dog. Alex took his cell phone out of his pocket and took a picture of the print, with his hand placed on the ground next to it for perspective. Then he sprinted back to the manor, glancing nervously behind him every stride or two.

"Look at that and tell me it isn't scary." Alex slammed his phone down on the desk in front of Sally. She looked down from the computer screen at the picture, and her eyebrows shot up.

"I confess, that's pretty scary," Sally said in agreement. "You took this in the orchard?"

"This thing was standing not four yards away from me."

"Just *now*? I guess this proves that they're corporeal then. Or that they can be. And, they must have some daytime activity...perhaps only in relative darkness? Heavy overcast? Mmmph. Well, that is unnerving. But the timing is impeccable."

"How so?"

"Look at this e-mail I just got."

Alex looked over her shoulder at the monitor. An open e-mail from someone named Clem G that read simply, "Watch yourself."

"Ooh. That doesn't sound good," Alex said. "Clem...isn't that the werewolf of London?"

"That's the one, Warren Zevon."

"For the love of God, do not get that song stuck in my head," Alex said. "But in all seriousness, do you trust this Clem guy?"

"He's always been reliable. Clem is one of my more loyal protégés. It's nice of him to warn me, but I would rather know what he's warning me about. The fact that he feels like he can't tell me over the 'net is perhaps more concerning than the message itself. Something is going on that I don't know about, Alex. I can't stand that."

"I assume you're going to ask Clem what he meant."

"Already done. But I don't expect an answer. I think I had a phone number for him somewhere. I'm going to dig around and see if I can find it. He probably won't talk over the phone either, but maybe we can agree to meet somewhere and discuss this face-to-face."

Alex nodded. "Where is Jason?".

"He's with Scarlet and one of the other werewolves, out in the field," Sally said.

"I'm going to go check on them."

"Good thought. And I need to talk to Hope about magical barriers. I don't want any Black Dog wandering around on my property, endangering my ward." Sally pushed the rolling office chair back and stood up. The conversation clearly over, Alex pivoted and exited the front door. From the porch he could just see some figures gallivanting about off in the distance.

Jason stood perfectly still, eyes closed, straining his ears. His enemy was out there, circling him. He knew it. But he couldn't hear it. He heard a faint pattering off to his left and whirled around. Immediately, he felt fingernails swipe against the side of his throat.

"Dead," he heard Scarlet say, and then sigh as he opened his eyes. She was right behind him, looking exasperated. "Again. Use *all* your senses, Jason. You can't always use your eyes. Darby, you try."

Jason slunk to the side while the young, violet-eyed werewolf took his place in the center of the imaginary circle. She shut her eyes and the training game began anew. Scarlet began to walk around Darby, keeping a wide berth. Scarlet placed each foot down softly and deliberately. Darby followed Scarlet as best she could. Her tall, slightly pointed ears—characteristic of a werewolf who was born, not Bitten—twitched and swiveled at the fringes of their range of motility. Every once in a while, Scarlet would make a noise loud enough that her trainee would hear, and Darby would lash out with sharpened fingernails toward the sound. Scarlet would leap backwards, out of her reach, and then begin again. After a few minutes, Scarlet repeated the trick that had gotten Jason—she picked up a stone and tossed it. Darby started to turn towards the impact, but she had seen what happened to Jason and turned back just in time to parry Scarlet's blow. The contact marked the end of that round.

"Good," Scarlet said in praise, and Darby glowed with pride. "But mostly because Jason went first. You both need to work on this. Next we—"

"I don't think there can be a 'next.'" Alex approached from the direction of the house. He looked worried, maybe even frightened, two emotions that Jason wasn't used to seeing from Alex.

"I found a paw print in the orchard," Alex explained when he reached them. "A really big, um...disembodied, source-less, you know what I mean, paw print. I think we need to take this operation indoors, or save it for another time."

"Eep!" Scarlet squeaked. Regaining her composure, she motioned her charges towards her. "Come on guys, we're going back to the house. Stay close."

"Training me is a waste of your time. I'm never going to be strong enough," Jason said in protest. They were sitting in Sally's kitchen while Alex did a sweep of the Kitch estate. If it was safe, then they would be sent straight home. If it wasn't, they might be spending the night at the Kitch Manor.

"It isn't just about muscle," Scarlet said. "If you fight smart, you can take down someone three times your size. Trust me, I've done it. We'll keep working. It'd be a lot easier if we could go outside...but of course not. There are a whole bunch of empty rooms here. I'm sure we can find one that'll work for training. It won't be like doing it outside, but oh well." She shrugged and returned to drawing dogs on a piece of printer paper. Jason thought that drawing dogs, even the friendly kind, was kind of inappropriate in the current climate, but he didn't say anything.

They sat for a few minutes without speaking: Scarlet doodling and Jason staring at the table and thinking about everything in the universe. I hope I get to go home soon. I still have a page of math problems to do. Not to mention practicing for the concert. Those fifth and sixth measures are killer. What if Alex finds the Black Dog? What do we do then? I can't fight. I don't care what Scarlet says, she can't train me out of being frail. Can I even do...whatever I have to do to save the world? What is it that I have to do anyway? Are the other Guardians this pathetic? I wonder if any of them even know. If we can't go outside anymore, can I still meet Sammy for soccer on Sundays? What do I say if I can't? They shouldn't be out there either if it's not safe, but I don't know how to explain it. I don't even know what "it" is. Are we really any safer inside? I mean, can Black Dogs not come into buildings? He thought this last question seemed of immediate importance and merited being addressed out loud.

"How come we're safer inside the house?" he asked. Scarlet paused in her drawing and looked up at Jason with wide eyes.

"Sally!" she called. "Why are we safer in the house?"

"We aren't." Sally walked through from the living room. "Black Dogs can come right on in here if they want. The only difference is that it's easier for us to keep track of and protect you when you're in an enclosed space," she told Jason. She crossed the kitchen and opened the refrigerator. "Hope is working on a more effective solution as we speak. It may be a while coming, but she's developing a spell to keep Black Dogs out of the manor." Sally took a fruit smoothie out of the fridge, screwed off the cap, and took a gulp. She looked totally calm, even though she had just admitted that a huge supernatural beast could burst in at any moment and make mincemeat of them all.

"If a Black Dog did come through the front door, what would we do?" Scarlet asked. It didn't make Jason feel any better to know that she was as clueless as him.

"If it has a physical body, then it can be wounded," Sally said as she reasoned through the situation. "And since Black Dogs are loners, it would be outnumbered by far. I see no reason why we couldn't prevail."

"Could we kill it?" Scarlet asked.

"Possibly," Sally replied vaguely, her gaze going a little unfocused as she mulled it over. "Probably not. We can chase it off. Perhaps make it weaker. The point is to protect Jason, and I'm fairly confident that we can do that."

Fairly confident. Wonderful. But Jason was too tired of worrying to really dwell on it. He watched Sally down her smoothie and tried not to think so much. Sally tensed, and tilted her head like she was listening for something.

"Alex says the coast is clear. Y'all can go back to the Drake place," she said, relaxing her muscles. She put the cap back on the drink and replaced it in the fridge, closing the door and walking back out into the adjoining room. Scarlet got to her feet and started cleaning up the mess of papers and colored pencils on the table, clearly ready to take Sally at her word.

"Wait, Sally," Jason called. She grabbed the doorframe and leaned back into the kitchen.

"Yes?"

"How do you know?"

"What Alex said? He just told me. Telepathically," she said. "He has a knack for that sort of thing, and we've been working on our connection for a good long while." She started to leave again, then changed her mind. "I should probably drive you. You shouldn't be walking out in the open and exposed. I suppose I ought to put some shoes on then. I'll be right back."

"You've got a VW bus?" Jason momentarily forgot to be overwhelmed by potential impending disaster as he feasted his eyes upon that marvel of transportation. His father had owned one when he met Pansy, but it had been turned to scrap metal before Jason had gotten to the second grade.

"Beautiful, isn't it? I bought it back in '64," Sally said proudly, running a hand along the metal body before opening the driver's side door and climbing in.

"It's almost impossible to keep running, though," Alex complained. He opened the side door and crawled in the back, and Jason followed.

"I've always wanted one of these things," Jason said. "Dad used to have one, when I was little. I bragged to all my friends about it..." He trailed off as he remembered what had happened to the old van. His father had crashed it, driving under the influence, and it had been smashed and twisted beyond any hope of repair.

"Yes, it's a pity they stopped making these things," Sally said, seemingly oblivious to the fact that the conversation had just gotten awkward. Scarlet buckled her seatbelt and Sally put the bus into gear, cautiously backing the cumbersome vehicle out of the driveway.

"Please," Alex said and snorted in derision. "VW buses are gas-guzzling hunks of junk that only go like fifty miles an hour, tops."

"At least I *have* a car," Sally shot back.

"What's wrong with my motorcycle?" he protested.

"Oh, yes, your minuscule locomotion device. I am so very impressed," Sally teased.

"Well you ride on the back of it to school with me every day. You can't hate it too much." The mindless banter continued all the way to Jason's house. Sally dropped them off at the end of the driveway and continued arguing back and forth with Alex until he had reached the doorstep. As she drove off, Alex unlocked the door with his copy of the house key, and they went inside.

The front door opened on the living room, which had lately become the realm of Scarlet and Alex. An interesting combination of Scarlet's animal books and Alex's heavy metal CDs lay strewn across the floor, with the occasional patch of green carpet visible in between. A card table had been set up in the middle of the room, upon which were the strategic documents that Sally insisted Alex and Scarlet have on hand. Computer printouts of the twelve prophecies, with handwritten notes scribbled in the margins and a little "x" in the upper right-hand corner of Jason's; photocopied pages from books, detailing the habits, strengths, and weaknesses of genies; and, as of recently, a few sheets of Black Dog lore.

Alex swore that it was all in some kind of order, but Jason was pretty sure that was merely an excuse for his inability to organize. Apparently Sally was the one who made sure every object was in its place at the Manor. It certainly wasn't a task delegated to either Scarlet or Alex, who seemed to live their lives in a state of semi-functional chaos.

"Pansy!" Alex called, setting the key down on the card table amongst the scattered papers. He waited a moment, but there was no reply.

"She did say she was going to run some errands while we were gone," Scarlet said.

"Oh yeah. I'll just have to talk to her when she gets back. Now, what to do in the meantime..."

"Math homework," Jason said, already en route to his textbook.

"I am too old to be doing math homework," Alex replied with obvious disgust.

"Excuses, excuses," Jason said in a scolding tone, enjoying the brief opportunity to be in charge. "If you're going to be in school, then you need to do your homework. How can you be my bodyguard if they flunk you and hold you back a year?"

This seemed to give Alex pause. After grumbling something that Jason was glad he didn't hear, Alex stomped down the hall and came back carrying his long-ignored backpack.

"There are more important things for me to be doing than math," Alex said in complaint, even as he started numbering a sheet of notebook paper. "It's a complete waste of time. As long as you can add and subtract, you can manage, that's what I say." Even so, he very unhappily started working the assigned math problems. Then the phone started ringing, and Alex gleefully threw the math book to the floor and answered it.

"Hello? One second. Scarlet, it's for you." Alex handed off the phone and glumly settled down to schoolwork again. After a few "uh-huh"s, Scarlet hung up.

"That was the leader of my pack," she explained. "He's scheduled for the whole pack to meet with Sally a couple nights from now, to talk about this Black Dog thing."

The leader of Scarlet's pack wasn't a very impressive-looking man, short and kind of tubby, with unfortunate hair loss so premature that even a werewolf bite hadn't prevented him from being almost bald. However, he conducted himself with a dignity and authority that indicated he was qualified for the job. Sally, however, had always thought him too pompous. His manners were exaggerated and he insisted upon being addressed only by a variety of titles, never by name. However, she usually kept her opinions to herself in his case, except for a point-blank refusal to refer to him as Mr. Alpha Wolf or Lord of the Brunswick Forest or any of the other monikers. She always called the pack leader simply "him," and the pattern was no different when she invited him to open the pack meeting at Kitch Manor.

"Is everyone here? Yes? Good. You all know why we're here, but I'll give you a quick reminder. People have been seeing an out-of-the-ordinary monster during the night, and it has been suggested that this monster could do some harm. Now, I'm sure you'll recall that our pack has had pleasant dealings with Miss Kitch in the past—if not for her protection, our pack might not have survived the mob of '82—so we are more than willing to lend a paw. If you please, Miss Kitch." He left the "stage"—a.k.a. the front porch of the Kitch Manor—with a bow and a flourish, an excessive and ineffective attempt at buttering Sally up. Sally lent him a polite nod as she mounted the porch.

"What we're dealing with is commonly called a Black Dog. The documentation on these creatures is vague and difficult to figure, but we do know this much: Black Dogs live to cause fear. This may be their weapon of choice, but I'm sure they wouldn't hesitate to employ their claws or teeth. Although the lore seems to suggest that they are merely spectres, one left a paw print in my orchard. Ghosts don't leave prints, so evidently they're corporeal at least part of the time. Now, normally Black Dogs only cause chaos for a while and then leave, their work done, but we are suspicious that this dog, or dogs, may have been summoned, and is doing someone's bidding, which would make it even more dangerous," Sally said in a lecturing tone. She paced as she spoke, but still managed to project her voice and make the occasional eye contact with her audience. Alex couldn't help thinking that his leader made a much better speech than Scarlet's. It was a petty thought, but that didn't make it any less true. With her intense eyes and captivating voice, Sally could hold an audience in thrall, even if she wasn't the best at communicating one-on-one.

"Before you even ask, I'm not going to tell you who we think is controlling it, or why, at least not until I know whether I'm right," Sally continued speaking. "I apologize for the inconvenience, but it is a matter that requires secrecy. Since I am leaving you somewhat out of the loop, I won't ask much. What I've been discussing with your leader is a system of patrols, not so much to defend as to watch. I haven't determined how a Black Dog is best disposed of, so directly confronting one would not be wise. I wish only for you to be my eyes and ears, though I would implore you to aid any civilians you see in direct danger. However, both of those requests are yours to accept or decline. Your leader has signed on with me, but I want to give each of you the opportunity to decide for yourselves. Tell me, Scarlet, or him," she gestured towards the werewolf in charge of the pack, "what your decision is. Thank you for your time and attention. I'll turn the meeting back over to your alpha now." Sally leapt off the porch and trotted up to Alex.

"How do you think it went?" she asked him, as the pack leader began to speak of other matters.

"You did amazing," he assured her. "I can't tell how the pack is reacting, though. I think some of them don't really like you."

"I'm quite certain that many of them very much dislike me," Sally said. "I've noticed that werewolves don't like taking orders from cats. I honestly think several wouldn't have shown up at all if the pack didn't owe me. Still, I'm holding out hope for a few recruits. It's not just me they would be doing this for. It's their own town that they're protecting. If werewolves are as loyal as they claim to be, surely they'll consider accepting our proposal."

"I accept!" cried a voice close behind.

"That was fast," Sally said. She and Alex turned to see a young werewolf, who didn't look to be any older than Jason. But then appearances could be deceiving.

"I want to help you," he said. "Actually, I kind of want to work for you, with what you're doing. You know, for the long haul." Alex looked at Sally at the same time as she looked at him, both clearly dubious.

"Um, kid..." Alex was trying to think of an intelligent thing to say in response. "I'm not sure that's really...I mean, why?"

"Well, Scarlet said you guys were working on something big, and then this guy at school, Sammy, we were talking to his brother, who mentioned this weird new girl at his school, and I realized he was talking about Scarlet. So then, Sammy, he wouldn't tell us exactly what was going on with you guys at the Manor, but he said that you guys were doing something really important. Like, survival of the universe kind of important. His brother just laughed, but I thought he was telling the truth. And I want in on it. Please?"

This was new. Getting a little reconnaissance out of the werewolves was one thing, taking on a new team member was quite another. And certainly something that would need to be discussed and debated. More importantly, in Alex's mind, how did this Sammy guy know what they were up to?

"Look, um, we'll have to talk about this as a group," Sally told him. "Tell us your name and how to contact you, and we'll get back to you soon, okay?"

"My name's Tyler..."

Jason shifted his weight from foot to foot uncomfortably under Alex's scathing gaze. Alex knew that he was just a child, and he hated to be tough on him, but he couldn't just let it go.

"I told him not to tell anybody," Jason said finally, barely more than a whimper.

"You shouldn't have told him in the first place," Alex said.

"He's my best friend! Sammy wouldn't tell anyone something I told him in the strictest confidence," Jason said in protest.

"Obviously he did, because I know about it."

"I'm sure he had his reasons." Jason stubbornly crossed his arms and tried to look like he was standing his ground. His wide, nervous eyes flitted like hyperactive butterflies from one spot to the next, but never summoned the courage to look directly at Alex.

"Apparently he was having an argument with his brother. That's not a very good reason. Fortunately, it worked out all right this time. Scarlet's going to go make sure he doesn't tell anybody else. And you had better not either." Alex looked Jason in the eyes with the sternest expression he could muster. Jason's gold-gleaming aura, now a familiar sight to Alex, swarmed inward, retreating protectively as Jason mentally submitted to Alex. It was a reaction Alex was used to seeing only from people who feared immediate physical harm, but he had already seen Jason's aura retract several times. He wondered if Jason had always been so frightened, or if the events of the past several months had broken him. Alex wished he could start this conversation over.

"Scarlet won't, you know, do anything to him? Will she?" Jason asked after a moment, looking up towards a point just above Alex's eyes.

"She won't hurt him, if that's what you mean," Alex said, the hardness melting from his demeanor. "She'll scare him, I'm sure, but she really doesn't like to bully. That's why I suggested Sally send her, rather than take care of it herself. Scarlet threatens people more humanely."

"Thank you," Jason said, dropping his eyes again. "And I'm sorry. I just wanted to talk to somebody...else. And Sammy makes everything seem less awful. But I won't do it again. I promise."

Great, now I feel like the worst person in the world, Alex thought. He glanced behind him to make sure that someone—namely Sally—wasn't nearby, listening. "Look, kid. I shouldn't say this, but I will. I've had a lot of secrets, so I know how it feels to want to tell someone. If you need to talk, find one person you can trust. Really trust. Someone you can be sure won't tell. And then tell them everything. You have to decide for yourself who that is, and it's an important choice, so think long and hard about it. I can't tell you who to choose, but if I may, I don't think it's Sammy. He probably didn't mean to betray you, but he can't understand what's at stake here. Not unless he becomes directly involved, and I know you don't want that."

"No! No. Of course not," Jason replied. A moment passed in silence, and Alex presumed the conversation had ended. But before he could leave the exceedingly uncomfortable situation, Jason spoke, so softly that Alex doubted any human could have picked up the words.

"I'm going to have to give it up, aren't I? The way things were before. I can't be like that. I'm not like that. I'm not the person Sammy used to know. Everything has to be different now."

Alex frantically searched for the right words, but there were none. What was there to say?

"I'm sorry, Jason," he whispered. He had never felt so helpless.

8

I call window!" Richie yelled, bouncing jubilantly into a seat adjacent to one of the tiny glass squares. He had never been on an airplane before, and he'd never imagined that he would be in a private plane if and when he finally did fly. Richie had imagined the interior would be something like a palace. In reality, the lounge was rather plain, but still elegant. A horseshoe of khaki couches surrounded a sleek metal table. A flat-screen television hung from the ceiling. Dracula's servants, some human and some less so, buzzed around like flies, attending to their master's every request.

Jack threw a suitcase into an overhead compartment and dropped onto the sofa next to Richie. He kept the box of Sally's books between his feet. Dracula landed in the couch across from them, limbs thrown onto the luxurious leather with purposeful disregard, a king sprawled over his throne.

The airplane started taxiing out onto the runway, and Richie watched out the window every step of the way. The takeoff was amazing. The cords of gravity snapped free from his body for a moment as they left the ground, and a giddy trill darted through his brain. Then out of the window the airport shrank away. For a minute he got a bird's eye view of the entire city of Budapest. The cars zoomed about the city as little colored blocks. The farther up they went, the more Richie saw of Romania, until eventually they broke through the clouds, and Richie quickly lost interest in staring at the banks of white fluffiness.

He sat back in his seat and wondered what to do now. The high was over, and he was bored. He knew he should read Sally's books, but what he wanted to do was check out that TV. He glanced over at Jack, wondering how much he would care if Richie chose to be lazy. Richie forgot about his dilemma when he noticed how freaked out

Jack looked. With his spine rigid and eyes closed, he sat stone-still, taking deep, deliberate breaths. The expression on his face indicated that the breathing exercise wasn't helping. It may have been the unflattering light, but Jack's skin tone looked kind of greenish.

"Jack...are you okay?" Richie asked. Jack nodded and opened his eyes.

"I'm fine," he said, trying for insist and sounding anything but.

"I assume neither of you have flown before?" Dracula said. Jack and Richie both replied in the affirmative. "Interesting how your reactions differ."

"The picture of the cotu you showed me had wings," Richie said, speaking to Jack. "So what, are you like penguins? Wings that don't work?"

"No," Jack said, opening his eyes to shoot Richie an insulted glare. "There is nothing wrong with my wings! But I've never flown with somebody else at the wheel...or this high..." He swallowed hard and hurriedly dug one of Sally's books and a fresh bottle of whiskey out of the box at his feet.

"Are you sure you should be drinking that?" Richie asked, thinking that liquor was probably not a recommended treatment for airsickness.

"Just need something to calm me down." Jack set the book in his lap and opened it to the candy wrapper he was using as a bookmark.

"Just don't ralph on me, okay?" Richie said after a minute.

"Your concern for my well-being is touching," Jack replied, not holding back on the sarcasm.

"Hey, um, Mr. Dracula, can I borrow your phone for a sec to check my e-mail?" Richie quickly looked around to make sure that nobody else in the airport restaurant had heard him call the man beside him "Dracula."

"Sure. And if you would rather call me Vlad, that is acceptable under the circumstances," Dracula responded, handing over his brand-new, high-tech cell phone. Trying not to think of the irony, Richie slid his finger across the screen to unlock it and then searched for the little icon that would take him to the Internet.

"Now, what was I saying before? Ah, yes. So, after New York we fly straight to West Virginia. If I remember correctly, we'll get there shortly after noon. The airport is in Lewisburg, in the southeastern part of the state." As he spoke, Dracula indicated each location on a map of North America that he had bought in the airport, preferring to plan his route the old-fashioned way. "Where do we need to go from there? Keep in mind that we'll most likely be horribly jet lagged for a day or two."

"We're looking for a woman named Clara Hawthorne," Jack said.

"That's a fair place to start," Dracula said. "Do you know where she lives?"

Richie finally found the right icon, and clicked on it. He logged into his e-mail and browsed his messages. Mostly spam and the usual handful of e-mails from his family and friends asking where he was. He deleted all of the above without reading them. Oh, look, Clement finally replied. Richie opened the message and stared blankly at it. "Watch yourself." Watch himself how? Why? Was there something else he needed worry about? Richie sent a quick e-mail back: What do you mean? Then he refocused his attention on the conversation at hand.

"I was told she's somewhere in the northwest of the state, but she lives where there aren't any towns, or at least not towns that have names. I'm talking deep backwoods. Which won't make her easy to find," Jack continued.

"I see. Fortunately, the 'backwoods,' as you call them, are a familiar environment to me, despite my aristocratic reputation, that is the sort of terrain in which I live. But before we get to that point, let's see, I'll need to rent a car at the airport. We should probably stay a night in Lewisburg, and then drive the next day..." Dracula continued to talk to himself as he planned out the particulars of the next leg of their journey.

Assuming the conversation to be over, Richie went back to reading. He put it off for as long as possible, but had finally given in. Sally's encyclopedia was certainly a lot different from that other guy's. It was a lot more detailed and told Richie some things that he actually wanted to know. For one, he had learned that not all cotus have wings, which was a bit disappointing to read. In fact, wings were considered a hideous deformity, although Sally claimed that was only because the flightless majority felt intimidated by their more muscular flying cousins whose wings remained a biological mystery.

He learned more than he really needed to know about the long love affair between the human and cotu races—a complicated history of misunderstandings, cultural exchange, and interbreeding—but what really interested him were the things he was learning about himself:

The Unofficial (But Vastly More Accurate) Encyclopedia of Cotus

...point. All cotus posess a crystalline structure, called simply the stone, which is nestled into a nook in their spines, right below the ribcage. This is where their elemental powers come from. The stone is like a second brain. It controls the body from the perspective of the cotu's particular power. It regulates things such as protein synthesis and body temperature, presumably through a form of as-yet-unidentified gene regulation. The stone is the only thing sacred to cotus. It is the most important part of all of us.

With that...

Without thinking about it, Richie put his hand over where the book said his stone should be. Even though it was deep inside his body, he thought he felt the heat coming from it. He removed his hand, feeling a little lightheaded. He tried to go back to reading, but was too distracted. Before, he had pushed the whole cotu thing to the back of his mind. He had still thought of himself as Richard McGill, human son of Ian and Hannah McGill. Now that he felt where his fire resided, his new reality was a lot more real to him. The identity crisis returned to the forefront of his mind, yet now he didn't feel as conflicted. He was Richie the Fire Cotu, on a quest to find The Lost City of Brunswick, with Jack the Ice Cotu and Count Dracula the *Primum* Vampire.

It sounded utterly ridiculous, like one of the comic books he read when he was younger. And yet it felt right, in an otherworldly, bizarre way. Maybe the insanity of it all made it easier to deal with. There weren't many other reasons Richie could think of that explained why he put up with this madness. After all, he had no clue where he was going, or whether getting there would be any help, and what on Earth did Jack have to do with any of this? And then there was Dracula— now *that* was truly insane. Richie looked over at Jack, who was bent over another of Sally's books, visibly engrossed. Richie didn't understand why, or what it was that Jack needed, but he knew for certain that Jack was at least as desperate as him. And of course Dracula had major parent-child issues to resolve. This adventure was weird, dangerous, and a wee bit creepy, and might not amount to anything, but Richie supposed he knew why they were on it. They each required something, more than anything else in the world, something that they couldn't catch for themselves. It seemed logical, in a twisted sense, that the only way to find what they had so hopelessly lost was to look in a place that couldn't be found.

But then what? Like a vine twining into the heart of a house, the truth began to dawn on Richie that he was never going to be the same. Now that he allowed himself to think it, it seemed so obvious. Had he really thought he could just run off, find a cure, and saunter back home like nothing had ever happened? How could he look his parents or his brothers in the eyes again, knowing they weren't his family? No. For better or for worse, Richie had crossed an invisible boundary when he had left home, and there was no going back. Needles pricked at the backs of his eyes, but no tears came to the surface. His childhood home was so remote, so unreal, he couldn't bring himself to truly mourn its passing. The worn book in his hands, the incessant drumming of Jack's heel, and a primordial vampire on a smart phone—somehow, that was real. His once-family swam like phantasms through a murky abyss somewhere in his memory, disconnected once and for all from his life.

Clement woke disoriented, with the bitter-sweet taste of magic in his mouth. At first, he couldn't see, even though he knew he had opened his eyes. His hearing was almost as bad; the only sounds were muffled and warped, like the underwater conversation of so many turtles. The clearest sound was of a repetitive impact, something colliding rhythmically with the floor, probably footsteps. His nose still worked, but all he could smell was magic and the cloying scent of genie, and he knew that much already. He was also unsurprised to find his hands bound behind his back. He struggled against his bonds as a matter of principle, but was less than shocked to find them too securely fastened.

"What do you want?" he said eventually. His senses were beginning to return, and he could discern his captor in silhouette, moving around in front of him.

"I want to know where those two cotu boys are going," replied a soft, lilting female voice, most certainly the genie he smelled. With his senses still clouded, it was difficult for Clement to hear her, but the sounds were becoming sharper by the second.

"It would be even better if you could tell me exactly where they *are*." Ah, there she was. Clement's vision had finally cleared. The genie paced back and forth, her long, tawny ponytail whipping the air with each turn. It took a moment for Clement to comprehend where he was, for he was expecting to be somewhere on the logical trajectory of his train ride. Instead, he was back in his office in London, tied to a wooden chair. By the feel of the coarse fibers chafing his wrists, he was bound with thick rope. Normally, that would not be anywhere near enough to hold him, yet his limbs lacked the strength to prevail. He suspected more magic was at work.

"I know quite a few cotus that come in pairs. To which are you referring?" Clement asked innocently, stalling while he tried to decide what to do. His eyes flashed about, looking for some means of escape. Nothing. He felt around the rope with his fingers, trying to see if he could undo the knots. No such luck. This genie knew what she was doing. He had to admit that he was stuck fast.

"You know who I'm talking about. The little Scottish child and his American companion. I know you've seen them, because I saw them enter this house a few weeks ago." Yes, Clement was well aware of *that* fact.

"Ah, yes, them. Why do you want to know?" This, for one, was a question he did not know the answer to. He only knew that a genie was chasing Jack and Richie, and rumor held she wasn't exactly looking to have tea and crumpets with them.

"That is none of your concern."

"Then, assuming I know something, which I don't, I wouldn't tell you," Clement replied. He was trying for a confident, steely tone, but his voice crawled forth trembling and reluctant.

"You will." The genie stopped pacing and walked over to a back corner of the room, where a canvas tote bag that didn't belong to Clement was leaning against the wall. Clement could feel his heart rate accelerating exponentially. He knew what came next. The genie pulled a leather case out of the bag and set it on the desk. She opened the clasp and pulled out a gleaming blade roughly the size of a pencil. It glinted menacingly in a ray of light that came through the closed blinds. Even from across the room, Clement could smell the chilly perfume of pure silver. The genie took the knife and stalked back to Clement, crouching in front of his chair.

"Let's try this again. Where are they?"

After the bustling, stifling scene at LaGuardia airport in New York City, the airport in Lewisburg seemed like a ghost town. It was the middle of the day, and yet there were only a few other people that Richie could see. It was probably just as well.

"It's just a suggestion, Jack. You don't have to get all defensive about it."

"You're as bad as Count Couture over there!" Jack said in accusation.

"I am not!"

"Are too!"

"What about when we meet Sally? What kind of impression are you going to make?" Richie knew immediately that he'd made the winning argument. Jack opened and closed his mouth a couple times like a confused fish, and then his shoulders sagged in surrender.

"Fine. I'll get the damn haircut."

"Wonderful! Bravo, Richie!" Dracula said, almost cheering as he approached from the car rental booth. Jack looked kind of hurt, like he thought Dracula had put Richie up to it.

"I didn't do it for *you*," Richie said in protest. Dracula looked back and forth between the two of them a couple times before realizing what an awkward situation he had just created.

"Yes, of course you didn't," Dracula said. "I am simply glad to have gotten my way, Jack. Now, come. We have a car."

"I'll be right here with you the whole time," Richie promised. Jack nodded, but his fingers continued to writhe over each other nervously. The stylist looked kind of weirded out by the whole thing. She kept glancing at Richie questioningly, as though asking him to account for Jack's strange behavior, and she regarded Jack's locks as though they were slugs. But she gamely pretended that nothing was amiss, most likely in the interest of assuring that she got a paycheck at the end of the week.

"So, how do you want it cut?" she asked as she vigorously washed Jack's hair with half a bottle of shampoo and an expression of disgust. Jack glanced helplessly at Richie. Richie examined Jack for a moment, trying to decide what cut would look best. He had a hard time imagining Jack without a couple feet of hair.

"Cut it a little shorter than mine," he finally decided. "And make it kind of spiky on top." The cosmetologist nodded, brushed a strand of her own bright pink hair out of her eyes, and grabbed her weapon of choice, a pair of massive scissors. The moment she started chopping, Jack squeezed his eyes shut. He sat stone-still, as instructed, but Richie flinched for him when the hairdresser began by unceremoniously lopping off a little more than twenty inches of thick, coal-black hair. Then she trimmed and trimmed and trimmed the rest away. Richie discovered that watching her work on Jack was far more antagonizing than any haircut he had ever had. Maybe Jack was rubbing off on him. Richie decided to preserve his nerves and turned his eyes to the floor, where a carpet of black hair was materializing one tuft at a time.

The hairdresser exhaled in relief as the light at the end of the tunnel finally appeared. She took an electric shaver and cleaned up the cut, gelled and hairsprayed it into the intended style, and then admired her quasi-miraculous success with a pleased smile. Richie risked a look in the mirror as she whipped off the protective apron and his jaw dropped.

"How is it?" Jack asked, keeping his eyes squeezed shut.

"You look amazing!" Richie said. "I'm not just saying that to make you feel better, I mean it. Open your eyes." Jack cautiously opened one eye a slit, and then blinked them both wide in surprise. The hairdresser had done a good job trying to apply Richie's suggestions to the disaster she'd been given—along the sides, she'd cut it pretty short, but left it a tad longer on top, and gelled it into stylish little peaks. Jack angled his head a little to the side and raised his hand to run it across the side of his head. He didn't say a word while Richie paid for the extensive operation and a bottle of hair gel, and then took Jack by the wrist and dragged him out of the salon.

"So what do you think? Can you stand it?" Richie asked once they were outside.

"I—I don't know. I think so. But it's so...*different.*" Jack ran a hand over the top of his head through his much-abbreviated mane, the expression on his face looking almost pained.

"Different is good. What fun is it if you always keep everything the same?" Richie said, starting to walk down the street to where they'd parked Dracula's rental car.

"I guess so." Jack conceded the point, but he didn't sound completely convinced. Richie let the conversation drop. He wondered if he'd been right to pressure Jack to lose the long hair. Of course it *looked* better now, and it would certainly be more hygienic. And there would be no more torturous hours on end of hair-brushing. But then Jack was so weird about things. One time Richie straightened up the room they were staying in, just for a change of pace, and Jack lost it when he realized that his spare sock wasn't where he'd left it. Richie was concerned that the hair thing might freak Jack out and over the edge, but it was far too late for Richie to change his mind.

"It really does look good on you," Richie said, reiterating quietly as he opened the door to the bright red Mustang convertible.

"You think so?" Jack asked.

"I do." Richie happened to look behind Jack, across the street. He smirked. "Apparently I'm not the only one." Jack followed Richie's pointing finger to a group of giggling girls who were not in the least trying to hide their admiration of Jack and Richie, and probably their car. Richie waved back with gusto. Jack, however, acted completely bewildered, maybe even frightened. He ducked into the passenger seat, sank down as low in the seat as he could, and drummed his fingers on the side of the car while he waited for Richie to get in and start the ignition.

"They were looking at me," Jack said, with amazement, peeking over the dash at the young women in question. Richie glanced over at him with an eyebrow raised.

"Yeah, they were. It's called 'checking you out.' We really need to get you a girl."

"I don't think that's such a good idea," Jack replied, looking down at the floorboard.

"Okay, then. Can I ask why?"

"I don't cope with women very well. It's a long story. I'd rather not talk about it."

"All right. Sure." Richie drove the rest of the way in silence, thinking about Jack's statement and what it would mean to not be able to 'cope' with women. The only reasonable conclusions Richie could reach were that Jack was either gay or impotent, but neither quite seemed to mesh with his strange reaction. Richie was once again reminded of just how very little he knew about Jack. He thought, after all this time together, he had the right to know who Jack really was. On the other hand, what had he told Jack about himself? Not much, even if it was more than Jack had divulged. There was no shortage of secrets between them.

Clement yelped as the silver knife cut into his arm, adding to a series of small, but painful, slits that the genie had made. The wounds burned as the silver seeped into his bloodstream, its poison sizzling through his veins.

"I already told you! Richie came to see me about the nightmares! That's it," Clement insisted, through tears of pain. The genie pulled back for a moment, looking thoughtful. "He probably went to find another doctor," Clement gasped out. It wasn't a lie. It just wasn't the whole truth. He hoped it would be enough to make her stop.

Kell looked at the werewolf thoughtfully. She had been at it for hours, and this was all she could get from him. She was wasting time, and wasting it on something unpleasant at that. She needed a quicker, cleaner way to find out where the target was. She put the knife back in its slot in the leather case and resumed pacing, to help herself think. If he ran away to keep me from using him to get to the kid, she thought, then he would have taken any evidence with him. Kell darted out into the hallway, where she had tossed Clement's luggage. It wasn't much, just two bags. Her eyes were drawn to one that looked just the right size and shape to hold a laptop. She extracted the computer carefully. Even though Kell was one of, if not the most skilled in her family when it came to computers, they still made her somewhat nervous. She went back into the office where she had Clement restrained and sat on the desk. She noticed that Clement blanched a shade paler at the sight of the genie with his laptop.

A good sign.

Kell powered on the laptop. A quick password-cracking algorithm later, she was skimming through his documents. Lots of patient records and a few medical eBooks. Kell skimmed through everything, but couldn't find anything about the young man in question. What was his name again? Richie, that was it. That would be a good thing to remember.

Kell searched every document for the name and other keywords, but came up dry. Undeterred, she switched her attention to the Internet. When she found that his Internet history had been wiped clean, she knew she was in the right place. His favorites list didn't include anything of note, leaving his e-mail as her best bet. The spirits must have been on her side, for Clement was already logged into his e-mail account. At the top of his in box there were about a dozen e-mails from patients, ranging from the calm and business-like—"I'm e-mailing to cancel my appointment on the 15th"—to the frantic—"I've been calling 4 days, WHERE R U?"

Mildly entertaining, but not very useful. Kell was going so fast that she almost skipped right over the message she needed. Such an innocuous title. "Re: You Know Who." She smiled as she read the address of the sender: RichieTheGr8. Richie. Kell couldn't hold back a little happy exclamation. The message itself wasn't significant, but the past e-mails threaded into it were.

Kell read and reread the correspondences. This was exactly what she was looking for. She was thrilled, but also fearful. The news was not ideal. Richard and his ruffian companion were hunting for Sally Kitch. As Clement said, Richie was trying to find a doctor to cure his night terror problem. If he found Sally, and Sally realized his importance, she would take Richie under her protection. Then it would be a hundred times harder to get to him.

Jasmine and the others must know immediately. As soon as the thought occurred to her, it was done. In her mind's ear, Kell could hear Jasmine giving orders to her remaining genies, telling them that pinning Richie down was the priority. *'Keep him far away from Sally, by whatever means necessary,'* Jasmine told Kell. *'Affirmative,'* Kell replied, and pulled back from the connection. She thought about the command for a moment. What could she do to delay Richie, when she still didn't know quite where he was? She cursed herself yet again for her failure to follow him. The anti-magic defenses around the elder vampire's property had been too great for her. So, she analyzed, I don't know where he is, but I know where he's going and who he's with. She mulled for a minute, and then an idea took form. She typed a website into the address bar. Kell went straight to the bulletin board and posted an anonymous tip, trying her best to sound credible:

Vampire Hunters' Guild—

Dracula is on the move, heading towards the East Coast of North America. He is traveling with a cotu adolescent named Richie and an adult ice cotu named Jack. If you find them, please inform me immediately. I will send a genie to your aid, posthaste. However, feel free to commence the hunt without her.

Vampire hunters were known for their speed and enthusiasm. Kell would know where Dracula and company were within hours. Even if the hunters didn't keep in touch, the trail of vampire carnage would let her know soon enough. She wasn't yet sure what she would do when she found them. The hunters would cause them untold grief and roadblocks, but that wouldn't stop the kid forever. Richie could always choose to leave Dracula to his own devices and go on alone, and then she would lose him again. It would be a happy coincidence if the hunters killed Richie for her, but most hunters were too self-righteous to put a stake into anything other than a vampire. No, she would need to take further action. But she could figure that out later. Right now, all she had to do was wait patiently. Kell smiled. It had turned into a good day after all. She put the laptop aside and turned her attention to Clement.

"Thank you for the help. I couldn't have done it without you," she told him. Her voice masqueraded as jest, but she couldn't quite take pleasure in the act like her Queen did. "May the earth-spirits welcome you into the beyond." Kell's words were sincere. She took a silver dagger from her bag of blades. Clement renewed his struggles as she crossed the room with it, and Kell had to cast a calming spell to keep him still. Once he had stopped moving, Kell put her left hand on his shoulder and with the right hand plunged the dagger into his heart.

The bite of the wind woke Richie up and reminded him of where he was. He opened his eyes and stared hollowly at the flashes of forest streaking by. His heart was still beating hard and fast, and he could still feel a stinging sensation on his face where the claws of the beast had torn him.

"Same dream?" he heard Jack ask softly from beside him. Richie turned his head in Jack's direction and nodded weakly.

"Anything new?" Dracula asked from behind the wheel of the Mustang. After Richie had woken up in the throes of a panic attack that morning, they had been obliged to tell Dracula about Richie's affliction. Dracula had tried to help interpret the recurring nightmare but could not make much of it either.

"It's getting worse. Longer and more vivid. Ever since New York,"

Richie said. "I think that means we're getting close to when it happens. Or where. Or both. I don't really know." Richie sighed heavily, laying his head back on the leather seat. "It'd be easier to think if I could get some sleep." He was used to having restless nights by now, but the night before he hadn't gotten a moment's sleep without the nightmare lurking behind his eyelids. Combined with the jet lag, this rendered Richie barely able to function.

"This woman we're going to see, you say she's a witch, yes?" Dracula asked.

"Yeah," Jack replied.

"Well, any witch worth an eye of newt knows how to do a sleeping potion. It would be an effective temporary solution," Dracula said. "That is, assuming we trust this Miss Hawthorne that much. I wouldn't know."

"I'm willing to try anything," Richie said. "How soon will we get there?"

"About fifteen more minutes," Dracula said. "Give or take. The exact location is difficult to pinpoint. But we'll be there soon."

Richie grumbled something in response—even he wasn't sure what it was—and then laid his head back and closed his eyes.

"This place *is* hard to find," Richie said in complaint, leaning against an ancient, warped tree. A few feet behind him, a battered and leaning mailbox by the driveway said C. Hawthorne, while a few yards ahead sat the indicated home. The house looked like it belonged to a witch. Massive writing spiders had made themselves at home in a languishing herb garden out front. A black rat snake lounged on the decaying porch rail. The chimney soared upward at a precarious angle. The walls were overgrown with vines and mosses and even a rather large fern on the roof, yet the structure still stood and unperturbed.

"These woods are thick and make an excellent place for a hermit to make her dwelling. I approve of her choice in real estate, if not her landscaping," Dracula said, perhaps to Richie, although he kept walking and didn't turn to look at whomever it was that he was addressing.

It had only taken them about three hours of wandering through the wilderness to find this place. The forest was indeed thick and choked with thorns such that they hadn't even seen the house until they were right upon it. On the bright side, that made it easier to conceal the convertible when they had to leave it behind.

Dracula tested the first stair with one foot. By some miracle, the rotting boards held his weight, and he ascended the last couple steps to the porch. He knocked on the front door. There was no response. After a few minutes, he knocked again, harder this time, with the same result.

Jack, tired of waiting, brushed past Dracula and tried the door-knob. It wasn't locked. Jack took this as his cue to barge on into the house. Richie and Dracula followed, the latter closing the door behind them.

"Whoa," Richie said, taking in the shelves of bizarre plant and animal parts. The objects were grotesque, yet fascinating in their exotic mysteriousness. In the center of the room sat a large, black cauldron. It was just like what Richie had thought a witch's hut would look like, which seemed strangely stereotypical after the shock of Dracula's not-so-creepy lair.

"Good ol' fashioned witchcraft," Jack said, taking one of the many suspicious-looking jars off of a shelf and turning it over in his hand.

"But no witch," Dracula said, stating the obvious. "Would she leave her door unlocked? I know I do occasionally, since the locals never give me any trouble, but I've come to realize that I'm an exception to most norms."

"Her soup's still on," Jack said, gesturing towards the cauldron. Richie peeked into it, and sure enough some sort of grayish-green liquid was bubbling inside. "Gross."

"Does anybody else see that envelope placed precisely in the middle of Miss Hawthorne's table, which we are quite obviously meant to notice?" Dracula asked. Jack turned from browsing the shelves and picked up the indicated document. He flipped the envelope over in his hands. There wasn't anything written on the outside. Jack glanced at his comrades, shrugged, and tore open the flap of the envelope. Richie flinched, half expecting the suspicious parcel to explode. It didn't, and Jack calmly removed the note inside.

"It's just one line," Jack said, bemused. "I'm not sure what language this is. German, maybe?"

"Allow me," Dracula said, swiping the sheet of paper. He read it, then flipped the note over and stared at the blank side with a puzzled expression.

"What is it?" Richie asked.

"Jack was right. It's German. It says 'Turn the page,' which, as you can see, I have, and there's nothing here." Dracula flipped back to the side with the vague message. "Perhaps it means something else."

"Like what?" Jack came over behind Dracula to look over his shoulder.

"It could be code," Dracula guessed, "or a clue. It could be a way of telling other witches how to remove a glamour to reveal the text underneath."

"Can we do that? Try to remove the...thing?" Richie was positive that he couldn't do anything witchy, but it might be possible for Dracula.

"No, even *vampira prima* don't have that sort of magic," Dracula replied. He replaced the sheet in the envelope and stuck it in the pocket of his coat. "I have people in Romania who could, but I would recommend following up any other leads we have on this side of the Atlantic before we fly back just to find out that this was Miss Hawthorne's grocery list." Richie glanced at Jack, waiting for him to make the decision.

"Well, we're pretty sure that Brunswick is somewhere in the Southeast, right?" he said, looking to Dracula for confirmation. Dracula nodded. "Then we should try our best to find it while we're here. Someone somewhere *must* know where it is. You said Alex used to send you letters. So how do they get their mail? Has anyone ever delivered furniture or something in Brunswick? Between the three of us, I'm sure we'll find a trail to follow. I didn't get very far by myself, but you two are smart. I don't want to give up and go back to Europe until we've scoured every inch from the Mason-Dixon line to Texas.

"I'm inclined to agree," Dracula said.

"Sounds fine," Richie said, secretly dreading more weeks on the road looking for a place that didn't want to be found.

"It's settled then!" Dracula declared. "Now we have to find our way back to the car."

Kell felt her phone vibrate and took it out of her pocket. You have mail it declared, showing a little envelope icon—as though she couldn't read. It was a notification that an admin had replied to her tip:

Thank you for the information. We have located Count Dracula and are mobilizing to attack. He is currently in West Virginia, U.S.A., heading south in a red convertible with his two companions.
--The Vampire Hunters' Guild, Chapter 47A

Kell smiled as she read the message. This was going better than she expected. Kell replaced the phone in her pocket and, checking to make sure no one was looking through the window of her motel room, Kell promptly began drawing a portal to West Virginia.

9

S carlet texted. She says the last holdout has agreed to lend a hand—or is it paw?" Jenna said, turning off her phone screen. "Either way, her pack has our backs. Sally, are you listening?"

"I'm with you," Sally said, still focusing on her computer screen with a frown. "Scarlet's pack. Lending paws. Gotcha."

"Did you find something interesting?" Hope asked, looking up from the three spell books she was flipping through. As soon as her eyes left the pages, the cloaking spell fell over the text again, and the pages started to become blank again from top to bottom.

"I think so," Sally answered, "but that's not what's bothering me. I checked the news feed on the Med Revolution site and found out that one of our own is dead. A walk-in patient found Clem's body in his office. It looks like he was tortured at length and then murdered."

"Oh, gosh, that's...I'm so sorry," Jenna said, knowing that Sally was likely to be more hurt than she was letting on. "Do they know why?"

"I don't think so. He was one of the least controversial people I know. The police aren't saying much. I know the coroner who did the autopsy. I don't know if he would tell me anything." Sally chewed her tongue for a few seconds, still locked onto the screen. Then she blinked a couple times and looked up at Jenna and Hope. "Sorry. I did find something that might be of interest to us. I had noticed a few cases reported of psychics losing their ability to foretell. I sent out a call for other reports of that nature, and the community has responded en masse. It looks like prophetic types are losing their third eye the world over. Dr. Johnson in Montreal also reported a patient who used to be able to speak in tongues who has lost every language except French and English. I don't know if that's a part of the same phenomenon or not. I'm not sure what this tells us, either. I don't think it's ever happened before, and it's all very recent, but it doesn't have to be Guardian-related simply because the cases cropped up shortly before we ID'ed Jason. Just might be something to keep an eye on." She shrugged and glanced at her two coworkers, waiting to see if they'd made any progress.

"I've been researching genies all day and haven't found anything that you didn't," Jenna said.

"I'm getting somewhere with a spell to catch us a hellhound, but none of these summoning spells are really what I had in mind." Hope started to point at a page in one of her books before she realized that it had timed out. "I'm having more luck with protective spells, but they all seem to be very temporary and localized. I'll let you know when I've got something more concrete. And, um, I'm sorry about your friend, Sally."

"Thanks, Hope." A flicker of a smile crossed Sally's face. "Keep up the good work, girls."

"Well then. Thank you, Mickey, you may be seated. Does anyone know what is wrong with that sentence?" Mrs. Adair gestured at the white board, where the hapless Latin student had just written *Frater est meus stultus* in large, scarcely legible, blue letters.

"There's nothing wrong," Cameron said in protest, brushing his mop of mousy hair out of his eyes to be sure. "Yeah, that grammar is *perfect*." Sometimes Jason couldn't tell whether Cameron was joking or not, but in this case the undertone of sarcasm was fairly self-evident. Technically, the grammar was correct, but the meaning was a little off the mark.

"It's wrong because it says 'The brother is my stupid,'" José blurted, as though the rest of the snickering class hadn't already figured that out.

"Oh! Yeah, adjective," Mickey said, blushing all over his meek, undersized personage. He slouched down in his seat to evade the ridicule of his classmates.

"Mrs. Adair?" Jason called. Most of the room went silent the moment he made a sound. Jason spoke out in class so rarely that they were a bit astounded. Even the teacher was somewhat taken aback, and it took her a few seconds to formulate a response.

"Yes, Jason?"

"Didn't you say that word order wasn't important in Latin?"

"Well, yes, that is true," she said.

"The only way you know which words go together is by whether or not they agree, right?" Again, Mrs. Adair confirmed Jason's observation. But Jason had lost his momentum, and suddenly found himself with the attention of an entire classroom trained upon him, lost for words. It was as if all the oxygen had been sucked out of his lungs and left him gasping like a fish out of water.

"What he means is, we're just assuming that 'meus' and 'stultus' go together," Cameron interjected, coming to Jason's rescue. "'Frater' is nominative masculine too, you know," he directed the comment towards José, "so 'meus' agrees with both of them. That sentence could say anything. We shouldn't apply English assumptions to Latin." He delivered his last sentence with exaggerated pedantic flair. Cameron was the most proficient student in the Latin class. The students turned their eyes to Mrs. Adair.

"Um, okay. You're not wrong, Cameron. Let's just move on," she said. The class returned to taking notes. José, comprehending Jason and Cameron's objective, mumbled an apology in Mickey's general direction. However, as soon as Mickey nodded in acknowledgment, José left the matter in the past and the usual grin returned to his broad, affable countenance. The momentary schoolroom crisis had passed, it seemed.

Jason wasn't quite over the incident, however. The instant of social panic had triggered his biological stress response, and there was no stopping it. Unbeknownst to Jason, inside him the tangled web of tough, silvery veins left from his cotu ancestry was reacting. They didn't coil tight together, like they usually did, such that Jason would feel the constriction. Perhaps the stress wasn't severe enough for the veins to retract. Perhaps the largely malfunctional system was just malfunctioning in a new way.

Whatever the reason, the veins chose to restrict blood flow to non-essential areas—a safe and normal procedure in the body of a cotu, but not that of a human being. The cotu veins went about their task methodically, instructed by the lumps of nerve tissue positioned periodically along their lengths. First the minor vessels in the hands and feet were sealed off. Then the blood supply to some of the less vital organs was reduced. Finally, the brain was attended. Veins in the section that processed tactile sensations closed their doors, redirecting a flood of hemoglobin into Jason's entirely unprepared visual cortex.

The last few letters he had written in his notebook looked like they'd been written by a monkey, or possibly Cameron. Jason shook his right hand with some irritation, trying to restore feeling to the fingers which seemed to have fallen asleep of their own accord. The palms of his hands had pins and needles, but the ends of his fingers might as well have been chunks of lead for all he could tell. He poked the pad of his left index finger with one fingernail. A little pink crescent on his skin proved that he had made contact, but neither finger gave him any sensation of pain or pressure. Come to think of it, his feet felt, or rather failed to feel, in much the same way. Jason was annoyed more than afraid, though. Numbness in his extremities was a familiar, if not common, symptom of his illness. It was going to make taking notes rather difficult, though. Jason glanced back to Sally's seat. Ah, good, she was taking notes. Jason had never understood why Sally took school so seriously when she had finished her formal education before he was born, but at the moment he was glad of it. He could just ask her for her notes later. Jason crossed his arms on his desk and rested his head on them, waiting for the feeling to return.

He must have dozed for a minute, because he awoke to a prod from Alex. *Are you okay?* Alex mouthed. Jason nodded, straightening up and fixing his eyes on Mrs. Adair. He wasn't really sure that he was all right, though. He still couldn't feel his fingers or toes. As he considered whether or not to call his mother to come get him, an iridescent pink blob engulfed Mrs. Adair's head. Jason blinked. The blob was gone. Nobody else had seen it, he presumed, because an attack by The Blob would probably have caused something of a stir among the class. Still, moments later another blob emerged from the floor, Carolina blue this time, and didn't disappear for several blinks. Jason was flummoxed.

What on Earth?

After the introduction and exit of a few small silvery blobs, the strange occurrence ended. But was it just him, or did the room seem brighter? Not just more light, but more color. Things were becoming progressively more vibrant, and more defined. Every object was infinitely separate from those around it, in a different dimension entirely, yet nothing had moved and everything was still in its natural spatial location. An intense ache emerged inside Jason's head, and he was forced to close his eyes and shut out the painful images. He was distantly aware of Sally getting up and murmuring something to Mrs. Adair. Jason felt a hand grasp his shoulder, gentle but firm.

"Stand up," Sally whispered. Jason complied and allowed her to lead him out of the room. At some point, Alex's cool, undead hand placed itself on Jason's other shoulder. In a few arduous seconds they were outside the classroom. Jason leaned against the wall and slid down to the floor. He curled up his knees and laced his arms on top of them, nesting his head inside this dark hollow to block out the too-radiant ghosts of images that pierced through his eyelids. He felt someone crouch down beside him.

"What's happening?" Alex seemed to be demanding of Sally. "Is this some kind of genie magic?"

"No magic, just pathology," Sally explained calmly, her voice right next to Jason's ear. "Jason is having a seizure of sorts. It's a fairly common human-cotu mixed-species problem. It should go away soon on its own, but if you'll allow me, Jason, I am an electric cotu. I can probably help calm down those neurons." Jason hadn't the slightest idea what she meant, but he nodded, just wanting it to quit. Sally laid a hand near the base of his skull, fingertips pressing lightly into his skin. Jason felt a mild electric crackling, humming from her flesh into his head. After a short while the colors playing upon his closed eyes abated, until he saw only the red-black glow he expected to see through shut eyelids. He refrained from opening his eyes, though, before sensation began to return to his hands and feet. When Jason finally did raise his head, the psychedelic aspect was absent from his vision. Sally removed her hand. The process had taken about five minutes.

"Thank you," Jason said and sighed. He stretched out his legs to speed the flow of blood to his feet.

"You're welcome," Sally replied. "But you need to know that I can't always make that work. The brain is a tricky organ, and much of the electrical over stimulation associated with syndromes like yours come from the peripheral nervous system. Most of your symptoms are going to be beyond my ability to calm with that little party trick."

Jason said that he understood, although he didn't really. He just understood that if he ever started seeing blobs again, he was going to go find Sally.

"I didn't know you could do that," Alex said, marveling. His voice contained both admiration and a deeper layer of resentment. Jason had to admit that he, too, was a little surprised that Alex wasn't aware of the extent of Sally's powers. How many decades had they been working together?

"It isn't a skill I like to advertise," Sally told him, "because people get to thinking that I can control minds or other such foolery. And then there's always someone who wants me to use my electricity for his own personal enjoyment. Or her enjoyment, I suppose, as the case may be."

"You think I would ask you to do that?" Alex's question quavered in the air between them. Sally looked right at him, her mask not allowing any obvious emotion through, while Alex stared back with his hurt plain for anyone to see. Sally shrugged, but her previous statements had spoken for themselves. Eventually, Jason couldn't stand the tension anymore.

"Hey, guys? Can I go to the office and call home?" he asked nervously. Sally instantly agreed that going home would be a good idea in order to prevent a relapse, and jumped to her feet ready to lead Jason in that direction. Alex followed more slowly, lagging behind without a word.

Alex stared uncomprehendingly at his homework. It was all Greek to him. Well, technically it was Latin, not Greek, but either one would have made just as much sense as the other. After a minute Alex violently crumpled the paper and threw it down in the slick red mud at his feet.

"Now what did that paper ever do to you?" Sally asked, settling beside Alex on the park bench.

"It was born," Alex answered. He looked up from the paper to Sally. She had abandoned her faux teenage morph for her usual form—Alex had always called it mature, but ageless. Sally sat—silent, hands in the pockets of her favorite plum-hued jacket, and bare feet crossed at the ankles. Like Scarlet, Sally almost never wore shoes if she could help it. They preferred to have their "claws" available at a moment's notice.

A rogue curl of Sally's chocolate hair was carried away from her in the wind. Alex raised a hand to catch it and tuck it behind her ear, a reflex left behind from more familiar days. Sally's eyes snapped to his hand—she might as well have caught him by the wrist. Chastised, Alex's arm drooped into his lap. He turned his eyes away, putting Scarlet and her frustrated apprentices in view instead. If he weren't a vampire, Alex felt certain that he would have flushed blazing crimson. He heard Sally sigh quietly, though whether in sadness or frustration he couldn't be sure.

"Jason seems to be learning fairly well," Sally said, nodding towards the spot where Scarlet was attempting to teach her three apprentices some sort of martial art. Alex mumbled agreement, appreciating the subject change. She wasn't wrong, either. Jason was picking up the movements quickly. There was no muscle behind the punches and kicks, of course, but Jason could execute them with more accuracy than his companions.

"At least Jason has the humility to try," Sally continued, casting a disapproving glance at the two young werewolves. While Jason was meticulously learning a complicated move from Scarlet, it looked as though Tyler and Darby had largely abandoned the effort and were conducting some sort of fist-fighting flirtation. Alex knew Jason would never be so insolent in front of a teacher, not even Scarlet.

"It bothers him that he's so powerless," Alex said, thinking aloud.

"Can't say as I'd blame him," Sally replied. "The last time I talked to Thomas was to diagnose a very young Jason with a nasty birth defect. Tangled Tube Syndrome, it's called. A deformity I identified myself. Strictly a phenomenon of cotus and cotu-mixes. The extracirculatory veins—the wiry ones that connect to a cotu's stone—grow incorrectly, all tangled and misplaced. Causes punctures, ulceration, organ scarring. It can be quite debilitating. I don't envy Jason one iota. I feel rather sorry for him, actually."

"Really?" Alex blurted, before he could stop himself. "I mean, you don't seem very understanding. With him. Usually."

"Alex, you know I don't do well with people," Sally said in protest, "especially when there's work to be done. After all these years bickering with Hope, I would have thought that was clear. If someone doesn't do things my way, I tend to get prickly. I've tried to fix that fault, but unfortunately I seem to be my mother's daughter."

"Having never met your mother, I don't know about that, but you *can* change. Since we arrived in Brunswick, you've become much more sympathetic. And if ever there was a time to learn cooperation, it would be now. There are about to be eleven more just like Jason, you know."

"Yes." She nodded. "I can try. I will. It'll be harder without you, though."

Alex wanted to say something, words of comfort maybe, but any such speech dried up before it left his brain. Never, not once since

Sally told Alex that she didn't love him, had she said anything to indicate that she regretted calling off their relationship. Unable to respond, he picked up the mud-stained Latin worksheet and started uncrumpling it while vainly trying to untangle his thoughts.

"Somehow Christmas decorations just seem inappropriate," Jason mused.

"I know what you mean," Pansy said in agreement, gingerly hanging a glass ball on the Christmas tree. "But I think a little Christmas cheer will do us good. The others seem to be enjoying themselves, at least." Jason glanced out the front window to where Scarlet was setting up luminaries. Alex was attaching strings of colored lights to the house. He waved at Jason from the top of the ladder. Jason gave a tiny wave back and returned to his ornamenting. As they labored, the plastic fir began taking on shades of vitality. A sky blue ceramic bear that said 'Baby's First Christmas,' a hula girl made of felt and grass from Pansy and Thomas's Hawaiian honeymoon, lacy snowflakes crocheted by Pansy's mother—the history of a family hung on a tree. For every year since Thomas and Pansy got married, there was a new ornament for the tree to mark the passage of time. Pansy and Jason had kept up the tradition even after Thomas was gone, but for the first time there was no ornament to commemorate the waning year. With the chaos as of late, there hadn't been time to find one.

"I'm sorry all this happened," Jason apologized, briefly catching his mother's eye. He wanted to say more. I'm sorry I've only ever been a problem. I'm sorry I'm not strong enough to take care of myself and keep you safe. I'm sorry I can't save the world. But he was afraid to trouble her with his true feelings. He knew from whom he'd inherited his overdeveloped sense of responsibility. His mother must think herself at fault as well. She blamed herself for everything already. It would be too selfish of him to burden her with the sinking-in-quicksand sensation that gripped him on the inside.

"I'm sorry, too," Pansy replied with a voice as brittle as snowflakes.

"At least we have Alex and them to take care of us." Even if we don't have Dad, he thought. Pansy had grown increasingly withdrawn ever since finding out that her son was in mortal danger, and Jason worried about her. Jason thought it strange that while he could be murdered any moment, it was his family that he was most concerned for.

"Yes. Alex and them," Pansy said, hollowly repeating his words and glancing outside. Scarlet and Alex were having a sword fight with the stakes that were supposed to secure the luminaries.

"What's wrong?" Jason asked. "You don't seem comforted."

"I—no, I shouldn't. They'll protect us, that's all you need to know."

"Mom, tell me what's bothering you," Jason asked. Pansy ignored him for a moment, placing a glittering glass angel on a tree branch, but Jason kept looking at her, and eventually she sighed, dropping her arms to her sides.

"I'm not sure they know what they're doing," Pansy admitted. "I don't doubt their intentions. But..." She glanced out the window. Having abandoned the fight, Alex was leaning back on the ladder and trying to read the instructions for the lights that he had somehow entangled around his head and both arms. Scarlet appeared to be talking to the plastic reindeer in the flower bed. Jason had to admit, they didn't give an appearance of great competence.

"I shouldn't have said anything," Pansy said. "They're fine. We're safe." She seemed to be talking to herself more than to Jason. He wanted to say something, to be the man of the house and assuage her fears, but the words simply weren't there.

"I wish Dad was here," Jason found himself whispering, although he hadn't really meant to say it out loud. Thomas could have protected them, no question. He was a pro with every kind of weapon from butter knives to rifles. More than ever, his family needed him back. In his palm Jason held a hand-carved wooden ornament in the shape of a guitar. Thomas had made it for his son's fifth Christmas. It was the first ornament Jason had ever hung on the tree himself. Jason carefully put the loop of string over one of the silken evergreen branches and for a moment he and his mother stood perfectly still, watching the little guitar spin slowly as physics pulled it to its resting place. When it stopped moving, time started again, and Jason and Pansy returned to their task, chatting about school and work and tacky purple Christmas trees, their previous comments left hanging in the air like an icy winter fog.

The bow was a part of him, one with his body. Jason pulled the bowstring taut, visually gauging the distance to the target. He aimed somewhat higher to compensate for the distance, and a few inches to the left to offset the wind. Then he released the string and watched with pleasure as the arrow flew flawlessly into the center of the target fifty feet away.

"Nice shot, Robin Hood." Alex's voice emanated from behind. Jason turned to face him and smiled, drinking in the praise.

"Thanks."

"Archery is a rare talent, you know," Alex said, walking up to Jason's side.

"I'm just glad I can finally do something useful."

Alex turned his eyes to the side and studied Jason with concern. "Physical ability isn't everything, you know. Other skills are important, too."

"What other skills do I *have?*" Jason sulked.

Alex thought about it for a second. "You're smart. You have a steady moral compass, which nobody does anymore. No one in the flute section can play like you. And I hear you're good at Latin...?"

"You need help with your homework?"

"Possibly."

"All right," Jason sighed, putting the rental longbow under his arm. "Let's go back to my house and we'll work some conjugations."

"That sounds so wrong."

"Alex, can we focus on the Latin?"

They trudged through the ice-encrusted grass of the park towards Jason's neighborhood beneath a heavy gray sky that threatened to drop more frozen water on them at any moment. The houses in Wolf's Run were all decked out for Christmas, which was now just a couple weeks away. There were Christmas trees in every window, some of them still glowing cheerfully in the early morning. One yard sported a giant inflatable Santa, though it had lost some of its air and was leaning drunkenly to the side. It had been that way since the week after Thanksgiving, and it gave Alex great amusement every time they passed it.

Jason never stopped to consider it odd that in a town populated with things that go bump in the night, Christmas was a big deal. In Brunswick it seemed perfectly natural; why not, when every other aspect of the place was in constant contrast and flux? Once in a while you would see a bell-ringing Santa with a tail or a snowman with fangs, but for the most part Brunswickans celebrated the holidays just like everyone else. As soon as November was past, lights started going up in trees along the streets, bows were tied on stop signs, and

Christmas trees were placed in a front window of every house. The trees were invariably artificial. The surrounding forest held plenty of good pine trees, but they didn't much appreciate being cut down and garnished with tinsel.

Alex and Jason were walking up Jason's driveway, still admiring the festive neighborhood Christmas spectacle, when they both saw the front door. They came to a stricken halt, staring at the chilling spectacle.

"What the—" Alex began. He pushed ahead of Jason protectively, coming to the door first. He inhaled deeply, gave the all-clear, and whipped through the door, presumably to search the house for further damage.

Jason ascended the front steps with painstaking slowness. Fear sapped sensation from his limbs and reduced his thoughts to an incoherent murmuring. Reaching the threshold, he ran his fingertips over the wounded door, a leaden dread settling into the pit of his stomach. Five mammoth claws had sliced through the red paint and left deep rifts in the soft flesh of the wood.

"If there was any doubt before, there isn't now. The Black Dog is definitely after Jason," Alex said. Too jittery to stand still, he started pacing up and down the room. He was meeting with Scarlet and Sally in the Drakes' living room, which had become a sort of secondary home base.

"Not necessarily," Sally said slowly. "But I have to admit that it would be quite the coincidence. How's Jason faring?"

"He's terrified," Alex answered. For the sake of his fragile ego, he neglected to mention his own mind-numbing fear.

"So is everyone else," Scarlet said. "We put a Christmas wreath over the scratches so they wouldn't be as obvious, but the neighbors still noticed."

"I'm concerned about what the neighbors are thinking," Alex said. "When they're scared, everyone wants someone to blame. Seeing as they can't catch the Black Dog, it would be just like people to demonize the Drakes, especially because they already think Thomas's son must be bad news like his daddy."

"As if that poor woman didn't have enough to worry about already," Sally said and sighed. She turned her gaze to a spot on the wall above

Alex's head and stared at it absently while her mental gears processed the new information.

"Perhaps there's something I can do," she said introspectively, meeting the eyes of her companions once more.

"What do you mean?" Scarlet asked, cocking her head to the side and looking very much like a confused puppy. Sometimes Alex thought that maybe Scarlet had been a werewolf for a little too long.

"It's been a good long while since I took an active role in Brunswick, but I'm sure a few still remember the good I did for the town. If they retain any faith in me, they will believe me when I say that their blame is misplaced," Sally explained.

"That's a big 'if,'" Alex said. "Recall that not everyone agreed with your methods, even if they agreed with your intentions." It had been sixty years since Sally imposed the Brunswick Codes, a strict series of laws to keep the different species in town living harmoniously. To be fair, she had put the proposal to a vote at a town meeting, and it had been almost unanimously supported. But Sally was not entirely clear at the meeting in describing what the punishments for breaking the codes would be. It wasn't really an issue anymore because none of the Brunswickans who refused to obey remained, but the same generation of citizens who would remember Sally's attempt at public service would also remember her tendency towards iron-fisted enforcement.

"The effort was successful, was it not?" Sally protested, crossing her arms. "Besides, I think my comprehension of social mores has grown considerably since then."

"*I* know that," Alex said, assuring her. "But that doesn't mean everyone else does."

"Perhaps you're right," Sally said, conceding after a reluctant pause. "But what do *you* propose? We have to protect Jason from every threat. If the townspeople make themselves a threat, in any capacity, we'll need to do something."

To this, Alex had no reply. He'd had more experience with angry mobs of citizens than he cared to think about. The world might have moved beyond pitchforks and torches, but people were still people. "I don't know."

"Do we *have* to do anything?" Scarlet asked. Alex and Sally stared at her, baffled.

"I just mean that maybe things will work themselves out," Scarlet added in explanation, blushing and fidgeting under their interrogative gaze. "We *think* that Jason's family is being blamed, but we don't really *know* that. Wouldn't it be smarter to wait and see what happens? Overreacting doesn't fix anything."

"Maybe," Sally replied after an awkward silent moment. "Alex?"

"Well...if we acknowledge the problem, people will have to respond to it," Alex said, "but I've noticed that most people, especially human people, have a knack for ignoring things that they don't want to deal with. If we don't tell them what's going on, they won't have an excuse to panic." He knew that was waxing overly optimistic, and like Sally, the idea of choosing not to take charge rubbed him the wrong way, but there had been occasions in which they had ignored Scarlet's peaceable thoughts and come out the worse for it. Her suggestions were simple but uncommonly effective, and thus worth taking into account. Besides, Alex knew well that his assessment of human denial was accurate. He had lived as a vampire among humans for nearly a thousand years, most of the time with other vampires alongside, and repeatedly avoided detection just by laying low and relying on the human capacity for deliberate ignorance.

"All right. We'll just have to keep a weather eye. That'd make my life easier. I have a Christmas party to plan," Sally said in conclusion.

"You still want to do that?" Alex asked and groaned. Sally had a bizarre obsession with organizing events. The annual Christmas party was her one chance to play the privileged hostess she was raised to be. For Alex, it meant risking life and limb to apply decorations and then risking sanity by socializing.

"Of course!" Sally exclaimed. "It is a time-honored tradition. Why stop now?"

"Because there's an evil spirit haunting the town and the world is getting ready to end?" Alex said, suggesting the obvious. But a little thing like that would never stop her.

"Culture yields to no catastrophe, Alex."

"A Christmas party?" Jason said, repeating the words and staring with disbelief at the invitation Alex had just handed him. Jason sounded like he too thought this party was untimely. Alex considered telling Sally this, but decided that he didn't want to start that argument up again. He hated fighting with Sally, and it was too late anyway.

"Formal or informal dress?" Pansy asked. Alex had to appreciate her ability to act normal in the midst of this madness. Perhaps it was easier for her to tackle a party than an apocalypse. Alex wasn't sure he could say the same.

"Just wear whatever," he answered with a shrug. "Sally and Hope wear something fancy, I wear the same things as always, Jenna puts on a crazy sweater, and Scarlet puts on reindeer antlers. Anything goes. Seriously."

He sat poised on a hill, diligently watching the large black-stone den. A small stream of two-legged animals arrived in their rolling metal machines and loped gaily through the den entrance. Lights shone brightly, echoes of laughter floated disembodied on the chill night air, and even from this distance he could imagine the atmosphere of frivolity taking shape inside. They had no idea what freedom it was to be able to celebrate. Why had that little she-demon insisted on attacking now? He had planned every move carefully, drawing on all his experience, but he wasn't fast enough for her. This wouldn't work. It was not the right way. Hopefully she would see that, when this failed. Perhaps then she would allow him to operate at his own discretion. Perhaps, but not likely. A guttural complaint, halfway between growl and moan, emerged from the back of his throat at the thought of her. The stars twinkled mockingly over his head.

Jason compulsively straightened the collar of his white button-up shirt, climbing the front steps of the Kitch Manor behind Alex. Parties weren't his forte, and even though he knew all the guests, he was jittery. Alex opened the front door and held it open for his guests. Jason crossed the porch, walking by the life-size stone gargoyle that guarded the door. He did a double-take when he realized that the statue was wearing a Santa hat.

"Interesting," Jason noted. From the first time he saw it, Jason had disliked that piece of sculpture. It was uncomfortably well-detailed and he felt as if those eerily realistic eyes were watching him. Somehow the cheery Christmas accessory made it all the creepier.

"Well, some people put sweaters on their dogs, some put hats on their gargoyles," Pansy said, passing Jason and crossing the threshold. With one last glance at Sally's rather unorthodox holiday porch display, Jason slunk into the house after her.

Jason hadn't been in the Manor since before Thanksgiving. Whenever there had been training, it was in the park by his house. Jason hadn't thought about it much, but now he realized why Sally had wanted them out of her way—her Christmas decorating would have made the denizens of Christmas Town itself jealous. It must have taken her weeks, especially as Alex and Scarlet wouldn't have been there to help most days. It reminded Jason of the time when his family had gone to see the Biltmore House in Asheville at Christmas time. Sally's Christmas tree didn't quite measure up to Biltmore's 35-foot giant, but Jason estimated that it was a good ten feet. And not only had Sally somehow managed to piece together multiple sections of *faux* pine up to that height, she had decorated almost every single branch of the tree, from top to bottom, with some sort of ornamentation. She had chosen red-and-gold as her color scheme—the ornaments, the tinsel, everything down to the wrapped presents under the tree was red, gold, or a combination thereof. The sofas that normally occupied the floor in the front room had been pushed aside, such that they were still available for use, but not in the way of mingling, or of the table of cookies and snacks set up in the center of the carpet. Sally had clearly gone to an enormous effort to arrange this party. Yet Jason and company had arrived a few minutes late, and he counted only seven other party goers, three of whom currently lived in the house. It appeared that aside from his household, the only nonresidential invitees were Tyler and that Darby girl. Judging by the way Tyler's arm was draped around her shoulders, Jason surmised that Darby was supposed to be his date.

"Merry Christmas, Drake contingent!" Sally had managed to sneak up beside Jason without his noticing. Jason flinched in surprise and turned to face his hostess who, true to her theme, was wearing a sparkling red dress and gleaming golden sash. He reflexively returned Sally's greeting, taken aback by her friendliness. In his experience, Sally wasn't usually upbeat or personable in any way. But that night she was the picture of holiday festivity, all aglow with Christmas spirit. Jason found it quite unnerving.

"So, how'd I do?" she asked, looking at Alex.

"Once again you have made the rest of us feel like underachievers with your magnificent décor," Alex replied, his flowery words a less-than-subtle satire of Sally's overblown speech and decorations.

"Overkill much?"

"It was overkill when the only people who came were the ones who couldn't get away. This year I have guests! Well, four of them. Which is more than can be said for the last ten years or so."

Because it was weird having Alex and Sally talk to each other through him, Jason decided to wander off. His usual strategy for social events was to find a corner to hover in and hope that nobody spoke to him. Apparently luck wasn't on his side.

"HEY, JASON!" Tyler raced over to him, dragging his date along.

"Oh, um, hey, Tyler. How're you doing?"

"I'm GREAT! Guess who my date is tonight?" Tyler gestured grandly at Darby, who was busy smoothing her skirt after the mad dash across the room.

"That's great," Jason replied, trying to sound surprised. As if anyone *didn't* know that those two fancied each other. The most striking girl and the most athletic guy, wasn't that how it always went? Darby meandered away shortly, but Jason was stuck listening to Tyler gush about his new girlfriend for a solid fifteen minutes. Once Tyler finally left to track Darby down, Jason quickly grabbed a plate of food and sank into the sofa seat farthest from the action. From his post he watched the others interact. Jenna had become Tyler's next victim and was politely pretending to listen to his ramblings. Meanwhile, Alex had taken the opportunity to whisk away Tyler's girl and pseudo-flirt with her by the Christmas tree, which Jason thought was extremely inappropriate, considering the vast age difference. Jason was so busy questioning Alex's state of mind that at first he didn't notice that Scarlet had sat beside him. In the big room full of bright decorations and noisy people, she just kind of disappeared.

"Not a party person?" Scarlet said, guessing and glancing at Jason. As Alex had said, there were in fact felt antlers affixed to a plastic band on her head.

"Nope, not a party person," Jason answered. "I'm not much of a people person at all."

"Yeah, me neither," Scarlet said, and took a bite of the snowflake-shaped cookie in her hand. They sat in silence for a long time, two wallflowers watching the world go by.

"Hey, Scarlet? I'm kind of curious. How'd you end up here? With Sally and the others, doing...whatever it is you do."

"Sally recruited me when she first came to Brunswick," Scarlet said, a note of pride seeping into her voice. "She decided to fix the place up, you know, lay down the law and make everybody get along.

She really made things better here, and I thought it was so nice of her. So I pledged my loyalty. I'm like Sally's personal warrior-bodyguard."

"Oh. Cool." Neither of them knew how to continue the conversation, so they dropped it, and spent the next few minutes focusing on everything but each other. All of a sudden, Jason felt the hairs on the back of his neck stand up, half a second before he heard a soft slithering sound, like the noise a ghost might make as it moved through the walls of a dream. It sounded like it was behind him, but when he glanced over the back of the sofa he couldn't see anything out of the ordinary. Maybe he was imagining it.

"Do you hear that?" Jason asked Scarlet, at the exact moment when she turned and asked the same question of him. They blinked at each other in surprise a few times.

"I think it's coming from the front porch," Scarlet said, shoving the awkward moment out of the way. She clambered over the back of the sofa, wiry muscles tensing. Jason followed her progress with his eyes. She stopped short of the front door and took a frantic step back. A nervous growl boiled up in her throat. She was staring fixedly at the bottom of the door. Jason drew up to his knees on the cushions so he could see what was going on. Coal-dark smoke was curling into the house from under the door and pooling on the poinsettia-patterned welcome mat.

"Um, Sally," Jason called loudly. The conversation died and every eye turned to him. He pointed a finger at the anomaly on the floor, unable to find words for it. Scarlet growled menacingly at the intruder and made small lunges, but could not figure out how to attack such an enemy.

"What on Earth?" In a few rapid strides Sally was beside Jason. He lowered his arm and shook his head, not knowing what to think. He hadn't the slightest idea what it was. Jason wondered if anybody knew. But they were all instinctively afraid. It was like so many amorphous snakes, writhing with vitality but entirely insubstantial. Something so strange could only mean danger. For a heartbeat everyone in the room stood stock still, the blades of an oblivious ceiling fan the only sound. Then Hope decided to take the initiative. She inched towards the roiling black substance, her hands beginning to glimmer and glow as she summoned her magic to them. Hope stopped when her lead foot was a mere six inches from the edge of the smoky circle. Having reached her destination, she seemed unsure, perching there indecisively. Another tendril spiraled languidly into the house and then in an indescribable and unnatural fashion, the smoke *opened its eyes*.

Looking back on the moment, Jason could never quite understand how. Up until that point it had been an entirely featureless mass, with no eyelids to pull back. But somehow, it did, revealing two glowing red orbs—fresh coals plucked from the fires of deepest Hell. There were no pupils, no way to tell what, if anything, the eyes were seeing; that's what Jason told himself. But when the eyes appeared, all the little hairs on the back of Jason's neck stood up and somehow he *knew* the black spirit was staring right at him. And, inexplicably, he was staring right back. Every nerve in his body was signaling manically, telling him to move, to run, to do *something*. Yet he couldn't. Fear had seeped through his skin and infected his blood, which his heart then pumped rapid-fire throughout his body. He was petrified by the terror. He had no idea where the mindless horror had come from, or exactly what he was afraid of—only that when he looked into those fiendish eyes, he was awash with fear.

All around, the story was the same. Nine people, enthralled by the power of the Black Dog. Darby fainted. Scarlet continued to growl, but the sound faded almost to a whimper. Alex's wings and hands twitched restlessly, as though trying to coerce the rest of his body into either fight or flight, to no avail.

Though Sally's muscles refused to cooperate, her mind raced on through the haze of fright. Black Dogs kill their victims by scaring them to death, she thought, and knew that she had to do something. So she performed the only movement her body would allow. She closed her eyes. Instantly the crushing terror lifted, but now she was blind. Beside her, she could smell the cinnamon tang of witch amidst the acridness of fear and reached out a hand to locate Hope. Sally found her shoulder, and quickly raised her hand to cover Hope's eyes. For a moment, Hope struggled against the hand on her face, until she realized that it had broken the trance. She closed her eyes and gently pushed Sally away. This time, Sally obliged. Hope needed no instruction. She murmured a few words in German and felt power bloom within her chest. She directed the energy towards her hands and felt the light magic obey. Her fingers warmed with a buttery inner glow. She plunged her open palms downward, creating a rectangle of effulgent magic barrier with which to push the creature back. The moment Hope's force-field touched the smoke, it let out a wail and rapidly retreated outside.

Even with the spell of fear broken, everyone remained terrified. It was still out there, God only knew where. Sally explained what it was, assuring everyone that it would be dormant as soon as the sun arose. In the meantime, she allowed the guests to stay at the manor. She hurriedly prepared rooms. The manor had no shortage of those. The party had died at heart with the entrance of the hellish exhaust fumes, so everyone went to bed as soon as possible. The exception was Scarlet, who offered to be the night guard. There was some debate as to the organization of the guests in their rooms. It was eventually decided that the kids would be divided into two rooms by gender and that Pansy would get her own.

Thus it was that Jason and Tyler were lying with their backs to each other, too freaked to be concerned with the awkwardness of two guys sharing the same bed. They could take some small measure of comfort from the fact that they weren't alone. Even so, there wasn't much comfort to be had. Sleep seemed impossible.

"W-what do you think it wanted?" Tyler whispered. His trembling voice was barely audible.

"I can't be sure," Jason told him honestly. He had been trying to figure it out, but he couldn't think of any creature that manifested like that. "But I'm pretty sure it wants me." Jason swallowed thickly, trying not to think what the Black Dog intended to do if it ever got ahold of him. The shadow of the fear he had felt earlier floated through his mind, and his wringing insides drew tighter.

"You? Why?"

"It's a long story…I don't think I'm supposed to tell you," Jason said in apology. He wasn't about to get in trouble for that again. He had enough to worry about as it was.

"Does it have anything to do with what Sammy almost told me?" Tyler asked.

"Yeah, how'd you know?" How much did Sammy tell?

"I got a long lecture from Alex about not telling anyone what Sammy told me. Sammy didn't say much of anything, but I figured whatever Alex thought he'd told me must be a big secret. And how many big secrets can there be in this one-horse town?" The waver was beginning to settle out of Tyler's voice. Talking about something else seemed to make him more his usual self.

"Alex sure gets around. He gave me that same lecture."

"So does that mean I never get to find out what grand cause I volunteered to champion?"

"I assume they'll tell you sometime," Jason said, although he wasn't confident of that. He realized that he really had no idea what his protectors were planning. He felt the dripping burn of blood in his abdomen as his nerve-wracked body cut into itself.

"I hope so! I would sure like to know what I'm getting into. It doesn't seem so much like a heroic adventure anymore."

"All right, that's the last window locked," Alex said. He was with Hope in the basement, securing the lone pane of glass while she put the house under a witch's brand of protection. Jenna had been relegated the task of playing therapist, particularly for Scarlet, who had been rather traumatized by meeting an adversary that she could not bite or punch. Alex couldn't blame her. He was abjectly shaken himself. He'd seen a lot of disturbing things in his lifetime, but tonight he had experienced a whole new kind of terror. It wasn't the smoke creeping under the door. That wasn't particularly shocking to him. It wasn't even just the Black Dog's contagious terror. What had frightened him most deeply was the thought of his charges being injured—Jason chiefly, but also the two juvenile werewolves, although they claimed to be independent and mature beings. This was something that Alex had never had to worry about before, and he was unprepared for the sensation.

"I've addressed all the doors," Sally said, descending the steps and joining them. "How's that spell coming, Hope?"

"Not too bad," Hope replied. "There are a lot of points of entry in this place. But in an hour or so I *should* have all of them magically alarmed. I'll know about everyone and everything that comes and goes." In front of her was a blueprint of the Manor. She was drawing glowing lines of magic across every opening visible on the map.

"Shouldn't we just cover the whole house?" Alex asked. "And what about Jason's place?"

"You know 'we' aren't doing anything," Hope pointed out testily. "I have to do all the magic by myself, and there's only so far I can stretch it."

"I'm not trying to be pushy, Hope. I just want to be thorough," Alex explained, holding up his hands in a gesture of surrender.

"He's developing Mother Hen syndrome. He can't help it," Sally told Hope, the words teasing but the delivery perfectly grave. Alex started to protest, but he knew that it was true. And he didn't like it. He felt guilty about not liking it, but couldn't deny that he was uncomfortable with the responsibility. He had always been sort of a lone ranger, even as a child. When he'd teamed up with the girls, he had still been accustomed to working in a loose collaboration with equals. But caring for a dependent? And this was just the beginning. There were eleven more like Jason out there somewhere. The more Alex thought about it, the more he sympathized with Atlas.

"I'm going to sleep," he said without preamble. Sally raised an eyebrow at him, but let him plod off down the hall to his bedroom without comment.

"You know, Alex isn't wrong," Sally said after he had left the room, looking pointedly at Hope.

"If you're suggesting that we recruit more witches to help me, you already know what I'm going to say," Hope said and sighed, with the tone of one talking to a small child. Her finger stabbed downward at the map, emphasizing to Sally that she was working. She didn't have time to talk about this again, especially given that she assumed that the conversation would go as it always did. Sally would get frustrated and walk out, allowing Hope yet another victory—that's what she thought, and they both knew it. Sally felt a spark of anger at Hope's insolence and an electric current began to hum quietly in her nerves. She repressed it, knowing how dangerous it was for her as an electric cotu to let herself be bothered. She might not agree with Hope sometimes, but in the grand scheme of things Sally did not want to electrocute her. A lifetime of carefully-constructed self-control would not go to waste now.

"What about someone we already know? Someone like Hawthorne, perhaps? We've both known her for years, and we know how trustworthy she is," Sally said. She lowered herself into the chair across from Hope, her intense gaze boring into the crown of Hope's straw-colored head.

"We also know how trustworthy she *isn't*," Hope replied. "Clara can be loyal, but she is above all a businesswoman, and a selfish one at that. She would be easily manipulated by the other side." Hope refused to give Sally the validation of looking at her. Sally drummed her fingers on the tabletop, her nails slicing into the wood.

"I find your affected superiority interesting. When we first met you were a scared little girl trying to hide from an angry village, out of her time and in over her head, or have you forgotten? And you haven't really changed. Your power has grown, certainly, but it's been over three hundred years since the people who hunted you were dead and buried, and you're still hiding. You'll always be running and hiding. And I'll always be the one who's not afraid to stand in the light and take the heat. It actually makes me feel a little bit sorry for you." Sally removed her hand from the maple wood and stood, her back to Hope. A tense minute passed—Hope didn't so much as twitch a muscle, watching Sally suck in and expel several calming breaths.

"Just...finish those force fields, please," Sally said tersely and left the room. Hope watched her leave, then slowly rotated her head to look at the five shallow crescent marks in the table. She stared at them for a long time. Her hands repeatedly fisted and unclenched. Eventually, her fingers relaxed and she returned to the blueprint, drawing her luminescent lines as though nothing had happened.

Shauna moved about her living room slowly, picking up various pieces of debris, ranging from bat wings to plastic cups. Solstice celebrations had changed quite a bit in the forty years she had been attending them. When her mother first took her to one, back in '71, it had been largely a gathering of stoned hippie girls who thought they were real witches. In the '80s the punks and goths came about, and by the 2000s, when Shauna began hosting her own parties, the witches who arrived were a heterogeneous mixture of devoted pagans, pseudo-Satanists, and moody teenage girls with nothing better to do on winter break. Shauna tossed a suspicious-looking mushroom into the trash bin and wished, not for the first time, that she had been born several hundred years earlier, when witchcraft was taken seriously.

Having cleared a roughly circular spot in the center of the floor, Shauna decided that it was about time for the most important part of Solstice. She sat down in the trash-free zone and reached underneath the nearby sofa. Her hands returned with a small wooden box. She opened the lid and carefully took out a small white candle and a box of matches. She lit the candle and softly began an incantation to invoke the energy of the moon. Shauna always closed her eyes when doing spells, as her mother had before her. This made her feel closer to the earth. She felt safe, and in tune with the world around her. The circle of light widened, encompassing Shauna. Then, suddenly, the light blew out. Her eyes snapped open. What had done that? In answer to the unspoken question, a patch of supreme darkness emerged from the night in front of her and slashed at her chest with its claws. It leaped on top of her, crushing the white candle with one paw and her ribcage with another.

"It's not the same without Scarlet and Alex here," came Sally's voice and a muffled sigh. She was crawling around under the Christmas tree, pulling out all the presents and categorizing them by recipient.

"For a long time it was just you and Alex and I," Hope reminded her. "This isn't all that different." In the course of her efforts, Sally elbowed into Hope. They recoiled from each other, but then returned to feigning holiday cheer for Jenna's benefit.

"Well, it's a little different than that, I think. I'm sure I'm much prettier than Alex," Jenna remarked good-naturedly, not acknowledging the spat. "I do miss Scarlet, though. She adds a wonderful element of childishness. It isn't quite as Christmasy without her."

"She is adorable, isn't she? Ah, finally, the last box!" Sally extricated herself from the green plastic boughs to bring out one more parcel to place on Jenna's pile.

"Now, who wants to start—" Sally was interrupted by the ringing of the doorbell.

"I'll get it," Hope said. "You go ahead."

Sally thanked her, carefully stepped over the boxes she'd surrounded herself with, and settled cross-legged on the floor beside Jenna.

Hope opened the ebony door, reflexively building a magic layer between her and whoever might be outside. There was no one there. She didn't think they were expecting any deliveries, but she looked down at the porch to be sure. There sat a rectangular package, plain cardboard tied with an ornate red-and-gold ribbon. There was a tag attached to the ribbon, and Hope crouched down to read it:

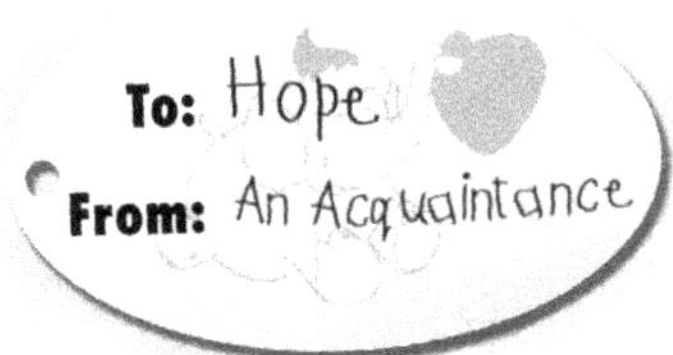

"Acquaintance?" Hope mentally scanned through the list of enemies, but there was no return address on the package to trace a particular person to. Now that she was looking more closely, Hope saw that there wasn't a sending address either. This hadn't been mailed. Someone had just dropped it in front of the door. Hope couldn't think of anyone in Brunswick that was against her, but so many red flags were going up. She crouched inside the doorway, indecisive. She was afraid to touch the unknown package, but afraid not to do anything with it either.

"What it is?" Jenna asked. She had come up behind Hope and was looking over her head at the delivery. Hope shrugged her shoulders helplessly.

"I don't know. It says it's for me, but it doesn't say who it's from. See?" Hope indicated the tag.

"Hmm. That is odd," Jenna remarked, her eyebrows furrowing.

"It is. I can't decide what I should do with it."

"Well I guess you kind of have to open it," Sally said, making Hope jump. She crawled over until she too could see out the door. "It might be something important, from someone who is afraid to state their identity. And no, I didn't have anything to do with it."

"Maybe you could cast some kind of protective charm and then open it?" Jenna suggested.

"All right. That sounds good." Hope closed her eyes and cast a quick spell on the box, to keep anything from coming out unexpectedly. Then, with trembling fingers, she untied the ribbon and opened the un-taped cardboard flaps. When she saw what was inside, she clapped a hand to her mouth to stifle the scream. Behind her, Jenna inhaled sharply and took a step back. Sally was the only one to lean in to investigate the gruesome display.

Inside the box was a pair of severed hands, arranged one atop the other on a bed of red tissue paper and gold tinsel. They were delicate, feminine hands, with pretty crimson-painted fingernails in stark contrast to the hue of the old blood caked on the severed wrists. One industrious drop of still-liquid red oozed lazily through a crack in the scabbing. Sitting on top of the hands was a note, in case the meaning wasn't clear enough:

Keep your paws to yourself, Witch

10

Alex lounged on the Drake's couch, flipping through channels on the television, trying in vain to find one that wasn't showing some sort of romance movie. Valentine's Day wouldn't be for another month, yet the pink, happy, lovey-dovey stuff was already becoming inescapable. Alex found the lot of it depressing.

In the kitchen, Jason was typing up his history paper. Alex glanced over every few minutes to check in on him. He couldn't help but worry. Jason had aged ten years since the autumn. The whole business with the young witch, Shauna—who'd lost her hands and her life to the Black Dog—had really taken a toll on him. Jason had never known the woman personally. Shauna's murder seemed to have simply been the last straw. The idea that his very existence had spawned death and destruction these past several months was more than the boy could withstand.

The SyFy channel was showing some sort of gory monster movie. Perfect. Alex watched something like a poorly-animated pterodactyl bite off the head of a hapless hiker, but he wasn't really paying attention. He glanced over at Jason again, and decided to try one more time. Alex strolled across to the computer desk. Jason had to have heard his footsteps, but chose to ignore them.

"You didn't kill her," Alex reminded him, lost for a more eloquent statement.

"So? It's still my fault. If I hadn't been born, she'd still be alive," Jason replied hollowly, not moving his eyes away from the computer screen.

"No, it's not your fault." Jason's refusal to see reason was beginning to anger him, and he had to struggle to keep his voice down. "She's dead because somebody decided they wanted to kill you, and because Hope and the rest of us decided that wasn't going to happen. You haven't done anything wrong. It's all because of how others react to you, and there isn't anything you can do to change that."

"What *can* I do?" Jason said. "Everybody makes all the decisions for me, and even if I had the opportunity to do something, I wouldn't be able to!"

"You're eleven years old. You aren't supposed to be able to do anything. Our job is to protect you until you're old enough to handle yourself. Just wait a few years."

"I don't want to wait. People are dying *now*."

"You say that, but it won't be long until you'll wish you were a kid again. Let others deal with things for now. We'll take care of it." Alex was trying his best to be wise and helpful, but Jason wasn't buying it. Alex thought he understood why, more or less. Even before Shauna, Jason had indicated over and over that he wished he was more useful. He wanted to make sure that no one got hurt on his behalf. Alex had to appreciate someone with such a heart of gold, but it didn't mean that he had to like trying to work with such a person.

"I'll tell you what you can do," Alex said. For the first time, Jason turned away from his homework to look straight at Alex. He had to take a steadying breath before he continued. "You aren't too young to learn. I've never gotten around to reading it, but I hear that there's some literature about the Guardians, and the genies, and everything else. Ask Sally. I'm sure she'd help."

"But isn't that kind of Sally's job?"

"Well, yes," Alex said in agreement. "But that doesn't mean you can't read up too. Besides, at least one of the actual Guardians should know what's going on. And you're the first, which means that all the others will look up to you, once we find them. You'll need to be able to answer their questions."

Jason nodded, biting his lip. "I guess you're right. Do you think we could go see Sally now?" He asked hopefully.

Seeing Sally was the last thing Alex wanted to do, but if it would make Jason feel better... "All right, sure. I'll tell Scarlet."

And once again, Alex found himself on the couch, watching the same strikingly bad monster movie. Down the hall, Jason and Sally were in the library. Sally was lecturing him enthusiastically, only stopping whenever Jason raised his hand to ask a question. Alex could just see the two of them through the open doorway, but unlike when he was at Jason's house, he wasn't checking up on them every ten seconds. Seeing Sally just added insult to injury. Usually Alex could swallow his feelings for her, but their anniversary, if you could rightly call it that, always killed him. He still remembered the last they celebrated together, their fifty-fourth. He had given her a dozen chocolate roses because whenever he bought her real flowers, their cat would eat them and then throw up on the carpet. It seemed like such a long time ago. Now their love, the roses, everything was gone. Even the cat was gone. It died the next year, not long after the relationship ended. A coincidence, to be sure, but a painfully appropriate one. In a few months it would be ten years since Sally broke his heart, but it still hurt like it had been yesterday. Alex sighed miserably and leaned his head back into the couch cushion, trying and failing not to think about how it used to be.

Hope cursed and rushed to take the sauce pan off the eye of the stove before the sludge inside boiled over. She turned on the exhaust hood to whisk the somewhat acrid, herb-scented smoke away from the interior of the house.

"Is that magic or dinner you're burning over there?" Jenna asked, calm as a coconut. She did glance up from her romance novel to make sure the kitchen wasn't actually on fire this time but returned to her leisure pursuit when she didn't spot any flames.

"It's magic," Hope said and huffed, cranking down the heat and placing the pot back on the eye, "although I guess there isn't anything in here that you couldn't eat. I'm trying to make charms to specifically ward off Black Dogs. There wasn't a whole lot in the literature to go on, but since we can't hide in here all day behind the wards, I have to come up with a portable solution."

"Will we have to *wear* it?" Scarlet asked, wrinkling her nose at the vegetal stench.

"Only if you don't want to die of fright," Hope reminded her, searching the drawers for a good stirring spoon.

"I think I'm gonna die of math first," Scarlet said, immune to Hope's brusqueness. She went back to work, looking at her textbook with as much loathing as she could muster.

"There's no need to be snappy, Hope." Jenna's tone was mildly scolding. "Check the towel drawer."

"Okay, I'm sorry. I'm stressed. You'll have to cut me some slack." Hope reached among the dishrags, hand towels, and potholders and frowned in confusion as she pulled out a wooden spoon. "Why'd you put this in here instead of with the serving utensils and spatulas?"

"I didn't. Alex was the last one to empty the dishwasher. He puts things in eclectic places," Jenna explained, turning a page. "And I don't think stress is the only thing bothering you."

Hope didn't want to admit that the splinter of guilt about her fellow witch's death was playing into her short temper and frantic potion-making. So she changed the subject. "Have you noticed that Alex and Sally are at it again?"

"It's that time of year again," Jenna said. "At least Alex is still sober."

"Maybe that's a good sign?" Scarlet replied.

Hope and Jenna shared a skeptical look.

"Maybe," Hope said, conceding the point. "There are four days left until the seventh, though, so there's plenty of time left for a breakdown. I give it forty-eight hours until we have to carry him in from the front porch again."

"Aw, Hope, be nice," Scarlet said, frowning. "I don't think he'll go off on a bender this time. There's too much at stake. Alex might be a little, um..."

"Emotionally unhinged?" Jenna said.

"Yeah, that sounds right," Scarlet said, nodding "but he knows how important it is that we keep on our toes these days. I think Alex will keep his head, now that he needs to. Might help if somebody would have a little faith in him." She glared pointedly at her housemates.

"We'll try to be supportive," Jenna promised. "Right, Hope?"

"Yeah, Alex deserves a little trust, I suppose. Say, Jenna, you aren't doing anything. How about you help me scoop this gunk into some little pouches?"

Jason cast his eyes around as he entered the school cafeteria. He scanned the smattering of ginger heads and found none of them to be Alex. Which was odd because Alex had been in all of the earlier classes they shared, but then he'd been acting a little off the past few days. Maybe he went home? But without telling Jason first? That couldn't be right. Confused and disinclined to spend lunch by himself, Jason carefully slipped beneath the radar of the teachers and sat down illegally at the table of another class, across from Sally.

"Hello, Jason," she greeted, moving her lunch box out of the way to give him more space. "I didn't know you were joining me in this sector of the cafeteria today. Have you been enjoying the book I lent you Thursday?"

"Yeah, it's great." Jason took his sandwich out his bag. "And it says *you* did the illustrations for the chapter on zombies?"

Sally nodded, twirling spaghetti noodles onto a plastic fork.

"They're really good," Jason said. "I had no idea you were an artist."

"I wouldn't say I'm an *artist*," Sally answered, the corners of her mouth turning up at the compliment. "My brother taught me the basics of drawing, and I taught myself how to use those skills to make accurate anatomical diagrams. No one does that anymore, I'm afraid. Cameras and computers have replaced drawings in medical texts." She sighed with a hint of melodrama. "If you consider it an art, then it is an art that is rapidly being lost."

"That's...a little depressing. Maybe you should teach someone to continue the tradition. Not me, though. I can't even draw stick figures." Jason took a bite of his sandwich and waited to see if Sally would notice Alex's conspicuous absence. She just kept eating her spaghetti, so he thought he should point it out.

"Hey, um, do you know where Alex is?" Jason asked, trying to sound as nonchalant as possible. Sally raised an eyebrow and set down her fork.

"He's not with you?" She crossed her arms on the table.

"No, he's not." Jason wondered how much trouble he was getting Alex into. "I haven't seen him since last period. It's not like him to wander off. He's been acting strange lately. More so than usual. It worries me."

"Oh. That." Sally sounded unsurprised and more than a little annoyed. "He always gets himself in a state around our...well, what was once our anniversary. Ever since we broke up."

"You and Alex were *together*?" This was news to Jason. He couldn't quite picture it. Then he remembered Alex getting all dreamy talking about Sally's eyes on the first day of school. Pieces started falling into place. Alex sitting beside Sally at strategy meetings. The way he would sometimes fix Sally's hair, and then jerk his hand away, like maybe he really shouldn't touch her. Now that the fact had been put right in front of him, Jason was starting to realize that if he was older and more mature, he would have noticed Alex's infatuation long ago.

"Yes." Sally sighed, as though it was an unpleasant confession. "For a long time. But the relationship wasn't healthy for either of us, so I broke it off about ten years ago. Alex has not coped well."

"If you don't mind my asking—I mean, I know I probably won't understand—but, why wasn't it working? Apparently Alex thinks it was." Jason felt warm pinkness creep up his cheeks for asking such an impertinent thing, but Sally wasn't bothered in the slightest.

"Alex did think so. He still thinks that we're perfect together. And he still loves me. Or that's what he says, anyways. Sometimes I think he's mostly just in love with the idea of being brokenhearted. Regardless, we couldn't have stayed together forever. We don't have much in common, not where it counts. And I never felt that kind of connection with him. And you are way too young to have any comprehension of what I'm saying, so why did you even ask?"

"I was going to try to talk to him, you know, about being so down. I thought maybe I should know what was what."

"Oh. Good luck," Sally replied. Jason couldn't tell if she was being sarcastic or sincere. Or both.

"Um, thanks. So do you know where he might be?"

Sally shrugged her shoulders and began peeling a banana with an undue degree of concentration. It made Jason uneasy that Alex would abandon his post like this. Jason didn't feel safe without him, and he wasn't sure Alex should be alone if he was that upset.

"Alex isn't the only one behaving in a worrisome manner." Sally's comment broke through Jason's musings.

"Hmm?"

"You've been different the last couple weeks," Sally said, looking up from her meal to nab him with her intense green gaze. "Hope as well. I can only think of one common denominator." Jason blinked but didn't respond. After a tense minute of silence in which Sally continued her lunch unperturbed, she decided to fill the vacuum herself. "Is that why Alex brought you to the library? I don't quite follow his reasoning, but it does seem to have helped. You talk more now."

"Alex thought I would feel more useful if I learned more about my role," Jason answered at last with a shrug.

"Do you?"

"I'm not sure." It was the truth. Jason knew a lot more about prophecies and supernatural history already than he had a couple weeks before, but he couldn't tell if putting together the pieces of where he fit in the world was actually making him feel better. Across the table, Sally chewed a bit of banana, her forehead furrowed as if deep in thought.

"Do you feel like it's something you want to keep doing?" she said at last.

"Well, yeah."

"Then it must be helping something. I'll have another key made so you can get into the library by yourself. As long as you're very careful with my books, you're welcome to them."

"Thanks." Jason favored her with a timid smile. "I'd like that."

"No problem. If you like these weird multigrain cardboard snack crackers, you're welcome to those, too. Just remind me never to let Scarlet do the grocery shopping unsupervised."

In the ground floor living room of Kitch Manor, Jason sat on the floor in a circle with his mother and their protectors. Inside the ring of people stood Hope with a paper bag. The last person to join them was Alex. He flopped onto the rug beside Pansy, carefully avoiding Jason's curious eyes. It had been two days since Alex's mysterious lunchtime disappearance, and Jason still couldn't weasel an explanation out of him. He had returned to next class period wearing a different color of eyeliner and never said a word. Jason hoped that this short meeting Hope had called would give him the opportunity to corner Alex. Jason didn't want an excuse or an apology so much as a chance to make sure that Alex wasn't about to fall apart on him.

Hope surveyed the room to make sure everyone was present. Satisfied with the gathered assembly, she reached into the paper bag, took out a tiny burlap sack tied with twine, and reached over to hand it to Jason. Jason held out his palm, and Hope dropped the strange object into his hand.

"These charms should ward off the Black Dog and any friends it might have," she explained, making her way around to deliver identical parcels to everyone else. "Traditionally, you'd wear something like this around your neck, but it would work just as well stuck in a pocket." Jason weighed the ad hoc protective amulet in his palm. Not a chance he was hanging that rough, itchy pouch on his neck. He could see that Hope had already done so, stringing a delicate gold chain through a loop of the twine. It didn't really mesh with her coiffed aesthetic.

"Are you sure these will keep it away?" Pansy cast a dubious gaze on the charm as Hope plunked it into her hand.

"Well, I couldn't test it," Hope admitted, shifting from one foot to the other, "so don't do anything crazy. No one has ever made anything like these before. I had to come up with my own recipe."

Recipe? Hmm. Jason didn't know much about witchcraft. He would have to take Hope's word that this funky jewelry would safeguard him. He bent his head and sniffed the sack, thinking to discern Hope's "recipe" for Black Dog protection. It smelled like someone dumped a bunch of lemon juice and his mother's whole spice cabinet onto a few sticks of beef jerky. Jason made a face but still sequestered the charm in his pocket as instructed.

"Sorry about the smell," Hope said. Jason started to apologize, then realized that Hope was talking to Scarlet and her none-too-subtle look of disgust. "I added lemon oil to try to mask it, but that won't help you very much. I'm, let's say, eighty-five percent certain these will protect you, so it's worth putting up with the odor."

"Eighty-five percent? I'll take those odds." Sally plopped her charm into the breast pocket of her shirt. "So what will it do? Vaporize any Black Dog in a ten-foot radius?"

"Probably not. I was going for more of a shielding effect, to prevent a Black Dog from ever noticing you. Other questions?" Hope scanned her audience. Jason raised his hand like a good little schoolboy, and Hope called on him.

"Do they have an expiration date?" he asked.

"I'll make new ones in a month just in case the herbs degrade, but spells can last centuries, so you shouldn't have to worry about it. If that's all, let's call it a day and go back to work."

Alex took a deep breath and tentatively pushed the buttons on the phone. He listened anxiously to the ringing, half hoping that Sally wouldn't pick up. But since he had dialed the extension to the personal phone in her lab, he wasn't surprised to hear her voice answer.

"Kitch Manor, Sally speaking."

"Hey, it's me," Alex answered. He'd rehearsed this conversation all afternoon but forgot everything he had planned to say as soon as he heard her speak.

"Something wrong?" Sally prompted after Alex spent a full noiseless minute trying to compose a sentence.

"No! Well, sort of. Jason made me call."

"Is this about you going AWOL the other day?"

"Yeah, right, about that..."

"It's fine," Sally said, cutting in. Her clipped tone attested to her frustration. "I took care of it. Just, please, don't do it again."

Alex couldn't help feeling a little wounded, as she was the one who drove him to such distraction again and again, but he fought not to let it show.

"I won't," he promised. "I wanted to apologize. I should never have left my post. It was childish and selfish, and I swear it won't happen again." For several seconds, there was nothing but a soft buzz of static on the other end of the line.

"Wow. Jason really put the fear of God into you, didn't he?" Sally finally said.

Alex laughed. The coolness had melted out of her voice, and Alex felt like he could breathe again. "Yeah, he kind of did. He's a persistent little bastard when he wants to be."

"Don't call him a bastard," Sally said, her voice almost a purr. "That boy is going to save the world someday. You'd do well to keep him happy." She paused for a moment. "At least one of us should."

"I don't know. I think *you* made him pretty happy today. He's excited about that library key. And he might never forgive me for abandoning him, so right now that makes you Number One," Alex told her, only about one-third joking.

"Oh, I'm sure he'll forgive you. He's a sweet kid. The kind I never was."

"Mmm, yeah, me neither. I'm sure my father would trade places with Pansy any day."

"Hey, Alex?"

"What?"

"Take care of yourself," Sally said—gentle but firm.

"Um, sure, I'll try. Thanks." Alex found himself floundering for words again. "And I guess...we both have work to do..."

"Yes."

"So I should probably go now. Yeah, so, bye. And, um, h—happy anniversary. I...I love you." He quickly turned off the phone before Sally could respond, or hear the catch in his throat.

11

Keep in mind, your hands are your best weapon. You can punch, claw, and light people on fire with them," Jack told him. "That being said, has anybody ever taught you how to make a proper fist?"

"Shouldn't it be obvious?"

"All right, make one, then.

Without thinking about it, Richie closed up his hand, wondering what this had to do with anything.

"Uh-huh, that's why I asked," Jack said. "Thumb has to be on the outside, otherwise it gets broken. Have you never been in a fight before?"

"I try not to pick fights with people bigger than me. Which is just about everyone." As much as Richie loved to argue, physical fights were something he avoided, knowing that he would inevitably lose. He was too shrimpy to have a chance. He doubted Jack was going to be able to remedy that, but it was more important than ever to try.

"Oh. All right, I can understand that. So fix the fist, and we'll work on throwing punches."

Richie tried to learn, sincerely, even though he thought from the beginning that it wasn't worth the effort. Jack taught him every kind of blow in the book. Getting the form down—not a problem. Blocking Jack's jabs or getting a punch through Jack's defenses—not a chance. After an hour of sparring, Richie was covered in bruises, and Jack was reaching for the whiskey again. Jack insisted on giving it one last try. Richie was determined to give it up. So Jack changed tactics.

"Hit me," Jack suddenly said, catching Richie off guard.

"What?"

"Hit me. If you're so piqued, sock me one."

Richie shook his head.

"What, are you afraid? C'mon, you lily-livered coward. Hit me!"

Jack kept insisting, taunting, and eventually Richie discovered that he did want to punch him. And why not? When had Richard McGill ever let someone get away with calling him a coward? Back in school his sharp tongue would have flayed alive anyone so brazen, or he would have had a couple meaty friends take up the fight for him. Had he really lost that much pride? The very thought was so repulsive—

TWACK! Jack staggered backwards and put a hand over his nose. The hand came back with a pool of blood in the palm. Jack stared at it in shock. Richie stared at his fist with equal amazement. For a moment, they were both too stunned to say anything. Then they both started speaking at the same time.

"I am *so* sorry—"

"Now *that's* what I'm talking about!" Jack grinned, even as he was pinching the bridge of his nose to stop the bleeding. The fact that Richie had just punched him in the face seemed to bother him surprisingly little. In fact, he seemed to be thrilled.

"Excellent hit. Although if I'd known it was coming, I could still have dodged. There is still work to be done. But now we know: you can do anything as long as you're mad enough. That's something I understand. It's something we can work with."

"I can't believe that you two lived in these conditions before you came to me. It's detestable," Dracula exclaimed as he ground a cockroach out of existence beneath his heel. Richie happened to think this place was pretty good. It was a legitimate hotel, after all, albeit an old and run-down one. They were even there legally, as paying customers. He was very much tempted to point out to Dracula that he too was living in those conditions, but he refrained. Dracula was clearly not in the mood to be jeered. Such had been the case for several weeks now, ever since their journey was so rudely interrupted.

"Do we know how much longer it'll be before we can get going?" Jack asked. He was sitting in the hollow made by broken springs on one of the beds, watching Dracula play whack-a-bug and flinching with every crunch as though they pained him physically. Distracted by the question, Dracula momentarily lay off of the helpless insect life and turned his attention to Jack.

"No, we do not." Dracula's voice nearly growled, although his anger was not directed at Jack. He took to pacing the length of the room in agitation. "I have been working day and night to get a new alias forged and make myself harder to track, but these vampire hunters are infuriatingly good at their jobs. I'm not sure how we can shake them, now that they've found me. Short of killing them, which is not the simple matter that it was in the old days. There would be police and lawyers and loose ends."

"Killing is always a reasonable solution," Jack replied. "Besides, aren't vampire hunters generally the loner type? It's easier to kill those without connections." He spoke very calmly, completely comfortable with the idea of murder. Richie found it hard to equate Jack the Killer with Jack the Bug Sympathizer. He wasn't paying much attention to the conversation itself. This wasn't the first time they'd had the discussion. They'd had it almost every day since they were attacked by a scruffy man with a wooden stake while leaving Clara's home. That particular hunter had been dealt with quickly and easily—Dracula had pinned him to a tree and snapped his neck without a moment's consideration. But he hadn't been the last. They still didn't know quite how the hunters had found Dracula, but whoever puzzled it out must have told all his friends. The hunters came with increasing frequency and Dracula began to balk at killing so many—someone was bound to notice.

Not that he didn't thoroughly enjoy exterminating the hunters. Dracula was quite pleased with himself every time he dispatched one more. Richie could understand that, sort of. These were Dracula's archenemies, so it made sense that Dracula would be happy to take them out. But the whole thing made Richie kind of queasy. He knew he would need to toughen up if this kept on. Jack was trying to help, teaching him to fight, but Richie didn't think it was working very well. Whenever a new hunter found where they were staying, Jack and Dracula jumped at the chance to fight, while Richie usually hid in the nearest available closet. It was all just a little more action than he'd bargained for, and in the universe's cruel irony, this was all happening right at Christmastime.

Christmas Eve. Richie was alone in the hotel room, a new one this time. They had just relocated after being found yet again. Dracula was busy trying to work out a kink in his new identity and Jack was on some mysterious errand of his own. So Richie was left staring mournfully out the window at the street one level below him. Snow was flurrying in the sky, but the ground was too warm for it to stick. On the sidewalk a few people rushed about performing last-minute preparations, going in and out of shops decked in their Christmas finest. This being the "bad" side of town, the decorations were not much to look at, but they were more than Richie had.

He hadn't wanted to put any further stress onto his companions, so Richie hadn't said anything, but right then he wanted to have Christmas more than anything else. They had always made a production of it at home. Even in the most meager years they would manage to be merry. When there wasn't enough money for presents, everyone made little crafts for each other. The second eldest son, Robin, had a knack for woodcarving. One year, he carved a tiny cat for Richie because that was his favorite animal, back in the days before he knew that he was one. Now that Richie thought about it, that was probably the best memory he had of Robin. The two of them usually didn't get along. Christmas was when their mother would make the five boys stop fighting and play nice with each other for once. That she could accomplish such a feat was miraculous, but somehow she could. The whole family would be harmonious and happy then, for about twelve hours. Richie wondered if he would ever have a family Christmas like that again, and he felt more homesick than ever. He felt the back of his eyes burning and didn't bother to stop the salty droplets from trickling down his face.

Richie heard the door open and shut behind him, and quickly tried to blink back the tears and compose himself. But there was no fooling Jack. He crossed the room and leaned against the wall facing Richie. Richie turned away, embarrassed that Jack had caught him in this moment of weakness.

"What's wrong?" Jack asked. The slight slur in his voice suggested that he and the wine bottle in his hand were already good friends. Richie sniffed and shrugged his shoulders.

"It's Christmas. I'm spending it in a motel room with a broken TV. My family is I don't even know how many thousands of miles away. You know what, don't worry about it."

"Too late. I am worried about it," Jack said in protest. "Missing your family is nothing to be ashamed of, if that's what you're thinking."

Richie had nothing to say, so he remained still and silent, but allowed himself to look at Jack out of the corner of his eye. Jack too was staring listlessly out the window, and for the first time Richie stopped to consider that Jack might miss his family as well. Jack didn't talk about his family much. Not at all, really—just the once, that time on the bank of the Danube. Then he had revealed what might have been his family's darkest secret. At no time, however, had he spoken of anything good that happened when he was with his family. Richie didn't talk about it, either. He knew that he didn't talk about his family because it hurt too much to voice aloud those things that he wished most to have back. Now Richie wondered if Jack felt the same way. Slowly, as his tears began to dry, Richie turned his head back to face Jack. Jack looked up once, quickly, meeting Richie's eyes for a fleeting moment, then casting them down and through the panes of glass once more. Richie didn't know how long they stood there, mute and immobile, before Jack worked up the courage to speak.

"We never celebrated Christmas," he murmured listlessly. "We weren't religious. But on the Winter Solstice, we had this tradition of gathering after dinner and extinguishing all the lights in the house except one candle in the center of the room that we would encircle. I don't think my mother ever showed, but the rest of us would tell stories and play games late into the night. The goal was to stay up until sunrise, but the little ones couldn't make it that long, so my father and I would put them to bed and then just sit together, talking. I don't even know why we did all that. We only got the chance a few times. I would give anything to be back there again."

Jack took a long draught from his bottle and then began drawing with his finger in the condensation on the window. He drew a snowflake, signed his name, put a zigzag border around the inside of one pane. Richie watched every movement, unable to formulate the words to respond. He watched Jack doodle, the gears of his mind turning sluggishly, until the urge to give a little of himself in return became too much to resist.

"My father insisted on cutting our own Christmas tree whenever we could afford one," Richie started, the memories so potent he could almost see them in front of him, dancing across the frosted window glass. "My father and brothers and I would drive a couple hours north to this man-made pine forest. I always got to pick the tree, because I was the baby. Then Father and my brothers would saw it down while I ran around and heckled them endlessly about taking so long. Mother was always afraid I'd get hurt, and wouldn't let me help cut the tree down until I was sixteen and my oldest brother had left home." Richie smiled weakly thinking about it.

"We're a pathetic little bunch here, aren't we? Every one of us away from our families." Jack sighed and shook his head. "I haven't seen mine in almost a century. Dracula seems to have lost most of his, and who knows if he'll ever see his son again." Jack fell silent, staring contemplatively out the window. Richie followed his gaze, watching the thin crescent of moon rise above the horizon.

"Where were you, anyway?" Richie asked. "You've been gone for hours. It couldn't have taken you that long to find a liquor store."

Jack snorted, a sound like a laugh's estranged, humorless cousin.

"I was trying to get you a Christmas present," Jack said after a while. "Or a holiday present. Whatever. You remember Dracula saying that Clara Hawthorne would have some sort of sleeping potion that we could get for you? Well, wouldn't you know she doesn't label anything? I've been looking for one ever since, but not a one of them is the least bit safe. So, Merry Christmas, I'm a failure. Does the thought count?"

"Yes, the thought does count," Richie managed to say, touched that Jack had gone to that much effort for his benefit. It had been weeks since they had examined Clara Hawthorne's house, and Richie had already forgotten about Dracula's rumored sleeping concoction. Not that he'd been sleeping any better—he was still plagued by the same vision, night after night—but he'd just given up the potion as a lost cause and put it out of his mind. Jack had not only remembered but kept searching. Richie admired his persistence. If only his efforts had paid off.

"When you say they weren't safe, what do you mean? I'm just curious," Richie asked, wondering if there was some way around this roadblock.

"Risk of addiction, coma, death in your sleep," Jack said, rattling off hazards, the bitter rasp of frustration in his voice. "And when I told sellers what the nature of your problem was, most immediately backpedaled. They said a potion wouldn't get rid of the nightmares. It would just keep you asleep while you kept dreaming. Apparently that would make you crazy. Trust me, you don't want that."

"Oh." Richie tried to imagine being unable to wake from his nightmares and shuddered. He had experienced the same vision for months now and still woke up absolutely terrified every time. He couldn't fathom being any more scared than that, but he was quite certain that he wouldn't be able to handle it, were it possible.

"That's the end of it, I guess," Richie said. "But thanks for trying."

"I just feel so useless," Jack said. A low growl sounded in the back of his throat. His hand, still resting on the frosted glass, clenched, producing small scratches on the window with a quiet shriek of protest from the abused surface.

"You're not useless," Richie replied in protest.

Jack gave him a doubtful sidelong glance.

To prove his point, Richie held up his hand, palm up. Almost instantaneously, a flame erupted on top of his skin. It was about two inches high and burned so hot that the center of it was blue-white. Jack's eyebrows rose.

"If you hadn't taught me, I would never have known I could do this," Richie said. "And if I hadn't met you, I wouldn't be on track to finding a cure. I wouldn't even be alive. You might be the most important thing that's ever happened to me." Richie hadn't intended to delve so deep, but now that it was out there he realized that he wasn't embarrassed he'd said it. He met Jack's astounded gaze.

"You really think so?" Jack asked.

Richie started to answer, but then Dracula burst into the room with his customary untimeliness.

"Gentlemen, we have a problem," he declared breathlessly. His overcoat was torn to shreds and his customarily perfect hair was in frazzled disarray.

"What happened to you?" Richie asked.

"We've been found again," Dracula answered. "Our friends the vampire hunters are a mere matter of minutes from reaching us and we haven't a second to spare."

Richie glanced around nervously. He knew this only made them appear even more suspicious, but he couldn't help it. There was nowhere around to rent a vehicle, so they were forced to walk, a mode of transport Richie had hoped he'd left behind in Europe. Normally they would have waited for a passing crowd to meld into, but Dracula had insisted on leaving immediately and there were no bustling streets in a small town at one o'clock, on the night before Christmas. Just like the poem says, "Not a creature was stirring," except for three painfully obvious men strolling down the sidewalk with suitcases. Therefore, Richie reserved the right to be jumpy.

"Where are we going?" Richie asked.

The total silence was eerie, and it was starting to creep him out. He had to say something.

"There's a house for sale that I spotted while I was out," Dracula told him. "I borrowed the realtor's key when she came by, in the interest of having a back-up plan. We need somewhere to reside for the night. These hunters still believe that I am strictly nocturnal, which means that they have taken up that same lifestyle. Tomorrow morning we need to move on. Where to, I am not entirely certain. I hadn't thought that far ahead yet. I'm afraid my superb organizational skills lose their potency when I'm profoundly stressed."

"We'll think of something," Jack said. "Or not, and we'll just wing it." The shock of their rush to leave had sobered him up, but his uncharacteristically cheerful optimism suggested that he was still a little under the influence.

"That's not the way I operate," Dracula said in protest. "I always have a plan."

"Forgive me for saying, but I think the time for planning is long past. Our situation is too unpredictable. You may have to try doing things my way," Jack replied.

"Maybe," Dracula said. "But not if I can help it. Your way frightens me."

Jack didn't respond, and for the better part of two blocks, no one spoke at all. As the moon proceeded on its downward arc, the night reached the point of deepest darkness, where even with superhuman night vision every shadow could hide anything.

"My God, what is wrong with these people?" Jack asked. "Oh, sorry, Richie. Didn't mean to give you a heart attack."

Jack reached to pull Richie up from the ground, where he had collapsed in sheer terror. Richie took the hand gratefully, mumbling curses at himself and his raw nerves. Between the nightmares while he slept and the vampire hunters while he was awake, he couldn't keep calm.

"But what I was saying," Jack said, continuing, "why are these hunters so damned determined to kill you? You said you haven't left your home turf in years. It's not like you're a public menace. Why can't they just leave us alone?"

"I don't know," Dracula said. "Maybe they think I've killed too many people to live, or they're out for revenge because I ate some relative of theirs. Maybe they're just sick of bad Christopher Lee sequels. Who knows?" He shrugged, an angry and disgusted toss of the shoulders. "Sometimes I wonder if they're just in it for the challenge. Five thousand years and no one has bested me yet. Everyone wants to be the first, the only man in the world who can honestly say 'I killed Dracula.' Never live past a thousand, boys. It gets to be more hassle than it's worth."

Richie couldn't imagine living to be one thousand years old. At the moment, he could hardly imagine living through the night. He thought he heard the crunch of a footstep behind him. Dracula looked over his shoulder—he'd heard it too. Richie opened his mouth to taste the air, like Jack had told him, but he didn't know what the scent of a vampire hunter would be. He might have caught a whiff of garlic, but the scent quickly disappeared into the background smells of the evening. Otherwise, there wasn't a trace of anyone following them. Jack volunteered to take up the rear, just in case.

Richie felt immeasurably safer when they reached the house Dracula had chosen for them. Without having to communicate a word, the three fugitives split off in different directions to lock every point of entry they could find. Richie found one window with the lock broken beyond repair, and in a moment of inspiration called his fire into his fingers and melted the vinyl window frame into the wall. The task completed to his satisfaction, Richie wandered back into the front room. Jack and Dracula were positioning the refrigerator against the front door, and with that the fortification was complete. They chose a room in the center of the first floor to sleep in. Jack elected to keep watch until dawn, which was not long distant, and bid his comrades do their best to sleep.

Richie must have dozed despite his frayed nerves, because the sparkling, mocking laughter of shattered glass woke him. In an instant he was wide awake. Dracula was already on his feet and Jack was halfway to the staircase to confront the intruder.

"Too late to run," Dracula said. "We're going to have to fight our way out."

Richie gulped. Jack had been preparing him for this, but he didn't feel ready. He clenched his hands—proper fists this time—as fear and fire flooded his arteries. The sound of Jack's furious yowl erupted upstairs. Dracula rushed to his aid while Richie followed haltingly. As Dracula began to ascend the stairs, he was met head-on by a machete-wielding young woman with more tattoos than skin. Not arresting his momentum for a moment, Dracula slashed the nails of one hand across her soft, beating throat. A few droplets of her blood sliced through the air and collided with Richie's face as her dying body plummeted down the stairs. But Richie didn't have time to think about that.

In another heartbeat, six hunters, dressed in every tradition from Van Helsing to Buffy, swarmed Dracula and a seventh slipped past with a stake aimed at Richie's chest. Something in Richie's brain clicked, and instincts he didn't even know he had roared to life. One hand snatched out to grasp the wooden missile. There was a crunch under his fingers—wood or bone?—as his fist closed tightly over his enemy's weapon and, in a gesture that would have been out of the question to his logical mind, he pulled the hunter closer. The hunter planted an arm against Richie's chest, trying to break free from a fight he now realized he never should have started. Half-bidden, heat boiled from Richie's skin, searing the adversary wherever they touched. Before his writhing enemy could squirm free, Richie snapped his jaws closed on the hunter's throat. He twisted his head, as Jack had taught him, to assure the kill shot wouldn't fail. Warm, thick liquid spilled over his body and filled his mouth. The sickening, coppery tang broke adrenaline's hold. He swallowed once, reflexively, before the reality sank in. Richie dropped the man's corpse in horror, unable to believe he had done this with his own hands. He was scared again, too—the animal within had died back. His instincts had vanished and left a yawning cavern of fear behind. Another vampire hunter had made his way down the stairs. He paused, observing in mute shock what had become of his comrade, and in that moment of inaction, Richie fled.

Richie crouched in the back corner of the coat closet, panting raggedly. Outside, he could still hear Jack and Dracula tussling with more than a dozen hunters, and he knew that he should be there with them. But he couldn't go back out there.

Something collided against the closet door with a resounding thud, making Richie flinch and his breathing come even faster. After a moment, whatever it was slithered down to the floor. The door to the closet flew open and one of the hunters appeared in its place. She reached in as though to grab at Richie, but Jack arrived in the nick of time, swiping at her face and leaving deep furrows in the wake of his fingernails. She screamed and vanished into thin air. Richie blinked, uncomprehending. He noticed belatedly that the sounds of fighting had ceased. Cautiously, he crawled forwards into what was left of the front room.

"It's over," Jack said, reaching down to help him up. Richie took Jack's hand gratefully, holding on for an extra second until he was sure his legs would hold. He looked around to take stock of the scene. The main room and kitchen had been turned into a battlefield. The furniture and stair rail had been demolished, the splinters scattered about the room. The prettily arranged artistic baubles meant to attract potential buyers were no more. Amongst the debris lay the two causalities of the battle on the stairs. Rendered harmless by death, they appeared as they really were: a girl scarcely old enough to be out of high school, her Gothic clothing congruent with her obsession, and an older man with thin, frail limbs. Richie wiped the blood off his lips with the back of his arm and tried to look at anything but the dead man's glassy eyes.

"Wait...where's Dracula?" Richie asked, his wandering eyes suddenly noticing the one thing that was missing.

"I don't know," Jack admitted. "We were fighting together, and then he was driven towards the back of the house, and the next thing I knew the hunters were gone and so was he." Jack's voice fractured at the end of his sentence.

"Dracula's *dead?*"

"No, there's no body. I guess they must have taken him."

"I don't understand. Why wouldn't they just kill him?" Richie asked, staring at the bottom of his empty shot glass as though he would find the answer there. In the periphery of his vision, he saw Jack shrug his shoulders and then take another swig straight from the bottle. The wine had run out long ago, so they'd gone elsewhere to lick their wounds and drown their guilt.

"They probably want to torture him first," Jack said wearily. "Those Dracula-hunting fanatics are mean sons-of-bitches." With that, he took a longer draught from the bottle and slumped down in his chair, eyes fixed on the floor. Richie knew how he felt. After everything

Dracula had done for them, they had let him down in the worst way. They had put up a good fight, sure—perhaps a better fight than Richie would ever be able to forgive himself for—but the end result was the same. Richie wanted nothing more than to follow Jack's example and drink himself into oblivion, but Richie knew he had to keep a clear head, at least mostly. He was trying his best to think of something they could do to amend their mistake. Nothing was coming to mind.

A man sitting at the bar dismounted his stool and crossed over to Richie and Jack's table. Richie didn't pay him much attention until his shadow fell over the tabletop. Richie tensed and looked up at this stranger who had gotten too close for comfort. The man's appearance was striking. He was easily the tallest person Richie had ever seen, and the thinnest. His long, spindly bones showed through translucently pale skin.

"Excuse me, I couldn't help but overhear—no, that's not true. I was eavesdropping. You say Count Dracula has been kidnapped? Perhaps I may be of service," the stranger said, speaking as though it were a perfectly natural topic of conversation.

Richie studied the bizarre man, trying to decide if he was insane or just very drunk. He sure didn't seem drunk.

"I'm serious," the stranger said, insisting. He pulled over a chair from a neighboring table and sat down with Jack and Richie. "You could say I'm a friend of the family. I'd noticed a stir over the count amongst the vampire hunting community. I had hoped to track him down before they did, but it sounds like I've arrived too late. What happened to him, and how do you know?"

His voice carried a whiff of vodka, but his eyes were sharp and intelligent. Richie and Jack exchanged an unsure glance. Was this guy for real? Richie wondered if he wasn't just a rival vampire hunter with the same agenda as the rest. But then, if he could lead them to Dracula, how much did his intentions really matter? Richie and Jack certainly didn't have any better ideas.

"We were traveling with him," Richie said, "and we were ambushed by vampire hunters. They'd been after us for a while. The two of us got separated from Vlad, and they took him." He spoke slowly to make sure he didn't let too many details slip out.

"Do you know *where* they took him?"

"No, we don't. We didn't see it," Richie told him. The stranger leaned his chair back onto two precarious legs, looking thoughtful.

"These hunters, what kind of weapons did they have?" he asked.

Richie looked to Jack, who had been in the fight long enough to know the answer.

"Knives, wooden stakes, I think I saw one guy with a crucifix," Jack said.

"Traditionalists, then," the stranger said in conclusion. "That means they'll be attracted to churches, where they feel safest and most in control. Abandoned churches are best. Less chance of an inconvenient discovery. And if they have taken the count to torture him to death, as you have suggested, then they would have a greater arsenal there. Not all vampires are wounded by holy objects, but the lore says that the count is. So that's where my search will begin. You two can come, if you're up to the task." He glanced doubtfully at Jack, who was evidently too drunk to catch the implication.

"Of course we're up to it!" Jack answered. He glanced at Richie. "We are, right?"

"Yes, we're coming," Richie said, firm in his resolution. Once again Richie found himself making an ill-advised alliance in a bar. It felt almost as if it were happening in a dream...no, Richie thought, if it were a dream of his, it wouldn't feel so unreal.

"Suit yourselves," the stranger said. "If we're going to be working together, then I should introduce myself. My name is Thomas. Thomas Drake."

Kell carefully applied her homemade herbal ointment to the scratches, wincing at the sting. What stung even more, however, was her frustration at having been *so close*. She'd had that boy cornered, arm's length from her, and failed to capture him. *And* she nearly lost an eye in the process. How humiliating. Her only consolation was that her hunters had succeeded. They hadn't been happy that she wanted them to take Dracula alive, but with the guarantee that they would be permitted to torment him however they chose, they complied. Now it was only a matter of waiting. Kell was fairly certain that Dracula's traveling companions would come to his rescue. Then she would have what *she* really wanted. Of course there was always a chance that she was wrong, but at least they wouldn't be able to outdistance her so well without the money for sophisticated transportation. Kell knew she should report this plan to Jasmine, but she was too ashamed to admit her failure. Finally, she gathered her courage and sent Jasmine a text from her burner phone, unable to bear the thought of engaging their direct mental link:

> Hunters have Dracula. The other two will come for him. Full report to be sent soon. ~K

Kell stowed the phone in her pocket and leaned back in her chair to look out the door. In the adjacent room, Count Dracula was chained—hanging from the wall hand and foot. The chains shimmered with their magical, reinforcing sheen. Two of the hunters were busy gleefully torturing their age-old enemy with knives, crucifixes, rusty nails, every device they could think of. Their only disappointment was that Dracula took it with dignity, never screaming and never begging. Kell was relieved. She had had enough of torture. But desperate times called for desperate measures. She picked a book off of the nearby shelf to read while she waited. It happened to be one of those Christian bibles, something that Kell had long been curious about, even if Christians were not often friends to her people. She settled down to read, doing her best to block out the unpleasant sounds of abuse and mocking voices coming from the other room.

Richie couldn't help but think that the noble Count Dracula deserved a much better rescue squad. Thomas at least seemed to be fairly capable. Richie, however, had already proven how unreliable he was in battle—murderous maniac one minute, hiding in the closet the next—and whatever merits Jack possessed had largely been drowned in alcohol. They were a pathetic team, yet they were all that Dracula had to hope for. It just didn't seem right.

"Maple Springs Baptist Church," Thomas spoke the introduction grandly, stopping in front of a small brick structure with a steeple. "It's our last candidate, so I hope it's the right one." He drew a sword out from beneath his trench coat and, ignoring Richie's startled expression, proceeded up the church walkway.

It didn't take long upon entering the church to find evidence of foul play. Scattered drops of crimson blood and a thick, milky substance among the countless muddy footprints told the tale. The air was thick with smells, including one that Richie's brain registered as the Count. Thomas led them towards the back of the church, heading down a hallway out of the sanctuary. Richie wasn't sure what trail

Thomas was following, but the farther they went, the stronger the miasma became. Without warning, Thomas halted, holding out an arm to stop his companions. Jack walked right into it. Thomas held a finger to his lips.

"You two are both cotus, right?" he whispered. "Tell me what you smell."

"I smell Dracula for sure," Jack said, opening his jaws to taste the atmosphere. "That and several humans and...something else. A witch, maybe?" He shrugged and glanced down at Richie. Richie shrugged, too. He'd never smelled a witch before as far he knew, so he couldn't tell.

"That's what I thought, too," Thomas agreed. "We're definitely outnumbered and, I think it's safe to say, outmatched. We'll need an intelligent plan."

"I don't think there's much chance of that," Richie said.

"Must I do everything myself?" Thomas asked and sighed. "All right then. Ice cotu, you're our diversion. Can you cause some chaos and lead them away from Dracula?" Jack nodded. "Great. Go for it. Now. Oh, and could you do it in cotu form? That'll cause more of a stir."

"A'ight," Jack answered. Before Richie's eyes, Jack's entire body melted into a viscous silvery substance. It was the same liquid that his tail had formed from the day after Richie met him. The goo which was Jack oozed out from his clothes and pooled on the floor. The garments slid over the slippery surface and off onto the hardwood. The puddle grew wider and thicker, then started to pile on top of itself, crawling upwards into a tower, a melting snowman played in reverse. Then the snowman sprouted four legs, a pair of large, round ears, and the familiar tail. As the detail of the blobby shape began to emerge, the liquid surface split into individual hairs, then solidified and turned a deep, raven black. The air caught in Richie's throat. It was the first time he had seen a cotu in its true form outside the pages of a book. It was a much more magnificent body than the human one, though the facial features, posture, and bleary eyes implied that the man inside was essentially unchanged. The thought fluttered through Richie's mind: *Is that what I really look like?*

Richie was afforded little time for consideration. Thomas gestured down the hallway as soon as the transformation was complete—a matter of at most five minutes—and the Jack-cat galloped off unsteadily in the indicated direction. Richie and Thomas only had to wait a couple minutes to hear Jack's handiwork. A hunter cursed, Jack yowled, and lots of crashing and clanging ensued. Thomas ushered Richie into an empty room along the hallway just in time for a dust cloud filled with hunters and Jack to come charging down the hall. They waited until the mob had passed out of hearing range, and then Thomas stepped silently out of the room, pulling Richie behind him by the shoulder. They crept carefully but hurriedly towards where Thomas said Dracula was. When they reached the end of the hallway, two rooms branched off across from each other.

"I think Dracula's in the one to the right," Thomas breathed, so softly that Richie could barely hear him. "There's someone in the room to the left too. Free your vampire or eliminate his guard—take your pick."

"I can't fight." Never again.

"Okay then. I'll go first. Once I'm in the left room, you go ahead and see what you can do about Dracula. I don't know how secured they have him, so it may take both of us to spring him." With that, Thomas left Richie behind and tiptoed towards the guard tower. As soon as Thomas entered, Richie sprinted into his own assigned room, terrified but also the tiniest bit exhilarated.

For a heartbeat Richie didn't recognize Dracula. His shirt had been removed in order to more effectively injure him. Every visible part of his body was covered with abrasions, slices, and burns, although strangely he did not bleed. This tattered and broken creature hardly resembled the Dracula Richie knew, but then it raised its head and fixed Richie with that familiar regal gaze.

"You two impress me. I was quite certain that I was to die here. I applaud your efforts," Dracula said calmly, with a voice far too clear for someone in so much pain. At that moment, Dracula officially attained godlike status in Richie's mind.

Richie wouldn't have thought there was anything he could do about Dracula's chains, if the vampire with the reputed strength of twenty men couldn't break free. He placed a limp hand upon one chain, looking for a break or other flaw in the iron. He found a few, but none caved when agitated. Then Richie had another idea. It was a crazy, stupid sort of idea, but what the hell, it might work. He wrapped a hand around a section of chain that contained a small crack in one link. Then he clasped the other hand on top, closed his eyes, and dug deep within for all the fire he could muster. He felt a sensation of suction in his stone, as though everything within him was gathering its forces. Then the thrilling warmth flared to life. He worked the fire into his hands and to his astonishment, the metal began to soften under his fingers like melting butter. Within a few minutes every chain was severed, leaving freckles of molten iron cooling on Richie's forelimbs.

Richie couldn't tell exactly what they had done to Dracula, but it must have been terrible, for the count couldn't stand on his own. Richie did his best to support the much larger man on one shoulder and led him into the hallway, where they almost bumped into Thomas.

"He's with us," Richie hastily explained to Dracula. "His name's Thomas." Dracula didn't look entirely convinced, but he didn't have the energy to object.

"There was just one guard in there," Thomas said. "She fought for a little bit, trying to defeat me with magic, before giving up and teleporting somewhere else. I got a good look at her face, though. I'll be sure to kill her if I ever see her again."

"Much appreciated," Dracula murmured.

"Any time. However, first we need to get out of here, which will be a good deal harder than getting in. We've lost the element of surprise, and I highly doubt our thoroughly wasted friend has had much luck with the hunters. Richie, do your best to protect Dracula. And stay behind me."

Richie stuck to his instructions, sending an open flame into his free hand to fend off any hunters who might make it past Thomas. That turned out to be unnecessary. Thomas fought with frightening efficiency, knocking aside a dead or unconscious adversary with nearly every movement. If Richie hadn't been so determined to bring Dracula out in one piece, he doubted he could have withstood the carnage. As it were, he spent much of the time with his eyes closed to the sight of blood, following Thomas by ear.

Thomas's trailer turned out to be a much more effective fortress than Richie could have imagined. The walls were covered with weapons— mostly swords, with a few shotguns—and a rudimentary system of cameras flashed scenes from the perimeter on Thomas's computer monitors. Richie, too physically and emotionally exhausted to do anything else, watched those pictures for any signs of intruders while Thomas patched up Dracula. Jack's clothes had never been recovered in the chaos, so he remained in his feline form. He repeatedly ran his tongue over the pad of a wounded paw as big as a dinner plate and as black as pitch.

"I'm afraid that's the best I can do," Thomas admitted, taping the end of the last bandage around Dracula's arm. "But the broken leg really needs professional attention. Also, I can tell by the smell that the knives they used were laced with werewolf venom, and I don't know how to treat that. I only know one person that can, assuming she still lives in the same place. And assuming I can still find it, which may be somewhat doubtful."

"Come again?" Richie asked, feeling like he'd missed something through his brain fog. He had never used so much fire at once, and he could barely summon the energy to breathe, much less listen critically.

"It's complicated," Thomas said. "The town isn't really part of this world, which makes it mighty hard to find, even if you know where to look. There's a brilliant physician there that I used to know, Dr. Kitch—"

"*Sally* Kitch?" Richie exclaimed, suddenly enlivened. Jack emitted a sharp meow, his already enormous eyes widening.

"Yes," Thomas said, mild shock registering on his face. "I thought she and the count might have met, but how do you know her?"

"It's really quite the story," Dracula said. "It seems half the world is looking for your Doctor Kitch today."

12

Richie buried slender feline fangs into his hand to keep from screaming, until the faces faded. Every single muscle was strained stiff, as though trying to rip away from his cursed bones. Steaming, vinegar blood flowed into his mouth and he jerked his palm free from his jaws. The feel of his tongue bathed in blood drew bile in his throat, and he swallowed harshly, blood and all.

"The dream again?" Dracula asked languidly.

Richie realized his eyes were squeezed shut. He forced them open. Jack was propped up on his elbows in the neighboring sleeping bag with wide, apprehensive eyes locked on Richie. Dracula lay on the only bed in the hotel room, staring vacantly at the ceiling, his eyes glassy and dull from the venom slowly corroding his body. Thomas had apparently been awake all night, examining his North Carolina map at the kitchen table. He gave Richie a cursory glance and then returned to his mulling. It was about the same reaction Richie got when he explained his dreams to Thomas and Dracula in the first place. They seemed mildly interested, perhaps somewhat sympathetic, but not astonished.

"It wasn't the same dream this time," Richie said, gingerly sitting up as he tried to unclench his tendons. "I think it was just a regular nightmare. That monster was there, and Thomas for some reason, and...never mind." Too late. He'd already started, and now Jack looked curious. Richie knew Jack wouldn't think twice about asking what he was supposed to "never mind," so Richie figured he might as well go ahead and say it.

"That hunter," Richie mumbled, his throat tightening as though to prevent the phrase from escaping. The image of those dead eyes, a spark of fear abruptly extinguished, was imprinted on his mind as indelibly as letters carved in stone.

"What hunter?" Jack asked. When Richie, who was busy trying not to vomit, failed to answer, Jack looked back and forth between the other two occupants of the room.

"The one he killed," Thomas said in clarification, finally looking up from his map. Jack continued to stare at him blankly. "He feels guilty."

"Why?"

"I presume it was his first," Dracula said.

"The first kill is almost always the hardest," Thomas reminded Jack. "You remember, don't you? How wrong it felt." Jack thought about it for a moment, eyes going foggy, unfocused, as he recalled the memory. He nodded.

"Yeah, I remember." He turned his gaze back to Richie, but Richie wasn't interested in discussing it. Knowing that everyone else in the room had gone through this once didn't make the way he felt any less painful. Richie wiggled down into his sleeping bag and pulled it over his head to escape Jack's haunted eyes. He felt Jack briefly, hesitantly, touch his shoulder through the fabric, trying in his own awkward way to be of comfort. But Richie's guilt wasn't assuaged in the least, and his dreams the rest of the night were no less troubled.

It had taken many days, but Kell had finally gathered all the ingredients she needed for the spell. This was a delicate and complex procedure: a sort of reverse summoning. If she had managed to get the boy's DNA, it would have been much simpler. She could have just taken him, from anywhere she pleased, and been done with it. But he hadn't left so much as an eyelash at the church. Fortunately, the adult cotu had changed forms and shed his clothes, leaving behind plenty of hair and skin cells to work with. Some retrograde magical engineering allowed her to isolate the distinct cotu DNA markers. After the addition of a few key ingredients, hours of careful tending, and a little spell-weaving, everything was ready.

There would be no more haphazard chasing, no need to send them more detainments. Now Kell could transport straight to them, grab the boy before they knew what was happening, and teleport elsewhere. *Then* she could kill him and complete her mission. Unbidden, the pitiful image of him cowering in a closet surfaced in Kell's brain, but she pushed it back, and began working her art.

The raucous blaring of the alarm clock woke Richie up. He crawled out of his sleeping bag, sluggish and sore from a night of wrestling monsters and morals. Jack and Thomas were already awake and prepared for the day. They stood on opposite sides of the kitchen table, Thomas talking thoughtfully about roads, Jack nodding every once in a while and shifting uncomfortably in the new jeans he had been obliged to get after losing the last pair at the church.

"Morning," Thomas said in greeting, while flicking Richie an unreadable glance. "So as I was saying, if we take the highway here, we should be within range of Brunswick by tonight. Of course, that's if we don't have any more calamities."

"Calamities are the only thing we seem to have plenty of," Dracula said. His voice had grown weak in his illness, but lost none of its acerbity. "I've seen more blocked roads, ice storms, and fallen trees in the past three weeks than in the past century."

"It's quite the coincidence," Thomas said. "I wonder if we're being purposely delayed."

"Who could *make* an ice storm?" Richie asked, the question emerging a bit harsher than he had intended. He never could keep himself in check these days.

"That would be the question, wouldn't it?" Thomas replied calmly, immune to Richie's tone. "I know that Dracula's guard was a creature of magic, given the way she escaped. A great many of her kind working together might be able to pull off weather of that scale. If we had time and money, I could throw together a simple protective charm, but unfortunately we don't have either. On that note, we really must be go—" Thomas stopped short, forehead creasing.

Before Richie could ask why, there was a flash—not a flash of light, but a flash of image, a complete obliteration of everything he was seeing. Not even one heartbeat passed before Richie's vision returned and he found that he was somewhere else altogether. Multicolored motes flitted across Richie's field of view as his brain tried to process the overwhelming flood of information the eyes had sent its way in the past second. On the floor in front of him stood a pair of feet, not Jack's shoeless monstrosities or Thomas's well-worn trainers but a girl's lavender flats. Richie looked up into the face of a young woman. It was a face he recognized, first from the bridge in London and then the fateful closet in West Virginia. He hadn't connected those two events before, but the visage elicited both snippets of memory. The tall, imperious face and wheat-hued ponytail swishing around her hips were uncomfortably familiar. She didn't look entirely like he remembered, however. Five angry red claw marks tore down the side of her face, culminating at the end of a stony mouth.

"Wha—who are you? Where am I?" Richie asked deliriously. It took a moment for him to realize that he should be afraid. Then he was terrified, and quickly scrambled backwards, away from the scarred woman. She didn't respond. She just stared, her dusty brown eyes fixed intently upon him. Richie backed away further and faster until he felt his shoulder blades grind against a wall. The breath rushed in and out of his airway. He did not immediately realize that panic wasn't the only reason his windpipe burned. At first it was a sort of itching, nothing near as concerning as the reappearance of this ominous woman. But then he could feel a vice closing in his throat, as though his own muscles were choking him. He thrashed, hands scrabbling to pull off the strangling force. His nails scraped against his own skin, powerless against this assailant. He turned pleading eyes to the woman before him. She diverted her gaze.

Why? Richie wanted to ask. She was one of the hunters. Maybe this was revenge for killing her friend. I'm sorry, I didn't mean to, he thought, concentrating on the words as though that might form them into sound. His jaws opened wide to scream the silent apologies, and he curled into a tight little knot to contain the agony in his chest.

The flash came again. Arms scooped Richie up under the shoulders and legs. Richie was lifted into the air and swung into something bright that cast blinding colors onto his retinas. The pressure ceased. The light faded. Richie was back in the hotel room, cheap carpet pressing into his side, air once again rushing into his chest. His throat stung with every inhalation and exhalation. Richie flinched at the light touch of Jack's examining fingers on his tender neck.

"What is going on?" Dracula inquired with worry in his feeble voice.

Jack didn't answer. He watched Richie carefully, not concerned with conversation. Eventually, Richie no longer felt like he was dying. His breathing slowed and he shifted into a sitting position.

"A transportation spell," Jack replied. "Fortunately, two can play that game. I opened a portal to retrieve him. Just in time, too. Richie, can you tell us what happened?"

"I, like, flashing, and then crazy woman, she was in London, and then last month…she was choking me, but not with her hands, just by *looking* at me," Richie stammered. To his astonishment, Jack seemed to understand his nonsense.

"The girl on the bridge, in London? The one following us."

"Yeah," Richie said, relieved he didn't have to explain further. Talking hurt.

"That's…weird," Jack muttered.

"Could you clue us in?" Thomas asked.

"Oh, right. Sure. She was tailing us before we got to Romania, and I thought maybe she was looking to enslave Richie for his prophetic powers. Or sell him. Anyways we lost her. And Richie thinks she was in the war party that took Vlad. And I think that's weird. Maybe she's some kind of hired hit-woman thing…but, if she wanted to kill *both* Richie and the Count, why just take the one today?"

"As much as it pains my ego to say this," Dracula said, "perhaps we should consider that setting a troupe of rabid vampire hunters on me was in fact a diversion? After all, I hadn't had serious problems with hunters for quite some time, until you fellows came along. For some unfathomable reason, Richie seems to be the more valuable target."

There was a blanket on the floorboard, which Richie eagerly cocooned in. The heat soothed his fraying nerves. In the front, Thomas's nimble hands hotwired the car. Jack loaded Dracula into the backseat with Richie and slid in beside Thomas as the engine gave a start.

"This is certainly an unexpected turn of events," Dracula was saying. "To think, Richie is who they want to kill, and not me! If it's true, this is *most* demeaning."

"Oh, get over it," Jack said, slamming the car door for emphasis.

"I'm sure I will, in a few centuries," Dracula replied calmly.

"If we don't get you to Brunswick fairly soon, you might not have a few more centuries," Jack reminded him sharply. The count's muscles stiffened, and Richie thought he perceived a flicker of real fear in his eyes.

"That wasn't necessary, Jack," Thomas said and glared. "I know everyone is under a great deal of stress, but if we start taking it out on each other, we'll probably get ourselves killed today. I don't know about you, but that is an ending I would like to avoid."

Jack gave him an impetuous glare in return, but declined to remark. Satisfied that Jack wouldn't cause any more trouble, Thomas shifted into gear, swung the vehicle out into the road, and accelerated.

"Now, it will take us most of the day to get there, even if I ignore speed limits," Thomas said after a while. Already the speedometer read 60 mph, and the last sign had read 35. Fortunately, it was early on a Saturday morning and most of the world was sleeping in. Not a single car had appeared to note how fast they were going. "Once we arrive, I know a witch I can contact. She'll protect Richie from any more magical attacks. In the meantime, we'll just have to hurry and keep an eye out for..." Thomas trailed off, unable to elaborate on what exactly they needed to watch for. Instead he focused his eyes on the road ahead and pressed the gas pedal harder.

Richie watched the world blur by outside the glass, and had a flashback of a simpler time—him and Jack in a freight car, Richie enjoying the wind in his hair and the thrill of the quest. Was that just this past fall? It seemed like ten years had passed. The world wasn't such a kind place anymore. Richie wondered how he'd managed to get himself into this mess. He hadn't asked for the nightmares. They came to him unbidden, and then they came true. First it was the dog, obliterated by a van, the same as he dreamt it. Then that girl in his math class had her finger slammed in the door. The widow down the road, Mrs. Cartwright, hung herself from a rafter in her attic. Every bad thing seen in his sleep had happened for real. One night he dreamed of scrambling for a handhold but failing to grasp anything, then falling from a great height, feeling one leg shatter beneath him as he hit the ground. Richie had tried to tell his family, told them about the dog and the finger, but they dismissed both as coincidences. Several weeks passed without anyone breaking a leg, and Richie had started to imagine they were right. Nothing was going to happen. He became so sure that he didn't think a thing of it when his brother Wesley announced that he would climb onto the roof and fix that pesky leak.

Richie closed his eyes and curled into a fetal position, wishing that the car and the asphalt and the dead hunter would just disappear. He would wake up back home with the dog licking his face and Wesley getting ready for work, whole and free from any wheelchair. Instead, he opened his eyes upon the too-familiar nighttime forest of his dreams, waiting for the monster to deliver his end once again.

13

Jason sat in a lawn chair in the park, watching Vanessa fetch a stick for Scarlet and thinking that this whole shindig was not a good idea. So what if it was his birthday? Did nobody remember what happened the last time they tried to have a party?

Obviously they did remember. Scarlet and Alex were attending as "guests" while the other three girls and several of Scarlet's pack members were scattered throughout the park. Jason could feel the shape of his sack of Hope's Black Dog repellant in his back pocket and took some comfort in that. He had tried to argue that he didn't really need a birthday party. He'd had eleven already. That ought to be enough. But his mother and Alex both insisted that he celebrate. Sally hadn't approved, but she hadn't vetoed the party, either, so here they were. The only stipulation, which hardly needed mentioning, was that everyone had to go home before dark. No children loose in the park after sundown.

"'Sup, J.D.?" Sammy dropped into a chair next to Jason, a soccer ball under one arm. The grin on his face was too sunny to be faked. At least someone was glad to be here. Jason did his best to smile back, but Sammy's cheerfulness didn't rub off on him like it used to.

"Nothing much," Jason answered. "Just, you know, getting older."

"Am I the first one here?"

"As always."

"Yes!" He thrust a victorious fist into the air. "Who else is coming?"

"Tyler, Darby, and two guys from my school that live here, José and Cameron," Jason said, ticking the names off on his fingers.

"Huh. Small crowd."

"Yeah, well, with everything going on around here, I thought I should stick to inviting just a few in-town friends," Jason explained. Plus, I don't really have any out-of-town friends.

"That's okay! We don't need a lot of people. We'll still have a great time!"

"Yeah, I guess. If you say so."

Jason pulled the last of the newspaper wrapping off of the last present and examined the object in his hands. It sort of looked like a birdhouse, but it was much taller than it was wide, and the entry holes were vertical slits that no bird he'd ever heard of would fit through. Flowers, greenery, and insects were painted all over the wooden surface.

"Okay, I feel like I should know what this is," he said, "but I'm drawing a blank." He glanced up at Scarlet, encouraging her to explain.

"It's a butterfly house," Scarlet's voice chirped. "Your mom plants all those flowers around your house, and she told me you liked butterflies, so I thought, 'butterfly house.'" She held out her arm to gesture at the box Jason held.

"He likes butterflies?" José whispered to Cameron, not as quietly as he thought he did. Jason chose to ignore him. What was so unmanly about butterflies? Jason ran his thumb across the lacquered surface, feeling the texture of the design beneath.

"Did you paint this yourself?" he asked, remembering a time when he saw Scarlet painting a canvas in the middle of the Drake's driveway.

"Yep! Do you like it?"

"Um, wow. Yeah, it's gorgeous. Thanks." Rather than put the piece of artwork beside him in the grass with the rest of his presents, Jason set it in his lap so it wouldn't get dirty.

"I think Scarlet wins," Alex said, seeing how Jason cradled the butterfly house. He mustn't have been too perturbed, for he continued lazily applying a coat of Midnight Satin nail polish. In the folding chair to his right, however, Sammy appeared a bit wounded that some girl he'd never met had one-upped him in the present department.

"Nobody *wins*," Jason said, correcting Alex and sending him an exasperated look. "You all gave me cool stuff, and I'm glad y'all came. But now it's getting late, so I think it's time to call it a day." There were several groans around the circle of mismatched lawn chairs.

"Hey, Mom and I still have to clean up and get everything packed in the car before dark," Jason said, reminding them while holding his hands up in surrender. Across from him, Darby pulled her phone out of her purse.

"My dad's here anyway," she said, standing up. "Tyler, do you want us to drop you off?"

"Nah, I'm on patrol tonight. I'll stay around and help Jason's mom."

"We can, too," Cameron said, pointing at José, who didn't look thrilled to be volunteered for clean-up duty. "We can walk home from here in ten minutes. We have plenty of time."

Cameron turned his eyes to the sky again. The sun was slowly sinking into the tree line in front of them, leaving streaks of crimson and fuchsia on the wispy clouds. The black silhouettes of branches stretched up and punctured the stellar orange disc in the heavens on its way down.

"Maybe we should have let Mrs. Drake drive us home…" Cameron said, looking at his friend with wide eyes.

"There's no point in calling her now," José replied. "We're almost home."

"What about the, you know, *the thing*?"

"Do you mean huge, black, red-eyed monster people keep talking about?" Jose snorted. "I haven't seen any monsters out here, have you?"

Cameron shook his head.

"They're just stories, Cam. Someone probably just saw a werewolf or someone's big, shaggy dog in the dark and got spooked. Or someone made it all up."

"We don't scare easy," Cameron said, referring to the people who comprised his otherworldly hometown. "You know that. And you saw how worried Mrs. Drake was when we said we would walk."

José was unusually quiet for a moment. "We'll be at your house in two minutes," he said at last.

Cameron couldn't argue with that. By unspoken agreement, the two picked up their pace. The fading daylight lent a reddish hue to the rooftops and cast long, distorted shadows on the concrete. A deep, throaty growl sounded at their backs. Both boys broke into a run.

Billows of smoke poured through a gutter, out a downspout, and onto the sidewalk in front of them. José skidded to a stop. Cameron's reflexes were clumsier and his shoes slicker—he slid into the mass of black like it was home base.

The smoke sucked inward and the creature materialized, swatting Cameron aside with a massive forepaw. Cameron's head cracked against the asphalt of the street and he lay still. The gigantic hound, swirls of vapor still curling off its fur, turned its snarling, salivating jaws on José. It enveloped the child with its cruel spell as he tried to run. Fear locked up his muscles, and the hellhound descended, digging its fangs into a victim too terror-stricken to scream.

An undulating howl, higher in pitch than most, pierced the thick air, causing the monster to raise its head and listen. Someone else was on the hunt tonight. A hunched, two-legged form hurtled over a nearby picket fence and launched itself at the Black Dog. His lupine scent flooded the monster's nostrils as he wrapped his arms around the Black Dog's neck and bit into its shoulder. Vile black ooze from the Black Dog's flesh filled Tyler's mouth, clogging his throat and choking him. The beast took advantage of his distraction. It dropped to the ground and rolled over, pinning Tyler underneath it and crushing him with its bulk. Overwhelmed by pain, the young werewolf stayed down, but his warning howl had not gone unheeded. The Black Dog heard at least four of his kind echoing the alarm. The creature surveyed the carnage around it, and decided that was enough for one night. Live rescuers could deliver the message better than corpses. The monster sublimated into smoke and streamed toward the shelter of the woods.

Jenna awoke to a cell phone emitting the wail of a siren. She fumbled on the nightstand for the device, answering it on the third shriek.

"Brunswick 911, what is your emergency?" she answered, feeling for her glasses with her free hand.

"There's something going on outside!" panted a shrill, desperate voice.

Jenna stuck her glasses on her face and swung out of bed, ready to alert the person most prepared to assist. "Ma'am, what is your location?"

"Two, Songbird Circle. They're just down the street."

"Who are they?" Jenna flicked on the light in the hall and headed for the stairwell. When in doubt, tell Sally.

"I—I'm not sure. I heard howling, and then someone screamed. I'm looking out my front window. Someone's on the ground. I think I see blood!"

"Try to stay calm. I'm sending help right...now." Jenna came face to face with Sally in the hallway at the foot of the stairs. She, too, was on her cell phone, with a look of consternation that mirrored Jenna's.

"Hold on one moment," Jenna said. She put her hand over the receiver. "Fight in the street at Songbird. You?"

"The same, maybe," Sally replied. "Three seriously injured. Two human, one werewolf. I was on the way to get you."

"Well, then, let's go." Jenna put the phone back to her head. "We're coming right now, ma'am. I have to drive, so I can't stay on the line with you, but I will let you know when it's taken care of. Thank you for reporting the incident."

Sally tumbled out of the passenger seat of Brunswick's only ambulance before Jenna had even put on the brakes. Three people weren't going to fit in the back, so one of the werewolves who first came upon the scene had brought his pick-up truck. Hope jumped out of the back of the ambulance when it reached a stop. Jenna put it in park and then followed the other two.

"Rosa, talk to us," Sally yelled, approaching the female werewolf who was in turn walking towards her with an air of authority.

"One of the humans is injured but conscious, may have a concussion," Rosa replied, pointing at a sandy-haired boy sitting on the curb beside one of the other werewolves. One of the alpha's right-hand wolves for over a decade, Rosa was no stranger to violence and no stranger to Sally.

"Jenna." Sally gestured toward the child Rosa indicated. Jenna gave a curt nod and went straight to him, a medical bag on her shoulder.

"The other two are much worse," Rosa said, continuing and leading Sally and Hope to them. "The one on the right is one of ours, Tyler. Lacerations, probably multiple broken bones, possible organ damage. On the left is the second human. Leg looks like it went under a lawnmower, compound fractures. We've been trying to stop the bleeding, as you said, but they aren't doing well. The human, something strange is happening to him. It looks like gangrene, but it's spread since we got here."

"I'll take strange, you take Tyler," Sally said. "Rosa, there are a couple of stretchers in the ambulance. Get them, and assign a couple of your people to keep any curious onlookers from getting in our way." Hope and Rosa did as they were told without comment, and Sally knelt beside a werewolf who was using her shirt to put pressure on the wounds on the human victim's left leg, but as Rosa had said, there wasn't much left to work with. Splinters of bone emerged from a wound pattern that suggested a single, powerful bite from something with jaws the size of a grizzly bear's. Sally slid her satchel onto the ground, her eyes never leaving the patient. Rosa was right. A black rot had set in around the teeth-marks left by his assailant, and as the seconds ticked by the blight was visibly spreading. Already the infection or chemical had eaten away much of the lower thigh and knee. Sally had never seen anything like it. She weighed the possibility of treating the mystery rot against the likelihood of it spreading beyond the ravaged leg. In a split second, she'd reached her decision. She turned to the werewolf beside her.

"I'm going to amputate this leg," Sally told her, quite matter-of-fact. "Will you be able to help me?" The werewolf thought a moment and nodded. "Good. He's unconscious, but I'm going to dose him with morphine just in case. I don't know what the hell has infected that leg, but it's necrotizing too fast. If it travels in the bloodstream, we may already be too late. We'll just have to be as sterile as possible, remove the rotting tissue, and hope for the best."

Sally rarely saw patients at the manor, spending most of her time consulting or doing scholarly work, but as the night's moon rise spilled its cold light through the tiny windows near the basement ceiling, the lowest floor of the Manor had become a tiny war hospital. Rosa and the werewolf who volunteered his truck had stayed to help; Sally let the rest go home and awoke the two remaining denizens of the Kitch estate to serve in their place.

Alex had been given the task of calling the parents of the three children and giving them the news. Cameron's family had been easy. Alex was able to tell them that there was every reason to believe their son would recover, though the psychological trauma was sure to linger. The reports he gave to José and Tyler's families were not so reassuring.

"Your son is in surgery right now," Alex explained to Tyler's father, "so you can't see him now, but you are welcome to come and sit in our waiting room until he's out. Do you know the address? All right, sir, the basement door will be unlocked. Someone can show you in when you arrive. You're welcome. Take care." Alex hung up and let the air out of his lungs slowly, calming himself down before making the worst call of the night. The scents of blood, anxiety, and fear carried into the tiny office space from the hallway, but the air carried less sound through the door than it had an hour ago. With one patient in an operating room with Hope and Sally, and only one left under observation, the scurrying and hollering had abated. Alex steeled himself and tapped the phone number onto the screen.

"Hello? Ms. Gutierrez? This is Alex at the Kitch Manor Emergency Clinic. It's about your son, José. Something attacked him on his way home tonight. No, ma'am. I'm so sorry to have to tell you this. He, um...he didn't make it."

Dark clouds obscured the sun and a light drizzle fell onto the funerary party. Jason experienced a moment of déjà vu as he watched his friend and classmate's casket lowered into the ground. Beside him, Cameron wept with one hand wrapped around his torso to prevent the wracking sobs from popping any of his stitches. Jason couldn't help wishing that it was him in that ornate wooden box. In a cruel twist of fate, José's grave was placed a stone's throw from Shauna's.

Jason was staring so intently into the six-foot hole, dug not quite long enough for an adult, that he didn't realize something was happening until he heard Cameron gasp. Jason looked up to see a swirl of black smoke materializing above José's headstone. Even before the shape was complete, Jason knew what it would be.

The Black Dog, huge and monstrous, was hovering in midair, glaring down on the assembly with its ember eyes. Around it smoke continued to swirl. Jason wanted to run, but felt the sensation of paralysis he had known once before, during the previous attempt on his life. Everyone around him was equally immobile, all forced to look upon the Dog's hideous visage.

"You've seen what I can do," it growled. Its voice was deep and rough, and full of malice. "Many more will die." It passed its gaze over every person present to drive home its point. "Your family, your friends, everyone in this town will rot, unless I get what I want." For a long time it said nothing, but simply allowed its words to sink in.

"What I want," it finally said, "is him!" With a snarl, the Black Dog swung its head to point right at Jason. "If Jason Drake is not delivered to me by midnight tonight, more of your children will die. Have him in the clearing east of this graveyard when the moon hits its peak." The smoke began to spiral inward, the Black Dog's shape dissolving with it, until it was just a pinprick.

Then the monster vanished.

"Obviously we aren't sending him to his death," Jenna said. "The question is: what *are* we going to do? If we don't figure out something pretty quick, the town may make the decision for us." Everyone in the meeting looked around at the others, hoping that someone else would answer. The silence among the five stretched out and still no one said a thing.

"We could send someone else in his place," Hope said at length. "Someone who could hold their own while looking like someone else. I can't do it, though. I've almost perfected a spell to capture the Black Dog. I'd need someone to keep it in one place long enough for me to cast."

"But, won't the Black Dog know the difference?" Scarlet asked. She retracted her head like a turtle, shrinking from the divisive role of Devil's Advocate.

"Probably," Hope said, "but I only need it to be stationary for about a minute."

"Well," Sally said, chewing her tongue, "I think there's an obvious choice here—"

"No, you don't have to," Alex said, interrupting her. "Hope could put a glamour over me, or anyone. Right?"

"I have no doubt that she could," Sally replied, "but what if it knows how to break a glamour? cotus are made to shapeshift. And—correct me if I'm wrong, Hope—I think she would prefer to be able to focus on one thing at a time." Hope nodded with vigor. Alex bit his tongue, knowing that he couldn't change Sally's mind once she'd set it.

"All right." Sally stood from the Drake's sofa, brushing imaginary dust off the black skirt she'd worn for the funeral. "I'll go in the kitchen and tell Pansy and Jason what the plan is. I'll need to borrow some of his clothes. Unwashed, preferably. Soak up his scent a little bit. Alex?"

"I'm on it."

"Good. Jenna, help Hope with whatever she needs. You can take the van back to the manor if you need to. Scarlet, stay here with the Drakes. We will have to do everything right and we only have a couple hours to have all our ducks squarely in a row. Make it happen."

Jenna carefully lit a circle of seven white candles on the stone floor. They were in the basement of the manor, in a room referred to as "The Dungeon," only half in jest. The purpose of the room was a mystery, even to Sally. The floor and walls, done rather artfully in dark granite masonry, outlined a cubical room ten feet on each side. In one wall was the entryway, a simple rectangular hole. Opposite there was a nook cut into the wall with a door of thick, horizontal iron bars—a single prison cell, two suspect rings of metal welded onto the back wall. Jenna had asked Sally once what the rings were for. Sally told her that there was a skeleton chained up there when she moved in with Hope and Alex. Since Jenna was often unsure whether or not Sally was joking, and Alex and Hope could neither confirm nor deny the story, she had generally given this room a wide berth. Now, she was not only in the room, but sitting on the floor within the cell itself. It was an uncomfortable situation, and an unavoidable one.

In the main room, Hope was slowly walking the perimeter, drawing a glowing line of magic along the walls' midline with her finger. There hadn't been time for her to examine every possible way their enemies might have eavesdropped. It was much faster, Hope explained, to apply several shielding spells around a room and only speak sensitive information in there. Of all the rooms in the manner, she had chosen this one for two reasons: the stone walls, since rock readily takes on magic, and the prison cell, in which she planned to capture the Black Dog at a moment's notice.

While Hope applied layers of protection, Jenna cast the circle into which the Black Dog would be teleported and sealed. Jenna didn't really have the touch for magic on a large scale, but a simple circle was within her capabilities. As Jenna lit the final wick, a thin loop of power bound the candles together. The thread wasn't visible like Hope's light magic ringing the walls, but it was there all the same: a cord of simple human energy tangible enough to pluck like a guitar string. Human magic and witch magic manifest very differently. By itself, Jenna's circle wouldn't hold a Golden Retriever. Hope would have to do the rest.

"I'm ready when you are," Jenna called softly. Across the room, Hope nodded and continued making her rounds, muttering a near-constant stream of archaic German incantations. A person could do magic in any language—Jenna preferred English, although she knew a few spells in French. Hope's mentor had taught her in German, so that was the tongue she always used. At last, Hope dropped her hand from the wall. The shimmering magic dissolved, fading from view while leaving the enchantments intact.

"All right. Let's get started!"

Sally made her way into the woods, forcing herself to trudge and drag her feet through the leaf litter even though every fiber of her being screamed at her to be more cautious. She had learned decades ago that shapeshifting was easy, but taking another person's place was nearly impossible. She would only have to keep up the charade for a short interval, true, but she didn't know what might tip the Black Dog off. It wasn't enough to mold herself into his shape and wear his scent. She would have to match his posture, his movements, and possibly his voice. It had been a long time since Sally felt this nervous. She consoled herself that a little anxiety would help. Any predator worth its claws can smell fear, and a teenager on his way to the gallows ought to reek of it. The more fearful she smelled, the better she would serve as a stand-in.

She stepped into the appointed clearing and checked Jason's watch. Seventeen minutes until midnight. Fashionably early. She sent a message to the minds of her cohorts: *I'm here. No Black Dog yet.* Sally jammed her hands into the pockets of Jason's jeans and studied her surroundings. Her adversary had chosen the location well. The vegetation was thick all around the oblong clearing, obstructing visibility and possibly thwarting any attempt to escape. It was a good place for an ambush, especially for a predator who could travel as a vapor, unhindered by the dense foliage.

Right on cue, dark smoke wafted in on the breeze. Sally had entered the clearing at one end of the long axis, the point farthest downwind. The hellhound was coming in at the other, putting a good three yards between them. As its legs began to take shape beneath the red embers of its eyes, it began to speak.

"Are you alone?" Its voice echoed from every particle of the swirling cloud. It lacked the booming quality of its voice in the cemetery, but Sally found this amorphous timbre more intimidating.

"I think so," Sally replied, allowing the shape of Jason's throat to help her fake his speech. *'He's here, Hope! Please tell me you're ready.'*

'Casting it right now,' Hope said.

"Have you made your peace?" the fiend rumbled, beginning to more closely resemble its solid, canine form. Sally thought it was an odd question, but the longer they stalled, the more likely she was to make it out of this alive.

"I have," Sally replied, planting her gaze at a point just beneath the Black Dog's face. "You promise not to hurt anyone else after I'm gone?" The creature, now fully materialized, opened its jaws to respond, when the wind changed. A gust whooshed from behind Sally's back, carrying her scent right into her enemy's nostrils.

The Black Dog snuffled, probably confused by the strange amalgamation of smells sent its way. Its eyes momentarily narrowed, then widened, as it realized what trick had been employed against it. It crouched, growling in fury. It launched itself into a gravity-defying leap across the clearing, but Sally wasn't about to wait. She whirled and ran back into the trees, tearing off branches and trampling ferns to break free of the wall around the clearing. Jason's disproportionate body was unwieldy, but under the skin thrummed Sally's own muscles, and her brother always said she was built for speed.

She was not, however, built for running straight through trees like the ghostly beast pursuing her. Sally could hear the Black Dog racing gaining on her even though its massive strides were much slower than hers. She could see the glimmer of the ring of bug-zapper lanterns she'd placed outside the forest to guide her home. If she could get that far, the Black Dog would be unable to follow into the circle of bright light, she hoped. The Black Dog's teeth snapped inches from the back of her neck. She couldn't reach the tree line before it would be on her. In a last desperate move, she shifted her momentum into a spin and came to a halt in her pursuers path. The Black Dog, not expecting the chase to end this way, collided with her, slamming her into the ground on her back. She raised a hand to block the inevitable lunge for her throat. As the monster's mouth closed on three of her fingers and jerked her arm out of its way, Sally reached inside into her stone and unleashed all the electricity her body could muster.

Miniature bolts of lightning exploded from the surface of her skin. Intense heat, light, and raging electrons sizzled into the earth, air, and Black Dog with all the force that comes from mortal fear. With a startled choking sound, the Black Dog's particles burst apart, sparks zipping between them. Sally scrambled to her feet, acrid blood dripping from her wounded hand, and made a final sprint for the glow at the end of the woods.

Jason checked the time on his phone. Nine minutes after midnight. He drummed on the kitchen table with his fingernails. He knew he should be asleep. Tomorrow would be a school day. But he couldn't rest until he knew this was over, and nobody else was going to die on his account. He'd seen the earth poured over a stranger and a friend. Most of Cameron's injuries were under his shirt or in his mind, but enough of the damage was plain to see. Jason hadn't seen Tyler since the attack. He couldn't bear to. All he knew from Scarlet was that Tyler would probably never walk again, and that alone was more than Jason's conscience could take. This had to end tonight.

"When do you think we'll hear from her?" Jason asked, raising his eyes to Scarlet's. She had to stop chewing her fingernail to speak.

"I guess it depends on how long it takes for Hope's spell," she replied. Every muscle in her body was drawn tight like piano wire. "The last thing I heard was Sally giving us the message that the Black Dog was there."

"How long ago was that?" Pansy was cutting biscuits out of dough next to the oven. In times of crisis, she couldn't stand by and do nothing. If there was nothing for her to do, she made food.

"About twenty minutes—" Scarlet was interrupted by the sound of the front door being flung open. She jumped to her feet, knocking her chair onto the ground in her haste.

"Just me!" Sally, still wearing Jason's clothes and his body, dashed into the kitchen so fast she barely touched the ground. "Didn't work. Need a Plan B. Start thinking." She stopped when she smashed into the counter by the back door. She frantically surveyed the counter back and forth before she snatched a wad of paper towels off the roll and a heavy-duty steak knife from the knife block.

"I was close, but the wind changed, and it pegged me," she said, panting and folding up the paper towels into a little paper pad on the counter. She set her left hand on it, the three fingers from pinky to middle pressed together, and took the knife in her right hand. Jason could see blood from her hand seeping into the paper towels.

"Okay," Scarlet said, watching Sally with a pained expression, "but what are you—?" Before Scarlet could finish, Sally set the tip-ward third of the knife beside her pinky and in one swift motion brought it down just above the third knuckle of the three wounded fingers.

Pansy screamed a word Jason had never heard her say in his presence before. Scarlet turned Easter-bunny white and grabbed the edge of the table to keep herself upright. Jason, already nauseated from anxiety, immediately vomited onto the vinyl tiles. Only Sally kept her composure, even as she murmured curses to herself and bled all over the kitchen counter. With jets of crimson spurting from the stumps of her fingers, she grabbed the sunflower-print hand towel hanging on the oven door and wrapped it around her left hand. Less rushed now, she carefully set the knife in the sink, scooped up the paper towels with fingers, and dumped them in the trash can.

"Um, sorry," she mumbled, looking at the mess she'd left on the floor and counter. "It got my hand in its mouth. I had to...to remove the contaminated tissue. I'll clean this up, if you've got some bleach I could use...and I'll buy you a new towel. Where's Alex?"

"B—bathroom," Pansy stammered, staring at Sally's sunflower-wrapped hand. "I'll go get the bleach." She hurried down the hall to the laundry room.

"And maybe some aspirin?" Sally called after her. "That...would be nice...Scarlet, can you call Hope or Jenna or somebody and tell them what happened? I'm, uh, probably not the best person to do the talking right now."

"Yeah, of course. I just have to find my cell phone." Scarlet took off for the living room, leaving Sally and Jason alone with each other and the puddles of bodily fluids. Sally leaned her back against the amputation counter, breathing heavily. Jason could only imagine what kind of pain she was in and gagged again just thinking about it.

"I'm sorry you had to be here for that," Sally said, face tilted toward her feet. "Your mom and I can probably take care of the...floor... problem, if you want to go someone, I mean, some*where* else." Jason nodded and shakily stood up from his seat. There was, in fact, somewhere else he needed to be.

Jack stared out the window of their latest rental car, watching trees and patches of wildflowers blur past. Richie's head lay on Jack's shoulder, and Jack's hand rested on Richie's head. Richie mewled, wriggling closer to Jack's side. Jack glanced down at him. He seemed to be asleep—he certainly had never been this snuggly while awake—but his eyes weren't quite closed. Underneath his eyelids, the young cotu's nictitating membranes came almost all the way across his dark brown irises. Jack wasn't sure what that meant, but he thought it didn't look good.

"We're almost there," Thomas said from behind the wheel. "I'm just looking for the turn-off."

Jack looked down the road, trying to see where this turn-off was supposed to be. He was still confused as to where they were going. After getting into North Carolina, they had started going toward the place where the Kitch Manor was built. Jack tried telling Thomas that the manor wasn't there anymore, but Thomas just said that it had "moved." Not it had *been* moved. "It moved," he said. Jack had heard of houses and even lighthouses being moved to new locations, but he'd never heard of a mansion moving itself. Then again, stranger things had probably happened.

Jack squinted. There was something funny about that big tree on the right side of the road. It looked...shimmery. Like a mirage, sort of, but a single mirage-y tree in the middle of a slew of other perfectly unexceptional trees. Jack started to say something about it, but Thomas had already noticed.

"Found it," Thomas announced with a tone of triumph and swung the rental car into a ninety-degree turn into the wavering tree. Jack hissed and recoiled into the leather seat at his back, but there was no collision. The atmosphere rippled as the front bumper went through the illusory trunk, and suddenly they were back on the road, passing through an opening in a low stone wall. There was no sign announcing their entry into the mysterious town of Brunswick, but there was no question that they had.

"You can feel it, can't you?" Thomas said, his eyes meeting Jack's in the rearview mirror.

"I can," Jack replied, putting his palm to the window so he could better feel the hum. "It, like, *buzzes*." The energy flowed through him, making his nerve endings tingle. Outside the car, a quaint little downtown greeted them. Everything from pastries to jars of eyes could be seen in the shop windows. It was getting late into the night, but many of the stores still had their lights on, and a few locals were meandering about. And what a mix of locals they were. Most were human, at least in appearance, but Jack also spotted an incubus, a wood nymph, and a couple of those lizard people from the deserts out west.

"This is amazing," he said, marveling. "And the manor is here?"

"Last time I checked," Thomas answered. "The town swallowed up the whole estate years before I was born."

"*Swallowed*?"

"That's how it was explained to me. Brunswick is a little universe of its own. Sometimes it moves, and sometimes it annexes things next to it when it moves back. I don't totally understand it myself. There's a lot about this town that you have to take on faith."

"As long as we find my, um, I mean Dr. Kitch, I guess I don't really care," Jack said.

"Well, we should be at her door before you know it, God willing."

"God's never done much for me," Dracula mumbled in the passenger seat, barely audible, "but there's always a first time."

Beside Jack, Richie stirred, blinking open groggy eyes.

"Oh, hey, you're awake." Jack withdrew his arm from behind Richie's shoulder. "Did you hear Thomas? We're almost there. We did it." Richie grunted and leaned forward to see out the front windshield. Tense muscles quivered under the skin of his arms, even though his manner seemed half-asleep.

"You okay?" Jack reached to smooth Richie's hair, but Richie batted his hand aside.

"I'm fine," he said, watching the road intently. Thomas came to a fork and flipped on the left turn signal. "No," Richie corrected, shaking his head. "Go the other way."

"What? Why?" Thomas stopped in the middle of the road and turned in his seat to see Richie.

"The thing," Richie said, "it's happening. Now." Thomas's face remained perplexed. Richie turned to Jack for support. "You know, the...thing. The forest, claws, red eyes, the thing. It's happening, it's about to happen, *right now*." The wheels spun in Jack's brain as he tried to understand Richie's sleep-deprived gibberish.

"Wait, do you mean the thing you keep dreaming about?" Jack guessed.

Richie nodded. His eyes were getting ever clearer and more pan-icked.

"I can feel it. Jack, I can see it." Richie gestured to the road splitting from the right side of the fork. "He's just a kid, Jack. We have to do something," he said, begging. Jack looked to Thomas. Thomas turned to Dracula, the one whose need for medical need was direst.

"If I've made it this long, I can make it another hour," Dracula said.

"Ohhh-kay." Thomas switched to a right turn signal. "Just tell me where I'm going."

A twig snagged in his hair. Jason stopped to untangle it, trying to keep his hands steady while he did so. He was so terrified that he worried he would faint before he reached the clearing, and he had to reach the clearing. Images of severed hands and fingers and fresh grave dirt played over and over in his head. It would end tonight. No one else was going to get hurt because of him.

He reached the spot sooner than he thought he would, even though the walk there had felt like a lifetime. He looked up at the heavy shield of moon visible in the sky—it was just rising. Jason took his place in the center of the small meadow. The blood pounding in his ears blocked out most of the forest sounds, but he thought he heard some-thing large passing through the undergrowth behind him. He closed his eyes, knowing this was the end, hoping Alex and his mom would understand. He couldn't possibly be doing them any good alive. He wasn't strong enough. He wasn't the hero they thought he was. Leaves rustled. The fiend was drawing closer, taking its time. The sounds of motion stopped. Jason felt warm breath at the back of his neck and heard snuffling sounds as the Black Dog made sure there would be no more tricks.

"You at last," it rumbled. "Have you made your peace, little one?"

"Yes, sir," Jason answered. He couldn't keep the tremble out of his voice or his muscles. His brain screamed at him to turn. He could al-most hear Scarlet's voice again. '*Never turn your back on an enemy,*' she would say. At last he couldn't stand it. Jason glanced over his shoul-der, just as the monster lunged for the kill.

Richie tore through the woods, ignoring the thorns that ripped through his clothes and skin. Adrenaline flooded every corner of his body. Fire filled his veins. He could pick out every scent in the forest and home in on the tantalizing smell of fear. His eyes picked out every root in his path and every flicker of movement around him. There wasn't a moth that could escape his notice, but his focus was unhampered by the deluge of sensory information. Deep inside, he burned with all the fury of a raging furnace. It didn't matter that his aim was to protect the prey, not to kill it. All his body needed to know is that it was time to hunt.

His eyes caught snippets of gold and white and black and red through the trees. Too far. Have to be faster. Months of exhaustion were a minor speed bump for his predatory instincts. Somewhere behind him, Jack was in pursuit, and farther back still Thomas sat idling in a Chevy with a man in the passenger seat who was watching his afterlife slip away. Have to be faster. One last push propelled Richie into the side of the human prey, and both crashed into a carpet of meadow grass.

The black beast of Richie's nightmares landed heavily on its forepaws, stunned that the twiggy human was no longer where it had just been. It only took the thing a moment to puzzle it out, and then it whirled to face Richie. Richie planted himself firmly between the monster and its victim, silently funneling his fire into his hands. As the hellhound charged, Richie's hands ignited into balls of flame. The inferno singed the beast's nose as it came to a hasty halt. It yelped and took a step back. Richie knew it was looking for a way through. He wasted no time dropping to his knees and spreading the fire to the grass at his feet. He drew a semicircle in front of himself and the boy at his back.

Richie stood, waiting for the monster to make the next move. If it decided to power through the wall of fire, there might not be much he could do to stop it. Now that he could see it in its entirety, he was struck by the sheer size of the creature. And it wasn't retreating. It was standing, staring, calculating. But something else was moving in the forest. The corner of Richie's mouth twitched up. I knew you wouldn't let me down.

Jack darted into the clearing, sized up the situation on the fly, and surprised Richie by curling his entire body around one of the monster's hind legs. As the jaws came for his throat, Jack rolled out of the way, leaving the beast's leg encased in ice—ice so cold it froze the very gases of the air. Ice cold enough to freeze Black Dog vapor. Ice that extended into the ground beneath and froze the leg in place. As Richie watched, half-listening to the panting of the boy behind him, the ice expanded, encroaching on the creature's hip and flank. Richie let the flames on his hands die as the Black Dog struggled in vain to escape. He turned to the hyperventilating boy at his back.

"Hi, my name's Richie. I'm here to save your life. Who are you?"

Hope's hands moved with the deft swiftness of great practice. In her head, she went over the incantation, modifying it as she went along. If they couldn't get the Black Dog to stand still for them, she was just going to have to be a little more inventive. The restraints were already in place. It had been a simple matter of amplifying Jenna's circle field. The challenge would be in the conjuring. Hope had no doubt that the Black Dog was stronger than she was. It had taken all she had to simply repel it at the Christmas party. Hope's advantage was her craftiness, not her raw power. She prayed it would not fail her now. It would have been easier with a familiar to bounce ideas off of, but Hope hadn't had one since Sally's last cat died. She had simply never taken the time to find and train another.

She sprinkled a pinch of powdered herbs onto each candle. The little fires grew taller and darkened to a deep maroon hue. Hope took a small vial of murky liquid from the floor beside her and poured it in her mouth before she could think about it too much. The potion contained the same herbs used to empower the candles, as well as the extract from the sort of vegetation Alex had been known to consume recreationally. For Hope, there was nothing fun about taking this serum. It would help her to focus and bring her power out of her body, a fairly unpleasant experience on the whole. As she swallowed the bitter potion, she became part of the circle, like another candle.

Hope began reciting the spell she had written that morning. With a single finger, she drew a five-pointed star in the air above the circle. The magic left a burning trail on the retina like a fourth-of-July sparkler. Inside the star, a vague image of a forest shimmered into view. The picture was too dark to see much more than shadows of tree trunks and two dull reddish glowings in one corner. Presumably, the Black Dog was somewhere there. Hope wished she could see more clearly. On the other hand, she didn't want to waste time tuning in, so she settled for repeating the visualizing spell once more. The crimson blobs moved to the center of the star. They narrowed, and Hope had the distinct impression that they were looking right back at her.

Hurrying so her adversary wouldn't have time to employ any countermeasures, Hope held the palm of her right hand to the star and uttered the simple demand—*come*. She felt power in her chest, unfurling into her arm like the frond of a fern. The stem straightened, lengthened, and left Hope entirely, reaching into the image in front of her. She closed her eyes and imagined the frond reaching the Black Dog, coiling around it—the ghost of a perturbed howl drifted to her ears—Hope tightened her hand into a fist, emphatically repeating the incantation she had found in one of Sally's dusty tomes. There was a sound, a sort of sizzle, and Hope felt her magic returning from the forest, the star she had drawn dissolving with the completion of its purpose. She opened her eyes. Inside the magic circle, a cloud of angry black smoke floated menacingly, with two blood-red eyes glaring out at her. In spite of herself, Hope smiled just a little, even as the exhaustion of an intense spell settled into her bones. She had done it.

Richie walked alongside Jason, his normal pace just meeting the blond kid's long-legged but benumbed strides. He claimed to be fine, but Richie hadn't forgotten the nightmare: the pain and the terror. He had been right in the midst of the dream when the fantastically clear hunch blasted through his mind. He had realized when and where the nightmare would come true, mere minutes before it very nearly did. The fact that he had stopped it and saved this guy—"Jason," whoever he was—gave him a warm, flickery feeling, like the fire inside him was doing a happy dance. He could almost swallow the bitter aftertaste of the murdered vampire hunter.

"So your dream led you to me?" Jason asked.

"Aye."

"And that's why you came to see Sally. The dreams."

"You've got it."

"I hope you'll forgive me for saying that I'm glad you found me first." Jason smiled weakly. "If you'd already found a cure, well, you know where I'd be."

Richie returned the smile. "You're welcome. I'm glad I was able to help. I've had a hard couple of years. I was starting to wonder if I was good for anything, erm, good."

"I know the feeling." Jason met Richie's gaze.

"But, I just have to ask," Richie said. "Why were you out there? You were just *waiting* for it. I've felt what you felt. You knew that thing was coming for you, and you weren't looking forward to it."

"I, uh, it's kind of a long story." Jason broke eye contact. "The Black Dog said that—"

"That thing could *talk*?"

"Yeah, and it said that if I gave myself up, it would stop attacking my friends."

"Damn." Richie shook his head. "That's a hell of a decision. I am so sorry. Why you? What'd you do to piss it off?"

Jason got a stricken expression, but before he tried to explain, Jack interrupted the conversation.

"This is it," Jack announced, his voice barely hissing through the filter of emotion.

"Sally's house?" Dracula asked, struggling to lift his head from Jack's shoulder. He had become so weak that Jack had to carry him.

"Yup," Jack said.

Richie felt his jaw loosen. *House* was the understatement of the century. Sally's home looked like a cross between one of those Gothic cathedrals and a medieval castle. It didn't measure up to Dracula's fortress, but it wasn't too far behind. Jack vaulted up the front steps and reached out to ring the doorbell. Richie thought he saw his hand shake a little before he pressed the button and rang the crisp tone out through the night.

Barely a second later a young woman threw open the door. She was the spitting image of the drawing in Jack's notebook. She scanned the crowd until she picked out Jason's golden curls.

"Jason, thank God—" Sally began. She halted, her brilliant green eyes traveling back to the man at the threshold. She and Jack locked gazes. Richie just had time to register that the two pairs of eyes were in fact the exact same shade.

"Oh my Lord," Sally exclaimed. "William—is that you?"

The gears in Richie's brain ground to a stop. William? The name struck some chord deep in his mind, but he couldn't put his finger on it.

"Sally, who's that at the door?"

Another woman, with carefully styled blondish hair and thick blue eye shadow, entered from another room, writing rapidly in a note-book. When no one answered, she looked up. She observed Jason, bruised and muddy; Sally, struck speechless; and a ragged gaggle of strange men outside the door, and summed up Richie's thoughts on the situation quite nicely:

"What in the holy name of Hecate is going on here?"

14

W hat do you mean, she's your sister?" Richie demanded. Jack clasped his hands and tucked them up under his chin. Richie knew his foot was tapping again, even though the carpet under their feet muffled the sound.

"I mean Sally is my little sister," Jack said, avoiding Richie's eyes. He must know that Richie felt his deception as a betrayal. For months, the only friend he had anymore had been stringing Richie along on false pretenses.

"Why did you lie to me? How hard would it have been to say 'I'm trying to find my missing sister'?"

"I'm sorry, okay? I didn't lie. I really was a patient of hers once, and that's part of the reason I wanted to find her again. I left out part of the story because I just...I couldn't. There are a lot of bad things attached to the family name, especially *my* name, and I didn't feel like I could tell you. I don't tell anyone if I can help it." Jack sat down heavily on the burgundy sofa and stared through the blank television screen across from him. Richie wanted to say something else, something about how much it hurt that Jack wouldn't trust him, after all this time, when they were interrupted. A black-clad ginger raced down the stairs and ran full-tilt into the room where Sally's newest patient was.

"Alexandru?"

"Tatăl!"

Sally and the young woman that seemed to be her assistant quietly exited the room and closed the door to lend some privacy to the reunion. They walked over to the waiting area in which Jack and Richie had been having their dispute.

"Well, that's all settled," Sally said. "Vlad will be fine. It's a good thing you brought him to me at once, though, or that might not be the case. The poisoning was quite severe." She plopped into the vacant armchair and looked at Jack and Richie expectantly. Her willowy blonde assistant sat cross-legged on the carpet nearby.

"I sense that there's an interesting story behind how you came to be in my house," Sally said. "I would very much like to hear it."

Abandoning the conflict for the moment, Richie sat at the other end of the sofa from Jack and they launched into the tale.

"Now how did you find your way into town exactly? It can be a challenge if you don't know where the road is," Sally said. Richie wasn't sure what to say. There wasn't any way he could think of to get around saying that Thomas had led them there, but when Richie and Jack emerged from the woods with Jason, only Dracula remained in the idling car. He passed on a request from their guide that he remain anonymous. Fortunately, Jack seemed to have prepared for this question.

"It took us a while, sure, but we stumbled upon it eventually, once we figured out what stretch of road to look along," Jack answered her. If Sally was skeptical, she didn't say. Something else was on her mind.

"Also, Richie, would you describe the woman who tried to strangle you?"

"Um, okay. She had long, dark blondish hair, in a ponytail," Richie told Sally. He felt a little ill recalling her face, and the memory of pain that accompanied it. "Light colored eyes, I think. And she was pretty short, maybe even half a head shorter than me."

"The world is full of coincidences lately," Sally said, raising her eyebrows. "If it weren't for Clement, I might think they were just that, but I'm certain there's a connection here. You see, I believe that woman is one of my new enemies, judging by her use of magic and your description of her. A similar creature was seen near Clement's home shortly after he was killed."

"Clement's dead?" Jack asked, aghast. Sally nodded. That yanked at Richie's heartstrings. Clement wasn't a close friend, but Richie had liked him. Thinking that the same woman who tried to murder him had taken Clement's life, Richie felt a sort of burning itch in his palms, and knew instinctively that his hands were moments away from releasing flames. He clenched them into fists to prevent it.

"Several others are dead, too, and it is all the work of genies," Sally said, continuing. "Not like genie-in-a-bottle, but real genia, powerful female mages whose species the rest of the world knows little about. They have suddenly taken a homicidal interest in a group of people called the Guardians. If what I suspect is true, Richie, and the genies are out for your blood, then the logical conclusion is that you, too, are a Guardian." Sally proceeded to tell Richie a story about magic and Infinites and spells that Richie could barely follow.

Alex's gaze swept over his father, not quite believing what he saw. Even after Sally's treatment, the count looked terrible. The incisions crisscrossing his flesh were all carefully stitched up with silvery medicinal threads, yet they still looked ragged and hostile. A slight greenish tone was blotched across his skin and his eyes were just a little too bright. But he was alive. Well, in an undead sort of way. As always. Alex knew that only his father could have survived such injuries. And Father had done it all for him. Alex couldn't remember anyone ever sacrificing so much on his account.

"Why did you have to come for me? I told you not to, and I am perfectly fine here," Alex complained, employing the antiquated form of Romanian he had spoken as a child. He couldn't really be upset, though. Not everyone had a father who loved them as strongly as his.

"You do not write, you do not call, what was I supposed to do? Leave it be? Never. It is my duty to interfere where I am not wanted." Dracula replied in the same tongue, smiling at his only son.

"I was trying to keep you out of it, so you would not come to any harm." Alex laughed softly at the irony. He should have known he could never hope to control Vlad Dracula.

"What are you working on that is so secret you cannot tell your own father?"

"I am helping Sally save the universe. It is a long story."

"Save the universe? Sally? That does not seem like her."

"She has changed...somewhat," Alex said. "So have I, I believe."

"Yes, I think you have." Dracula's dark eyes studied Alex carefully. "You are so much more mature; your own man. That makes me very proud of you. Although I still wish you would have been more communicative about it."

"I promise to stay in touch from now on," Alex said to assure him. He gently laid his hand overtop the count's.

"You will not get rid of me that easily," Dracula replied in warning. "Sally says I have to stay for at least another month, and I intend to stay far longer in order to spy on your every action."

Alex shook his head. He had no doubt that the count would do just that. "Oh how I have missed you, Father," Alex said with a roll of his eyes.

"That's interesting...but what does all that have to do with, erm, me?" Richie asked, stopping himself from saying "us" just for spite. He shot an evil look at Jack for emphasis. Jack watched his rapping left foot carefully, not meeting Richie's gaze.

"Well, it sort of determines your destiny," Sally told him. "And it would explain your prophetic nightmares. Other prophets have been losing their powers in the last several months, while you have been steadily developing an abnormally lucid ability to see the future. That is, you know, your Guardian gift, although I suppose it isn't a particularly pleasant 'gift' to have."

Richie struggled to absorb the flood of information. He was a Guardian, he had to save the world, that was why his dreams came true. It was more than he could swallow at once. As he took in Sally's words, trying his best to comprehend them, his frantic brain latched onto the one idea he could identify with.

"So, about the nightmares," Richie said. "You can get rid of them, can't you?" He held his breath while Sally considered.

"There is a remote, *very* remote, possibility that I can do it without killing you," Sally eventually conceded. Richie allowed himself to breathe, a wave of relief washing over him. Finally, he could be rid of this curse. "But I won't," she added bluntly.

Richie's entire world crunched to a halt. Time seemed to stop as his mind was absorbed into one solid, absent thought that he could not quite grasp. He thought some sort of syllable may have issued from his vocal chords, but words were beyond him. Sally watched his reaction with an expression he couldn't identify, chewing her tongue thoughtfully.

"Unless I learn otherwise, I must assume that you are a Guardian," she explained, in a voice that was cold but not entirely devoid of sympathy. "I have devoted my life to identifying and protecting the Guardians, in the interest of preserving the universe. The Guardians alone can keep the Infinites at bay. If I remove your gift, then the cause is doomed. Hate me for it if you want, but I'm not going to change my mind. I am sorry. That's the way it has to be."

Kitch Manor was always a little cool inside, but that wasn't why Jason was shivering. Sally had given him a clean bill of health, but the mental shock had infected his entire body. The evening had not gone as he had expected. This was a better ending than the one he had planned, certainly, but he still wasn't quite sure what to think. Scarlet had come up from the basement not long ago and congratulated Jason on having a new big brother. They weren't sure which prophecy he belonged to, but they were about ninety percent sure that Richie was a Guardian. Since genies were supposed to be peaceful, and Richie had been attacked by a magical midget, presumably a genie, then the logic went that he was a Guardian. Jason had difficulty following that train of thought, but he decided that was probably because he was tired and confused. Besides, the conclusion was Sally's, and apparently she was even smarter than Jason knew. If guys living in castles in the forests of Romania knew she was a medical genius, there had to be something to it. Jason supposed he had never really given Sally much credit, despite the vast knowledge she had displayed when tutoring him in the arcane at her library. He would need to remember to put more faith in her.

His eyes grazed past the circle of candles burning on the floor, and he decided to put more faith in Hope, as well. Even as he stood in the wet grass in the middle of the night waiting to die, they had figured out how to summon and trap the Black Dog without the need for a decoy. True to their word, his new friends were in fact going to protect him. Had he stuck around for fifteen more minutes instead of going on a suicide mission, he wouldn't have had to leave. Jason stretched out his legs on the couch, pulling the blanket tighter around his shoulders, thinking what an idiot he was.

Pansy paused while he adjusted. The moment Jason settled his head back on her lap, she resumed massaging his head. Jason was used to getting headaches from his illness, but this one was worse than most, if any, he'd had before. Thankfully the pain was only on one side. And the action of his mother's sympathetic digits did rub out some of the hurt. She didn't speak to him. Noise just made the headache worse, and neither had much to say. Nothing in their lives had prepared them for how they should speak that night. As his frazzled brain began drifting off, however, Jason thought of one thing he did want to say.

"Hey, Mom? I love you."

"I love you too," she replied, keeping her volume low for the sake of his sensitive eardrums. Pansy kissed his temple with the gentleness only a mother could have. Jason was already asleep.

Thomas stood outside the door for a long, long time, shifting from foot to foot. At last he worked up the courage. Removing the key from beneath the flowerpot that Jason had finger-painted a dinosaur on in preschool, he let himself in. No one was home, of course. Pansy was with their son at Kitch Manor, as Thomas knew she would be. He knew full well that he lacked the courage to speak with her, or Jason. Thomas still believed that leaving was the best thing he had ever done for his family. One day the shadow figures in his past would catch up with him, and he would make damn sure that his family wasn't there when they did.

He flipped on the lights. The house wasn't quite the same as he remembered. And he remembered very clearly—the couch had been on the other side of the room, the throw pillows had been blue, there had been a track and toy cars littering the center carpet, the last time he walked out that front door. The absence of the tiny race cars stung. He had forgotten how much of Jason's life he had missed. Now a card table stood in the middle of floor, topped with a couple textbooks, one of Alex's Sex Pistols CDs, and a pile of very official, very Sally-like documents. Thomas thumbed through the papers slowly, taking stock of the situation. Despite his best efforts, it seemed his family was in more danger than he could ever have imagined. He was aware of the Infinites and the Guardians. Sally had explained it at length when he was part of the manor. He had even helped them search. To think his own son was one of the Guardians they had looked for! It wasn't a sure thing, he supposed, but in his experience Sally was rarely wrong. Equal measures of pride and terror mingled in his mind. He vowed to do everything he could to protect Jason, albeit from afar. A salty droplet plummeted to the surface of the paper in his hand, one of the prophecies he had memorized as an adolescent—his son's name was inked in at the top of the page. Thomas replaced it on the table.

Although not certain he could take it, Thomas resolved to see Jason's room one last time. The door was open, but it still took a great deal of strength to go through. The walls were the same shade of cool green and the same soccer ball-patterned comforter covered the bed. Most of the boyish toys were gone, though Thomas recognized the plush Tyrannosaurus rex he had given Jason as a toddler, enshrined atop the dresser. Beside it hung a frame on the wall, one with places to put four pictures. In the top right was a photo of him and Jason together, probably one of the last ones taken. He thought he recognized Sammy in another picture, posing with an older Jason and a soccer ball. Where there used to be a younger image of that pair, there was a contemporary photograph of Jason and two boys Thomas didn't know. The fourth slot showed Jason and Pansy, a Christmas portrait from this year, or perhaps the year before. Pansy was a bit older, her face more drawn and a few worry lines developing around her mouth. The modest red dress she wore was somewhat shapeless, by far not the most flattering garment she had ever worn. Yet Thomas thought she was as beautiful as when they first met.

Thomas made for the closet, walking on tip-toe as if not to disturb the memories dusting the floor. If Jason had kept the dinosaur and the photo, perhaps the album was still in the same place. It was. Thomas lingered on every page of guitar picks, recalling the time and place of each. Finally he made it to the first empty slot. He reached into his pocket and pulled out the tiny rubber-banded parcel: a pick from the souvenir table at a Def Leppard concert and a simple message folded in paper. He removed the rubber band and slid both objects into the slot, wondering when Jason would notice. Did he even look at this old album anymore? For all he knew the most recent picks were months or years old. Maybe it would be better if Jason never found it.

Thomas put the pick album back in its place, padded down the stairs, and walked out the door again. It wasn't any easier the second time.

Richie sat morosely on the bed in his new room, unsure what to do with himself. He supposed he should be thankful that Sally was offering a room for him in her home, a place where he could be protected. But he was far too angry with her to be grateful. All along he had worried whether or not Sally *could* fix him. Never in a million years would it have occurred to him whether or not she *would*. He had wondered about money, but figured that he could always sign some sort of contract agreeing to pay her back later. But *that* wasn't the problem. Oh no, "money is no object" she'd said. But "prophecy is a gift, Richard" and he would need it when the time came for him to save the universe, so the nightmares had to stay. He had traveled thousands of miles, he had fought for his life, he had *killed a man*, in his efforts to get to Brunswick, to find out that Sally refused to help him. Why? Because she wanted him to be a hero. And maybe that was what angered him most of all, because in his heart Richie had always wanted to be the hero. Ever since he was a child, living in the shadow of his older brothers, he had wanted to be someone special. Well, he had gotten what he wanted. He was one of the most special people in the world, and now he wanted nothing more than to be normal again.

The sound of approaching footsteps echoed down the hallway. They were coming from the direction of Jack's room. Richie's flank muscles began to stiffen involuntarily—realizing half a second later that this was a very feline, non-human response only provoked him more.

The noise stopped just shy of Richie's open door. For a full five minutes, Richie didn't hear anything else. He had just started to relax, thinking his ears were mistaken, when Jack spoke.

"Richie?" he asked meekly. Richie glared at the door, thinking of all the things he wanted to say at that moment. The impulses were conflicting. Too many different emotions were boiling up. Richie was furious with Jack for deceiving him and with himself for being so easily taken in. He hated the world, he hated Jack for being in the world, and yet he knew Jack had tried to make his life better. Even knowing that Jack was a liar, Richie still felt like Jack had sincerely cared. And in his caring Jack had led Richie to disappointment. In exasperation, Richie silently screamed his most emphatic curse and gestured in Jack's general direction with one arm in an angry and abortive movement.

"I...Richie, I—I'm sorry..." Jack stuttered out. "You deserve better than this. You deserve better than me. I didn't want you to see me for who I am because you wouldn't like what I am on the inside, so I kept secrets. I needed you to bring me home, and I know it was selfish, but I really did think Sally could help you." A minute later the footsteps began again in the opposite direction, more rapid than before. The confrontation averted, Richie's hackles fell. His brain churned out a million things he could say to Jack, but none of them seemed right. Nothing in Richie's life had prepared him for today. The last twenty-four hours left him reeling. He had used his gift to save a life and maybe begin to atone for the life he had taken. Dr. Kitch could be right. If the nightmares could make him a hero, she was right to refuse to take them away. No matter what Jack thought, Richie knew he didn't deserve any better than that, but could he find it in him to keep suffering for the rest of his life and never see his adoptive family again in order to do some good in the world? Too tired and confused to do more than think in circles, Richie stretched out on the bed and closed his eyes, giving up on the inner battle for a while. For the first time in months, no dreams haunted his sleep.

"He hates me." Jack flopped down on his sister's bed and took a swig straight from the bottle of Alex's vodka he'd found in the kitchen. Sally glanced up from her book, first at her brother, then the bottle.

"Don't you think you're overreacting a little?"

"I'd hate me," Jack said, staring at the ceiling.

"You already hate you," Sally said, flipping to the next page. "You know you would get hurt much less often if you didn't get so attached to people."

"Thanks for the advice." Jack laughed humorlessly, an edge of hysteria in the sound. Sally was right on both counts, of course. "When you figure out how to confer your emotional invulnerability onto me, let me know and I'll try that out."

"Fair enough," Sally said, conceding the point. She stuck a bookmark between the pages and closed the book on her lap. "You didn't come here looking to get my stoicism by diffusion, and I don't suppose you're in the habit of picking up street urchins to go globetrotting with. So why did you come?" Jack shifted nervously and took another slug of liquor. He had mapped out this conversation in his head thousands of times, but now he couldn't find the words.

"What? I can't just drop in because I want to see my little sister?"

"It would be fairly unprecedented."

"Maybe I really missed you. It's been over fifty years," Jack said, shrugging. Sally closed her eyes and ran her hands through her hair.

"It's drugs again, isn't it?"

"No!" Jack sat up straight, pointing at his sister and one-time physician for emphasis. "No. I told you, I'm off the hard stuff for good. That's over and done with." He lowered his hand and put it down behind him to prop himself up.

"Well, then, what is it, William? I would like to think that you went to all this effort just because you missed me, but you didn't."

"No, I didn't," he admitted, laying back down on the mattress. "I...I'm not sure why I came. I just realized one day that I couldn't bear the monster I saw in the mirror, and I didn't have anyone else to turn to." He turned his eyes to Sally. "I know I'm a lost cause, but I had to try. I had to find somewhere safe to either work things out or, I don't know, finish drinking myself to death. You're the only person left in the world who might love me. I got my hopes up for Richie, but.... What I mean is, you're the only safe place I've got."

Sally nodded, frowning. "Sweetheart...you do realize that I have the emotional maturity of a zucchini, right?" She met her wayward brother's gaze. "A kidney stone I can fix. An existential crisis I cannot."

"I just need someone I can talk to. Someone who cares," Jack said, his expression pleading and willing her to understand. He thought he saw sympathy in her eyes, but it could've been wishful thinking on his part.

"I think you would be better off getting a dog," Sally said, "but I'm here for you. You're the only family I've got that I do care about. I'll do whatever I can. Now, are you going to tell me what's going on with you or not?"

Jack swallowed hard. Anxiety churned in his stomach at the thought of letting her in on his secrets. He wouldn't be able to take it if she turned him away, too.

"You promise you'll let me stay? No matter what?"

"Yes, I promise," Sally told him.

"Well, for starters, I've killed people."

"So I've heard. I'm afraid homicide does run in the family."

"It's worse than you think," Jack said in warning.

"I can handle it," she promised, but Jack shook his head. "Well, then, whenever you're ready. I'll be here."

Alex left his father's bedside to let him rest and went to a room down the hall. He had asked Sally once why there was a prison cell in her basement, and she just said that she thought her parents had installed it, and she didn't want to know why. Regardless, Alex was glad to have it now. He leaned in the doorway and watched Hope finish her incantation.

"All right," Hope said with finality, closing her spell book and turning to Alex. "It's trapped in there." Alex gazed at the curious contents of the cell. The Black Dog was alternating between smoke and canine. Alex thought it seemed annoyed, but it was hard to tell since it didn't have much in the way of facial expressions.

"You'll need this, I think," Hope said. She produced a wooden box from where she had stowed it under one slender arm. Alex took it, not understanding, but trusting in her knowledge. He brought a finger underneath the cast iron clasp, ready to see what magic lay inside.

"Don't open it yet!" Hope said.

Alex jerked away, afraid that whatever was in the box might jump out and bite him.

"I don't even know if it will work," she murmured, "but it might kill the Dog. When you're done asking questions, give it a try."

Alex nodded. Sally had established earlier that night that the Black Dog would be destroyed, if possible. The creature was too dangerous to let live, even if it would prove to be a valuable asset. Alex never liked to kill, but he was prepared to do so. He walked forward toward the cell while Hope exited behind him. Alex set the box on the floor, taking care not to jostle it too much, and started in with the interrogation. He couldn't see any aura with this particular prisoner, but he still knew how to ask some questions.

"So, are you going to talk?" he asked the apparition, crossing his arms in his most aggressive stance. The swirling thing behind the bars growled in reply. Alex didn't know how to interpret that, but figured he might as well charge ahead.

"All right then. Are you working for the genies?"

"Jasmine," it hissed. Once again Alex found himself stymied. That wasn't an answer he had expected to hear. He knew of a great many ways to say "yes" and "no," but "Jasmine" wasn't one of them.

"What do you mean by that?"

"The Queen," it replied. Its harsh, slithering voice sounded like acid dripping off a dead man's bones.

The worm of fear that wriggled up Alex's spine was nothing magical this time. Even immobilized and powerless, the Black Dog was darker and more menacing than any of the shadowy ghouls Alex had seen in the old forests of his youth. Worst was the thought that this thing could sneak up on him unobserved. No aura, no energy for him to sense. He remembered that time in the orchard and couldn't repress a shiver.

"The queen of whom?" Alex demanded, sheathing his fright in a leathery shell of toughness.

"Queen of the Little Ones."

"What little—wait. Do you mean she's the queen of the genies?" Now Alex was confused. Sally said a genie queen couldn't walk or talk. It probably couldn't even think. That was what the Black Dog was working for?

The black smoke solidified into the bust of the huge dog, lips baring angry teeth and the immense head nodding in confirmation. Alex wasn't aware that the genies had royalty. Might one of the Infinites have taken the genies under her tyranny? Can an Infinite be a "she?" The interrogation was going fantastic, inexplicably so. Alex decided to go for broke.

"What is Jasmine? What does she look like?" For several heartbeats there was no response, and Alex was starting to consider how to enhance his interrogation technique. Then he felt the Black Dog, inside his head, slipping past mental barriers—that Alex had spent centuries constructing—as readily as a water droplet sliding off waxed paper. An image was thrust into his consciousness.

Another prison, walls of earth instead of stone, lit with torches that glowed a cool violet. Watching from behind bars. In the center of the room, two small, human-like women: genies. One, dressed in ordinary big-box-store-issue clothes and with head bowed in deference and eyes widened in awe, listened as the other spoke. The other woman wore lavish purple robes, silken and stitched with a fanciful gold design. A slim black belt at her waist held a dagger. Skin darker than her companion's but still a very light shade. She threw her arm out to take in the whole of the dungeon, smirking at the brilliance of whatever plan she was explaining.

The morbid voice of the Black Dog hissed over the silent scene: 'Jasmine.'

The picture began to leach its vividness and then faded away. Alex was looking through his own eyes again, the Black Dog still floating before him like an abstract rendering of the Prince of Darkness himself. At first Alex was too shocked to react. He had believed his mind was impenetrable. The feeling of intense violation left his thoughts shattered.

Gradually, Alex realized that something was required of him. He pulled himself back together and focused his attention on the Black Dog with renewed harshness. This animal had invaded his mind; it couldn't be permitted to stay in the manor a moment longer. What secrets might it learn? What had it pulled from his mind already? Alex crouched down slowly, keeping his eyes trained on the prisoner, and felt for Hope's box. When he felt a wooden corner grate against his palm, Alex clenched his hand around his sole weapon and stood up straight, box clutched close to his chest. He flipped open the catch, held the box at arm's length toward the cell, and knocked the lid open.

The light mote gleefully shot into the air, jumping free from the box and spiraling towards the darkest part of the room. Alex's skin tingled when stray rays of light touched him, and he knew that Hope had created a ball of sunlight. Another invention of Hope's, an enchanted spur of metal through his eyebrow, protected Alex from the scathing light, but the Black Dog had no such shield. The Black Dog began to howl, and then to shriek, as the mote made contact and ejected streams of bright white light throughout its smoky body. Alex watched as the smoke began to disintegrate before his eyes, seemingly in slow motion, until nothing remained in the cell but a few drifting sparks. With a lingering feeling of unease, Alex turned to leave and report the new information to the girls, wishing he had something more definitive to tell them.

Jason gently deposited the cat carrier he'd borrowed from Alex on the lake shore. The cage rocked back and forth a little as Vanessa crawled around inside, making soft gurgling noises that sounded curious but not afraid. Jason was glad at least one of them was fine with this—he was worried sick. Vanessa had been his pet ever since she hatched in that pond in the park. Jason doubted she could take care of herself, but it had to be done. Sammy had been right; he couldn't keep a growing lake monster in a fish pond forever.

Jason crouched beside the carrier and pulled back the latch. The door swung open slowly, the rusty hinges creaking. Vanessa's rubbery snout poked out, followed soon by her head and neck. She placed her front pair of feet on the grass and began to pull the rest of her sinewy body free from its confinement. She was much bigger than she had been a few months ago, about three feet long. Jason was amazed that she fit in the small crate. Once outside, she stretched leisurely and sniffed the air. The smell of the lake hit her nose, and she squeaked with joy. She looked at Jason eagerly, as though asking his permission. He gave her rear a nudge with his hand. Vanessa was off like a shot, running towards the water on her short, clumsy legs. Once in the lake, however, she ceased to be clumsy. In one graceful movement, she dove into the green-blue surface, leaving a trail of ripples behind.

Jason stayed long enough to see that she surfaced again, and then a few minutes more, before he finally managed to tear himself away and walk back home. He paused in the park, staring at the pond where he had originally found the large, algae covered egg that became Vanessa. The first thing he had done was run to Sammy's house to show him. He thought maybe he should tell Sammy about letting Vanessa go, but instead went on to his house to return the cat carrier to Alex.

Surrounded by the journals of witches from innumerable generations, Hope scratched her florid handwriting across the thick, coarse paper. She had considered getting a new journal for the modern era, but the paper was always so flimsy. A witch's journal was meant to last.

With a final dot of punctuation, the entry was complete. From here on out, there would always be a way to kill a Black Dog. Hope swiped two fingers from right to left across the middle of the page. It was as if she was pulling a white sheet across the paper—in the wake of her touch, the letters faded away, hidden from prying eyes. For a moment Hope regretted that this information would be trapped in Sally's library, away from other witches who could benefit from it. Hope didn't trust Sally the way she used to, but she knew that Sally could be counted on to preserve a book for as long as possible, no matter who the author. A book to her was a sacred thing. As such, Hope had to conclude that the Kitch Library was, after all, the best place to secure her journal. As she slid the volume back into its customary slot on the shelves, she heard the bold snap of assertive footsteps coming down the hall, then the dim click of a doorknob unlatching. Hope turned to face Sally as she entered. Their eyes wandered into contact with false nonchalance. Hope was the first to look away, deflected by the intensity in Sally's gaze. She realized, with some surprise, that she was actually afraid of Sally. She wondered when that had happened.

Jason came in behind Sally, glancing nervously at the silent confrontation. Immediately, Sally came to life, continuing some half-told exposition and leading him to a particular section of the vast literary expanse. A little unnerved, Hope began the journey to the door. Halfway there she met with the other library-goers and in a moment of courage, or perhaps just curiosity, she hazarded a comment.

"Shouldn't you be bringing Richie down here, too?"

"Oh, certainly," Sally replied. Her face was smiling, but reserved. Hope couldn't tell what she was thinking. "He was raised as a human, apparently, so he has quite a lot to learn. But I'm letting him be for a while. Last week he got the shock of his life, and the preceding months weren't much kinder. I think the boy's earned some time alone for a nervous breakdown."

"So you'll talk to him when he's not mad at you anymore," Hope said, drawing a conclusion. Her tone came out a little more critical than she had intended.

"Well, that's the general idea, yes. As much as I enjoy arguing, I've noticed that sometimes it's better to just...not."

Hope wasn't sure whether or not that was supposed to be a hint. Bemused by the whole conversation, she nodded absently at Sally's statement and went on her way.

15

K ell perched stiffly on the ragged chair, anxiously twirling her blonde ponytail. She caught the creep across from her trying his best to look up her skirt, and she quickly curled her legs up beneath her. Everything about this place made her nervous. She wanted nothing more than to leave and run home to her sisters. Kell doubted any of the other genies had ever been in a place like this. Traditionally, trading on the black market was considered beneath the dignity and moral standards of her race. But she was determined to succeed in her mission.

The original plan had failed, and the Scotsman had found his way to Dr. Kitch. Queen Jasmine could take on Dr. Kitch and her friend the sorceress, but Kell knew that was beyond her personal capability. To try would be suicide. The magic shell around Brunswick and the witch's wards would interfere with any spell cast from the outside, and Kell would surely be killed if she tried to pluck the Guardian out of the enemy stronghold in person. So that was a lost cause. Kell was *not* going to return home empty-handed, however. She would find another nascent Guardian, and this time—

The door that led from the waiting room into the office opened and the merchant's scraggly lackey stuck his head through.

"Your turn, sweetheart," he called, his wandering eyes quickly finding Kell, the only female being in the waiting room. She again found herself regretting her choice of clothing.

Despite her misgivings, Kell took a deep, fortifying breath and followed the leering lackey through the door. He closed it behind her, sealing her in with him and his master.

When Kell saw Daemonicus, she immediately noticed two things about him: he was rather dark-skinned for a vampire, and he wasn't feeling her up with his eyes the way all his underlings had.

"Good evening, Miss," he greeted her with a warm smile and cold eyes. Amidst the decaying wooden walls of the building and the general filth, Daemonicus was a zone of glowing cleanliness. His pure white suit and black tie were spotless, not even a speck of dust to be seen on them. On the whole, he was a great relief, when compared with his surroundings. Then again, Kell suspected that this effect was carefully crafted.

"I need someone delivered to my Queen," Kell said. She hesitated, not sure what she was expected to say next. A lifetime in her comfortable genie nest had not prepared her for making deals in the outside world.

"At your service," Daemonicus assured her in a voice like velvet. "Just tell me who to find and where to send him."

"On the subject of payment..."

"Don't worry about it. I'll discuss payment with your queen upon delivery," he replied dismissively. "All I need from you is the barest of details..."

A timid knock sounded on the door, and Dr. Bloom looked up from his desk. The hazy silhouette of a person was framed in the frosted-glass window.

"Come in," Dr. Bloom called. His voice was rough with age but still warm and welcoming. The knob turned and the last interviewee of the day crept in. Her posture cried nervousness—head ducked, shoulders hunched, and textbook clutched to her chest. It wasn't the best way for a potential employee to present herself, but she was only an undergrad, and Dr. Bloom was looking for something other than confidence. His research assistant had to have just the right spark...

GRETCHEN THYRD: ON the BRIDGE

by Jason T. Graves

Gretchen Thyrd, foster kid since birth, hides from the brittle memories of a relationship gone wrong—a life torched. After the unthinkable happens and she becomes the bearer of the soul of the Red Prince, she finds herself pursued by winter freaks and ghosts, deep into the belly of the earth in search of the Fæ Realms.

THE GUARDIANS OF KNOWLEDGE
When the Books Go Bad

by Chip Putnam

Six kids have no idea that getting trapped in the school library marks the beginning of their training as **the Guardians of Knowledge**—those people who can travel into books. When it becomes clear that the books are taking on a life of their own, this unlikely group of friends must discover the source of the spreading chaos.

Meri Elena

Meri Elena is a North Carolina native and lifelong bibliophile. She started writing "seriously" in fourth grade, and her first published story, the horror novelette *Anew*, came out as a Kindle e-book in the summer of 2012. The e-book short story collection *These Four Walls* followed in October, 2013. Her short fiction has also been published in the *Off the Beaten Path* anthology series by Prospective Press.

She has won a Figment.com short story contest and been a finalist for another. Her essay on vampire mythology and the psychology of fear was selected for print in Teen Ink magazine. Her current project, first begun in fifth grade, is the Brunswick Prophecies series. The second book in the series, **Blood Magic**, will be published in 2017.

Meri attends North Carolina State University with majors in Plant Biology and Genetics and a minor in Creative Writing. In addition to literary and academic pursuits, she spends her time in used book stores and with *Buffy the Vampire Slayer*. She collects Bay City Rollers memorabilia and as many cats as she can reasonably keep up with.

www.ingramcontent.com/pod-product-compliance
Lightning Source LLC
Chambersburg PA
CBHW071250190726
48292CB00007B/2477